SCIENTIST DIS[barcode: S0-AXB-826] THAT CAUSES VAMPIRISM!

Recent advances in medicine have necessitated differentiating between clincial death, or cessation in heartbeat, and biological, or brain death. The distinction has been further complicated by the increasing use of heroic life support methodology. History reports rare cases in which clinical death was not followed by biological death, but was maintained in status. The affected undead individuals were called Nosferati, or vampires. The authors' investigation of this phenomenon has led to the discovery of a causative microorganism, Pseudobacteria augeria.

"Vampires?" I repeated, petting a white rabbit. "Come on, we did that one in med school. Funniest gag since Arlo left a piece of his cadaver in a confessional."

I looked around the lab, believing my eyes as little as Marlowe's story. They'd turned an old farm house into a modern-day Castle Frankenstein. Cages of lab animals faced a small computer, nestled amongst the centrifuges, particle counters, electron microscope, and spectrometers.

Marlowe handed me a stethoscope. "First, assure yourself that it works."

I put it over my fifth rib and heard a reassuring *lub dub lub dub*. "I'm alive."

"Try the rabbit."

No heartbeat. I stared at it, snuffling in my hands. Marlowe put out a saucer of what looked like blood. The fluffy little bunny tore free of my hold, dove at the bowl, and began lapping up the red liquid.

I said, "You boys just got yourself a surgeon."

—From "Born Again" by S.N. Dyer

TOMORROW SUCKS

Edited by
Greg Cox &
T.K.F.
Weisskopf

BAEN

TOMORROW SUCKS

Copyright © 1994 by Greg Cox and T.K.F. Weisskopf

A Baen Books Original

Baen Publishing Enterprises
P.O. Box 1403
Riverdale, N.Y. 10471

ISBN: 0-671-87626-0

Cover art by David Mattingly

First printing, October 1994

Distributed by
SIMON & SCHUSTER
1230 Avenue of the Americas
New York, N.Y. 10020

Printed in the United States of America

DEDICATIONS

T.K.F. Weisskopf
To my fellows at Baen Books: Jim, Hank, Jeanne, Jo, Eleanor, Marla, Bernie & Nancy; and to my proud parents.

Greg Cox
To the gang at Tor Books; and my family, too.

TABLE OF CONTENTS

ACKNOWLEDGMENTS

A Scientific History of Vampirism

GREG COX

Dracula nearly killed the vampire story.

Creatively, that is. Coming at the end of a wave of Victorian vampire tales that began in 1819 with John Polidori's "The Vampyre," Bram Stoker's classic horror novel, first published in 1897, quickly established itself as *the* definitive vampire story, encompassing and supplanting all that had been written before—and most of the vampire fiction to come. Dracula movies and plays popularized Stoker's vampire even more, and the Count cast an oppressive black shadow over more than fifty years of copycats and parodies. No vampire novels worth remembering were published for at least five decades after *Dracula*, and only a handful of short stories—such as Ray Bradbury's lyrical "Homecoming" (1946)—turned over fresh soil in an increasingly overcrowded literary graveyard.

Life—and unlife—was simpler then. Vampires were heartless creatures of hell, or, at best, tormented lost souls condemned forever by some unholy curse. Their motives and abilities were clearly defined, as were their weaknesses: sunlight, holy water, wooden stakes, and so on. They were the (mostly illegitimate) children of Dracula, and numbingly predictable for that reason.

Science proved the vampire's salvation. A few early stories pointed the way, like Mary Braddon's "Good Lady

Ducayne" (1896), an otherwise forgettable story about a
vicious old woman who preserves her life via frequent
blood transfusions. C. L. Moore's "Shambleau" (1933)
was possibly the first vampire of extraterrestrial origin,
unless one counts the blood-sucking Martians in H. G.
Wells' *The War of the Worlds* (1898)—and that's a bit
of a stretch. Wells also supplied "The Flowering of the
Strange Orchid" (1894), a ground-breaking tale of botani-
cal vampirism whose blood-sucking plant anticipated *The
Little Shop of Horrors* and other bizarre horrors.

It wasn't until the 1950s, though, that scientific vampires really came into their own. In the wake of Hiro-
shima and Sputnik, science fiction spread like fall-out
over the haunted castles and crypts of the Gothic tradition. On the silver screen, radioactive mutants and Things
from Outer Space suddenly outnumbered ghosts, werewolves, and undead. But what might have seemed like a
bad time for bloodsuckers proved instead a rebirth.

Forget curses, spells, and pacts with the Devil. Suddenly vampirism could be the result of bacteria, genetics,
mental illness, parallel evolution, atomic mutation,
robotics, or even an invasion from another planet. Anything was possible, and all the old rules were suddenly
subject to change. Even traditional, supernatural vampires suddenly found themselves confronted with such
unusual situations as time travel, space travel, and planets
with two or more suns. Somehow, Dorothy, they weren't in
Transylvania anymore. . . .

After years of stodgy cliches, vampire fiction received
a rejuvenating jolt of fresh blood. The new wave of scientific *nosferatu* included such instant classics as Richard
Matheson's *I am Legend* (1954), Theodore Sturgeon's
Some of Your Blood (1961), and, in a lighter vein,
"Blood" (1955) by Fredric Brown, about an old-fashioned
vamp's ill-fated attempt to drain blood from a sentient
turnip.

Perhaps most significantly, vampires didn't *have* to be
evil anymore. No longer a creature of hell by definition,
vampires could be villains, victims, or even heroes.

Science draws no moral distinctions, and what used to be an unnatural plague of darkness could now be treated as merely a handicap, an alternative lifestyle, or possibly the next stage in human evolution. Vampire stories became a lot more complicated ... and interesting.

Which doesn't mean, of course, that a scientific vampire couldn't be twice as scary as its supernatural brethren. If the old rules no longer applied, neither did the traditional defenses. And an entire species of non-human bloodsuckers, be they earthly or alien, might have less sympathy for mere *homo sapiens* than even the resurrected corpse of Vlad the Impaler.

In time, after the scientific vampire boom of the '50s, the children of Dracula eventually staged a comeback of sorts. Hammer Films beget a new generation of Gothic thrillers, while writers like Anne Rice and Stephen King found new ways to open the old graves. But vampirism would never be the same; the virus had escaped from the test tube, and a new, vital and sometimes virulent strain has entered the collective bloodstream of the genre, spawning memorable works like Suzy McKee Charnas's *The Vampire Tapestry* (1980), Whitley Strieber's *The Hunger* (1981), George R. R. Martin's *Fevre Dream* (1982), and continuing to mutate with each new novel, movie, short story, and comic book.

So throw away that crucifix. Pour your holy water down the drain. There's a new breed of vampire stalking your future, starting only a few pages away, and neither science nor sorcery can protect you from their unquenchable thirst.

Ray Bradbury is, of course, one of the best known sf authors in the world. "Pillar of Fire," originally published in 1948, is a chilling elegy for yesterday's monsters—and a case study in what can happen when science confronts the undead. Bradbury has written at least two other stories, "Usher II" and "The Exiles," set in the same (or similar) future.

Pillar of Fire

RAY BRADBURY

He came out of the earth, hating. Hate was his father; hate was his mother.

It was good to walk again. It was good to leap up out of the earth, off of your back, and stretch your cramped arms violently and try to take a deep breath!

He *tried*. He cried out.

He couldn't breathe. He flung his arms over his face and tried to breathe. It was impossible. He walked on the earth, he came out of the earth. But he was dead. He couldn't breathe. He could take air into his mouth and force it half down his throat, with withered moves of long-dormant muscles, wildly, wildly! And with this little air he could shout and cry! He wanted to have tears, but he couldn't make them come, either. All he knew was that he was standing upright, he was dead, he shouldn't be walking! He couldn't breathe and yet he stood.

The smells of the world were all about him. Frustratedly, he tried to smell the smells of autumn. Autumn was burning the land down into ruin. All across the country the ruins of summer lay; vast forests bloomed with flame, tumbled down timber on empty, unleafed timber. The smoke of the burning was rich, blue, and invisible.

He stood in the graveyard, hating. He walked through the world and yet could not taste nor smell of it. He heard, yes. The wind roared on his newly opened ears. But he was dead. Even though he walked he knew he was dead and should expect not too much of himself or this hateful living world.

He touched the tombstone over his own empty grave. He knew his own name again. It was a good job of carving.

WILLIAM LANTRY

That's what the gravestone said.
His fingers trembled on the cool stone surface.

BORN 1898—DIED 1933

Born *again* . . . ?

What year? He glared at the sky and the midnight autumnal stars moving in slow illuminations across the windy black. He read the tiltings of centuries in those stars. Orion thus and so, Aurega here! and where Taurus? *There!*

His eyes narrowed. His lips spelled out the year: "2349."

An odd number. Like a school sum. They used to say a man couldn't encompass any number over a hundred. After that it was all so damned abstract there was no use counting. This was the year 2349! A numeral, a sum. And here he was, a man who had lain in his hateful dark coffin, hating to be buried, hating the living people above who lived and lived and lived, hating them for all the centuries, until today, now, born out of hatred, he stood by his own freshly excavated grave, the smell of raw earth in the air, perhaps, but he could not smell it!

"I," he said, addressing a poplar tree that was shaken by the wind, "am an anachronism." He smiled faintly.

He looked at the graveyard. It was cold and empty. All of the stones had been ripped up and piled like so many flat bricks, one atop another, in the far corner of the wrought iron fence. This had been going on for two endless weeks. In his deep secret coffin he had heard the heartless, wild stirrings as the men jabbed the earth with cold spades and tore out the coffins and carried away the withered ancient bodies to be burned. Twisting with fear in his coffin, he had waited for them to come to him.

Today they had arrived at his coffin. But—late. They had dug down to within an inch of the lid. Five o'clock bell, time for quitting. Home to supper. The workers had gone off. Tomorrow they would finish the job, they said, shrugging into their coats.

Silence had come to the emptied tomb-yard.

Carefully, quietly, with a soft rattling of sod, the coffin lid had lifted.

William Lantry stood trembling now, in the last cemetery on Earth.

"Remember?" he asked himself, looking at the raw earth. "Remember those stories of the last man on earth? Those stories of men wandering in ruins, alone? Well you, William Lantry, are a switch on the old story. Do you *know* that? You are the last *dead* man in the whole damned world!"

There were no more dead people. Nowhere in any land was there a dead person. Impossible? Lantry did not smile at this. No, not impossible at all in this foolish, sterile, unimaginative, antiseptic age of cleansings and scientific methods! People died, oh my god, yes. But—*dead* people? Corpses? They didn't exist!

What *happened* to dead people?

The graveyard was on a hill. William Lantry walked

through the dark burning night until he reached the edge of the graveyard and looked down upon the new town of Salem. It was all illumination, all colour. Rocket ships cut fire above it, crossing the sky to all far ports of earth.

In his grave the new violence of this future world had driven down and seeped into William Lantry. He had been bathed in it for years. He knew all about it, with a hating dead man's knowledge of such things.

Most important of all, he knew what these fools did with dead men.

He lifted his eyes. In the centre of the town a massive stone finger pointed at the stars. It was three hundred feet high and fifty feet across. There was a wide entrance and a drive in front of it.

In the town, theoretically, thought William Lantry, say you have a dying man. In a moment he will be dead. What happens? No sooner is his pulse cold than a certificate is flourished, made out, his relatives pack him into a car-beetle and drive him swiftly to—

The Incinerator!

That functional finger, that Pillar of Fire pointing at the stars. Incinerator. A functional, terrible name. But truth is truth in this future world.

Like a stick of kindling your Mr. Dead Man is shot into the furnace.

Flume!

William Lantry looked at the top of the gigantic pistol shoving at the stars. A small pennant of smoke issued from the top.

There's where your dead people go.

"Take care of yourself, William Lantry," he murmured. "You're the last one, the rare item, the last dead man. All the other graveyards of earth have been blasted up. This is the last graveyard and you're the last dead man from the centuries. These people don't believe in having dead people about, much less walking dead people. Everything that can't be used goes up like a matchstick. Superstitions right along with it!"

He looked at the town. All right, he thought, quietly.

I hate you. You hate me, or you *would* if you knew I existed. You don't believe in such things as vampires or ghosts. Labels without referents, you cry! You snort. All right, snort! Frankly, I don't believe in *you*, either! I don't *like* you! You and your Incinerators.

He trembled. How very close it had been. Day after day they had hauled out the other dead ones, burned them like so much kindling. An edict had been broadcast around the world. He had heard the digging men talk as they worked!

"I guess it's a good idea, this cleaning up the graveyards," said one of the men.

"Guess so," said another. "Grisly custom. Can you imagine? Being buried, I mean! Unhealthy! All them germs!"

"Sort of a shame. Romantic, kind of. I mean, leaving just this one graveyard untouched all these centuries. The other graveyards were cleaned out, what year was it, Jim?"

"About 2260, I think. Yeah, that was it, 2260, almost a hundred years ago. But some Salem Committee they got on their high horse and they said, 'Look here, let's have just *one* graveyard left, to remind us of the customs of the barbarians.' And the gover'ment scratched its head, thunk it over, and said, 'Okay. Salem it is. But all other graveyards go, you understand, all!' "

"And away they went," said Bill.

"Sure, they sucked 'em out with fire and steam shovels and rocket-cleaners. If they knew a man was buried in a cow-pasture, they fixed him! Evacuated them, they did. Sort of cruel, I say."

"I hate to sound old-fashioned, but still there were a lot of tourists came here every year, just to see what a real graveyard was like."

"Right. We had nearly a million people in the last three years visiting. A good revenue. But—a government order is an order. The government says no more morbidity, so flush her out we do! Here we go. Hand me that spade, Bill."

* * *

William Lantry stood in the autumn wind, on the hill.
It was good to walk again, to feel the wind and to hear
the leaves scuttling like mice on the road ahead of him.
It was good to see the bitter cold stars almost blown
away by the wind.

It was even good to know fear again.

For fear rose in him now, and he could not put it
away. The very fact that he was walking made him an
enemy. And there was not another friend, another dead
man, in all of the world, to whom one could turn for
help or consolation. It was the whole melodramatic
living world against one William Lantry. It was the
whole vampire-disbelieving, body-burning, graveyard-
annihilating world against a man in a dark suit on a dark
autumn hill. He put out his pale cold hands into the city
illumination. You have pulled the tombstones, like teeth,
from the yard, he thought. Now I will find some way to
push your damnable Incinerators down into rubble. I will
make dead people again, and I will make friends in so
doing. I cannot be alone and lonely. I must start manu-
facturing friends very soon. Tonight.

"War is declared," he said, and laughed. It was pretty
silly, one man declaring war on an entire world.

The world did not answer back. A rocket crossed the
sky on a rush of flame, like an Incinerator taking wing.

Footsteps. Lantry hastened to the edge of the cemetery. The diggers, coming back to finish up their work?
No. Just someone, a man, walking by.

As the man came abreast the cemetery gate, Lantry
stepped swiftly out. "Good evening," said the man,
smiling.

Lantry struck the man in the face. The man fell. Lantry bent quietly down and hit the man a killing blow
across the neck with the side of his hand.

Dragging the body back into shadow, he stripped it,
changed clothes with it. It wouldn't do for a fellow to go
wandering about this future world with ancient clothing
on. He found a small pocket knife in the man's coat; not

much of a knife, but enough if you knew how to handle it properly. He knew how.

He rolled the body down into one of the already opened and exhumed graves. In a minute he had shovelled dirt down upon it, just enough to hide it. There was little chance of it being found. They wouldn't dig the same grave twice.

He adjusted himself in his new loose-fitting metallic suit. Fine, fine.

Hating, William Lantry walked down into town, to do battle with the Earth.

II

The Incinerator was open. It never closed. There was a wide entrance, all lighted up with hidden illumination, there was a helicopter landing table and a beetle drive. The town itself was dying down after another day of the dynamo. The lights were going dim, and the only quiet, lighted spot in the town now was the Incinerator. God, what a practical name, what an unromantic name.

William Lantry entered the wide, well-lighted door. It was an entrance, really; there were no doors to open or shut. People could go in and out, summer or winter, the inside was always warm. Warm from the fire that rushed whispering up the high round flue to where the whirlers, the propellers, the air-jets pushed the leafy grey ashes on away for a ten mile ride down the sky.

There was the warmth of the bakery here. The halls were floored with rubber parquet. You couldn't make a noise if you wanted to. Music played in hidden throats somewhere. Not music of death at all, but music of life and the way the sun lived inside the Incinerator; or the sun's brother, anyway. You could hear the flame floating inside the heavy brick wall.

William Lantry descended a ramp. Behind him he heard a whisper and turned in time to see a beetle stop before the entrance way. A bell rang. The music, as if at a signal, rose to ecstatic heights. There was joy in it.

From the beetle, which opened from the rear, some attendants stepped carrying a golden box. It was six feet long and there were sun symbols on it. From another beetle the relatives of the man in the box stepped and followed as the attendants took the golden box down a ramp to a kind of altar. On the side of the altar were the words, "WE THAT WERE BORN OF THE SUN RETURN TO THE SUN." The golden box was deposited upon the altar, the music leaped upward, the Guardian of this place spoke only a few words, then the attendants picked up the golden box, walked to a transparent wall, a safety lock also transparent, and opened it. The box was shoved into the glass slot. A moment later an inner lock opened, the box was injected into the interior of the flue and vanished instantly in quick flame.

The attendants walked away. The relatives without a word turned and walked out. The music played.

William Lantry approached the glass fire lock. He peered through the wall at the vast, glowing, never-ceasing heart of the Incinerator. It burned steadily without a flicker, singing to itself peacefully. It was so solid it was like a golden river flowing up out of the earth towards the sky. Anything you put into the river was borne upwards, vanished.

Lantry felt again his unreasoning hatred of this thing, this monster, cleansing fire.

A man stood at his elbow. "May I help you, sir?"

"What?" Lantry turned abruptly. "What did you say?"

"May I be of service?"

"I—that is—" Lantry looked quickly at the ramp and the door. His hands trembled at his sides. "I've never been in here before."

"Never?" The Attendant was surprised.

That had been the wrong thing to say, Lantry realized. But it was said, nevertheless. "I mean," he said. "Not really, I mean, when you're a child, somehow, you don't pay attention. I suddenly realized tonight that I didn't really *know* the Incinerator."

The Attendant smiled. "We never know anything, do we, really? I'll be glad to show you around."

"Oh, no. Never mind. It—it's a wonderful place."

"Yes, it is." The Attendant took pride in it. "One of the finest in the world, I think."

"I—" Lantry felt he must explain further. "I haven't had many relatives die on me since I was a child. In fact, none. So, you see I haven't been here for many years."

"I see." The Attendant's face seemed to darken somewhat.

What've I said now, thought Lantry. What in God's name is wrong? What've I done? If I'm not careful I'll get myself shoved right into that damnable fire trap. What's wrong with this fellow's face? He seems to be giving me more than the usual going over.

"You wouldn't be one of the men who've just returned from Mars, would you?" asked the Attendant.

"No. Why do you ask?"

"No matter." The Attendant began to walk off. "If you want to know anything, just ask me."

"Just one thing," said Lantry.

"What's that?"

"This."

Lantry dealt him a stunning blow across the neck.

He had watched the fire-trap operator with expert eyes. Now, with the sagging body in his arms, he touched the button that opened the warm outer lock, placed the body in, heard the music rise, and saw the inner lock open. The body shot out into the river of fire. The music softened.

"Well done, Lantry, well done."

Barely an instant later another attendant entered the room. Lantry was caught with an expression of pleased excitement on his face. The Attendant looked around as if expecting to find someone, then he walked towards Lantry. "May I help you?"

"Just looking," said Lantry.

"Rather late at night," said the Attendant.

"I couldn't sleep."

That was the wrong answer, too. Everybody slept in this world. Nobody had insomnia. If you did you simply turned on a hypno-ray, and, sixty seconds later, you were snoring. Oh, he was just *full* of wrong answers. First he had made the fatal error of saying he had never been in the Incinerator before, when he knew damned well that all children were brought here on tours, every year, from the time they were four, to instill the idea of the clean fire death and the Incinerator in their minds. Death was a bright fire, death was warmth and the sun. It was not a dark, shadowed thing. That was important in their education. And he, pale thoughtless fool, had immediately gabbled out his ignorance.

And another thing, this paleness of his. He looked at his hands and realised with growing terror that a pale man also was non-existent in this world. They would suspect his paleness. That was why the first Attendant had asked, "Are you one of those men newly returned from Mars?" Here, now, this new Attendant was clean and bright as a copper penny, his cheeks red with health and energy. Lantry hid his pale hands in his pockets. But he was fully aware of the searching the Attendant did on his face.

"I mean to say," said Lantry, "I didn't *want* to sleep. I wanted to think."

"Was there a service held here a moment ago?" asked the Attendant, looking about.

"I don't know, I just came in."

"I thought I heard the fire lock open and shut."

"I don't know," said Lantry.

The man pressed a wall button. "Anderson?"

A voice replied. "Yes."

"Locate Saul for me, will you?"

"I'll ring the corridors." A pause. "Can't find him."

"Thanks." The Attendant was puzzled. He was beginning to make little sniffing motions with his nose. "Do you—*smell* anything?"

Lantry sniffed. "No. Why?"

"I *smell* something."

Lantry took hold of the knife in his pocket. He waited.

"I remember once when I was a kid," said the man. "And we found a cow lying dead in the field. It had been there two days in the hot sun. That's what this smell is. I wonder what it's from?"

"Oh, I know what it is," said Lantry quietly. He held out his hand. "Here."

"What?"

"Me, of course."

"You?"

"Dead several hundred years."

"You're an odd joker." The Attendant was puzzled!

"Very." Lantry took out the knife. "Do you know what this is?"

"A knife."

"Do you ever use knives on people any more?"

"How do you mean?"

"I mean—killing them, with knives or guns or poison?"

"You *are* an odd joker!" The man giggled awkwardly.

"I'm going to kill you," said Lantry.

"Nobody kills anybody," said the man.

"Not any more they don't. But they used to, in the old days."

"I know they did."

"This will be the first murder in three hundred years. I just killed your friend. I just shoved him into the fire lock."

That remark had the desired effect. It numbed the man so completely, it shocked him so thoroughly with its illogical aspects that Lantry had time to walk forward. He put the knife against the man's chest. "I'm going to kill you."

"That's silly," said the man, numbly. "People don't do that."

"Like this," said Lantry. "You see?"

The knife slid into the chest. The man stared at it for a moment. Lantry caught the falling body.

III

The Salem flue exploded at six that morning. The great fire chimney shattered into ten thousand parts and flung itself into the earth and into the sky and into the houses of the sleeping people. There was fire and sound, more fire than autumn made burning in the hills.

William Lantry was five miles away at the time of the explosion. He saw the town ignited by the great spreading cremation of it. And he shook his head and laughed a little bit and clapped his hands smartly together.

Relatively simple. You walked around killing people who didn't believe in murder, had only heard of it indirectly as some dim gone custom of the old barbarian races. You walked into the control-room of the Incinerator and said, "How do you work this Incinerator?" and the control man told you, because everybody told the truth in this world of the future, nobody lied, there was no reason to lie, there was no danger to lie *against*. There was only one criminal in the world, and nobody knew *he* existed yet.

Oh, it was an incredibly beautiful set-up. The Control Man had told him just how the Incinerator worked, what pressure gauges controlled the flood of fire gases going up the flue, what levers were adjusted or readjusted. He and Lantry had had quite a talk. It was an easy free world. People trusted people. A moment later Lantry had shoved a knife in the Control Man also and set the pressure gauges for an overload to occur half an hour later, and walked out of the Incinerator halls, whistling.

Now even the sky was palled with the vast black cloud of the explosion.

"This is only the first," said Lantry, looking at the sky.

"I'll tear all the others down before they even suspect there's an unethical man loose in their society. They can't account for a variable like me. I'm beyond their understanding. I'm incomprehensible, impossible, therefore I do not exist. My God, I can kill hundreds of thousands of them before they even realize murder is out in the world again. I can make it look like an accident each time. Why, the idea is so huge, it's unbelievable!"

The fire burned the town. He sat under a tree for a long time, until morning. Then, he found a cave in the hills, and went in, to sleep.

He awoke at sunset with a sudden dream of fire. He saw himself pushed into the flue, cut into sections by flame, burned away to nothing. He sat up on the cave floor, laughing at himself. He had an idea.

He walked down into the town and stepped into an audio booth. He dialled *Operator*. "Give me the Police Department," he said.

"I beg your pardon?" said the operator.

He tried again. "The Law Force," he said.

"I will connect you with the Peace Control," she said, at last.

A little fear began ticking inside him like a tiny watch. Suppose the operator recognized the term Police Department as an anachronism, took his audio number, and sent someone out to investigate? No, she wouldn't do that. Why should she suspect? Paranoids were nonexistent in this civilization.

"Yes, the Peace Control," he said.

A buzz. A man's voice answered. "Peace Control. Stephens speaking."

"Give me the Homicide Detail," said Lantry, smiling.

"The *what*?"

"Who investigates murders?"

"I beg your pardon, what are you talking about?"

"Wrong number." Lantry hung up, chuckling. Ye gods, there was no such thing as a Homicide Detail. There were no murders, therefore they needed no detectives. Perfect, perfect!

The audio rang back. Lantry hesitated, then answered.

"Say," said the voice on the phone. "Who *are* you?"

"The man just left who called," said Lantry, and hung up again.

He ran. They would recognise his voice and perhaps send someone out to check. People didn't lie. *He* had just lied. They knew his voice. Anybody who lied needed a psychiatrist. They would come to pick him up to see why he was lying. For no *other* reason. They suspected him of nothing else. Therefore—he must run.

Oh, how very carefully he must act from now on. He knew nothing of this world, this odd straight truthful ethical world. Simply by looking pale you were suspect. Simply by not sleeping nights you were suspect. Simply by not bathing, by smelling like a—dead cow?—you were suspect. Anything.

He must go to a library. But that was dangerous, too. What were libraries like today? Did they have books or did they have film spools which projected books on a screen? Or did people have libraries at home, thus eliminating the necessity of keeping large main libraries?

He decided to chance it. His use of archaic terms might well make him suspect again, but now it was very important he learn all that could be learned of this foul world into which he had come again. He stopped a man on the street. "Which way to the library?"

The man was not surprised. "Two blocks east, one block north."

"Thank you."

Simple as that.

He walked into the library a few minutes later.

"May I help you?"

He looked at the librarian. May I help you, may I help you. What a world of helpful people! "I'd like to 'have' Edgar Allan Poe." His verb was carefully chosen. He didn't say "read." He was too afraid that books were passé, that printing itself was a lost art. Maybe all "books" today were in the form of fully delineated three-dimensional motion pictures. How in hell could you make a motion picture out of Socrates, Schopenhauer, Nietzsche and Freud?

"What was that name again?"

"Edgar Allan Poe."

"There is no such author listed in our files."

"Will you please check?"

She checked. "Oh, yes. There's a red mark on the file card. He was one of the authors in the Great Burning of 2265."

"How ignorant of me."

"That's all right," she said. "Have you heard much of him?"

"He had some interesting barbarian ideas on death," said Lantry.

"Horrible ones," she said, wrinkling her nose. "Ghastly."

"Yes. Ghastly. Abominable, in fact. Good thing he was burned. Unclean. By the way, do you have any of Lovecraft?"

"Is that a sex book?"

Lantry exploded with laughter. "No, no. It's a man."

She riffled the file. "He was burned, too. Along with Poe."

"I suppose that applies to Machen and a man named Derleth and one named Ambrose Bierce, also?"

"Yes." She shut the file cabinet. "All burned. And good riddance." She gave him an odd warm look of interest. "I bet you've just come back from Mars."

"Why do you say that?"

"There was another explorer in here yesterday. He'd just made the Mars hop and return. He was interested in supernatural literature, also. It seems there are actually 'tombs' on Mars."

"What are 'tombs'?" Lantry was learning to keep his mouth closed.

"You know, those things they once buried people in."

"Barbarian custom. Ghastly!"

"Isn't it? Well, seeing the Martian tombs made this young explorer curious. He came and asked if we had any of those authors you mentioned. Of course we haven't even a smitch of their stuff." She looked at his pale face. "You *are* one of the Martian rocket men, aren't you?"

"Yes," he said. "Got back on the ship the other day."

"The other young man's name was Burke."

"Of course. Burke! Good friend of mine!"

"Sorry I can't help you. You'd best get yourself some vitamin shots and some sun-lamp. You look terrible, Mr —?"

"Lantry. I'll be good. Thanks ever so much. See you next Hallows' Eve!"

"Aren't you the clever one." She laughed. "If there *were* a Hallows' Eve, I'd make it a date."

"But they burned *that*, too," he said.

"Oh, they burned everything," she said. "Good night."

"Good night." And he went out.

Oh, how carefully he was balanced in this world! Like some kind of dark gyroscope, whirling with never a murmur, a very silent man. As he walked along the eight o'clock evening street he noticed with particular interest that there was not an unusual amount of lights about. There were the usual street lights at each corner, but the blocks themselves were only faintly illuminated. Could it be that these remarkable people were not *afraid of the dark*? Incredible nonsense! *Everyone* was afraid of the dark. *Even he* himself had been afraid, as a child. It was as natural as eating.

A little boy ran by on pelting feet, followed by six others. They yelled and shouted and rolled on the dark cool October lawn, in the leaves. Lantry looked on for several minutes before addressing himself to one of the small boys who was for a moment taking a respite, gathering his breath into his small lungs, as a boy might blow to refill a punctured paper bag.

"Here, now," said Lantry. "You'll wear yourself out."

"Sure," said the boy.

"Could you tell me," said the man, "why there are not street lights in the middle of the blocks?"

"Why?" asked the boy.

"I'm a teacher, I thought I'd test your knowledge," said Lantry.

"Well," said the boy, "you don't need lights in the middle of the block, that's why."

"But it gets rather dark," said Lantry.

"So?" said the boy.

"Aren't you afraid?" asked Lantry.

"Of what?" asked the boy.

"The dark," said Lantry.

"Ho, ho," said the boy. "Why should I be?"

"Well," said Lantry. "It's black, it's dark. And after all, street lights were invented to take away the dark and take away fear."

"That's silly. Street lights were made so you could see where you were walking. Outside of that there's nothing."

"You miss the whole point—" said Lantry. "Do you mean to say you would sit in the middle of an empty lot all night and not be afraid?"

"Of what?"

"Of what, of what, of what, you little ninny! Of the dark!"

"Ho ho."

"Would you go out in the hills and stay all night in the dark?"

"Sure."

"Would you stay in a deserted house alone?"

"Sure."

"And not be afraid?"

"Sure."

"You're a liar!"

"Don't you call me nasty names!" shouted the boy. Liar was the improper noun, indeed. It seemed to be the worst thing you could call a person.

Lantry was completely furious with the little monster. "Look," he insisted. "Look into my eyes . . ."

The boy looked.

Lantry bared his teeth slightly. He put out his hands, making a clawlike gesture. He leered and gesticulated and wrinkled his face into a terrible mask of horror.

"Ho ho," said the boy. "You're funny."

"*What* did you say?"

"You're funny. Do it again. Hey, gang, c'mere! This man does funny things!"

"Never mind."

"Do it again, sir."

"Never mind, never mind. Good night!" Lantry ran off.

"Good night, sir. And mind the dark, sir!" called the little boy.

Of all the stupidity, of all the rank, gross, crawling, jelly-mouthed stupidity! He had never seen the like of it in his life! Bringing the children up without so much as an *ounce* of imagination! Where was the fun in being children if you didn't imagine things?

He stopped running. He slowed and for the first time began to appraise himself. He ran his hand over his face and bit his finger and found that he himself was standing midway in the block and he felt uncomfortable. He moved up to the street corner where there was a glowing lantern. "That's better," he said, holding his hands out like a man to an open warm fire.

He listened. There was not a sound except the night breathing of the crickets. Faintly there was a fire-hush as a rocket swept the sky. It was the sound a torch might make brandished gently on the dark air.

He listened to himself and for the first time he realized what there was so peculiar to himself. There was not a sound in him. The little nostril and lung noises were absent. His lungs did not take nor give oxygen or carbon-dioxide; they did not move. The hairs in his nostrils did not quiver with warm combing air. That faint purrling whisper of breathing did not sound in his nose. Strange. Funny. A noise you never heard when you were alive, the breath that fed your body, and yet, once dead, oh how you missed it!

The only other time you ever heard it was on deep dreamless awake nights when you wakened and listened and heard first your nose taking and gently poking out the air, and then the dull deep dim red thunder of the blood in your temples, in your eardrums, in your throat, in your aching wrists, in your warm loins, in your chest. All of those little rhythms, gone. The wrist beat gone, the throat pulse gone, the chest vibration gone. The sound of the blood coming up down around and through, up down around and through. Now it was like listening to a statue.

And yet he *lived*. Or, rather, moved about. And how was this done, over and above scientific explanations, theories, doubts?

By one thing, and one thing alone.

Hatred.

Hatred was a blood in him, it went up down around and through, up down around and through. It was a heart in him, not beating, true, but warm. He was—what? Resentment. Envy. They said he could not lie any longer in his coffin in the cemetery. He had *wanted* to. He had never had any particular desire to get up and walk around. It had been enough, all these centuries, to lie in the deep box and feel but *not feel* the ticking of the million insect watches in the earth around, the moves of worms like so many deep thoughts in the soil.

But then they had come and said, "Out you go and into the furnace!" And that is the worst thing you can say to any man. You cannot tell him what to do. If you say you are dead, he will want not to be dead. If you say there are no such things as vampires, by God, that man will try to *be* one just for spite. If you say a dead man cannot walk he will test his limbs. If you say murder is no longer occurring, he will make it occur. He was, *in toto*, all the impossible things. They had given birth to him with their damnable practices and ignorances. Oh, how wrong they were. They needed to be shown. He would *show* them! Sun is *good*, so is *night*, there is nothing wrong with dark, *they said*.

Dark is horror, he shouted, silently, facing the little houses. It is *meant* for contrast. You must fear, you hear! That has always been the way of this world. You destroyers of Edgar Allan Poe and fine big-worded Lovecraft, you burner of Hallowe'en masks and destroyer of pumpkin jack-o-lanterns! I will make night what it *once* was, the thing against which man built all his lanterned cities and his many children!

As if in answer to this, a rocket, flying low, trailed a long rakish feather of flame. It made Lantry flinch and draw back.

IV

It was but ten miles to the little town of Science Port. He made it by dawn, walking. But even this was not good. At four in the morning a silver beetle pulled up on the road beside him.

"Hello," called the man inside.

"Hello," said Lantry wearily.

"Why are you walking?" asked the man.

"I'm going to Science Port."

"Why don't you ride?"

"I *like* to walk."

"*Nobody* likes to walk. Are you sick? May I give you a ride?"

"Thanks, but I like to walk."

The man hesitated, then closed the beetle door. "Good night."

When the beetle was gone over the hill, Lantry retreated into a nearby forest. A world full of bungling helping people. By God, you couldn't even *walk* without being accused of sickness. That meant only one thing. He must not walk any longer, he had to ride. He should have accepted that fellow's offer.

The rest of the night he walked far enough off the highway so that if a beetle rushed by he had time to vanish in the underbrush. At dawn he crept into an empty dry water-drain and closed his eyes.

The dream was as perfect as a rimed snowflake.

He saw the graveyard where he had lain deep and ripe over the centuries. He heard the early morning footsteps of the labourers returning to finish their work.

"Would you mind passing me the shovel, Jim?"

"Here you go."

"Wait a minute, wait a minute."

"What's up?"

"Look here. We didn't finish last night, did we?"

"No."

"There was one more coffin, wasn't there?"

"Yes."

"Well, here it is, and open."

"You've got the wrong hole."

"What's the name say on the gravestone?"

"Lantry. William Lantry."

"That's him, that's the one! Gone!"

"What could have happened to it?"

"How do I know. The body was here last night."

"We can't be sure, we didn't look."

"God, man, people don't bury empty coffins. He was in his box. Now he isn't."

"Maybe this box was empty."

"Nonsense. Smell that smell? He was here all right."

A pause.

"Nobody would have taken the body, would they?"

"What for?"

"A curiosity, perhaps."

"Don't be ridiculous. People just don't steal. Nobody steals."

"Well, then, there's only one solution."

"And?"

"He got up and walked away."

A pause. In the dark dream, Lantry expected to hear

laughter. There was none. Instead, the voice of the gravedigger, after a thoughtful pause, said, "Yes. That's it, indeed. He got up and walked away."

"That's interesting to think about," said the other.

"Isn't it, though?"

Silence.

Lantry awoke. It had all been a dream, but God, how realistic. How strangely the two men had carried on. But not unnaturally, oh, no. That was exactly how you expected men of the future to talk. Men of the future. Lantry grinned wryly. That was an anachronism for you. This *was* the future. This was happening *now*. It wasn't 300 years from now, it was now, not then, or any other time. This wasn't the Twentieth Century. Oh, how calmly those two men in the dream had said, "He got up and walked away." "—interesting to think about." "*Isn't* it, though?" With never a quaver in their voices. With not so much as a glance over their shoulders or a tremble of spade in hand. But, of course, with their perfectly honest, logical minds, there was but one explanation; certainly nobody had *stolen* the corpse. "*Nobody* steals." The corpse had simply got up and walked off. The corpse was the only one who could have *possibly* moved the corpse. By the few casual slow words of the gravediggers Lantry knew what they were thinking. Here was a man that had lain in suspended animation, not really dead, for hundreds of years. The jarring about, the activity, had brought him back.

Everyone had heard of those little green toads that are sealed for centuries inside mud rocks or in ice patties, alive, alive oh! And how when scientists chipped them out and warmed them like marbles in their hands the little toads leapt about and frisked and blinked. Then it was only logical that the gravediggers think of William Lantry in like fashion.

But what if the various parts were fitted together in the next day or so? If the vanished body and the shattered, exploded Incinerator were connected? What if this fellow named Burke, who had returned pale from Mars, went to the library again and said to the young woman he wanted some books and she said, "Oh, your friend Lantry was in the other day." And he'd say, "Lantry who? Don't know anyone by that name." And she'd say, "Oh, he *lied*." And people in this time didn't lie. So it would all form and coalesce, item by item, bit by bit. A pale man who was pale and shouldn't be pale had lied and people don't lie, and a walking man on a lonely country road had walked and people don't walk anymore, and a body was missing from a cemetery, and the Incinerator had blown up and and—

They would come after him. They would find him. He would be easy to find. He walked. He lied. He was pale. They would find him and take him and stick him through the open fire lock of the nearest burner and that would be your Mr. William Lantry, like a Fourth of July set-piece!

There was only one thing to be done efficiently and completely. He arose in violent moves. His lips were wide and his dark eyes were flared and there was a trembling and burning all through him. He must kill and kill and kill and kill and kill. He must make his enemies into friends, into people like himself who walked but shouldn't walk, who were pale in a land of pinks. He must kill and then kill and then kill again. He must make bodies and dead people and corpses. He must destroy Incinerator after flue after burner after Incinerator. Explosion on explosion. Death on death. Then, when the Incinerators were all thrown in ruin, and the hastily established morgues were jammed with the bodies of people shattered by the explosion, then he would begin to make friends, his enrolment of the dead in his own cause.

Before they traced and found and killed him, they must be killed themselves. So far he was safe. He could kill and they would not kill back. People simply do not go around killing. That was his safety margin. He climbed out of the abandoned drain, stood in the road.

He took the knife from his pocket and hailed the next beetle.

It was like the Fourth of July! The biggest damned firecracker of them all. The Science Port Incinerator split down the middle and flew apart. It made a thousand small explosions that ended with a greater one. It fell upon the town and crushed houses and burned trees. It woke people from sleep and then put them to sleep again, forever, an instant later.

William Lantry, sitting in a beetle that was not his own, tuned idly to a station on the audio dial. The collapse of the Incinerator had killed some four hundred people. Many had been caught in flattened houses, others struck by flying metal. A temporary morgue was being set up at—

An address was given.

Lantry noted it with a pad and pencil.

He could go on this way, he thought, from town to town, from country to country, destroying the burners, the Pillars of Fire, until the whole clean magnificent framework of flame and cauterization was tumbled. He made a fair estimate—each explosion averaged five hundred dead. You could work up to a hundred thousand in no time.

He pressed the floor stud of the beetle. Smiling, he drove off through the dark streets of the city.

The city coroner had requisitioned an old warehouse. From midnight until four in the morning the grey beetles hissed down the rain-shiny streets, turned in, and the bodies were laid out on the cold concrete floors, with white sheets over them. It was a continuous flow until about four-thirty; then it stopped. There were about two hundred bodies there, white and cold.

The bodies were left alone; nobody stayed behind to tend them. There was no use tending the dead; it was a useless procedure; the dead could take care of themselves.

About five o'clock, with a touch of dawn in the east, the first trickle of relatives arrived to identify their sons or their fathers or their mothers or their uncles. The people moved quickly into the warehouse, made the identification, moved quickly out again. By six o'clock, with the sky still lighter in the east, this trickle had passed on, also.

William Lantry walked across the wide wet street and entered the warehouse.

He held a piece of blue chalk in one hand.

He walked by the coroner who stood in the entranceway talking to two others ". . . drive the bodies to the Incinerator in Mellin Town, tomorrow . . ." The voices faded.

Lantry moved, his feet echoing faintly on the cool concrete. A wave of sourceless relief came to him as he walked among the shrouded figures. He was among his own. And—better than that, by God! he had *created* these! He had made them dead! He had procured for himself a vast number of recumbent friends!

Was the coroner watching? Lantry turned his head. No. The warehouse was calm and quiet and shadowed in the dark morning. The coroner was walking away now, across the street, with his two attendants, a beetle had drawn up on the other side of the street, and the coroner was going over to talk with whomever was in the beetle.

William Lantry stood and made a blue chalk pentagram on the floor by each of the bodies. He moved swiftly, swiftly, without a sound, without blinking. In a few minutes, glancing up now and then to see if the coroner was still busy, he had chalked the floor by a hundred bodies. He straightened up and put the chalk in his pocket.

Now is the time for all good men to come to the aid of their party, now is the time for all good men to come to the aid of their party, now is the time for all good men to come to the aid of their party, now is the time. . . .

Lying in the earth, over the centuries, the processes and thoughts of passing peoples and passing times had seeped down to him, slowly, as into a deep-buried sponge. From some death-memory in him now, ironically, repeatedly, a black typewriter clacked out black even lines of pertinent words:

Now is the time for all good men, for all good men, to come to the aid of—

William Lantry.

other words—

Arise my love, and come away—

The quick brown fox jumped over ... *Paraphrase* it. The quick risen body jumped over the tumbled Incinerator. . . .

Lazarus, come forth from the tomb. . . .

He knew the right words. He need only speak them as they had been spoken over the centuries. He need only gesture with his hands and speak the words, the dark words that would cause these bodies to quiver, rise and walk!

And when they had risen he would take them through the town, they would kill others and the others would rise and walk. By the end of the day there would be thousands of good friends walking with him. And what of the naive, living people of this year, this day, this hour? They would be completely unprepared for it. They would go down to defeat because they would not be expecting war of any sort. They wouldn't believe it possible, it would all be over before they could convince themselves that such an illogical thing could happen.

He lifted his hands. His lips moved. He said the words. He began in a chanting whisper and then raised his voice, louder. He said the words again and again and again. His eyes were closed tightly. His body swayed. He spoke faster and faster. He began to move forward among the bodies. The dark words flowed from his mouth. He was enchanted with his own formulae. He stooped and made further blue symbols on the concrete, in the fashion of long-dead sorcerers, smiling, confident. Any moment now the first tremor of the still bodies, any moment now the rising, the leaping up of the cold ones!

His hands lifted in the air. His head nodded. He spoke, he spoke, he spoke. He gestured. He talked loudly over the bodies, his eyes flaring, his body tensed. "Now!" he cried violently. "Rise, *all* of you!"

Nothing happened.

"Rise!" he screamed, with a terrible torment in his voice.

The sheets lay in white blue-shadow folds over the silent bodies.

"Hear me, and act!" he shouted.

Far away, on the street, a beetle hissed along.

Again, again, again he shouted, pleaded. He got down by each body and asked of it his particular violent favour. No reply. He strode wildly between the even white rows, flinging his arms up, stooping again and again to make blue symbols!

Lantry was very pale. He licked his lips. "Come on, get up," he said. "They have, they always have, for a thousand years. When you make a mark—so! and speak a word—so! they always rise! Why not you now, why not you! Come on, come *on*, before *they* come back!"

The warehouse went up into shadow. There were steel beams across and down. In it, under the roof, there was not a sound, except the raving of a lonely man.

Lantry stopped.

Through the wide doors of the warehouse he caught a glimpse of the last cold star of morning.

This was the year 2349.

His eyes grew cold and his hands fell to his sides. He did not move.

Once upon a time people shuddered when they heard the wind about the house, once people raised crucifixes and wolfbane, and believed in walking dead and bats and loping white wolves. And as long as they believed, then so long did the dead, the bats, the loping wolves exist. The mind gave birth and reality to them.

But . . .

He looked at the white-sheeted bodies.

These people did not believe.

They had never believed. They would never believe.

They had never imagined that the dead might walk. The dead went up flues in flame. They had never heard superstition, never trembled or shuddered or doubted in the dark. Walking dead people could not exist, they were illogical. This was the year 2349, man, after all!

Therefore, these people could not rise, could not walk again. They were dead and flat and cold. Nothing, chalk, imprecation, superstition, could wind them up and set them walking. They were dead and *knew* they were dead!

He was alone.

There were live people in the world who moved and drove beetles and drank quiet drinks in little dimly illumined bars by country roads, and kissed women and talked much good talk all day and every day.

But he was not alive.

Friction gave him what little warmth he possessed.

There were two hundred dead people here in this warehouse now, cold upon the floor. The first dead people in a hundred years who were allowed to be corpses for an extra hour or more. The first not to be immediately trundled to the Incinerator and lit like so much phosphorus.

He should be happy with them, among them.

He was not.

They were completely dead. They did not know nor believe in walking once the heart had paused and stilled itself. They were deader than dead ever was.

He was indeed alone, more alone than any man had ever been. He felt the chill of his aloneness moving up into his chest, strangling him quietly.

William Lantry turned suddenly and gasped.

While he had stood there, someone had entered the warehouse. A tall man with white hair, wearing a lightweight tan overcoat and no hat. How long the man had been nearby there was no telling.

There was no reason to stay here. Lantry turned and started to walk slowly out. He looked hastily at the man as he passed and the man with the white hair looked back at him, curiously. Had he heard? The imprecations, the pleadings, the shoutings? Did he suspect? Lantry slowed his walk. Had this man seen him make the blue chalk marks? But then, would he interpret them as symbols of an ancient superstition? Probably not.

Reaching the door, Lantry paused. For a moment he did not want to do anything but lie down and be coldly, really dead again and be carried silently down the street to some distant burning flue and there dispatched in ash and whispering fire. If he was indeed alone and there was no chance to collect an army to his cause, what, then, existed as a reason for going on? Killing? Yes, he'd kill a few thousand more. But that wasn't enough. You can only do so much of that before they drag you down.

He looked at the cold sky.

A rocket went across the black heaven, trailing fire.

Mars burned red among a million stars.

Mars. The library. The librarian. Talk. Returning rocket men. Tombs.

Lantry almost gave a shout. He restrained his hand, which wanted so much to reach up into the sky and touch Mars. Lovely red star on the sky. Good star that gave him sudden new hope. If he had a living heart now it would be thrashing wildly, and sweat would be breaking out of him and his pulses would be stammering, and tears would be in his eyes!

He would go down to wherever the rockets sprang up into space. He would go to Mars, one way or another. He would go to the Martian tombs. There, there, by God, were bodies, he would bet his last hatred on it, that would rise and walk and work with him! Theirs was an ancient culture, much different from that of Earth, patterned on the Egyptian, if what the librarian had said was true. And the Egyptian—what a crucible of dark superstition and midnight terror that culture had been! Mars it *was*, then. Beautiful Mars!

But he must not attract attention to himself. He must move carefully. He wanted to run, yes, to get away, but that would be the worst possible move he could make. The man with the white hair was glancing at Lantry from time to time, in the entranceway. There were too many people about. If anything happened he would be outnumbered. So far he had taken on only *one* man at a time.

Lantry forced himself to stop and stand on the steps before the warehouse. The man with the white hair came out on to the steps also and stood, looking at the sky. He looked as if he was going to speak at any moment. He fumbled in his pockets, took out a packet of cigarettes.

V

They stood outside the morgue together, the tall pink, white-haired man, and Lantry, hands in their pockets. It was a cool night with a white shell of a moon that washed a house here, a road there and, further on, parts of a river.

"Cigarette?" The man offered Lantry one.

"Thanks."

They lit up together. The man glanced at Lantry's mouth. "Cool night."

"Cool."

They shifted their feet. "Terrible accident."

"Terrible."

"So many dead."

"So many."

Lantry felt himself some sort of delicate weight upon a scale. The other man did not seem to be looking at him, but rather listening and feeling towards him. There was a feathery balance here that made for vast discomfort. He wanted to move away and get out from under this balancing, weighing. The tall white-haired man said, "My name's McClure."

"Did you have any friends inside?" asked Lantry.

"No. A casual acquaintance. Awful accident."

"Awful."

They balanced each other. A beetle hissed by on the

road with its seventeen tires whirling quietly. The moon showed a little town further over in the black hills.

"I say," said the man McClure.

"Yes."

"Could you answer me a question?"

"Be glad to." He loosened the knife in his coat pocket, ready.

"Is your name Lantry?" asked the man at last.

"Yes."

"*William* Lantry?"

"Yes."

"Then you're the man who came out of the Salem graveyard day before yesterday, aren't you?"

"Yes."

"Good Lord, I'm glad to meet you, Lantry! We've been trying to find you for the past twenty-four hours!"

The man seized his hand, pumped it, slapped him on the back.

"What, what?" said Lantry.

"Good Lord, man, why did you run off? Do you realize what an instance this is? We want to talk to you!"

McClure was smiling, glowing. Another handshake, another slap. "I *thought* it was you!"

The man is mad, thought Lantry. Absolutely mad. Here I've toppled his incinerators, killed people, and he's shaking my hand. Mad, mad!

"Will you come along to the Hall?" said the man, taking his elbow.

"Wh-what hall?" Lantry stepped back.

"The Science Hall, of course. It isn't every year we get a real case of suspended animation. In small animals, yes, but in a man, hardly! Will you come?"

"What's the act!" demanded Lantry, glaring. "What's all this talk."

"My dear fellow, what do you mean?" the man was stunned.

"Never mind. Is that the only reason you want to see me?"

"What other reason would there be, Mr. Lantry? You

don't know how glad I am to see you!" He almost did a
little dance. "I suspected. When we were in there
together. You being so pale and all. And then the way
you smoked your cigarette, something about it, and a lot
of other things, all subliminal. But it is you, isn't it, it
is you!"

"It is I. William Lantry." Dryly.

"Good fellow! Come along!"

The beetle moved swiftly through the dawn streets.
McClure talked rapidly.

Lantry sat, listening, astounded. Here was this fool,
McClure, playing his cards for him! Here was this stupid
scientist, or whatever, accepting him not as a suspicious
baggage, a murderous item. Oh no! Quite the contrary!
Only as a suspended animation case was he considered!
Not as a dangerous man at all. Far from it!

"Of course," cried McClure, grinning, "you don't know
where to go, whom to turn to. It was all quite incredible
to you."

"Yes."

"I had a feeling you'd be there at the morgue tonight,"
said McClure, happily.

"Oh?" Lantry stiffened.

"Yes. Can't explain it. But you, how shall I put it?
Ancient Americans? You had funny ideas on death. And
you were among the dead so long, I felt you'd be drawn
back by the accident, by the morgue and all. It's not very
logical. Silly, in fact. It's just a feeling. I hate feelings
but there it was. I came on a, I guess you'd call it a
hunch, wouldn't you?"

"You might call it that."

"And there you were!"

"There I was," said Lantry.

"Are you hungry?"

"I've eaten."

"How did you get around?"

"I hitch-hiked."

"You *what*?"

"People gave me rides on the road."

"Remarkable."

"I imagine it sounds that way." He looked at the passing houses. "So this is the era of space travel, is it?"

"Oh, we've been travelling to Mars for some forty years now."

"Amazing. And those big funnels, those towers in the middle of every town?"

"Those. Haven't you heard? The Incinerators. Oh, of course, they hadn't anything of that sort in your time. Had some bad luck with them. An explosion in Salem and one here, all in a forty-eight hour period. You looked as if you were going to speak; what is it?"

"I was thinking," said Lantry. "How fortunate I got out of my coffin when I did. I might well have been thrown into one of your Incinerators and burned up."

"That would have been terrible, wouldn't it have?"

"Quite."

Lantry toyed with the dials of the beetle dash. He wouldn't go to Mars. His plans were changed. If this fool simply refused to recognize an act of violence when he stumbled upon it, then let him be a fool. If they didn't connect the two explosions with a man from the tomb, all well and good. Let them go on deluding themselves. If they couldn't imagine someone being mean and nasty and murderous, heaven help them. He rubbed his hands with satisfaction. No, no Martian trip for you, as yet, Lantry lad. First we'll see what can be done boring from the inside. Plenty of time. The Incinerators can wait an extra week or so. One has to be subtle, you know. Any more immediate explosions might cause quite a ripple of thought.

McClure was gabbling wildly on.

"Of course, you don't have to be examined immediately. You'll want a rest. I'll put you up at my place."

"Thanks. I don't feel up to being probed and pulled. Plenty of time in a week or so."

They drew up before a house and climbed out.

"You'll want sleep, naturally."

"I've been asleep for centuries. Be glad to stay awake. I'm not a bit tired."

"Good." McClure let them into the house. He headed for the drink bar. "A drink will fix us up."

"You have one," said Lantry. "Later for me. I just want to sit down."

"By all means sit." McClure mixed himself a drink. He looked around the room, looked at Lantry, paused for a moment with the drink in his hand, tilted his head to one side, and put his tongue in his cheek. Then he shrugged and stirred the drink. He walked slowly to a chair and sat, sipping the drink quietly. He seemed to be listening for something. "There are cigarettes on the table," he said.

"Thanks." Lantry took one and lit it and smoked it. He did not speak for some time.

Lantry thought, I'm taking this all too easily. Maybe I should kill and run. He's the only one that has found me, yet. Perhaps this is all a trap. Perhaps we're simply sitting here waiting for the police. Or whatever in hell they use for police these days. He looked at McClure. No. They weren't waiting for police. They were waiting for something else.

McClure didn't speak. He looked at Lantry's face and he looked at Lantry's hands. He looked at Lantry's chest a long time, with easy quietness. He sipped his drink. He looked at Lantry's feet.

Finally he said, "Where'd you get the clothing?"

"I asked someone for clothes and they gave these things to me. Darned nice of them."

"You'll find that's how we are in this world. All you have to do is ask."

McClure shut up again. His eyes moved. Only his eyes and nothing else. Once or twice he lifted his drink.

A little clock ticked somewhere in the distance.

"Tell me about yourself, Mr. Lantry."

"Nothing much to tell."

"You're modest."

"Hardly. You know about the past. I know nothing of

the future, or I should say 'today' and day before yesterday. You don't learn much in a coffin."

McClure did not speak. He suddenly sat forward in
his chair and then leaned back and shook his head.

They'll never suspect me, thought Lantry. They aren't
superstitious, they simply *can't* believe in a dead man
walking. Therefore, I'll be safe. I'll keep putting off the
physical checkup. They're polite. They won't force me.
Then, I'll work it so I can get to Mars. After that, the
tombs, in my own good time, and the plan. God, how
simple. How naive these people are.

McClure sat across the room for five minutes. A cold-
ness had come over him. The color was very slowly going
from his face, as one sees the color of medicine vanishing
as one presses the bulb at the top of a dropper. He
leaned forward, saying nothing, and offered another cigarette to Lantry.

"Thanks." Lantry took it. McClure sat deeply back into
his easy chair, his knees folded one over the other. He
did not look at Lantry, and yet somehow did. The feeling
of weighing and balancing returned. McClure was like a
tall thin master of hounds listening for something that
nobody else could hear. There are little silver whistles
you can blow that only dogs can hear. McClure seemed
to be listening acutely, sensitively for such an invisible
whistle, listening with his eyes and with his half-opened,
dry mouth, and with his aching, breathing nostrils.

Lantry sucked the cigarette, sucked the cigarette,
sucked the cigarette, and, as many times, blew out, blew
out, blew out. McClure was like some lean red-shagged
hound listening and listening with a slick slide of eyes to
one side, with an apprehension in that hand that was so
precisely microscopic that one only sensed it, as one
sensed the invisible whistle, with some part of the brain
deeper than eyes or nostril or ear. McClure was all chemist's scale, all antennae.

The room was so quiet the cigarette smoke made some
kind of invisible noise rising to the ceiling. McClure was

a thermometer, a chemist's scales, a listening hound, a
litmus paper, an antenna; all these. Lantry did not move.
Perhaps the feeling would pass. It had passed before.
McClure did not move for a long while and then, without
a word, he nodded at the sherry decanter, and Lantry
refused as silently. They sat looking but not looking at
each other, again and away, again and away.

McClure stiffened slowly. Lantry saw the color getting
paler in those lean cheeks, and the hand tightening on
the sherry glass, and a knowledge come at last to stay,
never to go away, into the eyes.

Lantry did not move. He could not. All of this was of
such a fascination that he wanted only to see, to hear,
what would happen next. It was McClure's show from
here on in.

McClure said, "At first I thought it was the finest psy-
chosis I have ever seen. You, I mean. I thought, he's
convinced himself, Lantry's convinced himself, he's quite
insane, he's told himself to do all these things." McClure
talked as if in a dream, and continued talking and
didn't stop.

"I said to myself, he purposely doesn't breathe through
his nose. I watched your nostrils, Lantry. The little nostril
hairs never once quivered in the last hour. That wasn't
enough. It was a fact I filed. It wasn't enough. He
breathes through his mouth, I said, on purpose. And then
I gave you a cigarette and you sucked and blew, sucked
and blew. None of it ever came out your nose. I told
myself, well, that's all right. He doesn't inhale. Is that
terrible, is that suspect? All in the mouth, all in the
mouth. And then, I looked at your chest. I watched. It
never moved up or down, it did nothing. He's convinced
himself, I said to myself. He's convinced himself about
all this. He doesn't move his chest, except slowly, when
he thinks you're not looking. That's what I told myself."

The words went on in the silent room, not pausing,
still in a dream. "And then I offered you a drink but you
don't drink and I thought, he doesn't drink, I thought.
Is *that* terrible? And I watched and watched you all this

time. Lantry holds his breath, he's fooling himself. But now, yes, now, I understand it quite well. Now I know everything the way it is. Do you know how I know? I do not hear breathing in the room. I wait and I hear nothing. There is no beat of heart or intake of lung. The room is so silent. Nonsense, one might say, but I know. At the Incinerator I knew. There is a difference. You enter a room where a man is on a bed and you know immediately whether he will look up and speak to you or whether he will not speak to you ever again. Laugh if you will, but one can tell. It is a subliminal thing. It is the whistle the dog hears when no human hears. It is the tick of a clock that has ticked so long one no longer notices. Something is in a room when a man lives in it. Something is not in the room when a man is dead in it."

McClure shut his eyes a moment. He put down his sherry glass. He waited a moment. He took up his cigarette and puffed it and then put it down in a black tray.

"I am alone in this room," he said.

Lantry did not move.

"You are dead," said McClure. "My mind does not know this. It is not a thinking thing. It is a thing of the senses and the subconscious. At first I thought, this man *thinks* he is dead, risen from the dead, a vampire. Is that not logical? Would not any man, buried as many centuries, raised in a superstitious, ignorant culture, think likewise of himself once risen from the tomb? Yes, that is logical. This man has hypnotized himself and fitted his bodily functions so that they would in no way interfere with his self-delusion, his great paranoia. He governs his breathing. He tells himself, I cannot hear my breathing, therefore I am dead. His inner mind censors the sound of breathing. He does not allow himself to eat or drink. These things he probably does in his sleep, with part of his mind, hiding the evidences of this humanity from his deluded mind at other times."

McClure finished it. "I was wrong. You are not insane. You are not deluding yourself. Nor me. This is all very illogical and—I must admit—almost frightening. Does that make you feel good, to think you frighten me? I have no label for you. You're a very odd man, Lantry. I'm glad to have met you. This will make an interesting report indeed."

"Is there anything wrong with me being dead?" said Lantry. "Is it a crime?"

"You must admit it's highly unusual."

"But, still now, is it a crime?" asked Lantry.

"We have no crime, no criminal court. We want to examine you, naturally, to find out how you have happened. It is like that chemical which, one minute inert, the next is living cell. Who can say where what happened to what. You are that impossibility. It is enough to drive a man quite insane."

"Will I be released when you are done fingering me?"

"You will not be held. If you don't wish to be examined, you will not be. But I am hoping you will help by offering us your services."

"I might," said Lantry.

"But tell me," said McClure. "What were you doing at the morgue?"

"Nothing."

"I heard you talking when I came in."

"I was merely curious."

"You're lying. That is very bad, Mr. Lantry. The truth is far better. The truth, is, is it not, that you are dead and, being the only one of your sort, were lonely. Therefore you killed people to have company."

"How does that follow?"

McClure laughed. "Logic, my dear fellow. Once I *knew* you were really dead, a moment ago, really a— what do you call it—a vampire (silly word!), I tied you immediately to the Incinerator blasts. Before that there was no reason to connect you. But once the piece fell into place, the fact that you were dead, then it was simple to guess your loneliness, your hate, your envy, all of the tawdry motivations of a walking corpse. It took only an instant then to see the Incinerators blown to blazes, and then to think of you, among the bodies at the morgue, seeking help, seeking friends and people like yourself to work with——"

"You're too damned smart!" Lantry was out of the chair. He was halfway to the other man when McClure rolled over and scuttled away, flinging the sherry decanter. With a great despair Lantry realized that, like a damned idiot, he had thrown away his one chance to kill McClure. He should have done it earlier. It had been Lantry's one weapon, his safety margin. If people in a society never *killed* each other, they never *suspected* one another. You could walk up to any one of them and kill them.

"Come back here!" Lantry threw the knife.

McClure got behind a chair. The idea of flight, of protection, of fighting, was still new to him. He had part of the idea, but there was still a bit of luck on Lantry's side if Lantry wanted to use it.

"Oh, no," said McClure, holding the chair between himself and the advancing man. "You want to kill me. It's odd, but true. I can't understand it. You want to cut me with that knife or something like that, and it's up to me to prevent you from doing such an odd thing."

"I *will* kill you!" Lantry let it slip out. He cursed himself. That was the worst possible thing to say.

Lantry lunged across the chair, clutching at McClure.

McClure was very logical. "It won't do you any good to kill me. You *know* that." They wrestled and held each other in a wild, toppling shuffle. Tables fell over, scattering articles. "You remember what happened in the morgue?"

"I don't care!" screamed Lantry.

"You didn't raise *those* dead, did you?"

"I don't care!" cried Lantry.

"Look here," said McClure, reasonably. "There will never be any more like you, ever, there's no use."

"Then I'll destroy all of you, all of you!" screamed Lantry.

"And then what? You'll still be alone, with no more like you about."

"I'll go to Mars. They have tombs there. I'll find more like myself!"

"No," said McClure. "The executive order went through yesterday. All of the tombs are being deprived of their bodies. They'll be burned in the next week."

They fell together to the floor. Lantry got his hands on McClure's throat.

"Please," said McClure. "Do you see, you'll *die*."

"What do you mean?" cried Lantry.

"Once you kill all of us, and you're alone, you'll die! The hate will die. That hate is what moves you, *nothing else*! That envy moves you. Nothing else! You'll die, inevitably. You're not immortal. You're not even alive, you're nothing but a moving hate."

"I don't care!" screamed Lantry, and began choking the man, beating his head with his fists, crouched on the defenseless body. McClure looked up at him with dying eyes.

The front door opened. Two men came in.

"I say," said one of them. "What's going on? A new game?"

Lantry jumped back and began to run.

"Yes, a new game!" said McClure, struggling up. "Catch him and you win!"

The two men caught Lantry. "We win," they said.

"Let me go!" Lantry thrashed, hitting them across their faces, bringing blood.

"Hold him tight!" cried McClure.

They held him.

"A rough game, what?" one of them said. "What do we do *now*?"

The beetle hissed along the shining road. Rain fell out of the sky and a wind ripped at the dark green wet trees. In the beetle, his hands on the half-wheel, McClure was talking. His voice was a susurrant, a whispering, a hypnotic thing. The two other men sat in the back seat. Lantry sat, or rather lay, in the front seat, his head back, his eyes faintly open, the glowing green light of the dash dials showing on his cheeks. His mouth was relaxed. He did not speak.

McClure talked quietly and logically, about life and moving, about death and not moving, about the sun and the great sun Incinerator, about the emptied tombyard, about hatred and how hate lived and made a clay man live and move, and how illogical it all was, it all was, it all was. One was dead, was dead, was dead, that was all, all, all. One did not try to be otherwise. The car whispered on the moving road. The rain spatted gently on the windshield. The men in the back seat conversed quietly. Where were they going, going? To the Incinerator, of course. Cigarette smoke moved slowly up on the air, curling and tying into itself in grey loops and spirals. One was dead and must accept it.

Lantry did not move. He was a marionette, the strings cut. There was only a tiny hatred in his heart, in his eyes, like twin coals, feeble, glowing, fading.

I am Poe, he thought. I am all that is left of Edgar Allan Poe, and I am all that is left of Ambrose Bierce and all that is left of a man named Lovecraft. I am a grey night bat with sharp teeth, and I am a square black monolith monster. I am Osiris and Bal and Set. I am the Necronomicon, the Book of the Dead. I am the house of Usher, falling into flame. I am the Red Death. I am the man mortared into the catacomb with a cask of Amontillado . . . I am a dancing skeleton. I am a coffin, a shroud, a lightning bolt reflected in an old house window. I am an autumn-empty tree, I am a rapping, flinging shutter. I am a yellowed volume turned by a claw hand. I am an organ played in an attic at midnight. I am a mask, a skull mask behind an oak tree on the last day of October. I am a poison apple bobbing in a water tub for child noses to bump at, for child teeth to snap . . . I am a black candle lighted before an inverted cross. I am a coffin lid, a sheet with eyes, a foot-step on a black stairwell. I am Dunsany and Machen and I am The Legend of Sleepy Hollow. I am The Monkey's Paw and I am The Phantom Rickshaw. I am The Cat and the

Canary, The Gorilla, The Bat. I am the ghost of Hamlet's father on the castle wall.

All of these things am I. And now these last things will be burned. While I lived *they* still lived. While I moved and hated and existed, *they* still existed. I am *all* that remembers them. I am all of them that *still* goes on, and will *not* go on after tonight. Tonight, all of us, Poe and Bierce and Hamlet's father, we burn together. They will make a big heap of us and burn us like a bonfire, like things of Guy Fawkes' day, gasoline, torchlight, cries and all!

And what a wailing will we put up. The world will be clean of us, but in our going we shall say, oh what is the world like, clean of fear, where is the dark imagination from the dark time, the thrill and the anticipation, the suspense of old October, gone, never more to come again, flattened and smashed and burned by the rocket people, by the Incinerator people, destroyed and obliterated, to be replaced by doors that open and close and lights that go on or off without fear. If only you could remember how once *we* lived, what Hallowe'en was to us, and what Poe was, and how we gloried in the dark morbidities. One more drink, dear friends, of Amontillado, before the burning. All of this, all, exists, but in one last brain on earth. A whole world dying tonight. One more drink, pray.

"Here we are," said McClure.

The Incinerator was brightly lighted. There was quiet music nearby. McClure got out of the beetle, came around to the other side. He opened the door. Lantry simply lay there. The talking and the logical talking had slowly drained him of life. He was no more than wax now, with a small glow in his eyes. This future world, how the men *talked* to you, how logically they reasoned away your life. They wouldn't believe in him. The force of their disbelief froze him. He could not move his arms or his legs. He could only mumble senselessly, coldly, eyes flickering.

McClure and the two others helped him out of the car, put him in a golden box and rolled him on a roller table into the warm glowing interior of the building.

I am Edgar Allan Poe, and I am Ambrose Bierce, I am Hallowe'en, I am a coffin, a shroud, a Monkey's Paw, a Phantom, a Vampire. . . .

"Yes, yes," said McClure, quietly, over him. "I know. I know."

The table glided. The walls swung over him and by him, the music played. You are dead, you are logically dead.

I am Usher, I am the Maelstrom, I am the MS Found In A Bottle, I am the Pit and I am the Pendulum, I am the Telltale Heart, I am the Raven nevermore, nevermore.

"Yes," said McClure, as they walked softly. "I know."

"I am in the catacomb," cried Lantry.

"Yes, the catacomb," said the walking man over him.

"I am being chained to a wall, and there is no bottle of Amontillado here!" cried Lantry weakly, eyes closed.

"Yes," someone said.

There was movement. The flame door opened.

"Now someone is mortaring up the cell, closing me in!"

"Yes, I *know*." A whisper.

The golden box slid into the flame lock.

"I'm being walled in! A very good joke indeed! Let us be gone!" A wild scream and much laughter.

"We know, we understand. . . ."

The inner flame lock opened. The golden coffin shot forth into flame.

"For the love of God, Montresor! For the love of God!"

This story is in this book because one of the editor's father read it aloud to him when he was just a kid. Greg didn't remember the title or the author, but he never forgot the story. It took years to track the story down, but we think you'll find it just as creepy today as it was when it was first published in 1953. Besides science fiction, Joe L. Hensley has written several acclaimed suspense novels.

And Not Quite Human

JOE L. HENSLEY

They won of course. One ship against a world, but they won easily.

The Regents would be pleased. Another planet for colonization—even a few specimens for the labs. Earthmen, who had incredibly lived through the attack.

Forward, in a part of the great ship where the complex control panels whirred and clicked, two of the Arcturians conferred together.

"How are the Earth specimens, Doctor?" the older one asked, his voice indifferent. He touched his splendid purple pants, straightening the already precise creases.

"They stare at the walls, Captain. They do not eat what we give them. They seem to look through the guards, say very little and use their bodies feebly. I do not think that all of them will live through the trip."

"They are weak. It only shows the laboratories are wrong. Our people are *not* related to them—despite the

44

similarity in appearance. No, we are cast in a stronger mold than that." He drummed his desk with impatient fingers. "Well—we can't let them die. Force-feed them if necessary. Our scientists demand specimens; we are lucky that some of them lived through the attack. I don't see how it was possible—it was such a splendid attack."

"They have no real sickness, not even a radiation burn in the lot of them," the doctor said. "But they are weak and morose."

"Keep them alive and well, Doctor."

The doctor searched the captain's metallic face. "Captain, do you ever have dreams?"

"Eh—dreams?" It took the captain a moment to comprehend. "Dreams are forbidden by the Regents! They show instability."

"The men, Sir ... some of the crew have been complaining."

"Complaining! Complaining's expressly forbidden in the rules. You know that, Doctor. Why haven't I been informed?"

"It was such a little thing, something psychological, I think. I've had a few in who've had nightmares." The doctor made a deprecatory gesture. "Space fear, I think. Most of the men complaining were first trippers."

"Make a list of the names and submit it to me. We have to eliminate such types, as you should know."

"Yes, Sir." The doctor got up to leave.

"Uh—Doctor—did they tell you what the dreams were about?"

"Blood, Sir." The doctor shook his head and clenched his antiseptic, scoured hands. "Skulls and bats and old women around a bubbling pot; bony shadows that trapped them when they ran."

"Rot."

"Yes, Sir."

The doctor walked down the gleaming passageway, seeing the men like well oiled machines; the talented men, each in his own technical job, each uniform precisely the same, the teeth, clean and white, each face and body cut from the same matrix, even the boots alike, dark shiny mirrors. Unlined faces—young, unlike the skeleton faces in the hold.

The first guard brought hand to forehead in a snappy salute. "Yes, Sir?"

"Prisoner inspection."

The door whined open and the doctor started through.

"Sir!" The urgency in the guard's voice detained him.

"Yes?" He remembered the man as one of the ones who had been at sick call that morning.

"May I be relieved? I feel ill. I've been sick since— since last sleep period."

The doctor looked impassively at the too-white eyes. *Better not let it start,* he thought.

"Stand your duty. I can't have you relieved. You know the rules."

"But, Sir!"

"Report to sickbay after you are relieved. For psycho-analysis—and I mean after you are *regularly* relieved!" The doctor again looked into the frightened eyes and considered making an exception this one time. *No, there'll be more then,* he thought.

The automatic salute reassured him. "Yes, Sir."

"Your name?" He wrote it in his prescription book and walked on.

First cell, second cell, the fifteenth; all the same. The listless faces, the hungry deadmen's eyes watching him. Eyes cut from coffins. Twenty-two cells—two to a cell, women segregated as they should be. Forty-four prisoners in all.

Eighty-eight eyes watching him. He shivered inwardly. *How many were there?* he thought. *Forty-four individuals left out of a billion or two?*

He read the guards' notebooks. "Man in cell fourteen, Name: Alexander Green. Was observed drawing strange patterns on the deck with chalk. Chalk taken away from him. No resistance."

"Woman in cell three, Name: Elizabeth Gout. Talking

to herself and to the walls. Was quieted by her cellmate, Meg Newcomb, on orders of Corporal of the Guard."

The shadows were thick in the prisoners' hold; the lights dim, the only sounds were the thrum of the rhythmic atomic engines and the click of the guards' heels as each one came to attention and presented his book for inspection.

The Corporal of the Guard walked silently behind him and took the orders down at the end of the cell block.

"Force-feed them. Bring the vitamin lights down here. Give them injections." The doctor paused and stared coldly. "The guard at cell four was inept in his salute. Place him on report."

"Yes, Sir."

"Anything else to report, Corporal?"

The man hesitated; then said, "Some of the guards are jumpy."

"And the prisoners?" the doctor asked caustically.

The corporal was flustered. "They seem stronger, Sir."

"They're getting acclimated to the conditions of the trip."

"They still haven't eaten anything."

"I said—in case you misunderstood me, Corporal— that they are getting acclimated to the trip. You may consider yourself on report too." The doctor enunciated each word savagely.

The corporal clicked his heels and the doctor went quickly back up the line of cells. He averted his head, not looking into the cells. An electronic device scanned him and opened the door as it read his identity.

He went through the hatch, felt it close quickly behind him, and disregarded the guard who had wanted to be relieved. He went on to his own office in the small, efficient sickbay. He slumped over his desk exhausted.

There was a sound of running feet outside. Then the door to his office was almost torn from its hinges as a soundless blast of energy struck it. The doctor leaped to his feet and flung open the metal door.

The sick guard stood there, weaving drunkenly on boneless legs. "Stand back, Doctor. I see one over by the wall. See it over there?" the man screamed. "It's coming for me. Can't get away—can't." He raised the pistol as the doctor watched.

"Stop—You damned fool!"

The man lay on the floor, gun pointed at his own shapeless body, his torso a mass of torn, charred tissue. His eyes were still open and they stared sightlessly at the small porthole, beyond which the luminous stars reeled.

The sight was not revolting to the doctor, but the implications were. He had seen too many dead, both of his own race and others, to care particularly about one more. It was what this death might mean to him personally that worried him—what the Regents might say.

He called the guard on watch and gave orders automatically until the task of examining and disposing was done. There were necessary papers to fill out and sign, the personal effects to be inventoried—and the report to the captain. And all the time he was engaged in the routine, his mind flashed the question: *I wonder what it will mean to me when we get back? The Regents will want to examine me. They'll say it was my fault.* He felt the panic begin to rise, but his body made the necessary responses and his face was imperturbable.

He went to the captain's office.

"Why did he do it, Doctor?" The captain was more perplexed than angry.

The doctor stonily replied, "We're in space."

"We have a hundred million men in space!" the captain exclaimed. "Few of them ever commit suicide. It's been bred out of the race. It just doesn't happen." He pounded his hand against his plastic desk, the almost muted sound incongruous with the angry gesture. "I want to know why. It's against the rules—*you* know that."

The doctor did not flinch. "He was a first tripper. First time away from home. A guard? No—a farmboy in uniform, that's what he was." The doctor found himself almost homicidally angry at the dead guard. *What right does he have to cause me all this trouble?*

The captain watched him strangely. "That's what most of our men are—men from farms. I'm from a farm myself." The captain eyed him dubiously while the insidious sounds of the machines rocked and jolted around them. "You're tired, Doctor. You need some rest."

The doctor ignored the remark. "Maybe it's the prisoners. All the guards who have complained have been standing prisoner watches."

"I've seen the prisoners." The barking voice was contemptuous.

Have you seen them? Have you seen the way they look at you? the doctor thought, but aloud he said, through regulated teeth: "Yes, Sir."

"Find out what's wrong."

"Yes, Sir. I'll do my best." *Spit and polish and everything according to the rules.*

"Report to me on everything."

"Of course, Captain."

"Do an autopsy—look at his brain."

"I did, Sir." He fought to keep his voice rational. "We kept his head. We always do in a case like this."

"Do it again." The captain stared penetratingly at him. "Find out what was wrong with his head, so that we can eliminate it from the race. Something was wrong with his head—that was it. Find out!"

"Yes, Sir!" *Feet together, salute, turn—keep your back straight. Be a soldier, be a spaceman, be an Arcturian, be strong—be a conqueror.*

The doctor went back to his own office and sat down shakily at his plastic desk. Then he fought his way upright again and looked in the room's small mirror.

Still the same. I'm still the same—but so tired—why am I so tired?

He touched his face. "Same face." *But it was more deeply marked and harsh now.*

His hair: "Like always." *Is that a streak of gray?*

His eyes: "They see." *What do they see? What? What?*

And then, for the first time, his tightly held mind barrier let down and he admitted the dreams and the long sleepless periods to himself. Remembered them for what they were. Knew he could no longer fool himself.

Insects crawling on him; a great gray rat with canine teeth at his throat, while bats eyed him evilly—and curious women who plied their trade around a bubbling pot, their thin-edged voices plotting more horrors. And always the shadows, shadows that leaped and tore at his unprotected body, shadows that had a definite form—shadows which faded disconcertingly just as he seemed to be able to make out the faces that were sickeningly familiar.

The nightmares became real to him.

Quite suddenly, the nightmares came close to him as he sat at the plastic desk and together they planned the ghastly joke, while they laughed together. He nicked, with surgical care, the arteries in his wrists and groins and smiled as he bubbled away on the metal desk.

"Goodby, Doctor," said a voice.

Goodby, Voice. And the sound echoed while the uniform became discolored, the boots greasy with death, the face too white—smiling and staring.

And the others—the many others—soon.

For three sleep periods the machines sighed as the carnage went on. The captain put out directives and took the guns away. After that they found other ways. Crewmen jumped out the escape hatches and into the atomic convertors—or smashed their heads against the steel bulkheads.

For three sleep periods.

Each time he heard the clicking of the guard's heels, the captain almost screamed. In his imagination, he was seeing the Arcturian Regents. They were pointing accusing fingers at him, while the extermination chambers waited.

"Your ship," they said.

"My ship," he admitted.

"The doctor, half of your crew dead. How—why did they die?"

"Suicide." He trembled under the blanket.

"It's against the rules, Captain," the voices said calmly, convicting him.

"I told them."

"But you are the captain. The captain is responsible. The rule says that."

"Yes—the doctor said it was the prisoners."

The Regents laughed. "For the good of the race, we have no choice but . . ."

The captain pulled the covers tighter over his aching head and lay stiffly on his cot. He drowned the voices in a sea of his own making, smiling as he saw each hand disappear under the stormy waves. For a while he lay that way, while the juggernaut shadows slippered carefully about the room, hovering and watchful.

And then, once again, he could hear the whine of the great engines. He sat up.

The old man—the one listed on the rolls as Adam Manning, one of the specimen Earthmen—sat on one of the stiff chairs by the captain's desk.

"Hello," the old man said.

"Guards!" screamed the captain.

But no one answered. Only the machines roared on, replying softly in their unhearing way.

"Guards!" the captain screamed again as he watched the old man's face.

"They can't hear you," the old man said.

The captain knew instinctively that it was true. "*You* did it!" He strained to leap from his cot at the old man. He could not move. His hands clenched as he fought against invisible bonds.

He began to cry. But the Regents' voices came, stopping it. "Crying's against the rules," they said stiffly, without pity.

The old man smiled at him from the chair. The shadows murmured softly, conferring in myriad groups, dirtying the aseptic bulkheads. They drew closer to the captain and he could only half-stifle a scream.

"What are you?" he managed.

"Something you've trained out of your people. You wouldn't understand even if we told you, because you don't believe that there ever was anything like us." The old man smiled. "We're your new Regents." The shadows smiled hideously, agreeing, and revealing their long, canine teeth.

"It was a wonderful attack, Captain," the old man said softly. The shadows nodded as they formed and faded. "Nothing human could have lived through it—nothing human did. Some of us were deep underground where they'd buried us long ago—the stakes through our hearts—they knew how to deal with us. But your fire burned the stakes away."

He waved a scaly hand at the shadows. They came down upon the Captain relentlessly.

The captain began to scream.

Then, there was only the automatic sound of the machines.

The ship roared on through space.

Not all scientific vampires live in the distant future, or even today. History is filled with bloodthirsty rulers, as well as scientists who refused to accept the superstitions of their times. British author and critic Brian Stableford mixes vampires with an intriguing alternate history in this story, which he later expanded into his acclaimed novel The Empire of Fear.

The Man Who
Loved the Vampire Lady

BRIAN STABLEFORD

A man who loves a vampire lady may not die young, but cannot live forever. (Walachian proverb)

It was the thirteenth of June in the Year of Our Lord 1623. Grand Normandy was in the grip of an early spell of warm weather, and the streets of London bathed in sunlight. There were crowds everywhere, and the port was busy with ships, three having docked that very day. One of the ships, the *Freemartin*, was from the Moorish enclave and had produce from the heart of Africa, including ivory and the skins of exotic animals. There were rumors, too, of secret and more precious goods: jewels and magical charms; but such rumors always attended the docking of any vessel from remote parts of the world. Beggars and street urchins had flocked to the dockland, responsive as ever to such whisperings, and were plaguing every sailor in the streets, as anxious for gossip as for copper coins. It seemed that the only faces not animated by excitement were those worn by the severed heads that dressed the spikes atop the Southwark Gate. The Tower of London, though, stood quite aloof from the hubbub, its tall and forbidding turrets so remote from the streets that they belonged to a different world.

Edmund Cordery, mechanician to the court of the Archduke Girard, tilted the small concave mirror on the brass device that rested on his workbench, catching the rays of the afternoon sun and deflecting the light through the system of lenses.

He turned away and directed his son, Noell, to take his place. "Tell me if all is well," he said tiredly. "I can hardly focus my eyes, let alone the instrument."

Noell closed his left eye and put his other to the microscope. He turned the wheel that adjusted the height of the stage. "It's perfect," he said. "What is it?"

"The wing of a moth." Edmund scanned the polished tabletop, checking that the other slides were in readiness for the demonstration. The prospect of Lady Carmilla's visit filled him with a complex anxiety that he resented in himself. Even in the old days, she had not come to his laboratory often. But to see her here—on his own territory, as it were—would be bound to awaken memories that were untouched by the glimpses that he caught of her in the public parts of the Tower and on ceremonial occasions.

"The water slide isn't ready," Noell pointed out.

Edmund shook his head. "I'll make a fresh one when the time comes," he said. "Living things are fragile, and the world that is in a water drop is all too easily destroyed."

He looked farther along the bench-top, and moved a crucible, placing it out of sight behind a row of jars. It was impossible—and unnecessary—to make the place tidy, but he felt it important to conserve some sense of order and control. To discourage himself from fidgeting, he went to the window and looked out at the sparkling

Thames and the strange gray sheen on the slate roofs of the houses beyond. From this high vantage point, the people were tiny; he was higher even than the cross on the steeple of the church beside the Leathermarket. Edmund was not a devout man, but such was the agitation within him, yearning for expression in action, that the sight of the cross on the church made him cross himself, murmuring the ritual devotion. As soon as he had done it, he cursed himself for childishness.

I am forty-four years old, he thought, *and a mechanician. I am no longer the boy who was favored with the love of the lady, and there is no need for this stupid trepidation.*

He was being deliberately unfair to himself in this private scolding. It was not simply the fact that he had once been Carmilla's lover that made him anxious. There was the microscope, and the ship from the Moorish country. He hoped that he would be able to judge by the lady's reaction how much cause there really was for fear.

The door opened then, and the lady entered. She half turned to indicate by a flutter of her hand that her attendant need not come in with her, and he withdrew, closing the door behind him. She was alone, with no friend or favorite in tow. She came across the room carefully, lifting the hem of her skirt a little, though the floor was not dusty. Her gaze flicked from side to side, to take note of the shelves, the beakers, the furnace, and the numerous tools of the mechanician's craft. To a commoner, it would have seemed a threatening environment, redolent with unholiness, but her attitude was cool and controlled. She arrived to stand before the brass instrument that Edmund had recently completed, but did not look long at it before raising her eyes to look fully into Edmund's face.

"You look well, Master Cordery," she said calmly. "But you are pale. You should not shut yourself in your rooms now that summer is come to Normandy."

Edmund bowed slightly, but met her gaze. She had not changed in the slightest degree, of course, since the days when he had been intimate with her. She was six hundred years old—hardly younger than the archduke—and the years were impotent as far as her appearance was concerned. Her complexion was much darker than his, her eyes a deep liquid brown, and her hair jet black. He had not stood so close to her for several years, and he could not help the tide of memories rising in his mind. For her, it would be different: his hair was gray now, his skin creased; he must seem an altogether different person. As he met her gaze, though, it seemed to him that she, too, was remembering, and not without fondness.

"My lady," he said, his voice quite steady, "may I present my son and apprentice, Noell."

Noell bowed more deeply than his father, blushing with embarrassment.

The Lady Carmilla favored the youth with a smile. "He has the look of you, Master Cordery," she said—a casual compliment. She returned her attention then to the instrument.

"The designer was correct?" she asked.

"Yes, indeed," he replied. "The device is most ingenious. I would dearly like to meet the man who thought of it. A fine discovery—though it taxed the talents of my lens grinder severely. I think we might make a better one, with much care and skill; this is but a poor example, as one must expect from a first attempt."

The Lady Carmilla seated herself at the bench, and Edmund showed her how to apply her eye to the instrument, and how to adjust the focusing wheel and the mirror. She expressed surprise at the appearance of the magnified moth's wing, and Edmund took her through the series of prepared slides, which included other parts of insects' bodies, and sections through the stems and seeds of plants.

"I need a sharper knife and a steadier hand, my lady," he told her. "The device exposes the clumsiness of my cutting."

"Oh no, Master Cordery," she assured him politely.

"These are quite pretty enough. But we were told that more interesting things might be seen. Living things too small for ordinary sight."

Edmund bowed in apology and explained about the preparation of water slides. He made a new one, using a pipette to take a drop from a jar full of dirty river water. Patiently, he helped the lady search the slide for the tiny creatures that human eyes were not equipped to perceive. He showed her one that flowed as if it were semiliquid itself, and tinier ones that moved by means of cilia. She was quite captivated, and watched for some time, moving the slide very gently with her painted fingernails.

Eventually she asked: "Have you looked at other fluids?"

"What kind of fluids?" he asked, though the question was quite clear to him and disturbed him.

She was not prepared to mince words with him. "Blood, Master Cordery," she said very softly. Her past acquaintance with him had taught her respect for his intelligence, and he half regretted it.

"Blood clots very quickly," he told her. "I could not produce a satisfactory slide. It would take unusual skill."

"I'm sure that it would," she replied.

"Noell has made drawings of many of the things we *have* looked at," said Edmund. "Would you like to see them?"

She accepted the change of subject, and indicated that she would. She moved to Noell's station and began sorting through the drawings, occasionally looking up at the boy to compliment him on his work. Edmund stood by, remembering how sensitive he once had been to her moods and desires, trying hard to work out now exactly what she was thinking. Something in one of her contemplative glances at Noell sent an icy pang of dread into Edmund's gut, and he found his more important fears momentarily displaced by what might have been anxiety for his son, or simply jealousy. He cursed himself again for his weakness.

"May I take these to show the archduke?" asked the Lady Carmilla, addressing the question to Noell rather than to his father. The boy nodded, still too embarrassed to construct a proper reply. She took a selection of the drawings and rolled them into a scroll. She stood and faced Edmund again.

"We are most interested in this apparatus," she informed him. "We must consider carefully whether to provide you with new assistants, to encourage development of the appropriate skills. In the meantime, you may return to your ordinary work. I will send someone for the instrument, so that the archduke can inspect it at his leisure. Your son draws very well, and must be encouraged. You and he may visit me in my chambers on Monday next; we will dine at seven o'clock, and you may tell me about all your recent work."

Edmund bowed to signal his acquiescence—it was, of course, a command rather than an invitation. He moved before her to the door in order to hold it open for her. The two exchanged another brief glance as she went past him.

When she had gone, it was as though something taut unwound inside him, leaving him relaxed and emptied. He felt strangely cool and distant as he considered the possibility—stronger now—that his life was in peril.

When the twilight had faded, Edmund lit a single candle on the bench and sat staring into the flame while he drank dark wine from a flask. He did not look up when Noell came into the room, but when the boy brought another stool close to his and sat down upon it, he offered the flask. Noell took it, but sipped rather gingerly.

"I'm old enough to drink now?" he commented dryly.

"You're old enough," Edmund assured him. "But beware of excess, and never drink alone. Conventional fatherly advice, I believe."

Noell reached across the bench so that he could stroke the barrel of the microscope with slender fingers.

"What are you afraid of?" he asked.

Edmund sighed. "You're old enough for that, too, I suppose?"

"I think you ought to tell me."

Edmund looked at the brass instrument and said: "It were better to keep things like this dark secret. Some human mechanician, I daresay, eager to please the vampire lords and ladies, showed off his cleverness as proud as a peacock. Thoughtless. Inevitable, though, now that all this play with lenses has become fashionable."

"You'll be glad of eyeglasses when your sight begins to fail," Noell told him. "In any case, I can't see the danger in this new toy."

Edmund smiled. "New toys," he mused. "Clocks to tell the time, mills to grind the corn, lenses to aid human sight. Produced by human craftsmen for the delight of their masters. I think we've finally succeeded in proving to the vampires just how very clever we are—and how much more there is to know than we know already."

"You think the vampires are beginning to fear us?"

Edmund gulped wine from the flask and passed it again to his son. "Their rule is founded in fear and superstition," he said quietly. "They're long-lived, suffer only mild attacks of diseases that are fatal to us, and have marvelous powers of regeneration. But they're not immortal, and they're vastly outnumbered by humans. Terror keeps them safe, but terror is based in ignorance, and behind their haughtiness and arrogance, there's a gnawing fear of what might happen if humans ever lost their supernatural reverence for vampirekind. It's very difficult for them to die, but they don't fear death any the less for that."

"There've been rebellions against vampire rule. They've always failed."

Edmund nodded to concede the point. "There are three million people in Grand Normandy," he said, "and less than five thousand vampires. There are only forty thousand vampires in the entire imperium of Gaul, and about the same number in the imperium of Byzantium—

no telling how many there may be in the khanate of Walachia and Cathay, but not so very many more. In Africa the vampires must be outnumbered three or four thousand to one. If people no longer saw them as demons and demi-gods, as unconquerable forces of evil, their empire would be fragile. The centuries through which they live give them wisdom, but longevity seems to be inimical to creative thought—they learn, but they don't *invent*. Humans remain the true masters of art and science, which are forces of change. They've tried to control that—to turn it to their advantage—but it remains a thorn in their side."

"But they do have power," insisted Noell. "They *are* vampires."

Edmund shrugged. "Their longevity is real—their powers of regeneration, too. But is it really their magic that makes them so? I don't know for sure what merit there is in their incantations and rituals, and I don't think even *they* know—they cling to their rites because they dare not abandon them, but where the power that makes humans into vampires really comes from, no one knows. From the devil? I think not. I don't believe in the devil— I think it's something in the blood. I think vampirism may be a kind of disease—but a disease that makes men stronger instead of weaker, insulates them against death instead of killing them. If that *is* the case—do you see now why the Lady Carmilla asked whether I had looked at blood beneath the microscope?"

Noell stared at the instrument for twenty seconds or so, mulling over the idea. Then he laughed.

"If we could *all* become vampires," he said lightly, "we'd have to suck one another's blood."

Edmund couldn't bring himself to look for such ironies. For him, the possibilities inherent in discovering the secrets of vampire nature were much more immediate, and utterly bleak.

"It's not true that they *need* to suck the blood of humans," he told the boy. "It's not nourishment. It gives them . . . a kind of pleasure that we can't understand.

And it's part of the mystique that makes them so terrible
... and hence so powerful." He stopped, feeling embarrassed. He did not know how much Noell knew about
his sources of information. He and his wife never talked
about the days of his affair with the Lady Carmilla, but
there was no way to keep gossip and rumor from reaching the boy's ears.

Noell took the flask again, and this time took a deeper
draft from it. "I've heard," he said distantly, "that
humans find pleasure, too ... in their blood being
drunk."

"No," replied Edmund calmly. "That's untrue. Unless
one counts the small pleasure of sacrifice. The pleasure
that a human man takes from a vampire lady is the same
pleasure that he takes from a human lover. It might be
different for the girls who entertain vampire men, but I
suspect it's just the excitement of hoping that they may
become vampires themselves."

Noell hesitated, and would probably have dropped the
subject, but Edmund realized suddenly that he did not
want the subject dropped. The boy had a right to know,
and perhaps might one day *need* to know.

"That's not entirely true," Edmund corrected himself.
"When the Lady Carmilla used to taste my blood, it did
give me pleasure, in a way. It pleased me because it
pleased *her*. There *is* an excitement in loving a vampire
lady, which makes it different from loving an ordinary
woman ... even though the chance that a vampire lady's
lover may himself become a vampire is so remote as to
be inconsiderable."

Noell blushed, not knowing how to react to this acceptance into his father's confidence. Finally he decided that
it was best to pretend a purely academic interest.

"Why are there so many more vampire women than
men?" he asked.

"No one knows for sure," Edmund said. "No humans,
at any rate. I can tell you what I believe, from hearsay
and from reasoning, but you must understand that it is a
dangerous thing to think about, let alone to speak about."

Noell nodded.

"The vampires keep their history secret," said Edmund, "and they try to control the writing of human history, but the following facts are probably true. Vampirism came to western Europe in the fifth century, with the vampire-led horde of Attila. Attila must have known well enough how to make more vampires—he converted both Aëtius, who became ruler of the imperium of Gaul, and Theodosius II, the emperor of the east who was later murdered. Of all the vampires that now exist, the vast majority must be converts. I have heard reports of vampire children born to vampire ladies, but it must be an extremely rare occurrence. Vampire men seem to be much less virile than human men—it is said that they couple very rarely. Nevertheless, they frequently take human consorts, and these consorts often become vampires. Vampires usually claim that this is a gift, bestowed deliberately by magic, but I am not so sure they can control the process. I think the semen of vampire men carries some kind of seed that communicates vampirism much as the semen of humans makes women pregnant—and just as haphazardly. That's why the male lovers of vampire ladies don't become vampires."

Noell considered this, and then asked: "Then where do vampire lords come from?"

"They're converted by other male vampires," Edmund said. "Just as Attila converted Aëtius and Theodosius." He did not elaborate, but waited to see whether Noell understood the implication. An expression of disgust crossed the boy's face and Edmund did not know whether to be glad or sorry that his son could follow the argument through.

"Because it doesn't always happen," Edmund went on, "it's easy for the vampires to pretend that they have some special magic. But some women never become pregnant, though they lie with their husbands for years. It is said, though, that a human may also become a vampire by drinking vampire's blood—if he knows the appropriate magic spell. That's a rumor the vampires don't like, and they exact terrible penalties if anyone is caught trying the experiment. The ladies of our own court, of course, are for the most part onetime lovers of the archduke or his cousins. It would be indelicate to speculate about the conversion of the archduke, though he is certainly acquainted with Aëtius."

Noell reached out a hand, palm downward, and made a few passes above the candle flame, making it flicker from side to side. He stared at the microscope.

"*Have* you looked at blood?" he asked.

"I have," replied Edmund. "And semen. Human blood, of course—and human semen."

"And?"

Edmund shook his head. "They're certainly not homogeneous fluids," he said, "but the instrument isn't good enough for really detailed inspection. There are small corpuscles—the ones in semen have long, writhing tails—but there's more . . . much more . . . to be seen, if I had the chance. By tomorrow this instrument will be gone— I don't think I'll be given the chance to build another."

"You're surely not in danger! You're an important man—and your loyalty has never been in question. People think of you as being almost a vampire yourself. A black magician. The kitchen girls are afraid of me because I'm your son—they cross themselves when they see me."

Edmund laughed, a little bitterly. "I've no doubt they suspect me of intercourse with demons, and avoid my gaze for fear of the spell of the evil eye. But none of that matters to the vampires. To them, I'm only a human, and for all that they value my skills, they'd kill me without a thought if they suspected that I might have dangerous knowledge."

Noell was clearly alarmed by this. "Wouldn't. . . ." He stopped, but saw Edmund waiting for him to ask, and carried on after only a brief pause. "The Lady Carmilla . . . wouldn't she . . . ?"

"Protect me?" Edmund shook his head. "Not even if I were her favorite still. Vampire loyalty is to vampires."

"She was human once."

"It counts for nothing. She's been a vampire for nearly six hundred years, but it wouldn't be any different if she were no older than I."

"But . . . she did love you?"

"In her way," said Edmund sadly. "In her way." He stood up then, no longer feeling the urgent desire to help his son to understand. There were things the boy could find out only for himself and might never have to. He took up the candle tray and shielded the flame with his hand as he walked to the door. Noell followed him, leaving the empty flask behind.

Edmund left the citadel by the so-called Traitor's Gate, and crossed the Thames by the Tower Bridge. The houses on the bridge were in darkness now, but there was still a trickle of traffic; even at two in the morning, the business of the great city did not come to a standstill. The night had clouded over, and a light drizzle had begun to fall. Some of the oil lamps that were supposed to keep the thoroughfare lit at all times had gone out, and there was not a lamplighter in sight. Edmund did not mind the shadows, though.

He was aware before he reached the south bank that two men were dogging his footsteps, and he dawdled in order to give them the impression that he would be easy to track. Once he entered the network of streets surrounding the Leathermarket, though, he gave them the slip. He knew the maze of filthy streets well enough— he had lived here as a child. It was while he was apprenticed to a local clockmaker that he had learned the cleverness with tools that had eventually brought him to the notice of his predecessor, and had sent him on the road to fortune and celebrity. He had a brother and a sister still living and working in the district, though he saw them very rarely. Neither one of them was proud to have a reputed magician for a brother, and they had not forgiven him his association with the Lady Carmilla.

He picked his way carefully through the garbage in

the dark alleys, unperturbed by the sound of scavenging rats. He kept his hands on the pommel of the dagger that was clasped to his belt, but he had no need to draw it. Because the stars were hidden, the night was pitch-dark, and few of the windows were lit from within by candlelight, but he was able to keep track of his progress by reaching out to touch familiar walls every now and again.

He came eventually to a tiny door set three steps down from a side street, and rapped upon it quickly, three times and then twice. There was a long pause before he felt the door yield beneath his fingers, and he stepped inside hurriedly. Until he relaxed when the door clicked shut again, he did not realize how tense he had been.

He waited for a candle to be lit.

The light, when it came, illuminated a thin face, crab-bed and wrinkled, the eyes very pale and the wispy white hair gathered imperfectly behind a linen bonnet.

"The lord be with you," he whispered.

"And with you, Edmund Cordery," she croaked.

He frowned at the use of his name—it was a deliberate breach of etiquette, a feeble and meaningless gesture of independence. She did not like him, though he had never been less than kind to her. She did not fear him as so many others did, but she considered him tainted. They had been bound together in the business of the Frater-nity for nearly twenty years, but she would never com-pletely trust him.

She lead him into an inner room, and left him there to take care of his business.

A stranger stepped from the shadows. He was short, stout, and bald, perhaps sixty years old. He made the special sign of the cross, and Edmund responded.

"I'm Cordery," he said.

"Were you followed?" The older man's tone was defer-ential and fearful.

"Not here. They followed me from the Tower, but it was easy to shake them loose."

"That's bad."

"Perhaps—but it has to do with another matter, not with our business. There's no danger to you. Do you have what I asked for?"

The stout man nodded uncertainly. "My masters are unhappy," he said. "I have been asked to tell you that they do not want you to take risks. You are too valuable to place yourself in peril."

"I am in peril already. Events are overtaking us. In any case, it is neither your concern nor that of your ... masters. It is for me to decide."

The stout man shook his head, but it was a gesture of resignation rather than a denial. He pulled something from beneath the chair where he had waited in the shadows. It was a large box, clad in leather. A row of small holes was set in the longer side, and there was a sound of scratching from within that testified to the presence of living creatures.

"You did exactly as I instructed?" asked Edmund.

The small man nodded, then put his hand on the mechanician's arm, fearfully. "Don't open it, sir, I beg you. Not here."

"There's nothing to fear," Edmund assured him.

"You haven't been in Africa, sir, as I have. Believe me, *everyone* is afraid—and not merely humans. They say that vampires are dying, too."

"Yes, I know," said Edmund distractedly. He shook off the older man's restraining hand and undid the straps that sealed the box. He lifted the lid, but not far—just enough to let the light in, and to let him see what was inside.

The box contained two big gray rats. They cowered from the light.

Edmund shut the lid again and fastened the straps.

"It's not my place, sir," said the little man hesitantly, "but I'm not sure that you really understand what you have there. I've seen the cities of West Africa—I've been in Corunna, too, and Marseilles. They remember other plagues in those cities, and all the horror stories are emerging again to haunt them. Sir, if any such thing ever came to London. . . ."

Edmund tested the weight of the box to see whether he could carry it comfortably. "It's not your concern," he said. "Forget everything that has happened. I will communicate with your masters. It is in my hands now."

"Forgive me," said the other, "but I must say this: there is naught to be gained from destroying vampires, if we destroy ourselves, too. It would be a pity to wipe out half of Europe in the cause of attacking our oppressors."

Edmund stared at the stout man coldly. "You talk too much," he said. "Indeed, you talk a *deal* too much."

"I beg your pardon, sire."

Edmund hesitated for a moment, wondering whether to reassure the messenger that his anxiety was understandable, but he had learned long ago that where the business of the Fraternity was concerned, it was best to say as little as possible. There was no way of knowing when this man would speak again of this affair, or to whom, or with what consequence.

The mechanician took up the box, making sure that he could carry it comfortably. The rats stirred inside, scrabbling with their small clawed feet. With his free hand, Edmund made the sign of the cross again.

"God go with you," said the messenger, with urgent sincerity.

"And with thy spirit," replied Edmund colorlessly.

Then he left, without pausing to exchange a ritual farewell with the crone. He had no difficulty in smuggling his burden back into the Tower, by means of a gate where the guard was long practiced in the art of turning a blind eye.

When Monday came, Edmund and Noell made their way to the Lady Carmilla's chambers. Noell had never been in such an apartment before, and it was a source of wonder to him. Edmund watched the boy's reactions to the carpets, the wall hangings, the mirrors and ornaments, and could not help but recall the first time *he* had entered these chambers. Nothing had changed here, and the rooms were full of provocations to stir and sharpen his faded memories.

Younger vampires tended to change their surroundings often, addicted to novelty, as if they feared the prospect of being changeless themselves. The Lady Carmilla had long since passed beyond this phase of her career. She had grown used to changelessness, had transcended the kind of attitude to the world that permitted boredom and ennui. She had adapted herself to a new aesthetic of existence, whereby her personal space became an extension of her own eternal sameness, and innovation was confined to tightly controlled areas of her life—including the irregular shifting of her erotic affections from one lover to another.

The sumptuousness of the lady's table was a further source of astonishment to Noell. Silver plates and forks he had imagined, and crystal goblets, and carved decanters of wine. But the lavishness of provision for just three diners—the casual waste—was something that obviously set him aback. He had always known that he was himself a member of a privileged elite, and that by the standards of the greater world, Master Cordery and his family ate well; the revelation that there was a further order of magnitude to distinguish the private world of the real aristocracy clearly made its impact upon him.

Edmund had been very careful in preparing his dress, fetching from his closet finery that he had not put on for many years. On official occasions he was always concerned to play the part of mechanician, and dressed in order to sustain that appearance. He never appeared as a courtier, always as a functionary. Now, though, he was reverting to a kind of performance that Noell had never seen him play, and though the boy had no idea of the subtleties of his father's performance, he clearly understood something of what was going on; he had complained acidly about the dull and plain way in which his father had made *him* dress.

Edmund ate and drank sparingly, and was pleased to note that Noell did likewise, obeying his father's instructions despite the obvious temptations of the lavish provision. For a while the lady was content to exchange routine courtesies, but she came quickly enough—by her standards—to the real business of the evening.

"My cousin Girard," she told Edmund, "is quite enraptured by your clever device. He finds it most interesting."

"Then I am pleased to make him a gift of it," Edmund replied. "And I would be pleased to make another, as a gift of Your Ladyship."

"That is not our desire," she said coolly. "In fact, we have other matters in mind. The archduke and his seneschal have discussed certain tasks that you might profitably carry out. Instructions will be communicated to you in due time, I have no doubt."

"Thank you, my lady," said Edmund.

"The ladies of the court were pleased with the drawings that I showed to them," said the Lady Carmilla, turning to look at Noell. "They marveled at the thought that a cupful of Thames water might contain thousands of tiny living creatures. Do you think that our bodies, too, might be the habitation of countless invisible insects?"

Noell opened his mouth to reply, because the question was addressed to him, but Edmund interrupted smoothly.

"There are creatures that may live upon our bodies," he said, "and worms that may live within. We are told that the macrocosm reproduces in essence the microcosm of human beings; perhaps there is a small microcosm within us, where our natures are reproduced again, incalculably small. I have read . . ."

"I have read, Master Cordery," she cut in, "that the illnesses that afflict humankind might be carried from person to person by means of these tiny creatures."

"The idea that diseases were communicated from one person to another by tiny seeds was produced in antiquity," Edmund replied, "but I do not know how such seeds might be recognized, and I think it very unlikely that the creatures we have seen in river water could possibly be of that character."

"It is a disquieting thought," she insisted, "that our bodies might be inhabited by creatures of which we can know nothing, and that every breath we take might be carrying into us seeds of all kinds of change, too small to be seen or tasted. It makes me feel uneasy."

"But there is no need," Edmund protested. "Seeds of corruptibility take root in human flesh, but yours is inviolate."

"You know that is not so, Master Cordery," she said levelly. "You have seen me ill yourself."

"That was a pox that killed many humans, my lady—yet it gave to you no more than a mild fever."

"We have reports from the imperium of Byzantium, and from the Moorish enclave, too, that there is plague in Africa, and that it has now reached the southern regions of the imperium of Gaul. It is said that this plague makes little distinction between human and vampire."

"Rumors, my lady," said Edmund soothingly. "You know how news becomes blacker as it travels."

The Lady Carmilla turned again to Noell, and this time addressed him by name so that there could be no opportunity for Edmund to usurp the privilege of answering her. "Are you afraid of me, Noell?" she asked.

The boy was startled, and stumbled slightly over his reply, which was in the negative.

"You must not lie to me," she told him. "You *are* afraid of me, because I am a vampire. Master Cordery is a skeptic, and must have told you that vampires have less magic than is commonly credited to us, but he must also have told you that I can do you harm if I will. Would you like to be a vampire yourself, Noell?"

Noell was still confused by the correction, and hesitated over his reply, but he eventually said: "Yes, I would."

"Of course you would," she purred. "All humans would be vampires if they could, no matter how they might pretend when they bend the knee in church. And men *can* become vampires; immortality is within our gift. Because of this, we have always enjoyed the loyalty and devotion of the greater number of our human subjects. We have always rewarded that devotion in some measure. Few have joined our ranks, but the many have enjoyed centuries of order and stability. The vampires rescued Europe from a Dark Age, and as long as vampires rule, barbarism will always be held in check. Our rule has not always been kind, because we cannot tolerate defiance, but the alternative would have been far worse. Even so, there are men who would destroy us—did you know that?"

Noell did not know how to reply to this, so he simply stared, waiting for her to continue. She seemed a little impatient with his gracelessness, and Edmund deliberately let the awkward pause go on. He saw a certain advantage in allowing Noell to make a poor impression.

"There is an organization of rebels," the Lady Carmilla went on. "A secret society, ambitious to discover the secret way by which vampires are made. They put about the idea that they would make all men immortal, but this is a lie, and foolish. The members of this brotherhood seek power for themselves."

The vampire lady paused to direct the clearing of one set of dishes and the bringing of another. She asked for a new wine, too. Her gaze wandered back and forth between the gauche youth and his self-assured father.

"The loyalty of your family is, of course, beyond question," she eventually continued. "No one understands the workings of society like a mechanician, who knows well enough how forces must be balanced and how the different parts of a machine must interlock and support one another. Master Cordery knows well how the cleverness of rulers resembles the cleverness of clockmasters, do you not?"

"Indeed, I do, my lady," replied Edmund.

"There might be a way," she said, in a strangely distant

tone, "that a good mechanician might earn a conversion to vampirism."

Edmund was wise enough not to interpret this as an offer or a promise. He accepted a measure of the new wine and said: "My lady, there are matters that it would be as well for us to discuss in private. May I send my son to his room?"

The Lady Carmilla's eyes narrowed just a little, but there was hardly any expression in her finely etched features. Edmund held his breath, knowing that he had forced a decision upon her that she had not intended to make so soon.

"The poor boy has not quite finished his meal," she said.

"I think he has had enough, my lady," Edmund countered. Noell did not disagree, and, after a brief hesitation, the lady bowed to signal her permission. Edmund asked Noell to leave, and, when he was gone, the Lady Carmilla rose from her seat and went from the dining room into an inner chamber. Edmund followed her.

"You were presumptuous, Master Cordery," she told him.

"I was carried away, my lady. There are too many memories here."

"The boy is mine," she said, "if I so choose. You do know that, do you not?"

Edmund bowed.

"I did not ask you here tonight to make you witness the seduction of your son. Nor do you think that I did. This matter that you would discuss with me—does it concern science or treason?"

"Science, my lady. As you have said yourself, my loyalty is not in question."

Carmilla laid herself upon a sofa and indicated that Edmund should take a chair nearby. This was the antechamber to her bedroom, and the air was sweet with the odor of cosmetics.

"Speak," she bade him.

"I believe that the archduke is afraid of what my little

device might reveal," he said. "He fears that it will expose to the eye such seeds as carry vampirism from one person to another, just as it might expose the seeds that carry disease. I think that the man who devised the instrument may have been put to death already, but I think you know well enough that a discovery once made is likely to be made again and again. You are uncertain as to what course of action would best serve your ends, because you cannot tell whence the greater threat to your rule might come. There is the Fraternity, which is dedicated to your destruction; there is plague in Africa, from which even vampires may die; and there is the new sight, which renders visible what previously lurked unseen. Do you want my advice, Lady Carmilla?"

"Do you *have* any advice, Edmund?"

"Yes. Do not try to control by terror and persecution the things that are happening. Let your rule be unkind *now*, as it has been before, and it will open the way to destruction. Should you concede power gently, you might live for centuries yet, but if you strike out . . . your enemies will strike back."

The vampire lady leaned back her head, looking at the ceiling. She contrived a small laugh.

"I cannot take advice such as that to the archduke," she told him flatly.

"I thought not, my lady," Edmund replied very calmly.

"You humans have your own immortality," she complained. "Your faith promises it, and you all affirm it. Your faith tells you that you must not covet the immortality that is ours, and we do no more than agree with you when we guard it so jealously. You should look to your Christ for fortune, not to us. I think you know well enough that we could not convert the world if we wanted to. Our magic is such that it can be used only sparingly. Are you distressed because it has never been offered to you? Are you bitter? Are you becoming our enemy because you cannot become our kin?"

"You have nothing to fear from me, my lady," he lied.

Then he added, not quite sure whether it was a lie or not: "I loved you faithfully. I still do."

She sat up straight then, and reached out a hand as though to stroke his cheek, though he was too far away for her to reach.

"That is what I told the archduke," she said, "when he suggested to me that you might be a traitor. I promised him that I could test your loyalty more keenly in my chambers than his officers in theirs. I do not think you could delude me, Edmund. Do you?"

"No, my lady," he replied.

"By morning," she told him gently, "I will know whether or not you are a traitor."

"That you will," he assured her. "That you will, my lady."

He woke before her, his mouth dry and his forehead burning. He was not sweating—indeed, he was possessed by a feeling of desiccation, as though the moisture were being squeezed out of his organs. His head was aching, and the light of the morning sun that streamed through the unshuttered window hurt his eyes.

He pulled himself up to a half-sitting position, pushing the coverlet back from his bare chest.

So soon! he thought. He had not expected to be consumed so quickly, but he was surprised to find that his reaction was one of relief rather than fear or regret. He had difficulty collecting his thoughts, and was perversely glad to accept that he did not need to.

He looked down at the cuts that she had made on his breast with her little silver knife; they were raw and red, and made a strange contrast with the faded scars whose crisscross pattern still engraved the story of unforgotten passions. He touched the new wounds gently with his fingers, and winced at the fiery pain.

She woke up then, and saw him inspecting the marks.

"Have you missed the knife?" she asked sleepily. "Were you hungry for its touch?"

There was no need to lie now, and there was a delicious sense of freedom in that knowledge. There was a joy in being able to face her, at last, quite naked in his thoughts as well as his flesh.

"Yes, my lady," he said with a slight croak in his voice. "I had missed the knife. Its touch . . . rekindled flames in my soul."

She had closed her eyes again, to allow herself to wake slowly. She laughed. "It is pleasant, sometimes, to return to forsaken pastures. You can have no notion how a particular *taste* may stir memories. I am glad to have seen you again, in this way. I had grown quite used to you as the gray mechanician. But now . . ."

He laughed, as lightly as she, but the laugh turned to a cough, and something in the sound alerted her to the fact that all was not as it should be. She opened her eyes and raised his head, turning toward him.

"Why, Edmund," she said, "you're as pale as death!"

She reached out to touch his cheek, and snatched her hand away again as she found it unexpectedly hot and dry. A blush of confusion spread across her own features. He took her hand and held it, looking steadily into her eyes.

"Edmund," she said softly. "What have you done?"

"I can't be sure," he said, "and I will not live to find out, but I have tried to kill you, my lady."

He was pleased by the way her mouth gaped in astonishment. He watched disbelief and anxiety mingle in her expression, as though fighting for control. She did not call out for help.

"This is nonsense," she whispered.

"Perhaps," he admitted. "Perhaps it was also nonsense that we talked last evening. Nonsense about treason. Why did you ask me to make the microscope, my lady, when you knew that making me a party to such a secret was as good as signing my death warrant?"

"Oh Edmund," she said with a sigh. "You could not think that it was my own idea? I tried to protect you, Edmund, from Girard's fears and suspicions. It was because I was your protector that I was made to bear the message. What have you done, Edmund?"

He began to reply, but the words turned into a fit of coughing.

She sat upright, wrenching her hand away from his enfeebled grip, and looked down at him as he sank back upon the pillow.

"For the love of God!" she exclaimed, as fearfully as any true believer. "It is the plague—the plague out of Africa!"

He tried to confirm her suspicion, but could do so only with a nod of his head as he fought for breath.

"But they held the *Freemartin* by the Essex coast for a full fortnight's quarantine," she protested. "There was no trace of plague aboard."

"The disease kills men," said Edmund in a shallow whisper. "But animals can carry it, in their blood, without dying."

"You cannot know this!"

Edmund managed a small laugh. "My lady," he said, "I am a member of that Fraternity that interests itself in everything that might kill a vampire. The information came to me in good time for me to arrange delivery of the rats—though when I asked for them, I had not in mind the means of using them that I eventually employed. More recent events. . . ." Again he was forced to stop, unable to draw sufficient breath even to sustain the thin whisper.

The Lady Carmilla put her hand to her throat, swallowing as if she expected to feel evidence already of her infection.

"You would destroy me, Edmund?" she asked, as though she genuinely found it difficult to believe.

"I would destroy you all," he told her. "I would bring disaster, turn the world upside down, to end your rule. . . . We cannot allow you to stamp out learning itself to preserve your empire forever. Order must be fought with chaos, and chaos is come, my lady."

When she tried to rise from the bed, he reached out to restrain her, and though there was no power left in him, she allowed herself to be checked. The coverlet fell away from her, to expose her breasts as she sat upright.

"The boy will die for this, Master Cordery," she said. "His mother, too."

"They're gone," he told her. "Noell went from your table to the custody of the society that I serve. By now they're beyond your reach. The archduke will never catch them."

She stared at him, and now he could see the beginnings of hate and fear in her stare.

"You came here last night to bring me poisoned blood," she said. "In the hope that this new disease might kill even me, you condemned yourself to death. What did you do, Edmund?"

He reached out again to touch her arm, and was pleased to see her flinch and draw away: that he had become dreadful.

"Only vampires live forever," he told her hoarsely. "But anyone may drink blood, if they have the stomach for it. I took full measure from my two sick rats ... and I pray to God that the seed of this fever is raging in my blood ... and in my semen, too. You, too, have received full measure, my lady ... and you are in God's hands now like any common mortal. I cannot know for sure whether you will catch the plague, or whether it will kill you, but I—an unbeliever—am not ashamed to pray. Perhaps you could pray, too, my lady, so that we may know how the Lord favors one unbeliever over another."

She looked down at him, her face gradually losing the expressions that had tugged at her features, becoming masklike in its steadiness.

"You could have taken our side, Edmund. I trusted you, and I could have made the archduke trust you, too. You could have become a vampire. We could have shared the centuries, you and I."

This was dissimulation, and they both knew it. He had been her lover, and had ceased to be, and had grown older for so many years that now she remembered him as much in his son as in himself. The promises were all too obviously hollow now, and she realized that she could not even taunt him with them.

From beside the bed she took up the small silver knife that she had used to let his blood. She held it now as if it were a dagger, not a delicate instrument to be used with care and love.

"I thought you still loved me," she told him. "I really did."

That, at least, he thought, might be true.

He actually put his head farther back, to expose his throat to the expected thrust. He wanted her to strike him—angrily, brutally, passionately. He had nothing more to say, and would not confirm or deny that he did still love her.

He admitted to himself now that his motives had been mixed, and that he really did not know whether it was loyalty to the Fraternity that had made him submit to this extraordinary experiment. It did not matter.

She cut his throat, and he watched her for a few long seconds while she stared at the blood gouting from the wound. When he saw her put stained fingers to her lips, knowing what she knew, he realized that after her own fashion, she still loved him.

Is biology destiny? A doctor ought to know.... "S.N. Dyer" is the pseudonym of a practicing M.D. She is also known for her Hugo-winning tales of life as a resident in an inner city hospital.

Born Again

S.N. DYER

ABSTRACT. *The historical condition vampirism is found to be caused by a microörganism which revamps the host's physiology and metabolism through negentropic processes. Evolution of the organism is conjectured and potential uses of the discovery suggested.*

TITLE. *Haematophagic Adaptation is* Homo Nosferatus, *with Notes Upon the Geographical Distribution of Super-gene-moderated Mimicking Morphs in* Homo Lycanthropus.

I'd forgotten the pitch black of a country road at night. Overhead, between the aisles of trees, you can see the stars; but otherwise it's the same as being blind. Totally different from the hospital where I'd just completed my residency, an oasis of fluorescent light in an urban jungle. You couldn't walk down the best lit streets in safety there. It felt good to be home, even just for a short vacation.

I walked by the feel of the asphalt under my feet. At the bend there'd be an almost subliminal glimmer of

79

starlight on the mailbox at the foot of the drive to my family's farm. The halo of an approaching car rounded the bend, illuminating the road. I discovered I was standing directly in the center, and moved to the side of the road. Headlights washed over me. I shut my eyes to keep my nightsight.

The car hung a sharp left into the driveway of the old Riggen place, and stopped.

City-conditioned nerves made my heart pound faster.

The car door swung open, the overhead lighting up a seated man in his late twenties. He had dark hair and a bushy moustache.

"Are you lost?" he asked.

"No, I'm close enough to home to call the dog."

He chuckled, and his smile turned him handsome. "Don't be so paranoid. Hmmm ... you must be the Sangers' famous daughter who went to the Big City to become a doctor."

"Guilty as accused. And you must be the Mad Scientist renting the Riggen spread."

"No, I'm just a humble master's in microbiology. Kevin Marlowe. My boss Auger is the mad scientist."

"*The* Auger?"

He flashed another grin. "Ah. Why don't you come to tea tomorrow, Doctor, and see."

AUTHORS. *Alastair Auger, Ph.D.*
Kevin Marlowe, M.A.
Mae Sanger, M.D.
Asterisk. Funded by a grant from the Institute for the Study of Esoterica.

INTRODUCTION. *Recent advances in medicine have necessitated differentiating between clinical death, or cessation of heartbeat, and biological, or brain death. The distinction has been further complicated by the increasing use of heroic life support methodology.*

History reports rare cases in which clinical death was not followed by biological death, but was maintained in

status. The affected undead individuals were called Nos-
ferati, or vampires. The authors' investigation of this
phenomenon has led to the discovery of a causative
microörganism, Pseudobacteria augeria.

"Dr. Sanger, Dr. Auger."

"Charmed." The great Professor Alastair Auger smiled down at me. He was tall, gray-haired but with dark eyebrows, somewhat out of shape, a couple of decades older than Marlowe and I. He had the clipped words, riveting eyes, and radiating intellect of the perfect lecturer.

He continued, "At last we meet someone in this semi-civilized intellectual backwash who at least aspires to the level of pseudo-science."

"You must come by sometime and see my herb-and-rattle collection," I replied.

He raised an eyebrow. "I understand that you've heard of me."

"Sure. Everyone knows about Professor Auger, brilliant—"

He preened.

"But nuts."

Auger said, "You see, Kevin? She has retained the delightful candor of the local rednecks, untempered by her exposure to the hypocritical milieu of higher education. She'll do fine."

My turn to raise an eyebrow.

The doorbell rang. Marlowe looked out the window and groaned. "Hell. It's Weems."

I followed his gaze. Leaning on the bell was a small ferret-faced man, with a gray suit and a loud tie.

Auger grimaced with pain and clutched his abdomen for a few seconds, then recovered. "I'll get rid of him. Take her on a tour of the lab."

METHODS AND MATERIALS. The Pseudobacteria
augeria *was stored in isotonic saline solution kept at*
37°C, at which temperature it is inactive. Titers of inac-
tive P. augeria *were injected into host animals, which*
were then sacrificed. After a critical period, depending

*on the number of injected pseudobacteria and the genera-
tions (Graph 1) necessary to achieve the species specific
ratio of pseudo-bacteria/kg body weight (Table A), the
dead host animal was reanimated. The mean latency was
three days. The dotted line indicates the threshold number of primary infecting pseudobacteria necessary to rep-
licate sufficient progeny in order to reanimate the body
before irreversible decay occurs. In vivo, a number of
vampiric attacks or "bites," ensuring a large founding
colony, would increase chances of postmortem revivification.*

"Vampires?" I repeated, petting a white rabbit. "Come
on, we did that one in med school. Funniest gag since
Arlo left a piece of his cadaver in a confessional."

I looked around the lab, believing my eyes as little as
Marlowe's story. They'd turned an old farm house into a
modern-day Castle Frankenstein. Cages of lab animals
faced a small computer, nestled amongst the centrifuges,
particle counters, electron microscope, and spectrometers. Automatic stirrers clacked away in the background.

Marlowe handed me a stethoscope. "First, assure yourself that it works."

I put it over my fifth rib and heard a reassuring *lub
dub lub dub*.

"I'm alive."

"Try the rabbit."

No heartbeat.

I stared at it, snuffling in my hands. Marlowe put out
a saucer of what looked like blood. The fluffy little bunny
tore free of my hold, dove at the bowl, and began lapping
up the red liquid.

"Okay, I believe you. How? I mean, its brain is obviously getting oxygenated or it wouldn't be hopping
around. But how does the blood circulate if the heart's
not pumping?"

"We're not sure." He waved at a garbage can. There
was a former rabbit inside.

"Were you dissecting it or dicing it?"

"Auger's a biochemist, and me . . . well, neither of us can even carve a roast."

"I see. You need someone who feels at home with a scalpel, right? Look, this is my first real vacation in seven years, and I have a job that starts Back East in a month. . . ."

Weems and Auger entered the lab.

"I am certain, Mr. Weems, that even you will notice that we have not had recourse to the pawnshop," Auger said, gesturing expansively.

Weems pointed to a coffee mug sitting on the infrared spectrometer. "Is that any way to treat the Foundation's equip— Who's she?"

"Our new associate," Auger said.

Weems looked at me contemptuously.

"You wanna see my credentials?"

He sneered. "I think I see them."

I said, "You boys just got yourselves a surgeon."

The progressive effect of vampirism upon host physiology was studied in rats. One group was injected with a threshold number of P. augeria, *sacrificed, and placed in an incubation chamber held at 15°C to hasten replication. Ninety-seven percent of the infected rats reanimated between 54 and 73 hours post-mortem. Specimens were sacrificed at intervals of 0, 6, 12, 24, etc., hours post-revivification, and the gross anatomy, pathology, and serology studied.*

Another group of control rats was injected with normal saline, sacrificed, and placed in the 15°C incubation chamber. These under-went classical necrotic decay, and were disposed of on the sixth day.

"Whew. Smells like a charnel house," Marlowe said. "How do you stand it?"

"It's obvious you never worked in an inner-city clinic, Kevin. Or lived on a farm." I pointed to the rat I had pinned open on the table and was dissecting under red light.

"See that? They may not be using the heart as a pump, but it's still the crossroads of the circulatory system. That must be why the old stake-in-the-heart routine works."

"Only as a temporary measure," Marlowe said. "The microörganisms seem able to repair tissue. Remember, the classical method of killing vampires is staking, followed closely by decapitation or burning."

"Mmm. Stake, season well with garlic, and place in a hot oven until thoroughly cooked. Look at those little buggies move."

"Please do not call my *Pseudobacteria augeria* 'buggies,' " Auger said, walking in on us. He was good at that.

"Oh, you'll want to see this, sir," Marlowe said, handing the taller man an electronmicrograph.

"Beautiful!"

I stood on tiptoe to see. The micrograph showed the bug, with its bacteria-like lack of a nucleus, its amoeba-like pseudopods and irregular cellular borders, and its just-plain-weird ribosome clusters and endoplasmic reticulum, plus some things not even Marlowe could identify. There was a smooth, anucleate disc attached to the outer membrane.

"Wow! That's got an erythrocyte hooked on!"

"I let them settle out instead of centrifuging," Marlowe said proudly. "The spinning must dislodge the red blood cells from the surface."

"Well, that explains how the blood is transported," I said. Auger lifted his eyebrow slightly, to signify intellectual condescension.

We heard a car drive up.

"Hell and damn!" Auger said. "It must be Weems again." He scowled and left the room.

"How about seeing the movie in town tonight, Mae?" Marlowe suggested.

"We've seen it, twice, unless you mean the new Disney over South-County."

"Lord, what a dull area. How do you stand it?"

"Well, in three weeks—when I'm in a Manhattan emergency room and up to my ears in blood—I'll cherish these nice quiet memories. Why don't we take a day off and drive down to the city—"

"*Idiot!*"

Outside in the garden, Professor Auger was shouting. We heard Weems shouting back. Marlowe and I ran out.

"It's revoked," Weems was yelling. The little man had ducked behind his car for protection. Auger looked mad enough to throttle him. His face was livid, and he was breathing as if he'd just run the four-minute mile. I didn't even want to imagine what his blood pressure was up to.

"Calm down, you'll give yourself a stroke," I said.

Weems turned to us triumphantly. "The Foundation's revoked the grant. We'll want a total accounting."

"You bastard!" Auger bellowed, and lunged across the car at Weems. He halted in mid-stride, a confused expression on his face, grabbed his stomach, and collapsed.

I leapt over and began examining him. He was pale and breathing rapidly, with a weak, racing pulse. Shock.

"Is it a heart attack?" Weems asked. The little rodent sounded happy.

Marlowe knelt on the other side. "What can I do?" he asked. I ripped open Auger's shirt and felt his abdomen. It was hot, pink and firm. Internal hemorrhage.

"Oh, Christ." I reached inside his pants and felt for the femoral pulse. There was none. "Well, that's it. Damn." I realized I was crying.

Auger stopped breathing, and Marlowe began mouth-to-mouth resuscitation. I reached to the neck and felt for the carotid pulse. It fluttered weakly and then faded.

"It's no use, Kevin. He's dead."

Weems chortled gleefully, jumped in his car, and sped up the driveway in reverse. Marlowe began external heart massage, anxiously doing it 'way too fast.

I pulled him off and shook his shoulders. "Stop it, Kevin. It won't help. Remember those stomach pains he had? It was an aneurysm, a weakness in the wall of his abdominal aorta. It burst, Kevin; he's bled to death internally. CPR won't help, dammit, nothing can."

"Ambulance, call a—"

"Listen. Even if they could get here within a half-hour, it wouldn't do any good. Look, Kevin, five minutes ago, if I'd had him on the table in a fully equipped operating room, with a good team, we could have tried a DeBakey graft. But the chances of saving him would have been maybe five percent."

Marlowe stood and stared down at the body. Then he turned and ran inside the house, leaving me with the corpse. Dead, Auger was devoid of charisma. His features were bloodless white; he looked like a horror waxwork. I closed his mouth and rearranged the clothes to give him more dignity.

Marlowe returned with a huge cardiac syringe and a bottle of milky liquid.

"You're crazy."

"It would work, Mae. We can bring him back. I centrifuged them down to a concentrate. There are enough pseudobacteria here to repair the damage and reanimate him almost immediately."

The implications were terrifying. Vampire rabbits were bizarre enough, but he was preparing to do it to a human being.

"You can save his life! Come on, do it."

Typical Marlowe, always leaving the decisions to someone else. I filled the syringe and plunged the six-inch needle deep into the blood-distended abdomen. Marlowe looked ill, and turned away. It was hard work pushing in the fluid. I pulled the needle out, and a small amount of blood welled up through the puncture. Two more syringes full and the bottle was empty.

We carried the body into the lab and packed it in ice to lower the body temperature quicker. Marlowe went away to vomit. I brewed some coffee and added a stiff jolt of medicinal Scotch.

"Here's to a fellow future inmate of Sing Sing," I toasted Marlowe.

Half an hour later we were feeling no pain.

"We'll have to buy him a black cape," I was saying. "Lessons in Transylvanian diction, too."

"I vant to suck your blood," Marlowe said, and leapt on me. We collapsed on the floor together, laughing.

The doorbell rang. Weems had returned with a sheriff's deputy.

"Hey, Fred!"

"Uh, hi, Mae. Long time no see." The deputy looked embarrassed.

"We went to high school together," I announced to no one in particular.

"Sorry to have to disturb you, but this guy says you've got a stiff here."

Marlowe giggled from the floor. "A body? I don't see anybody." He adopted a stern voice. "The only thing dead around here is the night life in town."

Weems piped up with, "They're drunk."

"Brilliant, Weems, an astonishing deduction," I cried.

"They've hidden the body! Alastair Auger was dead. She even said so." He pointed at me accusatorily.

"Remove your finger."

The deputy stepped between us. "Uh, I'm sorry, Mae, uh, Doc, but I have to make a report."

"Professor Auger's not feeling well, Fred; he shouldn't be disturbed. Hey, you can believe me when I say he's alive. I'm a doctor. We're trained to know these things."

"They're faking. I won't leave until I see Auger's body."

"Yes, it is awe-inspiring. But I'm afraid you're just not my type, Weems."

Weems's face blanched at the sight of Auger, leaning in the doorway to the lab, and smiling malevolently at us all. He was glistening from the ice, and was wearing a towel.

"She's done something to him," Weems stuttered. "He was dead."

The deputy took Weems's elbow and propelled the little man out the door. "Sorry, Mae, Professors—" He headed for the patrol car, saying, "Okay, mister, there's a little matter of making false reports."

Marlowe laughed hysterically.

"If you hadn't woken up right then," I said, "you'd have woken up in the county morgue."

Auger said, "If you'll excuse me, this light is most unpleasant and I'm starving."

I offered to fetch him a pint of blood.

"Yes, please, please, Doctor. I'm finding myself uncomfortably attracted to your neck."

RESULTS AND DISCUSSION. The vampire is tradition-ally considered a body occupied by a demon. We may now modify that picture to encompass a mammal, dead in that its heart does not beat and its body temperature is abnormally, indeed fatally, low, but still functioning as an organism due to the presence of a colony of symbiotes. The pseudobacteria function as metabolizers and as transporters of oxygen, nutrients, and wastes, functions assumed in uninfected organisms by the circulatory and digestive systems. P. augeria is a weak infective agent, requiring the special environment found after death, and susceptible to most common antibacterial drugs. Folklore documents the vampire's aversion to garlic, a mild antibiotic.

The host physiology undergoes changes which seem to eliminate unnecessary systems and increase efficiency for vampiric adaptations. These changes appear to be pro-gressive, but must await long-term studies.

The first major change is the atrophy of the digestive tract. Nutrients pass directly from the stomach to the blood-stream, with the concurrent necessity that only iso-tonic solutions be ingested, to avoid the osmotic destruc-tion of the blood cells. As the only isotonic solution available in nature is blood, the vampire's fluid intake has traditionally been in this form. An external blood source is also necessary for other reasons. Because blood transport is pseudobacterial rather than hydrostatic, and

hence much slower, the body requires more red cells than
can be produced by the host's bone marrow.

"All the great men are dead—myself, for instance."

"Breathe in," I replied.

Marlowe walked in, saw us, and blushed. The longer
I knew Kevin, the more I realized how anal retentive he
could be.

"Am I interrupting?"

"Yes," Auger said. When he spoke, I could see his
sharp canine teeth.

"No. Pass me that, yeah, the sphygmomanometer.
You don't realize what a pleasure it is to have a patient
who doesn't complain about the stethoscope being
cold."

I joked as I put on the blood pressure cuff, trying to
hide the creepy feeling Auger gave me. Intellectually, I
knew he was the same man I'd met a week before, but
emotionally I had problems relating to a patient with a
current body temperature of 30°C—midway between
what it should be, and the temperature of the room. And
because of the vagaries of his circulation, even in the
warmest room Auger's hands felt like he'd been out in
a snowstorm without his mittens.

"Must we do this again?" Auger winced as I pumped
up the cuff. I nodded, and listened with the stethoscope.
I just couldn't get used to the fact that his heart didn't
beat, and that he had no blood pressure.

"No diastolic, no systolic," I said. "Sir, your b.p.'s holding steady at zero over zero."

"Ah, normal," Auger said, reaching for his shirt.
"Enough time wasted. Shall we return to the lab?"

He hated medical exams (and, I was convinced, doctors as well). I argued in vain for the opportunity to take
him to a hospital and run some *real* tests on him: X-rays,
metabolic studies, EEGs. . . .

"It's three in the morning," Marlowe complained. "I
need some coffee."

"Can't get used to working graveyard shift?"

He acknowledged my joke with a weak smile. This nocturnal living was tough to get used to. Auger had acquired the vampiric dislike of daylight. Another thing that needed more study: was it because of the temperature, or the infrared radiation? In any case, my parents seemed to think my new hours were the result of an affair with Kevin Marlowe, and this made things fairly uncomfortable on the home front.

Auger accepted a cup of coffee, and stirred in a spoonful of salt, to make it osmotically similar to blood.

"There aren't enough metabolites and nutrients in the blood you drink to sustain you, Professor. Where the hell do you get your energy?"

"It's a negentropic process, similar to the one which allows my *Pseudobacteria augeria* to be dormant over 35°, while ordinary enzymatic processes become accelerated," he told me. "How much calculus have you had, Dr. Sanger?"

"Two semesters."

"You'd need at least four to understand. Hadn't we better return to work?"

As human populations grew, they tended to eliminate competing species, creating a niche for a predator. It may be possible to remutate Pseudobacteria augeria *to its hypothetical ancestor,* P. lycanthropica, *which could survive at normal body temperature and changed its hosts into carnivorous animals. The body type was probably mediated by a supergene complex similar in principle to those found in butterfly mimicry, resulting in discrete morphs with a lack of intermediate types. Examination of the literature suggests the morph adopted was that of the major natural predator of the geographical area, leading to werewolves in Northern Europe, were-bears in Scandinavia, and were-tigers in India. Some cases have been reported of werewolves becoming vampires after death, suggesting either concurrent infection, or evolution in progress.*

*   *   *

I was driving back from town when I saw police cars lined up along the road. I slowed up and yelled out the window.

"Need a doctor?"

My deputy friend Fred flagged me in behind a patrol car. "Remember the wimp who accused the big guy of being dead?"

He led me through a swarm of cops, down the gully to the creek.

Weems lay with his arm dangling in the creek. His wrist had been slashed, and he had bled to death.

"Not much blood," I finally commented. "It usually gets all over when someone exsanguinates."

"Washed away downstream," the sheriff said. "They always have to come on my territory to kill themselves. How long would you say he's been dead?"

The body was cold. Rigor mortis was complete but not yet passing off. I estimated twenty hours, maybe less allowing for the cold.

"Damned suicides," the sheriff muttered.

"Big goddamn nuisance." I agreed, and we all stood around for a few minutes swapping gross-out stories.

Then I sped home, parked the car, and walked over to the lab. It was dusk when I arrived.

Marlowe was in an elated mood. "We've started on the last draft of the article. We'll submit simultaneously to *Science* and *Nature*. Well, Mae, start working up an appetite because I hear they have great food at the Nobel awards."

I stomped past him to Auger's bedroom. Auger was lying on his bed, absolutely straight, like a corpse already laid out. As I stood there, clenching my fists, he awoke and sat up.

"Well, Dr. Sanger. To what do I owe the honor of—"

"You killed him."

"Whom?"

Oh he could be suave.

"You were clever making it look like suicide. The cops have swallowed it."

He gave me his most charming smile, not realizing how his long teeth spoiled the effect. "I had no alternative. The man was our enemy. He convinced the Foundation to revoke our funding."

"His death won't get the grant back, Auger. You just killed him out of spite."

He laid a cold hand on my arm. "Calm down. By next week we'll all be famous. You won't have to take that cheap job in New York. You'll be the most pre-eminent witchdoctor in America."

"You're making me sick." I wrenched my arm away and walked out. "Good-bye, Kevin. It was swell while it lasted. Leave my name off the article. I want to forget that any of this happened."

Marlowe had a hurt-little-boy look on his face. "But you can't just leave."

"Watch me," I muttered.

It was pitch black already, but I'd walked it a dozen times. When my feet felt asphalt instead of gravel, I turned right and headed uphill. A passing car lit up the road, and I moved to the side. The tail-lights dwindled in the distance, and in their faint afterglow I saw a tall figure come from the driveway.

Auger.

Following me.

Then it was black again. I saw two eyes, shining like a deer's, only red. They were all I could see: the stars above, the two red eyes. They stared right at me, the nightsight of the predator.

Auger spoke softly, his voice carrying in the stillness. "It won't hurt. You know you want it."

I panicked and started running, going by the sound of my feet on the blacktop, my hands outstretched as I ran blind. My heart was pounding with fear and cold sweat poured down my body, but the supercharge of adrenalin kept me going.

I saw the glimmer of light on the mailbox. I could turn down the driveway, run the quarter-mile to my home. Home, light, safety. . . .

Something cut off the glow of the mailbox; and I knew it was Auger, in front of me now, blocking the driveway. Six feet above the ground, two red eyes.

I swerved and plunged into the forest. Branches whipped against my face and caught in my clothes and hair. I tripped and fell in the stream, got up and kept running.

Hands caught me from behind and pulled me against a body, invisible in the dark. I was conscious of an inhumanly strong grip, and a coat smelling of wool and chemicals. I started pounding and flailing, but he ignored my blows.

He caught my hands and held them in one ice-like hand.

"Don't fight it," he whispered. "You'll enjoy it."

I felt his breath on my neck, and tried to scream, but I couldn't. I was too scared.

This can't be happening to me, I thought. *Not me.*

The bite was sharp and painful, followed by a warm sensation as my blood welled up through the punctures. I started struggling again, but he was oblivious to everything but the blood he was greedily sucking in.

My mind went clinical on me. *Two pints equals fifteen percent blood volume. Moderate shock will set in.* I could feel the symptoms start. *He's killing me.*

My knees gave out and I sank to the ground, Auger still drinking from my left jugular. Over the roaring in my ears I could hear my gasping breath and the vampire's gross panting and slobbering. I was too weak to fight any more. The summer constellations gazed down uncaring, and became part of a light show as lack of oxygen brought hallucinations, and a strange feeling of euphoria.

The dying started to feel good.

CONCLUSIONS. Throughout history the vampire has been maligned as a villain and demon. Now that the etiology of the condition is understood, there is no reason why the vampire cannot take his place as a functioning member of society. With prescription availability of blood, the disease will be limited to present victims. Under these conditions it need not even be classified as contagious.

I woke up under an oak tree. A spider had used my left arm to anchor its web, and earwigs were nesting in my hair.

"Ohhh. I must have tied one on good," I groaned, and pulled myself into a sitting position, leaning against the oak. I felt like hell. Weak, cold, splitting headache, and hungry. Never so hungry in all my life. The feeling of hunger seemed to fill every inch of my body.

Absently, I put two fingers to my wrist to take my pulse.

There was none.

I reached up to check the carotid. Every movement hurt.

My heart wasn't beating.

I withdrew my hand and stared at my fingers. They were pale: dead white.

I was dead. I was a vampire. I tongued my canines and felt their new sharpness.

Auger did this to me. I remembered it all, and felt nauseated.

He'd be in the lab.

And blood. They had blood there. Whole refrigerators full. Rabbit blood. Rat blood.

Human blood.

The new moon is still a sliver in the sky, but I can see in the dark now. A deer crosses my path and freezes in terror until I pass. As I approach the house I can hear Marlowe typing the article the damned article.

It will even be possible, through a controlled infection of Pseudo-bacteria augeria, *to conquer death, allowing us to revive and preserve indefinitely great minds and*

*   *   *

"Kevin. Get me some blood. Quick, before I bite you."

I clutch at a chair to control myself. When I look down, I see that my new vampiric strength has crushed the hard plastic.

Marlowe tremulously hands me a liter of O-negative. I gulp it down. It's cold, cramping my stomach.

"More."

It takes six liters before I can look at Marlowe without wanting to attack him. Then I clean up some, comb my hair, cover my filthy clothes with a lab coat, and slip a filled syringe into the pocket.

"Where is he, Kevin?"

"You're alive, Mae, that's what counts. Let's not—"

"He sucked me damn near dry. Where is he?"

"It didn't hurt you. He said it wouldn't—"

I grab his arm, and he flinches at the touch. "Feel it, Kevin, dead flesh. Is a Nobel going to keep either of us warm at night?"

"Add this to the conclusion, Kevin: 'Where there is no longer any death, murder must be redefined.' Welcome back, Dr. Sanger."

Auger stands in the lab doorway. I realize that I'm shaking.

He can't hurt me now, I repeat over and over. But I want to flee. Or else cry.

"Refrigerated blood is nothing. Wait until you've drunk warm, pulsing, living blood."

"Shut up," I whisper.

"And the power. The strength. You've always admired strength. You'll enjoy being a vampire, Dr. Sanger."

"No. No, I won't become power-crazy. I won't kill. I'm trained to save, to heal . . . I won't be like you!"

He laughs.

"Biology isn't destiny!" I scream.

He laughs more. I almost don't blame him.

"I thought we'd give you a chance. All right, Kevin, stake her."

I spin around. Marlowe has a wooden stake and a

mallet, but he's vacillating, as usual. I pick him up and toss him to the floor before Auger.

Auger curses and snatches up the stake.

"Am I to assume this won't hurt either?" I ask.

"I've always admired the late doctor's resilient sense of humor," he says.

I pull the syringe from my pocket, duck in close, ram it into his side and push the plunger.

"Admire that—twenty cc of tetracycline."

He roars and throws a table at me. I duck, and it crashes into a shelf of chemicals.

"You're cured, Auger. I've killed those little bugs, the ones that are keeping you alive."

He picks up a 200-pound spectrometer and tosses it at me. It bowls me into the cages, liberating a half-dozen specimens. Vampire rabbits scurry about underfoot. I get up and dust myself off.

"Temper, temper. That's Foundation equipment."

Marlowe watches dumbfounded as Auger throws the gas chromatograph at me. It shatters on the floor, sparks igniting the spilled chemicals. A brisk fire begins, punctuated by explosions of bottled reagents.

Auger closes in and grabs me, but this time I push him back, pick up the wooden stake, and shove it into his heart.

He looks surprised.

"Why me?" he asks, and dies again.

"Kevin. Come on. The place is burning up."

"Get away from me," he yells. "Don't touch me, vampire!" He pulls open his shirt to show a cross on a chain.

"Don't be stupid, Kevin."

The fire has reached the chemical stockroom. I run for the window, and plunge through in a cloud of glass. The lab behind me explodes.

Marlowe's screams die out.

Charred paper blows away as heated air rushes out the shattered windows. The plastic on the typewriter melts and runs, laying bare the sparking wires inside. The metal letters writhe and bend and wrap around each other, and then melt into an indistinguishable lump.

I go home and clean up, and get back in time to watch the firemen. Not much is left of the old farmhouse.

"I'm a physician. Can I help?"

"They're beyond help, Mae." The fire chief remembers me from 4H. "Think you could identify the bodies?"

They've covered them with yellow plastic blankets, two gross, body-shaped chunks of charred meat. The fire chief looks at me sympathetically.

"I guess their own mothers wouldn't know them ... you're pale, Mae. Johnny, you better walk her home."

A husky young fireman takes my arm and steers me up the path, away from the lights and smoke.

"They were scientists?" he asks. "What were they doing in there?"

"Working on things man was not meant to know," I say. He doesn't recognize the quote.

I stare sideways at my escort.

He's young and strong and healthy.

He won't miss a pint at all.

There is an exquisite pain on becoming a parent, and not just the physical labor pangs of the mother. Fathers feel the supreme joy and incredible burden of responsibility for bringing a new life into the world, too. Possibly the only experience more sharply felt than the birth of a child is its premature death. . . .

Kaeti's Nights

KEITH ROBERTS

This isn't one of Kaeti's nights. So I can get a bit of work done.

Wind's getting up again, blustering round the pub. Sign starting to creak a bit in the big gusts. That means Force Eight, Nine. We've got our own Beaufort scale here. Raining again too, hard. Hear it rattle on the windows. Been a funny old year for weather. Trees didn't drop their leaves till near on Christmas. Fields were still green too. Vivid. Sort of sickly.

Just seen to Chota, got her her bits. Saucer of milk and that. Funny little beggar. Born the wrong side of the door, I reckon. Any door. Some cats are like that. I never thought Kaeti would rear her. She did though. Kept on. Even after we'd all written her off. Even her Mum. Used to come back midmornings, give her her feed. Never knew how she got away with it. That's Kaeti though.

Kaeti's my daughter. She's dead, by the way. Just three weeks before Christmas, it was.

Funny. Me writing. Not my sort of thing at all. Couldn't

98

see the point at first. Kaeti explained all that though.
About actions. Said we weren't *supposed* to see the point.
None of us. She said—let's get this right—she said what
matters about actions is just that they're *done*. She said
if she, well, spilled a glass of milk or scratched her knee
or anything, anything at all, then it was always true it
was *going* to happen. At that place, and at that point of
time. Very particular about that she was. Because there
are other Points, apart from those in Time. She said it
was always true it *would* happen, no matter how many
millions of years you went back. And it would always be
true it *had* happened, no matter how far you went forward. Something about going on from where Gotama
stopped. Sitting right across from me she was, curled up
on the settee. And looking solemn, solemn as I'd ever
seen her. She'd lost me a bit by then. She said that didn't
matter though, nobody could get it all first time off. What
mattered was that I believed. Another sort of belief.
Something quite new.

She talked a lot about Time. Said you could *feel* it
passing, if you tried. The minutes, all the seconds in 'em,
all those actions going on, getting themselves recorded.
Building something that was huge and getting bigger,
something that could never be stopped or hurt. It doesn't
need us, it never needed us. But we all belong to it. She
said it was called the One, that everything belongs to it.
The atoms in a chair leg, all whistling about. They're
Events as well. Sometimes one explodes, and that's a
Nova. She said to read the neo-Platonists, they knew a
bit about it. I wondered where she'd had time for stuff
like that. I thought Sixth Form College was nothing but
skiving and Business English.

Doesn't make sense? That isn't important. Not really.
Because it makes sense to me. Just in flashes. When a
pendulum swings, there's shadows. Like those trick titles
you see now on the Box. Some are in the future, some
are in the past.

It's the bar clock I can hear. The big one in the saloon.

Funny how you can hear it right up here. Sort of trick of the building.

Came from Pete's Dad's place, that clock did. His pride and joy. Parliament clocks, they call them. Go back to the days when some silly blighter put a tax on time-pieces. Seems governments weren't any smarter then. All that happened was they all chucked their clocks out, had one thundering great big thing everybody could see. Worth a packet these days. That bent little sod from the brewery offered me two hundred cash to knock it off the inventory. He must have been joking.

That's another funny idea. *Worth*. Value, price. If you knew the half of what I do—but maybe you will one day. If you get the time.

Looked in on Pete on the way up. She's asleep. Real sleep, not that halfway, floating stuff you get from pills. Hair spread on the pillow, looks about twenty. As if the years don't matter. But they don't, not really. That's what's so bloody marvelous. They don't matter at all.

Asked Kaeti what I should write *about*. She just grinned though. "Anything," she said. "You, Mum. The pub. It's all Actions. Anything you like." So I'll start with me.

I wasn't born in these parts. London, that's where I hail from. The Smoke. Only they shifted me out. Five or six I was, and the Blitz just really starting to warm up.

Funny how clear some of it still is. The sirens going and us trailing out from school, lining up in the yard. Then down the shelters, shoving and pushing, and the whistles going and all us with the gasmasks on our shoulders. We used to sit sometimes and hope there'd be a raid. Like holidays they were. Half days off, courtesy of old Adolf. We didn't know of course. Not really. Bombs don't mean anything to kids. They're just something that happens on the films.

I remember the shelters too. Lines of slatted seats, and the voices everywhere. Puddles on the floor, and that stink there always was of wet cement. And the lamps in their wellglasses, lines and lines of little yellow bulbs.

Funny, thinking back. The school was a damned sight better built than those bloody shelters, we'd have been better off staying where we were.

That's what my old man reckoned. We'd got an Anderson out the back, they all had. Only, we only ever used ours the once. After that, if there was a raid on, he'd sit downstairs with his mates and just play cards. You'd hear the rumble of voices and the laughing. Sounded louder than the bombs sometimes. They'd always get me up though, make me dress. I'd got a siren suit made out of bright blue blankets, just like old Churchill. They'd get me into it and zip the front, then Jerry could do what he bloody liked. That was all we bothered.

I was only ever really scared once. And that wasn't at anything that could hurt. Typical. Mam put the bedroom light out one night and opened the curtains and took me to the window. "Look, Bill," she said, "we'll be all right now. It's the *serchlie!*" I didn't know what she meant, not to start with. Then I saw these two beams of misty blue, reaching up there miles across the housetops, and for some reason, God knows why, they looked like horns on the head of a bloody great ghost. Then they swung and dipped, and I knew the *serchlie* was nosing about looking for me and started yelling the place down. Poor old Mam, she never did understand it. They tied the labels on our coats next morning and shipped us out. Evacuation, they called it. Sis kept bawling but I was just glad I was getting out, where the *serchlie* couldn't get me. Ghosts were a lot worse than bombs. That's where we all went wrong of course, years and years ago. Teaching kids a load of muck like that.

That's how I got to Blackwell the first time. Blackwell, Hants. Just over the border, on the edge of the big common. Queer little place it is. Not much to it, not even a church. Just little red-brick cottages scattered about and a couple of pubs, and the lane up to the farm. There's one big house, at the other end of the village. That's where we all stayed. The Stantons have got it now, had it for years, but in those days it was owned by an old biddy called Olivia Devenish. Left over from the Raj, she was. Indian stuff all stood about, and a big old overgrown garden that even had canebrakes in it. You could play lions and tigers through there a treat. Or Spitfires and Messerschmitts. We did too, me and Sis and about a dozen more. Right little perishers, we were. Mrs. Devenish never bothered though, just sat in the middle of it all and mended socks and clipped ears when she had to. I reckon that was her War Effort. Auntie we called her, and we all got on fine. Knew when to stop of course. Not like these days.

It was a bit queer to start with, green fields all over and the birds every morning. Most of us never took to it. I know Sis didn't, she was off back to London first chance she got. It suited me though somehow. They'd got ack-ack guns on the common then, and a searchlight unit. I knew what they were by then of course. Used to hang round every chance I got, scrounge off the soldiers. Got to be a sort of company mascot in the end. Even had my picture in the paper once, sitting at one of the guns complete with oversize tin hat. Plus some bloody drivel about the next generation and Building for the Future. Still got it somewhere.

Nobody ever bombed Blackwell though; and after a while the unit was moved out. It was real quiet after that.

I could have gone back, I suppose. A lot of them did. I probably would have if I'd had the chance. But Dad always said no, not till they blew the whistle. Reckoned Jerry had still got some stuff left up his sleeve. As it turned out, he was right. V-2 it was, took the whole row out. The war finished a few weeks later.

I lived with Auntie May and her lot till I finished school. I got myself a garage apprenticeship then. Used to hang round Douggie Caswell's old place in the village, I'd got used to the smell of motor oil. After that it was national service of course. For some reason they decided I wasn't quite A-1 so it was the pay corps and like it. Two years counting plasters, watching camels float down the Sweetwater bloody Canal. When I got back to London, there was nothing to stay for any more. What mates I'd had had all drifted off; Sis had married and moved out, damn near to Epping, and the Council had really got their teeth into our neighborhood. I reckon they finished Jerry's job for him. All the stuff he hadn't had a go at, they did. My old man would have turned in his grave. If he'd ever had one. Auntie was slated for a high-rise block, and there wouldn't have been room for me even if I'd wanted to go. That's how I turned up again one bright day in Blackwell. I've been here ever since.

Always liked the common. Not that there's all that much to see. Just flat ground, undulating a bit, the tussocky grass, big stands of gorse and bramble. Swarms with adders in the summer, the cottage hospital always used to keep the serum. Lazy little beggars, bite rather than move, the kids would step straight on 'em. Autumn's the time to see it though. Autumn, and early winter. It sort of comes into its own then. The pub fronts it square-on, you can see the mist lie on it like milk, the humps and bushes sticking up out of it dark. The mist's nearly always there, hanging low. Till the wind gets up and shreds it. They say it's to do with the subsoil. Which I suppose is as good a story as the next. Sometimes it comes creeping across the road, big blue tongues that push out sudden, no more than a foot or two off the ground. It was a night like that old Teddy saw the ghost. Tall swirling pillar it was, come squirting straight out the ground. I can remember him saying it. "Swirling," he kept on saying. "Swirling, it was." Took half a bottle of Scotch to set him to rights. But Teddy was an old trooper, sarn't-major farrier in the Bengal Lancers. Never needed much in the way of excuses at the best of times.

I first met Pete on the common. I used to walk there whenever I had the time. Which wasn't all that often. I was working for Douggie Caswell then, been with him getting on four years. He was at the garage all hours himself so if an urgent job came in, which they often did, I never bothered much about staying on as well. Not much else to do in Blackwell anyway. But I used to stroll that way when I could. You could still see the pads where they stood the anti-aircraft guns, and close by were some concrete bunkers they'd never got round to knocking down. Even some rusty coils of wire, with the weeds all growing through them. I'd sit and smoke a fag and think about the old times. Mam and Dad, what he'd have made of it all. I suppose I'd turned into a bit of a loner. I was like it in the mob, they always reckoned I was a funny sort of blighter. Even for a Londoner.

Pete was a bit the same. Though to start with I never realized why. She's got this scar on her face. Down one cheek and across her chin. Pulls her lip up one side, into a little pucker. Pony did it, when she was a nipper. Must have nearly split her in half, poor little devil. They'd make a better job of it now. But those days plastic surgery was something not even money could buy. Took us a war to really find out about that.

Funny, but that first time I never even noticed it. Maybe because she had a knack of keeping her face half turned away. She was very good at it too, never made it obvious. All I saw was this tall blonde piece in flat slippers and a belted mac, mooching along on her own. Her collar was turned up against the drizzle, her hands were rammed in her pockets. But, do you know, I fancied what I saw. When I finally did see the mark—well, it was just a part of her, wasn't it? It didn't worry me one little bit, not ever. I sometimes think I thought more of her because of it. But perhaps I'm funny that way.

Her Dad kept a ramshackle old pub the other side of Camberley. The Hoops, it was called. Been knocked down for years now, to make way for a by-pass. Her Mum was dead and there weren't any other kids, so Sunday afternoons were about the only free time she had. That's when we used to meet, up on the common. Meet, and just walk. Sometimes we'd talk, sometimes we wouldn't bother. I expect you'll think that's a funny sort of courtship. But then I never looked on it as courting. I don't think she did either. I'd tell her about Cairo and the army, and being in London in the war, and she'd come out with bits about herself. Her great grandparents were Norwegian, which was where she got her figure and her looks. Proud of it too, in a funny sort of way. She still spelled her name the same, "Petersen" with an "e." She hadn't got much of a life though. Just the pub really. Her Dad enjoyed the gout, he'd got pills for it but the awkward old blighter wouldn't take 'em. They didn't do much trade, not enough to run to bar help. So the nights he couldn't hobble, she'd got the place to run on her own. That's why I took to dropping in, latish sometimes, to do a bit of cellar work for them. Rack the barrels for tapping, get the empties into the yard. I suppose they got to rely on me. But we didn't think too much about that either.

It was over a year before I popped the question. Even then I don't think I would have, only I'd had just one or two over the odds. Christmas it was, they'd asked me over to stay, help out with the bars because for once they were going to be busy. Anyway, when we finally got the doors shut and the old man had tottered off for some kip, we just flopped out, both of us, either side the fire. Turkey was on, there wasn't anything else to do. We watched the windows bluing for a while; then she fetched another drink and we got to talking. She was really tired. I knew because she was rubbing the scar, a thing she never did. Sliding her fingers along it, touching at her lip.

I don't know why but I felt a sense of urgency. As if a moment was coming—an Event—that would never come again. Not ever, not in a thousand million years. I'd never imagined myself marrying anybody, let alone *asking*. I'd thought about it odd times, I suppose everybody does, but the image had just refused to form. But now I somehow knew it wouldn't wait. Every second was precious and they were rushing past faster and faster, all the while I sat. So I just came out with it. No time even to be scared.

I'll never forget the look on her face. "What?" she said. "What?" As if she hadn't heard right. So I said it again. Told her some other things as well, that had been waiting a very long time. They all came out in a rush. I wasn't any bloody capture, not for anybody. Let alone a girl like her. It was a cheek even to think about it, and I told her that as well.

She still looked sort of dazed. "Me?" she said. "Me?" I found out then what that silly little mark on her face had come to mean to her over the years. Because she grabbed my hand, pressed my fingers on it. "You'd be marrying this as well," she said. "This. Wake up every morning, have to look at it."

I knew I'd had too much then because I just got blazing mad. Not *at* her though. Sort of for her. "Yes," I said, "and aren't I the lucky one? Think of all the fun I'm going to have, trying to kiss it better."

She started laughing at that. Then she was crying, then we were both laughing again. "Why not?" she said. "Why bloody not?" Then I think we both went a bit mad. All that lot bottled up, then the cork came out the bubbly. Afterwards she said, "I love you, Bill, I love you," and I said, "I love you." Silly bloody words, aren't they? But words are all we've got. We lay and said them and said them and the radio was playing in the lounge because we hadn't turned it off, and there's a carol that still stands my back hairs straight on end. I was the King of Bethlehem that night, because I'd just been born; and she was the Queen.

We made part of the top floor of the Hoops into a flat. It wasn't ideal but there really wasn't anything else to do. Kaeti was born just over a year later. That wasn't a good time either. Pete got her second scar. Afterwards, she could never ever have any more.

They say it never rains but what it bloody pours. A few weeks later Douggie called me into his rabbit hutch of an office. I'd been expecting it. I'd lost a lot of hours, work was piling up, we were going to have to sort something out. It wasn't that though. He beat about the bush for a while, which wasn't like him; then he came out with it. He hadn't been feeling too good for a year or more; he'd been thinking it was time to call it quits. Now he'd had an offer he couldn't turn down. So he was selling up.

He'd started to look his age, I granted that. I'd seen it, so had one or two more. But the first thing in my mind was Pete and the kid. I said, "Who to?"

He looked away again. Finally he said, "Jacobsons." Then he looked back. He said, "I'm sorry about it, Bill, I know just how you feel. I feel the same. But that's the way it's got to be."

A by-word in the district, they were. Right crowd of Flash Harrys. Made it pay though, got a big place out on the A-30, couple more down Frimley way. Believed in fast turnover. Small profits, quick returns. Or so the saying goes. The fast turnover included staff. I couldn't imagine what they wanted our dump for. I found out fast enough though. First thing in was the time clock. Second was a smartyboots little manager. His main job was corner-cutting. If there was a fast way round anything, that was the way you took. Not sawdust in the axles, rubbish like that; they were far too smart. But some of the bits were bloody near as bad. There were four of us by then. Five including the foreman. Which naturally wasn't me. They extended the old workshop, pushed an ugly great prefab across what used to be the Waterfords' greenhouse. General consensus was, it spoiled the village. Which in fact it did. There are such things as planning authorities of course, but a bob or two in the right place always did work wonders.

Maybe I should have got out before I did. But jobs in my line weren't all that thick on the ground. I did prospect a couple, but I couldn't see myself being any better off. And it had to be local because Pete was tied to the pub. Her old man was worse than ever, in addition to which he'd started hitting the bottle. We'd had to take on a fulltime girl, and another to cover her days off. The combined wages made a hefty dent in the family income. All in all, we'd got ourselves into a right bloody tangle.

I stood it for a year. Then Douggie rang one night with a proposition. I didn't fancy it at first. I'd never seen myself as a shopkeeper, I don't now. But the way he put it, it made sense. "You know the trade's changing, boy. It's not repairs any more, it's just replacements. You don't *do* any bloody engineering, one month's end to the next. Why not face facts?"

He'd got property all over, bought in the days when you could get a nice little cottage for a couple of hundred quid. Nice little shop it was too, just off Camberley High Street. Caswell Autospares. Did well right from the start, I was surprised. Leather steering wheels, poncy little car vacs; lot of stuff I wouldn't have bothered with myself. I always stopped short at Dolly Danglers though.

Funny, sometimes when you hit a bit of rough. It seems you cop for the lot. Then you get through it and it all goes smooth and straight and you know it's going to stay that way, for a little while at least. Though I expect Kaeti would have a smart answer for that as well. Something to do with Perception of Reality.

She was seven when we came up here. Right little tomboy, spitting image of her Mum. Darker coloring, but the same big grey-blue eyes. Her Grandad had been dead five years or more. We brought the big clock out and an old carved box full of family letters, and that was the last I wanted to see of the Hoops. We settled down to build the business up and make ourselves a home. The first real one we'd had.

Pete was over the other thing as well. About never having any more kids. It hit her hard to start with. She never said all that much, but I could tell. I knew she was over it when she stood in front of the mirror one night. "You know," she said, "I think it's working."

I couldn't think what she meant, not to start with. I said, "What's working?" and she grinned at me. She said, "What you told me that first night. It must be mind over matter."

I'd been going through some of the papers and they'd given me an idea. "Pete," I said, "have you ever been home?"

"What?" she said. "I am home."

"No," I said, "I didn't mean that. I ment Norway."

It didn't sink in for a minute. Then her eyes started to change. She said, "We can't afford it."

"No," I said, "we can't. When shall we go?"

She didn't answer straight off. Just sort of swallowed. Then she said, "It'll have to be a ship. Grandad always said it had to be a ship."

And so a ship it was. Kaeti and Pete and me, all on a great big ship. And Norway?

It's funny, but it's a place where there's only Now. Because the winter's coming and it's dark, it lasts forever. So you live a marvelous, vivid Now. And there's the mountains, the huge mountains, and the sea. It's a place to be in love. On a ship, under the Midnight Sun.

Wind's dropped a bit. Rain's easing too. Put the light out just now, stood till my eyes got used to the dark. Nothing to see though. Dim gleam of the lane and the common stretching out, big humps of bushes. Nothing moving at all.

Douggie died in sixty-nine. I'd been expecting it but it still came as a shock. After all, I'd known him most of my life. I got a bigger shock a few days later though. He'd left us the shop. The lot, lock, stock and barrel. I knew there weren't any relatives, just a sister somewhere down Brighton way; but I still never expected that. About the same time the word went round the Greyhound would be changing hands, old Bill was going to retire. Good old boy he was, ex-copper. Had it since just after the War.

Pete grinned when I told her about it. She said, "Going to have a go then?"

"A go," I said, "what do you mean?" and she looked at me. "The pub," she said. "You know you want it."

I think my mouth must have dropped open. I *did* want it, I wanted it a lot, but till that minute I don't think I'd faced up to it. I said, "Haven't you seen enough of pubs?"

She started clearing away. "We're not talking about me," she said. "We're talking about you."

"We're talking about both of us," I said. "You wouldn't want to go back into a pub, not after what you put up with."

She leaned on the table. "Look, Bill Fredericks," she said, "I've never told you what I want, one way or the other. So don't go putting words in my mouth." She looked thoughtful. "Matter of fact, I wouldn't mind running a pub," she said. "*Running* one. My way. And you could make that place go."

"But there's nothing up there," I said. "Only the village."

"There's the new estates," she said. "And that other one they started up Yately way. Came by the other day, there's people in already."

"They're no good," I said. "Up to here in mortgages. Anyway we couldn't afford it, the ingoing's bound to be sky high. It'd mean selling up."

She looked scornful. "Course it wouldn't," she said. "Get it off the bank, you've got collateral now. Then put somebody in here. I don't see how you could lose."

And that was the first time I realized Pete's got a far better business head than me.

I didn't think we stood much of a chance. Heard later they had twenty couples after it. But Pete got herself done up to kill and that was the end of it. Perhaps the brewery thought they owed her a favor.

I suppose the Greyhound isn't everybody's idea of a country pub. Big gaunt red-brick place it is, stands back on its own facing the common. Wood-paneled walls, vintage nineteen twenty, and the two big bars. There's more to it than meets the eye though. Had a horse in the Public one night, new pony from the riding school. Old Teddy's fault, that was. Little lass on board couldn't get it past; then he clicked to it and in it came for its ale. Reckoned later he could tell it was a beer drinker by the look in its eye. And there it was plunging about with the little lass looking distraught and Teddy up the corner having the croup. He got it back outside finally with the lure of a pine, after which of course it never would go by the pub. Used to have to hack along the other road.

Thursdays were the highlights. They were the barter nights; unspoken thing it was, among the locals. They'd all slope in, starting about eight, dump polythene sacks on the long bench just inside the door. Peas and beans, cabbages, onions and spuds, cauliflowers. Looked like a budding harvest festival sometimes. They'd have a pint or two apiece, not hurrying, then it would start." "Nice-looking collies you got there," Jesse Philips would say, and somebody else would take it up. "See your beans done all right then, Jesse." After a while the swap would be made, and that would set the tone for the rest. Peas would change place with cabbages, potatoes with onions, till everybody was suited. The incomers from the new estate cottoned after a while and tried to join in. But all they brought were bunches of flowers. Jesse Philips summed it up one night. "Can't eat bloody chrysanths," he said, after which they took the hint and tried for vegetables. But the new plots couldn't compete. The builders dumped the rubbish from the footings, they'd lost their topsoil. The ring closed up. They'd sell, at fair Camberley prices, but they would not trade. So Blackwell became two villages. We watched that happen as well.

We made our mistakes of course, like everybody else. But they weren't too serious. We kept the old trade and built on it. The lads from Jacobsons started dropping in when they heard I'd taken over. And there was the new place, the annex to the Agricultural College. Weekends they'd bring their wives and girlfriends, and so the word spread round. Sundays there were the trippers and hikers. We catered for them, forty or fifty at a time, so the word spread that way too. After the first couple of years we could afford bar help two or three nights a week, and we were taking holidays again. Never get rich, not from a pub like the Greyhound; but we were comfortable. And of course there was the shop as well.

I've heard people say bringing up teen-age boys is bloody murder. I wouldn't know. All I can say is, try

bringing up a teen-age girl. I can't remember noticing
the change as such, but suddenly it seemed we hadn't
got a pretty little kid any more. Instead there was this
gawky twelve- or thirteen-year-old, all knees and elbows
and bloody bad temper. Tantrums every morning, tears
every night. Or so it seemed to me. And never a reason
for it, not that I could see. She'd got all the things most
kids of her age want, but it was never enough. So-and-
so had got this, somebody else had got that. Such-and-
such was going on a school exchange to Germany, why
couldn't she? So we sent her to Germany, though she
didn't seem much better suited when she got back. Then
it was a pony, she had to have a pony. Horses morning
noon and night, six months or more. So we got her a
pony, rented grazing from old Frank the diddy. The fad
lasted another three or four months, after which she
never went near. So there was trouble over that as well.
Her mother got fed up in the end, sold the thing over
her head. The row that followed was the best so far. I
left them to it, opened up on my own. The public bar
was beginning to seem more and more a haven of rest.

Then it was boys of course. First was young Davey
Woodford from the farm. Nice enough kid in his way,
but, oh Gawd, teen-age romance! "Wasn't you ever
young, Mr. Fredericks," he asked me once. "Wasn't you
ever *young*?" I'm afraid I made things worse, laughing
the way I did. Course I was young, but I can't remember
any episodes like that. Never had time, to start with. His
age I was out in the bundu, counting bloody shekels.

Got worse rather than better when the thing with him
blew up. She attracted 'em, from as far away as Frimley.
Acted like a magnet. She was starting to be a looker, I
granted that. But some of 'em weren't very wholesome
types at all. I could see our nice clean reputation taking
a sudden dive. That finished when her mother turned
her out the bar one night. "Get upstairs," I heard her
say, "you're not coming in here like that." After which
there was a constant grinding of rock from her room till
suppertime, at which we had the row to end all rows.

That was also the first time in my life I saw Pete really lose her temper. She didn't stop at one either, she beat the daylights out of her.

I'll admit it, I got out. Made myself a John Collins, went and sat in the snug and had a smoke. There's something about voices raised in anger that I've always found chilling. Not so much the violence, the pointlessness. We act, sometimes, as if we're all immortal. It reminds me, or reminded me, of the shortness of life.

Pete came through about half an hour later, got herself a drink as well. She looked at me a minute, then came and put her hand on my shoulder. "Sorry," she said, "but it had to come. I wasn't being spoken to like that."

I said, "What's happened?" and she smiled. "Nothing," she said. "She'll be all right. She's gone to bed."

I said before, sometimes you seem to cop for the lot. Then you come through it and it all seems to sail along again. Just as suddenly, or so it seemed to me, Kaeti was a young woman. Taller than her mother, couple of inches with her heels on, and just as pretty. Same mannerisms, same turn of the head, same po-faced sense of humor. Like turning the clock back somehow. All the rest was behind her. She was smoking but not too much, she liked a drink, she was going to Sixth Form College. Knew just what she wanted and how to get it. Mornings when she had a free period, Pete would nip down to Camberley, have coffee with her there. They'd come back together. Two women, joking and laughing. Close. I suppose we were a family again. Though this time we didn't have very long to enjoy it.

April it was, when she first got ill. She'd been looking off-color for days; finally she didn't come down to breakfast. Said her throat was bad, she couldn't hardly swallow. Didn't clear up either. So finally I called Doc Jamieson. He came down shaking his head. Said it was thrush, first adult case he'd seen in years. He left her some stuff, but it didn't seem to do much for her. She was off a couple of weeks. When she finally went back she just seemed listless. Preoccupied. You'd speak to her, and odds she wouldn't answer. Sometimes have to speak two or three times, then she'd come round with a jump. But she wouldn't know what you'd said. The other thing was starting by then of course. But at the time we didn't realize.

It was the most perfect summer I can remember. Day after day cloudless, the nights warm, with the breeze bringing the scents in off the common. Made it even more ironic. Kaeti lying upstairs there, dozing or staring out at the sky. I rigged a television for her, put the control where she could reach it without moving her arm. But she never bothered with it. "I'm all right, Dad," she kept on saying. "Just a bit tired, that's all. Don't worry, I'll be all right." She wasn't all right though; she was far from all right. She looked bloodless somehow. Like a marble statue.

Doc Jamieson was worried as well. I could see that. Had a drink with me one night just before we opened. Said it was the listlessness that had got him bothered more than the rest. There wasn't much physically wrong at that stage. Touch of anemia certainly, but that did sometimes happen after a bad infection. He finally said he'd like her taken in for tests. Asked him what sort of tests but I might as well have saved my breath. Lawyers and accountants can both be vague enough when it suits their book. But the medical profession leaves 'em at the post.

I don't know how many tests she did have. We both lost count. They were all inconclusive. Or maybe there were too many conclusions. Agranulocytosis without ulceration. She'd got the experts thoroughly baffled as well. So I did a bit of reading for myself. Afterwards I wished I hadn't. There's a lot of words for it but they all add up to one thing. If it goes on long enough, the blood turns yellow-green, like pus. I still don't like to use the phrase they have for it. Even though I know by now they got it wrong.

The mist came back with the autumn. Long white tongues of it, creeping round the pub. Even then though she wouldn't have her windows closed. It was the only thing that roused her. The Doc shrugged finally and said to let it be. The rest was left unspoken but I had a horrible feeling I knew what it was. Nothing would do much harm now; she was past any help he thought he could give her.

The locals were very good. There were always things being left for her, jam, preserves, whole load of stuff. We'd got a cupboard full. Not that she ever touched it. Wasn't eating enough to keep a mouse alive. She'd ask sometimes how they all were, Jesse and old Teddy and the rest. And they'd ask after her of course. All except Frank Smith, which was odd. Funny little bloke he was, a lot of gypsies are. But he'd always been one of the most concerned. Till I told him, quite early on, there was a touch of anemia but the Doc thought she'd be fine. After that he didn't come in again. I didn't give it much thought for a couple of weeks; then I asked Jesse if he was bad. I thought he gave me a funny sort of look. He said no he was fine, been talking to him that morning in the village. Saw him myself a couple of times after that, out on his rounds, but he wouldn't speak. First time he looked the other way; second time he whipped the horse up. Which was a thing I'd never seen him do. His place was put up for sale a few days later; we didn't see him again.

Last thing they tried was x-ray treatment. I didn't like the idea of it, neither did Pete. But Kaeti just laughed. "That's all right," she said. "it won't matter, I shall be back for Christmas, you see." Funny, but she looked really perky. Sitting up with a woolly on, brighter than she'd been for weeks. Made a fuss about having all her bits and pieces, books to read and such. Even got her mother to do her hair. Two days later the hospital phoned. I knew it somehow before I picked the damned thing up. Our daughter was dead.

They all said afterwards how good we both were. You know, carrying on. It wasn't like that at all though; there was nothing good about it. When a thing like that happens, it turns all your ideas upside down. You carry on because you've got to. Would you mind telling me what else there is to do?

It was a big turnout. Sis came down of course, and Auntie May's lot, and some other cousins I hadn't seen for years. Plus the brewery outside manager, and nearly everybody from the pub.

It was raining. People always say it rains on days like that. And somehow it nearly always seems to. I don't remember very much else about it. I know I stared at the wreaths laid out on the grass and caught myself wondering what I was doing there. And there was a little chapel set among the graves, and a trolley with rubber-tired wheels that didn't squeak. That didn't get to me either though. It was like acting in a film somehow, it was nothing to do with us. Me and Pete and Kaeti. I was waiting for somebody with a megaphone to jump up and shout cut. Then we could all go home. But the film kept grinding on.

Sis stayed a fortnight, helped out with the bars. Then she had to get back. I didn't blame her. She'd already done more than most.

Hardest thing was convincing myself it had really happened. I knew I'd got to of course, but in a queer way I still couldn't believe it. Kaeti's life just stopping like that, a breath that went in and didn't come back out. And letting the box down on its webbings, and going home for tea. It couldn't be all there was to it; it just wasn't possible. So none of it had really happened; I was in some sort of dream. I kept trying to wake up but I couldn't. Coming to terms, they call it. What a bloody phrase. Though you can't blame them for that. Like I said before, words are all we've got.

Nights were the worst. I was tired and getting tireder, but I wasn't sleeping worth mentioning. I'd doze off sometimes toward dawn, get an hour or two. Then it was daylight, and I'd wake up and realize the dream was still going on and just want to go to sleep again, and sometimes I'd manage it. Then I'd be late for the dray or the Cash and Carry, and the bottling up wouldn't be done by opening time. I remember thinking sometimes it had to have an end. But there's never an end to anything. Any more than there's a beginning. We went to London for the Christmas, just one night. Then back again first thing to open up. Another year would be starting soon. That was beginning to get to me as well.

Pete was worrying me too. The day after the funeral she stripped the display units in both bars, washed them down. The morning after she did it all again. And the morning after that. We always used to do them pretty often. You've got to, the smoke gets to them mirrors. But not every day God sent. Then she shampooed the carpets. Scrounged one of those big industrial units from a little bloke who used to come in now and then. After that it was the kitchen's turn. She scrubbed it down, walls, floor and ceiling. Then the upstairs bathroom. Then a load of paint arrived from the brewery. I thought the van driver looked a bit shifty. Turned out she'd fixed it without telling me. The upstairs had to be done up. All of it, right through. She started on it in the afternoons. Which meant she was working eighteen hour days. And she wasn't sleeping either.

I thought at least she'd leave Kaeti's room till last. She didn't though. Went up one day, found all her things parceled in heaps. Ready for the jumble. She just shrugged when I said about it. Asked what was the point of keeping them, they weren't any use to us. I said, "But, Pete," and she turned and looked at me. Nothing behind her eyes, not any more. They looked—well, sort of dead. So I didn't say anything else. But it still hurt plenty.

It had to end of course. Nobody can just keep on going like that, week after week. I was in the Public when it happened, talking to Jesse and one or two more. Dick Stanton had come down with his sister-in-law, the one who used to be an opera singer. I could hear his distinctive voice in the saloon. There was quite a crowd in, mostly youngsters from the college, but Pete had shoved me out. Said she could cope. So I left her to it. She was always better working on her own; we saw too much of each other the rest of the time.

I wasn't really registering the buzz of voices till it stopped. There was a crash then, like a bar stool going over. I half turned, and Pete was standing in the door-way. I've never seen a face like it. There's a phrase for it they use in lousy novels. *Blazing* white. Well, it was. She opened her mouth, sort of half pointed behind her, then she just crumpled. I jumped forward, but I was nowhere near quick enough. Bottles went flying, then Dick ran through. He said, "My God, Bill, what happened?"

We got her to the bedroom somehow, and his sister-in-law came up. I left them, ran to call the Doc. I thought she was a goner, straight. But by the time he arrived she was sitting up. Still looked pale as death but she swore she was all right, she just passed out. He left her some stuff, and I followed him down. "Doc," I said, "what's wrong?"

He shook his head. Nothing, apparently, that he could find. He said, "How's she been? Since . . ."

I told him what had happened and he nodded. He said what I'd been thinking, that nobody could keep on indefinitely. It catches up with them. He said, "Can you get some help in?"

"Sure," I said, "George Swallow will always do an extra night. Glad of the cash."

He opened his car door. "Get him then," he said, "and try and keep her in bed. It would do you both good to get away for a few days. I'll look in again tomorrow." He drove off and I went back inside. Good bloke, is Doc Jamieson. After all, we were only ever NHS.

I got the bars closed finally and went upstairs. I thought she was asleep but she opened her eyes when she heard me. They were huge and dark. "No, Bill," she said. "I don't want no pills." She grabbed my wrist. She said, "Bill, I *saw* her. . . ."

"What?" I said. "Saw who?"

She swallowed and tightened her grip. "Kaeti," she said. "She was in the bar. . . ."

Things seemed to spin round a bit for me as well. I sat on the bed. "Look, Pete," I said. "you've got to face it. Kaeti's dead. . . ."

She pushed her hair back. "You don't understand," she said. "I *saw* her, it *was* her. Don't you think I know my own daughter?"

I got her a bit more settled after a while and went back down. I got myself a stiff drink and sat and smoked a fag. I didn't know what to do. Or think. But I had to talk to somebody. Finally I rang Dick Stanton. He's always been a late bird. I didn't think he'd mind. He said at once, "How is she?"

I hesitated. I said, "She's fine, the Doc thinks she'll be OK. Just been overdoing it, you know what it's been like."

"Yes," he said, "I think I've got the picture."

I hesitated again. "Look, Dick, *did* anything happen? In the other bar? The way she came through . . ."

He didn't answer for a minute. I sensed he was puzzled as well. Finally he said, "Not that I saw. She was talking to us, seemed quite OK. Then suddenly . . . it was as if she'd seen a ghost."

Level-headed man is Dick. I've always had a lot of time for him. And he knows how to keep his mouth shut. I swallowed and took the plunge. I said, "She did."

The phone said, "What?"

I said, "She thinks she saw our daughter. She saw Kaeti."

A pause. Then he said, "Just a minute." I stood and listened to the atmospherics on the line. They were bad that night. Like voices nearly, whispering and hissing. Finally he said, "Hello? You still there?"

"Look, Bill," he said, "there was one funny thing. There were some youngsters in, looked like students. Over in the far corner, I didn't pay 'em much attention. They'd just got up to leave. Jilly says there was a girl with them. Tall, brown haired."

So that explained it.

"No," he said, "not quite. When Pete ran through like that, Jill went out after them. She thought they might have done some damage or nicked something. She was only a second or two behind. But there wasn't anybody outside. No cars moving either."

"What?" I said. "There must have been."

I could sense him shrugging. He said, "It's probably not important. Like you said, she just made a mistake. She's been under a lot of strain." Another pause. Then he said, "Look, Susan's at the college. My eldest. I'll get her to ask round on the quiet. See if anybody was there. If they remember."

"Thanks," I said, "thanks a lot. And, Dick . . . keep it under your hat, will you? I wouldn't want it getting about."

He said, "I didn't hear a thing. Take it steady, Bill. I'm sure she'll be OK."

Oddly enough, for once I got a good night's sleep. When I woke up, Pete wasn't in the room, I ran downstairs but she wasn't in the pub either. I was just starting to get really worried when the side door clicked. She came in looking different somehow. Brighter. She said, "I went for a walk on the common. It's a lovely morning. I think spring's coming."

I've never seen anybody perk up the way she did. She went down to Camberley that same day, came back with an armful of flowers. She made up bowls for each of the bars, and one for the sitting room upstairs. When Doc Jamieson arrived she was dashing about like a two-year-old. He raised his eyebrows but he didn't say anything. I'd have given a lot to know what he was thinking though.

That night I heard her laughing in the saloon. Just like the old times. That hurt as well, deep down. She couldn't have forgotten Kaeti already. Not as quick as that.

She didn't touch her bedroom again. The fad seemed to have ended as quickly as it started. The clothes she'd sorted out had vanished, but I hadn't seen her take them anywhere. I slipped in on the quiet one morning. They were all back in the chest of drawers, and sprigs of lavender to keep them fresh. Apart from some she took down to the kitchen. She washed and ironed them, did some mending; then she put them with the rest.

She didn't stop the redecorating. Instead she worked harder than ever. Seemed to have got fresh strength from somewhere. I argued with her about it once, but she just smiled. "Got to have it looking nice," she said. "Never know, somebody might come."

"Who?" I said. "There's only us." But she carried on regardless. So I got stuck in as well. It was April by the time we'd finished, nearly May. And the common brightening with the new spring grass.

I thought she'd forgotten our daughter. She hadn't though. Far from it. After we closed one night, I caught her taking a cup of tea upstairs. I asked her where she thought she was going and she grinned at me. "Where do you think?" she said. "It's for Kaeti."

I opened my mouth and shut it. Couldn't think of anything to say. Next day I made an excuse to go out, called on Doc Jamieson. After that the pills changed color. She said she didn't need them. She took them sometimes, when she couldn't get out of it, but most of the while she just flushed them down the loo. Those were the nights she took to wandering. I'd see the light on under Kaeti's door, hear her talking inside and laughing. I never interrupted her, because I couldn't face what was happening.

I won't say that was the worst part of all because it wasn't. But it did come near to being the last straw. She was in a private world of her own, somewhere I could never go. We were drifting apart as well, and there wasn't a single thing I could do.

It's been a funny old year for weather. Trees didn't drop their leaves till near on Christmas. Fields were still green too. Vivid. Sort of sickly.

The mist we sometimes used to get hung round right through the summer. Mostly by the pub. Jesse remarked

on it more than once, said it was clear up by his place.
Which was only a couple of hundred yards along the
road. Teddy noticed it too. Only he wasn't coming in so
much. He'd had a bad go of asthma; he said it played
his chest up.

Used to sit and watch it sometimes. When I didn't
fancy sleeping. Long tendrils, white as milk, and always
moving. Flowing. Organic almost. I'd moved my desk
into the sitting room, so I could hear if Pete got too
restless. I'd finish the day's booking, then put the light
out, just sit and smoke a cigarette and stare. Get hypnotized almost. Sometimes I'd doze. I'd always have bad
dreams then. Only they weren't bad at the time. Just
when I woke up. I'd be talking to Kaeti, remembering
little things. All sorts of things. Then I'd sit up and the
room would be empty again. Sometimes I'd think I could
still hear her voice, that she was still there. Sitting across
from me, curled on the settee. But it was only patches
of moonlight on the wall.

Pete bought her a skipping rope once. Just after she
started college. Kaeti swore she was getting fat, went on
and on. I even dreamed about that.

Real jute it was, it said so on the carton. With handles
made from old loom spindles. There was a booklet too,
all about children's rhymes. It became her prize posses-
sion. She'd play with it for hours, up in her room. Clear
all the stuff away first so she could get a good swing.
The bumping and thumping would echo right through
the pub. Like the old clock ticking. And you'd hear
her chanting, getting steadily more out of breath.
"Salt-mustard-vinegar-pepper, salt-mustard-vinegar-pepper. . . ." Then an extra thump as she tried for the big
one, four turns under, and usually a faint *"Damnit. . . ."*
After which she'd start all over. Right nut case she was,
I told her so more than once. But it never had any effect.

When I opened my eyes that time, I could still hear the
scuff of her feet. Even the faint whistle of the rope. The
sounds took ages to die away. When I went out onto the landing, the door of her room stood ajar, and the light was

on again. I reached in, turned it off and pulled the door shut. I didn't look back, because if it came back on I would have to go and see. I did turn by our bedroom. The room had stayed dark of course.

Next night I was seeing to Chota. I'd got her her bits as usual, saucer of milk and that. She had a good drink, thought about the meat, then changed her mind and ran to the back door. "Oh, no," I said, "you can't want out this time of night." But she was mewing, scratching at the frame as if her life depended on it.

"All right," I said, "be quick then." I was wasting my breath though; I opened the door a few inches and she was through it like a streak and away.

I swore and went to fetch a torch. I walked outside and called but there was no sign of her. The mist was moving fast, streaming toward the pub. I flicked the torch about but it was useless, the beam just refracted back. I thought I heard her again somewhere ahead. I walked till I could see the common stretching out vague and blue-white. Then I heard the door slam shut behind me.

I gave up and went back. First thing I saw was the cat, finishing the saucer as if nothing had occurred. Ears laid back, really tucking in. I called her a few names under my breath, shot the bolts on the door and went upstairs. It was late but I didn't want to sleep. I went into the sitting room instead, sat down at my desk. I watched the mist flow in after me under the door. For some reason I wasn't really surprised.

There wasn't much of a crack but it had found it. It swirled round my ankles, spread across the room. Once I put my hand down to it. I expected it to feel cold but it didn't. Not much sensation from it at all.

More came, and more. There seemed no end to it. I thought for a while the room would fill right up. It didn't though. It was as if it was congealing somewhere, out of my line of sight. I watched the pattern on the carpet become visible again, heard the soft footsteps pad across the room. My old dressing gown was slung across a chair.

I heard it rustle, then the steps came back. Finally I looked up. Kaeti was sitting on the settee with the dressing gown wrapped round her. It was too long by a foot or more. She said, "Hello, Dad." Then she smiled. She said, "You always was a gent."

My cigarettes were lying on the desk top. I picked the packet up and opened it. But I didn't really want it. So I put it back. When I looked up again she hadn't gone away. I said, "What's happening?" I don't know quite what I meant by that. Some sort of a time-slip idea I think.

She pushed her hair back. She said, "Don't tell me you didn't know." She got up, walked toward me. She said, "Hello" again and held her hands out. I took them. They were warm.

I said, "It is you, isn't it?" and she said, "Yes." Then she scotched on my lap, put her arms round my neck. She hadn't done that since she was about eight. She said, "I know it's a bit of a shock. But I did try and warn you. You must have heard me the other night."

I said. "I couldn't be sure." Then it got to me. "Kaeti," I said, "it was raining," and she said, "I know," and hugged me. "Don't, Dad," she said, "it's all right," and I said, "Kaeti, oh my God." We said a lot more then, the both of us, but I don't remember any of it. Neither did I care. I'd got her back, you see, I'd got my kid back. And she was warm.

Afterwards I said, "Kaeti, what about your mother," and she put her head back and laughed. "She knows," she said, "she's known for ages. We were only worried about breaking it to you." I did pull away a bit then because I'd seen the faint hypertrophy of the eyeteeth, the lovely little pearly fangs she'd grown. But she only laughed again. "Dad," she said, "you are a twit. I'm not going to *chumph* you, that's only on the films." She sat up then and looked at me solemnly. She said, "You look as if you need a drink. And I'd like something too, it don't half make you thirsty. Can I make some tea?"

I said, "Can you *drink*?" and she giggled. "What do

you think I do," she said, "pour it in my ear?" She got up and I caught her hand. I said, "I'll get it," but she shook her head. "It's OK," she said. "You've been dashing about all day."

I still didn't want her out of my sight though. I stood outside her bedroom and waited. She came out pulling a woolly over her head. "I'm sorry about Mum," she said, "I gave her a right turn that first time; you'll have to make it up to her." I said, "I thought you'd killed her," and she turned back looking troubled. "I know," she said, "but there was nothing I could do. I had to stop her getting rid of all my things. I wouldn't have had anything left to wear. . . ."

She put the kettle on, fetched the bottle of Paddy I keep for special occasions. Broke me up a bit that she'd remembered. She mashed the tea, stood the pot on a tray, then scooped Chota onto her shoulder. "Let's go back upstairs," she said, "it's warmer." And so we sat and talked, till there was grey light in the sky. And that was the first of Kaeti's nights.

Those teeth were the only thing that worried me. But that always sent her into fits. "Come on, Dad," she used to say, "they're kinky. Don't you think they suit me?" They did too, in a funny sort of way. Made her look, I don't know, like a healthy young animal. Which I suppose was what she'd always been. I think I was seeing things clearer. A lot of things. Hard to see straight, when you're trying to earn a living. Deal with bloody VAT and all the rest.

That's what I mean, about seeing straight. We had the VAT boys in a few days later. Played hell because I'd been supplying Dick with spirits by the crate; it had knocked my profit margin back a bit. Part of their job is keeping inflation on course though. Or perhaps you knew. There was a time when I'd have blown my stack. But not any more. I don't think I even listened very much; they were like radio static a long way off. All I could think of was K eti was coming back; it was going to be another of her Nights. Horses in blinkers, that's what we'd all been. Anger is for mortals.

She told me early on, the legend's wrong. Cocked up from start to finish. It's not what's taken from you, it's what they *give*. And they don't leave marks, any more than an acupuncture needle leaves a mark. "It's a sort of Contact really," she said. "It changes the flow. It all goes on from there. . . ." I asked her what flow she meant, but she only grinned. "Ask a Chinaman," she said. "They knew a bit as well. Everybody knew bits. Even the bloke who wrote the book. But nobody ever got it all together." She pulled a face. "Then they found out about those grotty little bats in South America, the ones that bite the donkeys, and that was that. It's just a different lifestyle, Dad, that's all. . . ."

It did take a little while to get used to. But that was OK too; she said I'd got a million years of prejudice to get rid of. Atavism, that was the word she used. Her vocabulary was going up by leaps and bounds; she'd left me standing. "Bashing saber-tooths over the head with hatchets," she said. "That's why you're scared of the night. It's the days you ought to be frightened of though really. That's when the bad things happen. . . ."

Sometimes she'd come three or four nights together. Then we wouldn't see her for a week or more. She said there were long resting periods, there had to be; but she was never too clear about that. I don't think myself it was that at all. She was being considerate. After all, we'd still got the pub to run. It worried me a bit sometimes. Her not being there. I'd sit and stare out at the common and watch the rain and wonder what she was doing, where she was. But she put me right about that as well. "Look, Dad," she said, "if I'm not here with you I'm not *anywhere*. Well, nowhere you could understand just yet. What do you think I'm doing, running about getting soaked?" In any case, they don't experience Time the way we do. "I'm always here," she said to me once. "I never went away. Think of it like that. . . ." Also, she warned me about Desire. It seemed a queer word somehow for her to use, but she didn't mean it quite the way I thought. "You mustn't *want* me to come every night," she said. "You mustn't *want* anything. Then I'll be here." That's what she meant, about going on from the Gotama. "He knew as well," she said. "They all knew really. . . ." After that I'd go down to the kitchen afterwards and pick her clothes up where they'd fallen and bring them back upstairs and put them away and just not think of anything at all. I reckon I'd reached stage one of the Enlightenment.

She never let me see the transformation except for that first time. Not that there was anything horrible about it; she was very clear on that. It was just that there were certain things I wasn't ready for. And watching her turn to protoplasmic mist was one of them. "It might give you the wrong idea," she said. "You might start thinking about those grotty films again. . . ."

That was funny too, coming from her. She always used to be a sucker for them. Even badgered us into getting a color telly so she could see the blood better. Gruesome little devil. But now it just seemed sad. I mean, that anybody had bothered with rubbish like that. "Think of a chrysalis," she told me once. "You crawl out on a branch and hang yourself up and squidge down into a sort of porridge. Then you wait a million seconds, and out you come a butterfly. Those were the things we should have been looking at. . . ." It was one of her metaphors; she'd developed quite a knack for them. She was the butterfly now, riding high night.

I'll tell you what it was like. It was like being in love. I don't mean with *her*, that sort of thing. It was like the first time ever, waking up and seeing colors, the atoms of things vibrating. And knowing there are textures, your feet are pressing the ground, things are *real*. And you send up thanks. Not unto the Lord, that sort of stuff, just thanks. For being. That's when you see the One. Only there's gravity, it all falls away. And you can never get it back. I lived it every day though. Like a dream that didn't stop. I told her that too once, and she grabbed my hand. "That's *right*, Dad," she said. "You're coming

on. Everything's a dream, they all knew that. Jesus, the
Gotama, everybody. They're all One." I said, "*The* One?"
and she nodded. "That's right," she said, "*The* One. . . ."

They know so much more than us of course. They're
homo superior, they have been all along. The next stage
on. Only we got confused. Couldn't see the wood for a
few spooky trees. We hounded them, wherever we
thought they were. That's why there's still so few of
them. But that's going to change a bit. She made that
very clear.

She raised the subject herself one night. Her birthday,
it was. We hadn't forgotten, we were hardly likely to.
But she made sure anyway. Talk about nudge nudge,
wink wink. Pete made her a cake, and didn't she tuck
into it. I'd seen some healthy appetites before, but that
was a classic demo. No weight-watching problems any
more, you see. They trade off excess molecules the same
way they take in nutrients, usually while passing through
earth. The age enzymes go with them, which is why
they're immortal. They don't really need to eat at all,
not in the ordinary sense. She finished with a cuppa
nonetheless, then asked if she could have a cigarette. She
was looking thoughtful. "Dad," she said, "I want to talk
to you. It's a bit serious."

I didn't have much doubt what it was about. I'd been
reading the papers, watching the whole world getting
ready to tear itself to bits. We hadn't got very long.

I thought when she did finally raise the matter, I'd at
least need time to think. I didn't though. Funny. Or
maybe it's not really so odd. I didn't want to be parted
from her again, you see. But now it was me that was at
risk. The only thing that worried me was having to go
through what she'd had to first. And that was honestly
more for her mother's sake than mine. But she shook
her head. "It's nothing, Dad," she said. "It looks worse
than it is; you really don't feel a thing. I was a bit scared
right at the start, but you'll know what's happening. Anyway, it takes different people different ways. You won't
have the time I had." They remember the future too of

course, in bits and pieces; so I knew she wasn't talking without a book.

There was still one other thing though. I didn't know quite how to put it. She waited, grinning, and finally I said, "Kaeti, will it ... be you?" The grin got broader then, and she shook her head. "No, Dad," she said, "it won't be me. Be a bit intimate, wouldn't it? Don't worry about it though, somebody'll come."

Nice young kid she was too. A few years older than Kaeti. And really pretty, jet-black hair all done in sort of ringlets. Looked up-to-date enough apart from that, jeans and a sweater. But they were Kaeti's things of course, picked up from just next door. She knew a lot about the Thirty Years' War, said they tied one of her brothers across a cannon mouth. She wasn't bitter about it though; she wasn't bitter about anything. Of course she was looking at things from a different point of view.

I didn't really know what was expected of me. Not till she suddenly popped a finger into my mouth. It went through me then like an electric shock. She needn't have done it that way, I'm pretty sure. It was just to make things easier. Maybe she kissed me sometime, I can't remember. I think she must have, because suddenly I wasn't on the earth at all. I was out in space, and there were stars and suns, and mountains and a rubber-tired trolley going by, and a bank of flowers bigger than a planet. Everything was expanding, but it was shrinking too, all at the same time, reducing to a tiny shining dot. That was the One as well.

She talked a lot afterwards about love. Said what we know can only be a shadow. When two clouds merge, that's Joining. I said they must be Gods and Goddesses then, but that was muddle-headed. She said there was still something outside, they were still looking. So nothing really changes. Afterwards I laughed so loud I woke Pete up. Because I'd never left my bed, that was for sure. So it was still the dream. There was a disco running. Somewhere in the village. Been thumping and crashing nearly all the night. I ask you, when Folk have to be up by six.

But that's the human race all over for you. I sometimes think it deserves what it's going to get.

We had a letter in the post next morning. First time I'd actually seen copperplate handwriting, it was just a phrase before. Done on some sort of parchment too, though the English was modern enough. It begged an interview on a most urgent matter, said that the writer would call that afternoon at three.

I know what I'd have said about that in the good old days. Afternoons are sacred for a publican; it's the only chance the poor blighter has to get some kip. But the way we were living that sort of thing had ceased to matter, and Pete was curious as well. Mainly because of the writing. She asked who it was from, but we could neither of us make it out. Address was a good class London hotel, but the signature was the only indecipherable part. It was just a florid scrawl, it could have been anything.

He was punctual to the minute. I heard the taxi pull up and went to the door. Tall, bony-looking bloke he was, wearing one of those funny old-fashioned Inverness capes. His suit looked dated too; good tweed, but with a queer-looking cut to it. And he was wearing a cravat and one of those high stiff collars, the sort you only see now on the films. "Good afternoon," he said, "it is kind of you to see me. My name is van Helsing. You may perhaps have heard of my great-grandfather. He was a man of some renown, in his own highly specialized field."

It didn't ring a bell with me at all. Not to start with anyway. I sized him up instead. His hair was pale, so pale I took it to be white at first. Then I decided it was the color of bleached-out straw. His eyes were indeterminate too, pale-lashed and with an odd sort of sunken gleam. I started to wonder just what sort of a nut case we'd lumbered ourselves with. His voice was pleasant enough though, deep and well modulated, and his manners were impeccable. As old-world as his style of dress.

Pete looked at me. She said, "Van who?" and he said "Helsing" again and gave a little bow. She glanced back to me, then shrugged and turned away, got busy with the teapot. I said, "So what can we do for you?"

He was staring round, chin raised in a searching sort of way. And snuffing, for all the world like a dog looking for a scent. Finally he nodded. "Yes," he said, "this is indeed the place. I sense it. . . ."

I toyed with the idea that he might be from the Council after all, that somebody had made a complaint about the drains. I dismissed it straight away. He just hadn't got the right air of petty officialdom. There was something about him though. Sort of an authority. He turned to me gravely. "First," he said, "let me commiserate with you in your time of loss."

Pete froze in the act of pouring a cuppa. She said, "We don't want to talk about it. It's over and done with."

He leaned forward earnestly. "But, Mrs. Fredericks, it is not over," he said. "You know, and I know, that it is far from over. . . ."

"Bill," she said, "have we got to listen to this?" But I shushed her. "All right," I said, "let him have his little say." I turned to the van Whatsit bloke. "And you'd better make it good, my friend," I said. "Wishing yourself on us like this, upsetting my wife. Who the hell do you think you are anyway?"

He said, "I have told you who I am." He shook his head, and I swear his voice was vibrating with sympathy. "Believe me," he said, "I do understand. Nothing would normally induce me to intrude on such a time of sorrow. . . ."

"Look," I said, "get to the point, or get out." The name was still going round in the back of my mind. I was beginning to have a nasty feeling I had heard it before.

He got to the point. His way. It took a bit of time. He used a fair few high-flown words, but phrases like "the undead" were never far away. "To bring peace to that poor tormented soul," he said finally, "that is truly my only aim. It will be unpleasant, I realize that. Repugnant perhaps to any thinking being. But mercifully it is soon ended, and your child will be at rest. My apparatus is in the village, but I must have your consent. . . ."

I think it was the word apparatus that did it. I remembered all the films I'd seen then. The mallets and pointed stakes. I didn't think I was hearing right at first. I couldn't speak for a minute; then I was on my feet. "Let's get this straight," I said. "You want to *open* our kid's grave. . . ."

Pete was ahead of me though. She was always quicker on the uptake. A knife lay on the draining board; she snatched it up. "I'll give you graves," she said. "Get out that door, you bastard—"

He'd jumped up himself. "Mrs. Fredericks," he said, "you are making a terrible mistake—" That was as far as he got though. I yelled at her, but she'd already lunged.

How it missed him I shall never know. He eeled back somehow; then he was making for the door. "Deluded souls," he said. "You poor deluded souls. . . ."

I grappled with Pete but she wrenched away. He didn't wait for anything else; he was through the door like a long dog. Next minute he was legging it down the lane. He didn't look back either, not till he turned the corner out of sight.

I went back. "It's all right, love," I said. "We shan't be seeing any more of him." Pete threw the knife down, sat back at the table. She put her face in her hands, then and started to cry. Later she said, "Bill call the police."

"The police," I said. "What do you think they could do?"

"Stop him," she said. "There must be something they can get him on. Whoever he is."

"They wouldn't believe us to start with," I said. "Just think we'd been watching too much late-night telly. Anyway, think what he could do us for if they did catch up with him."

She stared at me. She said, "What do you mean?"

"Well," I said, "assault with a deadly weapon for a start."

"But it wasn't like that," she said, "It wasn't . . ."

"So you got upset," I said. "That's no reason to start waving knives about though. Leastways, that's how they'd see it."

She sat and looked at me miserably. "It's Kaeti," she said. "I was only thinking of Kaeti." Then the tears welled up again. "Bill," she said, "I'm afraid. I've never been so afraid. . . ."

Kaeti laughed about it when I told her. "Oh, him," she said. "We know all about him; he's been mooning round for days. He's out of his tiny Chinese; there isn't a van Helsing. There never was. His real name's McMorrow or something. He's cleared off now though; we don't know where he went. I reckon Mum put the frighteners on him for good."

I hesitated. "Kaeti," I said, "you know what you told me once. About everybody knowing little bits. Would it . . . is it a sort of formula? The stakes and that?"

She looked me straight in the eye. "Well," she said brightly, "look at it like this. If somebody rammed a dirty great spike through you, then cut your head off, you wouldn't be feeling too chipper, would you? Not to mention the garlic. . . ."

I must admit I'd never looked at it like that.

After she'd gone I watched the dawn come up. I knew if I went to bed I wouldn't sleep. She'd been airy enough, dismissed the whole affair; but there was something at the backs of her eyes that I just didn't like. She was scared as well.

I went down to Camberley in the afternoon, had a look at the grave. I'm ashamed to admit I'd never been near before. At first I couldn't face it; then later there never seemed a need. Everything was neat, the marble curbs in place and the new lead lettering. KAETI LINDA FREDERICKS, it read. 1962—1979. And on the other side something Pete had dreamed up later, a line from a Roman poet. LIE LIGHTLY ON HER EARTH, SHE NEVER LAY HEAVY ON THEE. It brought it all a bit too close again. Even—well, knowing what I did. I walked back into town, bought a bunch of flowers, arranged them for her

in the little zinc pot. The sun was shining, there were
birds all over. Bit different from last time. I wondered
if she—no, I didn't wonder anything. Anything at all.

It all seemed ridiculous, going back to the car. People
with spades and dark lanterns. I mean, not in the twentieth century. I had a word with the old boy in the gate-
house nonetheless. He said the gates were padlocked
seven sharp, he saw to it himself. There were high stout
railings, and, anyway, the main road ran outside; there
were streetlamps every few yards. Nobody would break
in *there*.

All the same, the unease didn't go away. It stayed with
me right through the day. By the time we got the bars
shut I felt flaked out. Pete was looking tired as well; we
decided we'd have an early night. Well, early for us. I
was asleep as soon as my head hit the pillow.

I had the most appalling dream. About van Helsing.
He was stooping down, doing something near the
ground. I couldn't see what. I shouted at him, but he
didn't take any notice. So I shouted again. It seemed my
voice went rushing out over a huge empty space. He
turned at that and held something up. I still couldn't see.
So he clicked a torch on for me. It was Kaeti's head.
She was grinning, but her eyes were terrified. Her mouth
was stuffed full of what looked like leaves, and a dreadful
vivid beard ran down her chin. I grappled with the bastard then, tried to choke the life out of him. He fought
back. He was stronger than he looked. I threshed about;
then Pete was yelling at me. She said, "Wake up, for
Christ's sake, Bill, *wake up!*"

I sat up. I felt groggy. I said, "I had this Godawful
dream," and she yelled again. "It wasn't a dream, don't
you know anything yet? Bill, *for Christ's sake. . . .*"

She was dressing already. I said, "What is it love,
what's wrong?" and she glared at me. She said, "She's
in trouble. He's already there. The bastard's *there. . . .*"

That sort of fear is infectious. I grabbed for my trousers and a shirt, flew downstairs and rammed a pair of
shoes on. I still didn't believe it was happening to me. I

ran the car back and she dived onto the front seat before
I'd finished braking. She'd got the big old shotgun I
bought once from Dick Stanton when I fancied trying
my hand at a bit of rough-shooting. I said, "Jesus, what
do you want that for? We can't take that. . . ." But she
just shouted at me. "Bill, get *going*. . . !"

The main gates of the cemetery were standing open.
Padlock hanging from one of them, and a length of chain.
I slewed the car through thinking I'd woken the street.
The headlights jizzed on obelisks, stone angels. I hauled
the wheel again, slashed beneath an overhanging tree.
Then I was running two wheels up on grass, along a
tarmac path. She yelled, "Right, go *right*. . . ." A wire
basket flew up in the air, a watering can went bowling
across the path. Then I saw him. Just a glimpse, his
head and shoulders as he straightened. Behind him the
headlamps lit the mound of fresh-turned earth. He took
one look and ducked out of sight again. I knew what he
was doing somehow without seeing. He was wrestling
with the lid.

Pete was out again before I'd stopped, and running.
Her shadow went jumping ahead across the grass. I followed, leaping over graves. A curbstone caught my foot
and I measured my length. It knocked the breath out of
me for a minute. I could only watch.

It was as if it was all happening in slow motion. She
yelled at him, just like I'd done in the dream. He showed
his teeth but he didn't stop what he was doing. He raised
the mallet; then the gun exploded. Both barrels. Among
the echoes there seemed to be a tinkling. He was flung
backwards, and the lamp that stood at the grave rim
went out abruptly. Which was just as well. I'd never seen
anybody hit at close range with a charge of shot before.
I don't want to again.

I jumped down. God, but she was looking pretty. Like
a rose, complete with scent and thorns. I lifted her. She
was limp and warm. I looked at Pete and we didn't have
to speak. No way was she going back down there again.
Not ever.

One thing you can say for graves. They're great for getting rid of bodies in. Neither did I feel too much remorse. I reckoned he'd got about what he deserved. Even to the second-hand coffin.

We worked like demons, the pair of us. I knew we couldn't possibly fill it all back in, get it squared off by daylight. There wasn't a chance. We did it though, somehow.

Pete drove us back. I was seeing to Kaeti. I kissed her once and she opened her big eyes. She said, "Thanks, Dad," and went to sleep again.

The roads were all deserted, no lights showing anywhere. The one car we did meet had its headlamps masked to slits. I wondered what they must have thought of us. I didn't pay that much attention though. Not till we got back in sight of Blackwell. I did look out then. Dawn was in the sky, sort of a pale grey flush. It showed me the outlines of the ack-ack guns, the long slim barrels pointing up. I looked the other way, to the sullen glow low down that meant London had had its nightly pasting again.

I went back in the morning. Didn't know quite what I would see. It was all right though. Just the lines of graves, the bright, tidy grass. All signs of the disturbance had long since gone. Nor did the gatekeeper say anything about the padlock. But I hardly expected he'd remember a little thing like that. After all, a lot of stuff went missing in the blackout.

She woke a few times crying after that. There was always one of us on hand to soothe. She tried to tell me once what it was like. Hearing the spade, from wherever she had been. Scraping coming closer, then the thumping on the lid. "I never did no harm to him," she said. "None of us did. . . ." I held her till she was quiet. "It's all right, love," I said, "it won't come again, not ever. It's over. . . ."

Next night she wasn't there. Gone out to recharge. Only now she had her own place to come back to, a room where we always kept the curtains drawn. The locals thought it was a sudden sign of mourning. Only Dick Stanton guessed. Or maybe it was more. He hasn't been too well this last couple of weeks. Throat infection that doesn't seem to clear. I heard they had the Doc the other day.

I think Time's wearing thin for all of us. Sometimes I hear the guns now, from a war I don't remember. Sometimes there's other things. The mushroom clouds all rising, and the fireballs. The walls of the pub all glow then, like bright glass. It happened a minute ago. In the old reckoning of Time. It didn't worry us though. I took Pete by the hand, and Kaeti, and we floated down, stood and watched the common light up and burn. There were others coming and then more, a great big crowd. There was one we called the Master. Not Vlad the Impaler though. He'll give the signal, when he's good and ready; and we'll all be away and gone. Headed for the dark side of another World. It won't take long. Because there isn't really Space, any more than there's Time.

There. It happened again. The paper I was writing on was burning, curling and blackening at the edges. But that don't matter either. All it means is that the One has grown a bit bigger. By something short of fifteen thousand human words. And a boat is setting sail, but not for Norway. And we stand on it and see the atoms dance, locked in a sort of brilliant, breathless Now.

Callahan's Bar attracts all types, from time travellers to vampires. Spider Robinson has written several books about Callahan's and its denizens, including the recent Off the Wall at Callahan's Place. *Need a drink, and maybe a laugh or two? Then come back to that famous bar where everybody knows your vein. . . .*

Pyotr's Story

SPIDER ROBINSON

Two total drunks in a single week is much higher than average for anyone who goes to Callahan's Place—no pun intended.

Surely there is nothing odd about a man going to a bar in search of oblivion. Understatement of the decade. But Callahan's Place is what cured me of being a lush, and it's done the same for others. Hell, it's helped keep Tommy Janssen off of *heroin* for years now. I've gotten high there, and once or twice I've gotten tight, but it's been a good many years since I've been flat-out, helpless drunk—or yearned to be. A true drunk is a rare sight at Callahan's. Mike Callahan doesn't just pour his liquor, he serves it; to get pissed in his Place you must convince him you have a need to, persuade him to take responsibility for you. Most bars, people go to in order to get blind. Mike's customers go there to see better.

But that night I had a need to completely dismantle my higher faculties, and he knew that as I crossed the threshold. Because I was carrying in my arms the ruined body of Lady Macbeth. Her head dangled crazily, her proud neck broken clean through, and a hush fell upon Callahan's Place as the door closed behind me.

Mike recovered quickly; he always does. He nodded, a nod which meant both hello and something else, and glanced up and down the bar until he found an untenanted stretch. He pointed to it, I nodded back, and by the time I reached it he had the free lunch and the beer nuts moved out of the way. Not a word was said in the bar—everyone there understood my feelings as well as Callahan did. Do you begin to see how one could stop being an alcoholic there? Someone, I think it was Fast Eddie, made a subvocal sound of empathy as I laid the Lady on the bar-top.

I don't know just how old she is. I could find out by writing the Gibson people and asking when serial number 427248 was sent out into the world, but somehow I don't want to. Somewhere in the twenty-to-thirty range, I'd guess, and she can't be less than fifteen, for I met her in 1966. But she was a treasure even then, and the man I bought her from cheated himself horribly. He was getting married *much* too quickly and needed folding money in a hurry. All I can say is, I hope he got one hell of a wife—because I sure got one hell of a guitar.

She's a J-45, a red sunburst with a custom neck, and she clearly predates the Great Guitar Boom of the Sixties. She is *hand-made*, not machine-stamped, and she is some forgotten artisan's masterpiece. The very best, top-of-the-line Gibson made today could not touch her; there are very few guitars you can buy that would. She has been my other voice and the basic tool of my trade for a decade and a half. Now her neck, and my heart, were broken clean through.

Long-Drink McGonnigle was at my side, looking mournfully down past me at the pitiful thing on the bar. He touched one of the sprawled strings. It rattled. Death rattle. "Aw," he murmured.

Callahan put a triple Bushmill's in my hand, closed my fingers around it. I made it a double, and then I turned and walked to the chalk line on the floor, faced the merrily crackling fireplace from a distance of twenty feet. People waited respectfully. I drank again while I considered my toast. Then I raised my glass, and everybody followed suit.

"To the Lady," I said, and drained my glass and threw it at the back of the fireplace, and then I said, "Sorry folks," because it's very difficult to make Mike's fireplace emit shards of glass—it's designed like a parabolic reflector with a shallow focus—but I had thrown hard enough to spatter four tables just the same. I know better than to throw that hard.

Nobody paid the least mind; as one they chorused, "To the Lady" and drank, and when the barrage was finished, *eight* tables were littered with shards.

Then there was a pause, while everybody waited to see if I could talk about it yet. The certain knowledge that they were prepared to swallow their curiosity, go back to their drinking and ignore me if that were what I needed, made it possible to speak.

"I was coming offstage. The Purple Cat, over in Easthampton. Tripped over a cable in the dark. Knew I was going down, tried to get her out from under me. The stage there is waist-high, her head just cleared it and wedged in under the monitor speaker. Then my weight came down on her ..." I was sobbing. "... and she *screamed*, and I ..."

Long-Drink wrapped me in his great long arms and hugged tight. I buried my face in his shirt and wept. Someone else hugged us both from behind me. When I was back under control, both let go and I found a drink in my hand. I gulped it gratefully.

"I hate to ask, Jake," Callahan rumbled. "I'm afraid I already know. Is there any chance she could be fixed?"

"Tell him, Eddie." But Eddie wasn't there; his piano stool was empty. "All right, look, Mike: There are probably ten shops right here on Long Island that'd accept the commission and my money, and maybe an equal number who'd be honest enough to turn me away. There are maybe five real guitar-makers in the whole New York area, and they'd all tell me to forget it. There might be four Master-class artisans still alive in all of North America, and their bill would run to four figures, maybe five, assuming they thought they could save her at all." Noah Gonzalez had removed his hat, with a view toward passing it; he put it back on. "*Look at her*. You can't *get* wood like that anymore. She's got a custom neck and fingerboard, skinnier'n usual, puts the strings closer together—when I play a normal guitar it's like my fingers shrunk. So a rebuilt neck would have less strength, and the fingerboard'd have to be hand-made ..."

Long-Drink burst into tears. Callahan nodded and looked sad, and passed me another big drink. He poured one for himself, and *he* toasted the Lady, and when that barrage was over he set 'em up for the house.

The folks treated me right; we had a proper Irish wake for the Lady, and it got pretty drunk out. We laughed and danced and reminisced and swapped lies, created grand toasts; everyone did it up nice. The only thing it lacked was Eddie on the piano; he had disappeared and none knew where. But a wake for Lady Macbeth *must* include the voice of her long-time colleague—so Callahan surprised us all by sitting down and turning out some creditable barrelhouse. I hadn't known he could play a note, and I'd have sworn his fingers were too big to hit only one key at a time, but he did okay.

Anyhow, when the smoke cleared, Pyotr ended up driving better than half of his home, in groups of three—a task I wouldn't wish on my senator.

I guess I should explain about Pyotr. . . .

The thing about a joint like Callahan's Place is that it could not possibly function without the cooperation of all its patrons. It takes a lot of volunteer effort to make the Place work the way it does.

Some of this is obvious. Clearly, if a barkeep is going to allow his patrons to smash their empties in the fireplace, they must all be responsible enough to exercise prudence in this pursuit—and furthermore they must have better than average aim. But perhaps it is not obvious, and so I should mention, that there is a broom-and-scoop set on either side of the hearth, and whenever an occasional wild shard ricochets across the room, one of those broom-and-scoops just naturally finds its way into the hands of whoever happens to be nearest, without anything being said.

Similarly, if you like a parking lot in which anarchy reigns, with cars parked every which way like goats in a pen, you must all be prepared to pile outside together six or ten times a night, and back-and-fill in series until whoever is trying to leave can get his car out. This recurring scene looks rather like a grand-scale Chinese Fire Drill, or perhaps like Bumper Cars for Grownups; Doc Webster points out that to a Martian it would probably look like some vast robot orgy, and insists on referring to it as Auto-Eroticism.

Then there's closing ritual. Along about fifteen minutes before closing, somebody, usually Fast Eddie Costigan the piano player, comes around to all the tables with a big plastic-lined trash barrel. Each table has one of those funnel-and-tin-can ashtrays; someone at each table unscrews it and dumps the butts into the barrel. Then Eddie inserts two corners of the plastic tablecloth into the barrel, the customer lifts the other two corners into the air, and Eddie sluices off the cloth with a seltzer bottle. Other cleanup jobs, mopping and straightening and the like, just seem to get done by somebody or other every night; all Mike Callahan ever had to do is polish the bartop, turn out the lights and go home. Consequently, although he is scrupulous about ceasing to sell booze at legal curfew, Mike is in no hurry to chase his friends out, and indeed I know of several occasions on which he kept the Place open round the clock, giving away nose-paint until the hour arrived at which it became legal to sell it again.

And finally, of course, there's old Pyotr. You see, no one tight drives home from Callahan's bar. When Mike decides that you've had enough—and they'll never make a Breathalyzer as accurate as his professional judgment—the only way in the world you will get another drink from him is to surrender your car keys and then let Pyotr, who drinks only distilled water, drive you home when you fold. The next morning you drive Pyotr back to his cottage, which is just up the street from Callahan's, and if this seems like too much trouble, you can always go drink somewhere else and see what that gets you.

For the first couple of years after Pyotr started coming around, some of us used to wonder what he got out of the arrangement. None of us ever managed to get him to accept so much as a free breakfast the morning after, and how do you buy a drink for a man who drinks distilled water? Oh, Mike gave him the water for free, but a gallon or so of water a night is pretty poor wages for all the hours of driving Pyotr put in, in the company of at least occasionally troublesome drunks, not to mention the inconvenience of spending many nights sleeping on a strange bed or couch or floor. (Some of the boys, and especially the ones who want to get pie-eyed once in a while, are married. Almost to a woman, their wives worship Pyotr; are happy to put him up now and then.)

For that matter, none of us could ever figure out what old Pyotr did for a living. He never had to be anywhere at any particular time next morning, and he was never late arriving at Callahan's. If asked what he did he would say, "Oh, a little bit of everything, whenever I can get it," and drop the subject. Yet he never seemed to be in need of money, and in all the time I knew him I never once saw him take so much as a peanut from the Free Lunch.

(In Callahan's Place there *is* a free lunch—supported by donations. The value of the change in the jar is almost always greater than the value of the Free Lunch next to it, but nobody watches to make sure it stays that way. I mind me of a bad two weeks when that Free Lunch was the only protein I had, and nobody so much as frowned at me.)

But while he is a bit on the pale side for a man of Middle European stock, Pyotr certainly never looks undernourished, and so there was never any need for us to pry into his personal affairs. Me, I figured him for some kind of a pensioner with a streak of pure altruism, and let it go.

He certainly looks old enough to be a pensioner. Oh, he's in very good shape for his age, and not overly afflicted with wrinkles, but his complexion has that old-leather look. And when you notice his habit of speaking into his cupped hand, and hear the slight lisp in his speech, and you realize that his smiles never seen to pry his lips apart, you get the idea that he's missing some bridgework. And there's something old about his eyes. . . .

Anyway, Pyotr was busier than usual that night, ferrying home all the casualties of Lady Macbeth's wake. It took quite a while. He took three at a time, using the vehicle of whoever lived furthest away, and taxied back for the next load. Two out of every three drunks would have to taxi back to Callahan's the next day for their cars. I was proud of the honor being paid my dead Lady. Pyotr and Callahan decided to save me for last. Perhaps on the principle that the worst should come last—I was *pissed*, and at the stage of being offensively cheerful and hearty. At last all the other wounded had been choppered out, and Pyotr tapped me on one weaving shoulder.

"So they weld—well hell, hi, Pyotr, wait a half while I finish telling Mike this story—they weld manacles on this giant alien, and they haul him into court for trial, and the first thing he does, they go to swear him in and he swallows the bailiff whole."

Mike had told *me* this gag, but he is a very compassionate man. He relit his cheroot and gave me the straight line, "What'd the bailiff do?"

"His job, o'course—he swore, in the witness. Haw haw!" Pyotr joined in the polite laughter and took my arm. "Time to bottle it up, Pyotr you old lovable Litvak?

Time to scamper, is it? Why should you have to haul my old ashes, huh? Gimme my keys, Mike, I'm not nearly so drunk as you think—I mean, so thunk as you drink. Shit, I said it right, I *must* be drink. All right, just let me find my pants—"

It took both of them to get me to the car. I noticed that every time one of my feet came unstuck from the ground, it seemed to take enormous effort to force it back down again. A car seat leaped up and hit me in the ass, and a door slammed. "Make sure he takes two aspirins before he passes out for good," Callahan's voice said from a mile away.

"Right," Pyotr said from only a few blocks distant, and my old Pontiac woke up grumbling. The world lurched suddenly, and we fell off a cliff, landing a million years later in white water. I felt nausea coming up, chattered merrily to stave it off.

"Splendid business, Pyotr old sock, absolutionly magnelephant. You drive well, and this car handles well on ice, but if you keep spinning like this we're going to dend up in the itch—mean, we'll rote off the ride, right? Let's go to the Brooklyn Navy Yard and try to buy a drink for every sailor on the *U.S.S. Missouri*—as a songwriter I'm always hoping to find the Moe juiced. Left her right there on the bartop, by all the gods! Jus' left her and— turn around, God damn it, I left my Lady back there!"

"It's all right, Jake. Mr. Callahan will leave her locked up. We will wake her for several days, correct Irish custom, yes? Even those not present tonight should have opportunity to pay their respects."

"Hey, yeah, sure. Hey! *Funeral.* How? Bury or cremate?"

"Cremation would seem appropriate."

"*Strings?* Gearboxes? Heavy metal air pollution? Fuggoff. Bury her, dissolve in acid, heave her into the ocean off Montauk Point and let the fish lay eggs in her sounding box. Know why I called her Lady Macbeth?"

"No, I never knew."

"Used to sneak up and stab me inna back when didn't

expect it. Bust a string, go out of tune, start to buzz on the high frets for no reason at all. Treacherous bitch. Oh, *Lady!*"

"You used each other well, Jake. Be glad. Not many have ever touched so fine an instrument."

"Goddam right. Stop the car, please. I want to review inputs."

"Open the window."

"I'll get it all over the—"

"It's raining. Go ahead."

"Oh. Not sure I like Finn's magic. Have to pay attention to notice it's raining. Right ho. *Oh.*"

Eventually the car stopped complaining and rain sprinkled everything but Pyotr and me and then my house opened up and swallowed me. "Forget aspirins," I mumbled as my bed rushed at me. "Don' need 'em."

"You'll be sorry tomorrow."

"I'm sorry now."

The bed and I went inertialess together, spun end over end across the macrocosmic Universe.

I was awakened by the deafening thunder of my pulse.

I knew that I was awake long before I had the power to raise my eyelids. I knew it because I knew I lacked the imagination to dream a taste like that in my mouth. But I was quite prepared to believe that the sleep had lasted at least a century; I felt *old.* That made me wonder if I had snored right through the wake—*the wake!* Everything came back in a rush; I flung open my eyes, and two large icicles were rammed into the apertures as far as they would go, the points inches deep in my forebrain. I screamed. That is, I tried to scream, and it sounded like a scream—but my pulse sounded like an empty oil tank being hit with at maul, so more likely what I did was bleat or whimper.

Something heavy and bristly lay across me; it felt like horsehair, with the horse still attached. I strained at it, could not budge it. I wept.

The voice spoke in an earsplitting whisper. "Good morning, Jake."

"Fuck you too," I croaked savagely, wincing as the smell of my breath went past my nose.

"I warned you," Pyotr said sadly.

"Fuck you twice. Jesus, my eyelashes hurt. What is *lying* on me?"

"A cotton sheet."

"Gaah."

"You should have accepted the aspirins."

"You don't understand. I don't get hangovers."

Pyotr made no reply.

"Damn it, I don't! Not even when I was a lush, not the first time I ever got smashed, not *ever*. Trick metabolism. Worst that ever happens is I wake up not hungry—but no head, no nausea, no weakness, never."

Pyotr was silent a long time. Then, "You drank a good deal more than usual last night."

"Hell, I been drunker'n *that*. Too many times, man."

"Never since I have known you."

"Well, that's true. Maybe that's . . . no, I've fallen off the wagon before. I just don't get hangovers."

He left the room, was gone awhile. I passed the time working on a comprehensive catalog of all the places that hurt, beginning with my thumbnails. I got quite a lot of work done before Pyotr returned; I had gotten halfway through the hairs on my forearms when he came in the door with a heavily laden tray in his hands. I opened my mouth to scream, "Get that *food* out of here!"—and the smell reached me. I sat up and began to salivate. He set the tray down on my lap and I ignored the pain and annihilated bacon, sausage, eggs, cheese, onions, green peppers, hot peppers, bread, butter, English muffins, jam, orange juice, coffee, and assorted condiments so fast I think I frightened him a little. When I sank back against the pillows the tray contained a plate licked clean, an empty cup and glass, and a fork. I was exhausted, and still hurt in all the same places—that is, in all places—but I was beginning to believe that I wanted to live. "This is crazy," I said. "If I *am* hung over, the concept of food ought to be obscene. I never ate that much breakfast in my life, not even the morning after my wedding night."

I could *see* Pyotr now, and he looked embarrassed, as though my appetite were his fault.

"What time is it?"

"Seven P.M."

"God's teeth."

"It was four in the morning when we arrived here. You have slept for thirteen hours. I fell asleep at noon and have just awakened. Do you feel better now that you have eaten?"

"No, but I concede the trick is possible. What's good for total bodily agony?"

"Well, there is no cure. But certain medications are said to alleviate the symptoms."

"And Callahan's has opened by now. Well, how do we get me to the car?"

In due course we got to Callahan's where Lady Macbeth lay in state on top of the bar. The wake was already in full swing when we arrived and were greeted with tipsy cheers. I saw that it was Riddle Night: The big blackboard stood near the door, tonight's game scrawled on it in the handwriting of Doc Webster. On Riddle Night the previous week's winner is Riddle Master; each solved riddle is good for a drink on the Riddle Master's tab. The Doc looked fairly happy—every *un*solved riddle is a free drink for him, on the house.

The board was headed "PUBLIC PERSONALITIES." Beneath that were inscribed the following runes:

I.

    a) Hindu ascetic; masculine profession
    b) tramp; crane
    c) profligate; cheat
    d) span; tavern, money
    e) fish; Jamaican or Scottish male, caviar
    f) certainly; Irish street
    g) handtruck; forgiveness

II.

   a) pry; manager
   b) smart guy; Stout
   c) chicken coop; more loving
   d) bandit; crimson car
   e) coffin; baby boy
   f) tote; subsidy
   g) moaning; achieve

III.

   a) irrigated; laser pistol
   b) Nazi; cook lightly
   c) British punk; knowledge, current
   d) chicken coop; foreplay
   e) wealthier; nuts to

IV.

   a) Italian beauty; stead, depart, witness
   b) toilet; auto, senior member
   c) be dull; Carmina Burana
   d) grass; apprentice, younger
   e) valley; odd
   f) burns; leer at

Example: penis; truck = peter; lorry = Peter Lorre.
Extra drinks for identifying Categories I–IV.

People were staring at the board, seemed to have *been* staring at it for some time, but none of the riddles were checked off yet. I paid my respects to the Lady, said hello to Mike, accepted a large glass of dog-hair. Then, deliberately, I turned away from the Lady and toward the board. (Why don't you take a crack at it before reading further?)

"Got one," I said at once, and allowed Long-Drink to help me to the board. "First one in line," I said, marking with chalk. "Hindu ascetic; masculine profession. That's Jain; Man's Field, and Category One is Actresses."

Doc Webster looked pained. "Say Film Women," he suggested. "More accurate. Mike, one for Jake on me."

Given the category Section I was fairly simple. I got b) 'Bo; Derrick. Long-Drink McGonnigle got c) Rakehell; Welsh. Tommy Janssen figured out that d) and e) were Bridge It; Bar Dough and Marlin; Mon Roe. Josie Bauer took f) Surely; Mick Lane and g) Dolly; Pardon. We collected our drinks gleefully.

I suspected that the second category would be Male Actors (or Film Men), but kept my mouth shut, hoping I could figure them all out and do a sweep before anyone else twigged. This turned out to be poor tactics; I got a), b), d) and f), but while I was puzzling over the rest, Shorty Steinitz spoke up. "The category is Male Film Stars, and the first one is Jimmy; Steward!" I tried to jump in at once, but Long-Drink drowned me out. "Got b): Alec; Guinness! Hey, and f) has to be Carry; Grant."

"And d)," I said irritably, "is Robber; Red Ford. But what about the others?" We stared at them in silence for awhile.

"A hint," Doc Webster said at last. "With reference to g), the first name is what I'll be doing if you do the second."

"Got it!" Long-Drink cried. "Keenin'; Win." The Doc grimaced. Callahan was busy keeping score and distributing the prizes, but he had attention left to spare. "That third one there, c): That has to be Hennery; Fonder."

There was a pause, then. Nobody could figure out "coffin; baby boy." (Can you?) After awhile we turned our attention to the remaining two categories, but the silence remained unbroken. The Doc looked smug. "No hurry, gents and ladies," he said. "Closing time isn't for several hours yet." We all glared at him and thought hard.

Surprisingly, it was Pyotr who spoke up. "I have a sweep," he stated. "Category IV in its entirety."

Folks regarded him with respectful interest. He was committed now: if he missed *one*, he would owe the Doc all six drinks. The Doc looked startled but game—he seemed to think he had an ace up his sleeve. "Go ahead, Pyotr."

"The category is Famous Monsters." The Doc winced. "The first is Bella; Lieu Go See.' Applause. "Then John; Car a Dean." More applause.

"Not bad," the Doc admitted. "Keep going."

"The next two, of course, are among the most famous of all. Be dull; Carmina Burana *has* to be Bore Us; Carl Orff. . . ." He paused to sip one of the three drinks Callahan had passed him.

"Brilliant, Pyotr," I said, slapping him on the back. "But I'm still stumped for the last three."

"That is because they are tricky. The first is tortured, and the last two are obscure."

"Go ahead," Doc Webster said grimly.

"The first is the famous Wolfman: Lawn; Trainee Junior." Delighted laughter and applause came from all sides. "The others are both Frankenstein's Creature, but it would require an historian of horror films to guess both. Glenn Strange played the Monster in at least three movies . . ." The Doc swore. ". . . and the last shall be first; the man who played the Monster in the very first film version of *Frankenstein*."

"But we already had Karloff," I protested.

"No, Jake," Pyotr said patiently. "That was the first *talkie* version. The very first was released in 1910, and the Monster was played by a man with the unusual name of Charles Ogle. Read 'chars' for 'burns' and you come close enough."

We gave him a standing ovation—in which the Doc joined.

All of this had admirably occupied my attention, from almost the moment of my arrival. But before I turned to a study of Category III, I turned to the bar to begin the third of the four drinks I had won—and my gaze fell on the ruined Lady. She lay there in tragic splendor, mutely reproaching me for enjoying myself so much while she was broken. All at once I lost all interest in the game, in everything but the pressing business of locating and obtaining oblivion. I gulped the drink in my hand and reached for the next one, and a very elderly man came in the door of Callahan's Place with his hands high in the air, an expression of infinite weariness on his face. He was closely followed by Fast Eddie Costigan, whose head just about came up to the level of the elderly man's shoulder blades. Conversations began to peter out.

I just had time to recall that Eddie had vanished mysteriously the night before, and then the two of them moved closer and I saw why everybody was getting quiet. And why the old gent had his hands in the air. I didn't get a real good look, but what Eddie had in his right hand, nestled up against the other man's fourth lumbar vertebra, looked an awful lot like a Charter Arms .38. The gun that got Johnny Lennon and George Wallace.

I decided which way I would jump and put on my blandest expression. "Hi, Eddie."

"Hi, Jake," he said shortly, all his attention on his prisoner.

"I tell you for the last time, Edward—" the old gent began in a Spanish accent.

"Shaddap! Nobody ast you nuttin'. Get over here by de bar an' get to it, see?"

"Eddie," Callahan began gently.

"Shaddap, I said."

I was shocked. Eddie *worships* Callahan. The runty little piano man prodded with his piece, and the old Spaniard sighed in resignation and came toward me.

But as he came past me, his expression changed suddenly and utterly. If aged Odysseus had come round one last weary corner and found Penelope in a bower, legs spread and a sweet smile on her lips, his face might have gone through such a change. The old gent was staring past me in joyous disbelief at the Holy Grail, at the Golden Fleece, at the Promised Land, at—

—at the ruined Lady Macbeth.

"*Santa Maria,*" he breathed. "*Madre de Dios.*"

Years lifted from his shoulders, bitter years, and years

smoothed away from his face. His hands came down slowly to his sides, and I saw those hands, really *saw* them for the first time. All at once I knew who he was. My eyes widened.

"Montoya," I said. "Domingo Montoya."

He nodded absently.

"But you're dead."

He nodded again, and moved forward. His eyes were dreamy, but his step was firm. Eddie stood his ground. Montoya stopped before the Lady, and he actually bowed to her. And then he looked at her.

First he let his eyes travel up her length the way a man takes in a woman, from the toes up. I watched his face. He almost smiled when he reached the bridge. He almost frowned when he got to the scars around the sounding hole that said I had once been foolish enough to clamp a pick-up onto her. He did smile as his gaze reached the fingerboard and frets, and he marveled at the lines of the neck. Then his eyes reached the awful fracture, and they shut for an instant. His face became totally expressionless; his eyes opened again, studied the wreck with dispassionate thoroughness, and went on to study the head.

That first look took him perhaps eight seconds. He straightened up, closed his eyes again, clearly fixing the memory forever in his brain. Then he turned to me. "Thank you, sir," he said with great formality. "You are a very fortunate man."

I thought about it. "Yes, I believe I am."

He turned back and looked at her again, and now he *looked*. From several angles, from up close and far away. The joining of neck to body. The joining of head to neckstub. "Light," he said, and held out his hand. Callahan put a flashlight into it, and Montoya inspected what he could of Lady Macbeth's interior bracings through her open mouth. I had the damnedest feeling that he was going to tell her to stick out her tongue and say "Ah!" He tossed the flashlight over his shoulder—Eddie caught it with his free hand—and stooped to sight along

the neck. "Towel," he said, straightening. Callahan produced a clean one. He wiped his hands very carefully,
finger by finger, and then with the tenderness of a
mother bathing her child he began to touch the Lady
here and there.

"Jake," Long-Drink said in hushed tones. "What the
hell is going on? Who *is* this guy?"

Montoya gave no sign of hearing; he was absorbed.

"Remember what I said last night? That there are only
maybe four Master-class guitar makers left in the
country?"

"Yeah. This guy's a Master?"

"*No*," I cried, scandalized.

"Well then?"

"There is one rank higher than Master. Wizard. There
have been a dozen or so in all the history of the world.
Domingo Montoya is the only one now living." I gulped
Irish whiskey. "Except that he died five years ago."

"The hell you say."

Fast Eddie stuffed the gun into his belt and sat down
on his piano stool. "He didn't die," he said, signalling
Callahan for a rum. "He went underground."

I nodded. "I think I understand."

Long-Drink shook his head. "I don't."

"Okay, Drink, think about it a second. Put yourself in
his shoes. You're Domingo Montoya, the last living guitar
Wizard. *And all they bring you to work on is shit*. There
are maybe fifty or a hundred guitars left on the planet
worthy of your skill, most of which you made yourself,
and they're all being *well* cared for by careful and
wealthy owners. Meanwhile, fools keep coming in the
door with their broken toys, their machine-stamped
trash, asking Paul Dirac to do their physics homework
for them. Damnfool Marquises who want a guitar with
the name of their mistress spelled out in jewels on the
neck; idiot rock stars who want a guitar shaped like a
Swiss Army knife; stupid rich kids who want their stupid
Martins and stupid Goyas outfitted with day-glo pick-
guards by the man everyone knows is the last living

Wizard. Nobody wants to pay what honest materials cost nowadays, nobody wants to wait as long as true Quality requires, everybody wants their goddamn lily gilded, and *still* you can't beat them off with a club, because you're Domingo Montoya. You triple your fee, and then triple it again, and then square the result, and still they keep coming with their stupid broken trash—or worse, they purchase one of your own handmade masterworks, and use it ignobly, fail to respect it properly, treat it like some sort of common utensil." I glanced at Montoya. "No wonder he retired."

Montoya looked up. "I have not retired. If God is kind I never will. But I no longer sell my skills or its fruits, and I use another name. I did not believe it was possible to locate me."

"Then how—"

"Two years ago I accepted an apprentice." My brows went up; I would not have thought there was anyone worthy to be the pupil of Domingo Montoya. "He is impatient and lacks serenity, but both of these are curable with age. He is not clumsy, and his attitude is good." He glowered at Eddie. *"Was* good. He swore secrecy to me."

"I went ta school wit' 'im," Eddie said. "P.S. Eighty-t'ree. He hadda tell *some*body."

"Yes," Montoya said, nodding slowly. "I suppose I can see how that would be so."

"He come back ta de old neighborhood ta see his Ma. I run into 'im on de street an' we go to a gin mill an' pretty soon he's tellin' me de whole story, how he's never been so happy in his life. He tells me ta come out to Ohio an' meetcha sometime, an' he gimme yer address." Eddie glanced down at the gun in his belt and looked sheepish. "I guess he sh'unta done dat."

Montoya looked at him, and then at Lady Macbeth, and then at me. He looked me over very carefully, and to my great relief I passed muster. "No harm done," he said to Eddie, and for the first time I noticed that

Montoya was wearing a sweater, pajamas, and bedroom slippers.

I was bursting with the need to ask, and I *could not ask*, I was afraid to ask, and it must have showed in my face, at least to a gaze as piercing as his, because all of a sudden his own face got all remorseful and compassionate. My heart sank. It was beyond even his skill—

"Forgive me, sir," he said mournfully. "I have kept you waiting for my prognosis. I am old, my mind is full of fur. I will take you, how is it said, off the tender hooks."

I finished my drink in a swallow, lobbed the empty into the fireplace for luck, and gripped both arms of my chair. "Shoot."

"You do not want to know, can this guitar be mended. This is not at issue. You know that any imbecile can butt the two ends together and brace and glue and tinker and give you back something which looks just like a guitar. What you want to know is, can this guitar ever be what she was two days ago, and I tell you the answer is never in this world."

I closed my eyes and inhaled sharply; all the tiny various outposts of hangover throughout my body rose up and *throbbed* all at once.

Montoya was still speaking. "—trauma so great as this must have subtle effects all throughout the instrument, microscopic ruptures, tiny weakenings. No man could trace them all, nor heal them if he did. But if you ask me can I, Domingo Montoya, make this guitar so *close* to what it was that you yourself cannot detect any difference, then I tell you that I believe I can; also I can fix that buzz I see in the twelfth fret and replace your pegs."

My ears roared.

"I cannot guarantee success! But I believe I can do it. At worst I will have to redesign the head. It will take me two months. For that period I will loan you one of my guitars. You must keep your hands in shape for her, while she is healing for you. You have treated her with kindness, I can see; she will not malinger."

I could not speak. It was Callahan who said, "What is your fee, Don Domingo?"

He shook his head. "There is no charge. My eyes and hands tell me that this guitar was made by an old pupil of mine, Goldman. He went to work for Gibson, and then he saw the way the industry was going and got into another line. I always thought that if he had kept working, kept learning, he might have taught me one day." He caressed the guitar. "It is good to see his handiwork. I *want* to mend her. How daring the neck! She must be a pleasure to play once you are used to her, eh?"

"She is. Thank you, Don Domingo."

"Nobody here will reveal your secret," Callahan added. "Oh, and say, I've got a jug of fine old Spanish wine in the back I been saving for a gentleman such as yourself— could I pour you a glass on the house? Maybe a sandwich to go with it?"

Montoya smiled.

I swiveled my chair away from him. *"Eddie!"* I cried.

The little piano man read my expression, and his eyes widened in shock and horror. "Aw Jeez," he said, shaking his head, "aw, *naw,*" and I left my chair like a stone leaving a slingshot. Eddie bolted for cover, but strong volunteers grabbed him and prevented his escape. I was on him like a stooping falcon, wrapping him up in my arms and kissing him on the mouth before he could turn his face away. An explosion of laughter and cheers shook the room, and he turned bright red. "Aw *jeez!*" he said again.

"Eddie," I cried, "there is no way I will *ever* be able to repay you."

"Sure dere is," he yelled. "Leggo o' me."

More laughter and cheers. Then Doc Webster spoke up.

"Eddie, that was a good thing you did, and I love you for it. And I know you tend to use direct methods, and I can't argue with results. But frankly I'm a little disappointed to learn that you own a handgun."

"I bought it on de way to Ohio," Eddie said, struggling

free of my embrace. "I figger maybe de Wizard don' wanna get up at seven inna mornin' an' drive five hunnert miles to look at no busted axe. Sure enough, he don't."

"But dammit, Eddie, those things are dangerous. Over the course of a five-hundred-mile drive ... suppose he tried to get that gun away from you, and it went off?"

Eddie pulled the gun, aimed it at the ceiling, and pulled the trigger. There was no explosion. Only a small clacking sound as the hammer fell and then an inexplicable loud hiss. Eddie rotated the cylinder slightly. In a loud voice with too much treble, the gun offered to clear up my pimples overnight without messy creams or oily pads.

It actually had time to finish its pitch, give the time and call-letters, and begin Number Three on the Hot Line of Hits before the tidal wave of laughter and applause drowned it out. Montoya left off soothing the wounded Lady to join in, and when he could make himself heard, he called, "You could have threatened me with nothing more fearsome, my friend, than forced exposure to AM radio," at which Eddie broke up and flung the "gun" into the fireplace.

Eventually it got worked out that Eddie and Montoya would bring Lady Macbeth back to Eddie's place together, get some sleep, and set out the next morning for Montoya's home, where he could begin work. Eddie would bring me back the promised loaner, would be back with it by the night after next, and on his return we would jam together. Montoya made me promise to tape that jam and send him a dupe.

What with one thing and another, I finished up that evening just about as pickled as I'd been the night before. But it was happy drunk rather than sad drunk, an altogether different experience, in kind if not in degree. Popular myth to the contrary, drink is not really a good drug for pain. That is, it can numb physical pain, but will not blunt the edge of sorrow; it can help that latter only by making it easier for a man to curse or weep. But alcohol is great for happiness: it can actually intensify joy. It was perfect for the occasion, then; it anesthetized me against the unaccustomed aches of my first hangover, and enhanced my euphoria. My Lady was saved, she would sing again. My friends, who had shared my loss, shared my joy. I danced with Josie and Eddie and Rachel and Leslie; I solved Category III of Doc's riddle and swept it without a mistake; I jollied Tommy out of being worried about some old friend of his, and made him laugh; with Eddie on piano and everybody else in the joint as the Raelettes I sang "What'd I Say" for seventeen choruses; for at least half an hour I studied the grain on the bartop and learned therefrom a great deal about the structure and purpose of the Universe; I leaped up on the same bartop and performed a hornpipe—on my hands. After that it all got a bit vague and hallucinatory— at least, I don't *think* there were any real horses present.

A short while later it seemed to be unusually quiet. The only sound was the steady cursing of my Pontiac and the hissing of the air that it sliced through. I opened my eyes and watched white lines come at me.

"Pyotr. Stout fellow. No—water fellow, won't drink stout. Why don't you drink, Pyotr? S'*nice.*"

"Weak stomach. Rest, Jake. Soon we are home."

"Hope I'm not hung over again tomorrow. That was awful. Cripes, my neck still hurts. . . ." I started to rub it; Pyotr took my hand away.

"Leave it alone, Jake. Rest. Tonight I will make sure you take two aspirins."

"Yeah. You're the lily of the valley, man."

A short while later wetness occurred within my mouth in alarming proportions, and when I swallowed I felt the aspirins going down. "Good old Pyotr." Then the ship's engines shut down and we went into free fall.

Next morning I decided that hangovers are like sex— the second time isn't *quite* as painful. If the analogy held, by tomorrow, I'd be enjoying it.

Oh, I hurt, all right. No mistake about that. But I hurt like a man with a medium bad case of the flu, whereas the day before I had hurt like a man systematically tortured for information over a period of weeks. This time sensory stimuli were only about twice the intensity I could handle, and a considerably younger and smaller mouse had died in my mouth, and my skull was no more than a half size too small. The only thing that hurt as much as it had the previous morning was my neck, as I learned when I made an ill-advised attempt to consult the clock beside me on the night table. For a horrified moment I actually *believed* that I had unscrewed my skull and now it was falling off. I put it back on with my hands, and it felt like I nearly stripped the threads until I got it right.

I must have emitted sound. The door opened and Pyotr looked in. "Are you all right, Jake?"

"Of course not—half of me is left. Saved me for last again, eh?"

"You insisted. In fact you could not be persuaded to leave at all, until you lost consciousness altogether."

"Well, I—OH! *My guitar.* Oh, Pyotr, I think I'm going to do something that will hurt me very much."

"What?"

"I am going to smile."

It did hurt. If you don't happen to be hung over, relax your face and put a finger just behind and beneath each ear, and concentrate. Now smile. The back of my neck was a knot of pain, and those two muscles you just felt move were the ends of a knot. Smiling tightened it. But I had to smile, and didn't mind the pain. Lady Macbeth was alive! Life was good.

That didn't last; my metabolism just wasn't up to supporting good cheer. The Lady was *not* alive. Back from the dead, perhaps—but still in deep coma in Intensive Care. Attended, to be sure, by the world's best surgeon. But she did not have youth going for her—and neither did the surgeon.

Pyotr must have seen the smile fade and guessed why, because he said exactly the right thing.

"There is hope, my friend."

I took my first real good look at him.

"Thanks, Pyotr. Gawd, you look worse than I do. I must have woken you up, what time is it, I don't dare turn my head and look."

"Much like yesterday. You have slept the clock 'round, and I have just finished my customary six hours. I admit I do not feel very rested."

"You must be coming down with something. Truly, man, you look like I feel."

'How *do* you feel?"

"Uh—oddly enough, not as bad as I expected to. Those aspirins must have helped. Thanks, brother."

He ducked his head in what I took to be modesty or shyness.

"You should take a couple yourself."

He shook his head. "I am one of those people who can't take asp—"

"No problem, I've got the other kind, good for all stomachs."

"Thank you, no."

"You sure? What time did you say it was?"

"Normal people are eating their dinners."

"Their—*dinner*!" I sat up, ignoring all agony, got to my feet and staggered headlong out of the room, down the hall to the kitchen. I wept with joy at the sight of so much food in one place. That same eerie, voracious hunger of the morning before, except that today I was not going to make Pyotr do the cooking. I was ashamed enough to note that he had cleaned up the previous night's breaker (a compound word formed along the same lines as "brunch"), apparently before he had gone to sleep.

I designed a megaomelet and began amassing construction materials. I designed for twin occupants. "Pyotr, you old Slovak Samaritan, I know you have this thing about not letting people stand you to a meal the next day, and I can dig that, makes the generosity more pure, but I've been with you now close to forty hours and you've had bugger all to eat, so what you're gonna do is sit down and shut up and eat this omelet or I'm gonna shove it up your nose, right?"

He stared in horror at the growing pile on the cutting board. "Jake, no, thank you! No."

"Well, God damn it, Pyotr, I ain't asking for a structural analysis of your digestion! Just tell me what ingredients to leave out and I'll double up on the rest."

"No, truly—"

"Damn it, anybody can eat *eggs*."

"Jake, thank you, I truly am not at all hungry."

I gave up. By that time all eight eggs had already been cracked, so I cut enough other things to fill an eight-egg omelet anyhow, figuring I'd give the other half to the cats. But to my surprise, when I paused to wipe my mouth, there was nothing left before me that I could legitimately eat except for a piece of ham gristle I had rejected once already. So I ate it, and finished the pot of coffee, and looked up.

"Cripes, maybe you really are sick. I'm gonna call Doc Webster—"

"Thank you, no, Jake, I would appreciate only a ride home, if you please, and to lie down and rest. If you are up to it. . . ."

"Hell, I feel practically vertebrate. Only thing still sore is the back of my neck. Just let me shower and change and we'll hit the road."

I pulled up in front of Pyotr's place, a small dark cottage all by itself about a half a block from Callahan's Place. I got out with him. "I'll just come in with you for a second, Pyotr, get you squared away."

"You are kind to offer, but I am fine now. I will sleep tonight, and see you tomorrow. Goodbye, Jake—I am glad your guitar is not lost."

So I got back into the car and drove the half block to Callahan's.

"Evenin', Jake. What'll it be?"

"Coffee, please, light and sweet."

Callahan nodded approvingly. "Coming up."

Long-Drink snorted next to me. "Can't take the gaff, huh, youngster?"

"I guess not, Drink. These last two mornings I've had the first two hangovers of my life. I guess I'm getting old."

"Hah!" The Drink looked suddenly puzzled. "You know, now I come to think of it . . . Huh. I never thought."

"And no one ever accused you of it, either."

"No, I mean I just now come to realize what a blessed long time it's been since I been hung over myself."

"Really? You?" The Drink is one of Pyotr's steadiest (or unsteadiest) customers. "You must have the same funny metabolism I have—ouch!" I rubbed the back of my neck. "Used to have."

"No," he said thoughtfully. "No, I've *had* hangovers. Lots of 'em. Only I just realized I can't remember when was the last *time* I had one."

Slippery Joe Maser had overheard. "I can. Remember *my* last hangover, I mean. About four years ago. Just before I started comin' here. Boy, it was a honey—"

"Ain't that funny?" Noah Gonzalez put in. "Damned if I can remember a hangover since I started drinking here myself. Used to get 'em all the time. I sort of figured it had something to do with the vibes in this joint."

Joe nodded. "That's what I thought. This Place is kinda magic, everybody knows that. Boy, I always wake up hungry after a toot, though. Hell of a stiff neck, too."

"Magic, hell," Long-Drink said. "Callahan, you thievin' spalpeen, we've got you red-handed! Waterin' your drinks, by God, not an honest hangover in a hogshead. Admit it."

"I'll admit you got a hog's head, all right," Callahan growled back, returning with my coffee. He stuck his seven o'clock shadow an inch from Long-Drink's and exhaled rancorous cigar smoke. "If my booze is watered down, how the hell come it gets you so damn pie-faced?"

"Power of suggestion," the Drink roared. "Placebo

effect. Contact high from these other rummies. Tell him, Doc."

Doc Webster, who had been sitting quietly hunched over his drink, chose this moment to throw back his head and shout, *"Woe is me!"*

"Hey, Doc, what's wrong?" two or three of us asked at once.

"I'm ruined."

"How so?"

He turned his immense bulk to face us. "I've been moonlighting on the side, as a theatrical agent."

"No foolin'?"

"Yeah, and my most promising client, Dum Dum the Human Cannonball, just decided to retire."

Long-Drink looked puzzled. "Hey, what the hell, unemployment and everything, you shouldn't have any trouble lining up a replacement. Hell, if the money's right, *I'll* do it."

The Doc shook his head. "Dum-Dum is a midget. They cast the cannon special for him." He sipped bourbon and sighed. "I'm afraid we'll never see an artist of his caliber again."

Callahan howled, and the rest of us accorded the Doc the penultimate compliment: we held our noses and wept. He sat there in his special-built oversize chair and he looked grave, but you could see he was laughing, because he shook like jello. "Now I've got my own back for last night," he said. "Guess my riddles, will you?" He finished his bourbon. "Well, I'm off. Filling in tonight over at Smithtown General." His glass hit the exact center of the fireplace, and he strode out amid a thunderous silence.

We all crept back to our original seats and placed fresh orders. Callahan had barely finished medicating the wounded when the door banged open again. We turned, figuring that the Doc had thought of a topper, and were surprised.

Because young Tommy Janssen stood in the doorway,

and tears were running down his face, and he was *stink-ing* drunk.

I got to him first. "Jesus, pal, what is it? Here, let me help you."

"Ricky's been kicking the gong—" he sang, quoting that old James Taylor song, "Junkie's Lament," and my blood ran cold. Could Tommy possibly have been stupid enough to . . . but no, that was booze on his breath, all right, and his sleeves were rolled up. I got him to a chair, and Callahan drew him a beer. He inhaled half of it, and cried some more. "Ricky," he sobbed. "Oh, Ricky, you stupid shit. He taught me how to smoke cigarettes, you know that?"

"Ricky who?"

"Ricky Maresca. We grew up together. We . . . we were junkies together once." He giggled through tears. "I turned him on, can you dig it? He turned me on to tobacco, I gave him his first taste of smack." His face broke. "Oh, *Christ!*"

"What's the matter with Ricky?" Callahan asked him.

"Nothing," he cried. "Nothing on Earth, baby. Ricky's got no problems at all."

"Jesus," I breathed.

"Oh, man. I *tried* to get him to come down here, do you know how hard I tried? I figured you guys could do it for him the way you did for me. Shit, I did everything but drag him here. I shoulda dragged him!" He broke down, and Josie hugged him.

After a while Callahan said, "Overdose?"

Tommy reached for his beer and knocked it spinning. "Shit, no. He tried to take off a gas station last night, for the monkey, and the pump jock had a piece in the desk. Ricky's down, man, he's down. All gone. Callahan, gimme a fucking whiskey!"

"Tommy," Callahan said gently, "let's talk awhile first, have a little java, then we'll drink, OK?"

Tommy lurched to his feet and grabbed the bar for support. "Don't goddammit ever try to con a junkie! You think I've had enough, and you are seriously mistaken.

Gimme a fuckin' whiskey or I'll come over there an' get it."

"Take it easy, son."

I tried to put my arm around Tommy.

"Hey, pal—"

He shoved me away. "Don't patronize me, Jake! *You* got wasted two nights running, why can't I?"

"I'll keep serving 'em as long as you can order 'em," Callahan sad. "But son, you're close to the line now. Why don't you talk it out first? Whole idea of getting drunk is to talk it out before you pass out."

"Screw this," Tommy cried. "What the hell did I come here for, anyway? I can drink at home." He lurched in the general direction of the door.

"Tommy," I called, "wait up—"

"No," he roared. "Damn it, leave me alone, all of you! You hear me? I wanna be by myself, I—I'm not ready to talk about it yet. Just leave me the hell alone!" And he was gone, slamming the door behind him.

"Mike?" I asked.

"Hmmm." Callahan seemed of two minds. "Well, I guess you can't help a man who don't want to be helped. Let him go; he'll be in tomorrow." He mopped the bartop and looked troubled.

"You don't think he'll—"

"Go back to smack himself? I don't think so. Tommy hates that shit now. I'm just a little worried he might go look up Ricky's connection and try to kill him."

"Sounds like a good plan to me," Long-Drink muttered.

"But he's too drunk to function. More likely *he'll* go down. Or do a clumsy job and get busted for it."

"Be his second fall," I said.

"Damn it," the Drink burst out, "I'm goin' after him."

But when he was halfway to the door and we all heard the sound of a vehicle door slamming out in the parking lot, and he pulled up short. "It's okay," he said. "That's my pickup, I'd know that noise anywhere. Tommy knows I keep a couple bottles under the seat in case of snakebite.

He'll be okay—after a while I'll go find him and put him in the truckbed and take him home."

"Good man, Drink," I said. "Pyotr's out with the bug, we've got to cover for him."

Callahan nodded slowly. "Yeah, I guess that'll do it." The Place began to buzz again. I wanted a drink, and ordered more coffee instead, my seventh cup of the day so far. As it arrived, one of those accidental lulls in the conversation occurred, and we all plainly heard the sound of glass breaking out in the parking lot. Callahan winced, but spilled no coffee.

"How do you figure a thing like heroin, Mike? It seems to weed out the very stupid and the very talented. Bird, Lady Day, Tim Hardin, Janis, a dozen others we both know—and a half a million anonymous losers, dead in alleys and pay toilets and gas stations and other people's bedrooms. Once in every few thousand of 'em comes a Ray Charles or a James Taylor, able to put it down and keep on working."

"Tells you something about the world we're making. The very stupid and the very sensitive can't seem to live in it. Both kinds need dangerous doses of anesthetic just to get through a day. Be a lot less bother for all concerned if they could get it legal, I figure. If that Ricky wanted to die, okay—but he shouldn't have had to make some poor gas jockey have to shoot him."

Another sound of shattering glass from outside, as loud as the first.

"Hey, Drink," Callahan said suddenly, "*how* much juice you say you keep in that truck?"

Long-Drink broke off a conversation with Margie Shorter. "Well, how I figure is, I got two hands—and besides, I might end up sharing the cab with somebody fastidious."

"Two *full* bottles?"

All of us got it at once, but the Drink was the first to move, and those long legs of his can really eat distance when they start swinging. He was out the door before the rest of us were in gear, and by the time we got outside he was just visible in the darkness, kneeling up on the tailgate of his pickup, shaking his head. Everybody started for the truck, but I waved them back and they heeded me. When I got to the truck there was just enough light to locate the two heaps of glass that had been full quarts of Jack Daniels once. The question was, how recently? I got down on my hands and knees, swept my fingers gingerly through the shards, accepting a few small cuts in exchange for the answer to the question, is the ground at all damp here abouts?

It was not.

"Jesus, Drink, he's sucked down two quarts of high test! Get him inside!"

"Can a man die from that?"

"Get him inside." Tommy has one of those funny stomachs, that won't puke even when it ought to; I was already running.

"Where are you—oh, right." I could hear him hauling Tommy off the truck. Callahan's phone was out of service that week, so the Drink knew where I had to be headed. He was only half right. I left the parking lot in a spray of gravel, slipped in dogshit just off the curb, nearly got creamed by a Friday-night cowboy in a Camaro, went up over the hood of a parked Caddy and burst in the door of the all-night deli across the street from Callahan's. The counterman spun around, startled.

"Bernie," I roared, "call the Doc at Smithtown. Alcohol overdose across the street, *stat,*" and then I was out the door again and sprinting up the dark street, heading for my second and most important destination.

Because I knew. Don't ask me how, I just knew. They say a hunch is an integration of data you did not know you possessed. Maybe I'd subconsciously begun to suspect just before the Doc had distracted me with his rotten pun—I'd had a lot of coffee, and they say coffee increases the I.Q. some. Maybe not—maybe I'd never have figured it out if I hadn't *needed* to just then, if figuring it all out hadn't been the only thing that could save my silly-ass friend Tommy. I had no evidence that would stand up in any kind of court—only hints and guesswork. All I can tell you is that when I first cleared the doorway of Callahan's Place, I knew where I would end up going—hipping Bernie was only for backup, and because it took so little time and was on the way.

Half a block is a short distance. Practically no distance at all. But to a man dreadfully hung over, afraid that his friend is dying, and above all absolutely, preternaturally *certain* of something that he cannot believe, a half block can take forever to run. By the time I got there, I believed. And then for the second time that day I was looking at a small, dark cottage with carven-Swiss droller-ies around the windows and doors. This time I didn't care if I was welcome.

I didn't waste time on the door bell or the door. There was a big wooden lawn chair, maybe sixty or seventy pounds I learned later, but right then it felt like balsa as I heaved it up over my head and flung it through the big living room window. It took out the bulk of the win-dow and the drapes behind; I followed it like Dum-Dum the Human Cannonball, at a slight angle, and God was kind: I landed on nothing but rug. I heard a distant shout in a language I did not know but was prepared to bet was Rumanian, and followed it through unfamiliar darkness, banging myself several times on hard objects, destroying an end table. Total dark, no moon or starlight, no time for matches, a door was before me and I kicked it open and there he was, just turning on a bedside lamp.

"I know," I said. "There's no more time for lying."

Pyotr tried to look uncomprehending, and failed, and there just wasn't any time for it.

"You don't drink blood. You *filter* it." He went white with shock. "I can even see how it must have happened, your trip at Callahan's, I mean. When you first got over here to the States, you must have landed in New York and got a job as a technician in a blood bank, right? Leach a *little* bit of nourishment out of a *lot* of whole blood you can feed without giving serious anemia to the transfusion patients. An ethical vampire—with a digestion that has trouble with beef broth. I'll bet you've even got big canines like the movie vampires—not because size makes them any more efficient at *letting* blood, but because there're some damned unusual glands in 'em. You interface with foreign blood and filter out the nourishment it carries in solution. Only you couldn't have known how they got blood in New York City, who the typical donor is, and before you knew it it was too late, you were a stone alcoholic." I was talking a mile a minute, but I could see every single shot strike home. I had no time to spare for his anguish: I grabbed him and hauled him off the bed, threw clothes at him. "Well, I don't give a shit about that now! You know young Tommy Janssen, well he's down the block with about three quarts of hooch in him, and the last two went down in a gulp apiece, so you move your skinny Transylvanian ass or I'll kick it off your spine, you got me? *Jump, goddammit!*"

He caught on at once, and without a word he pulled his clothes on, fast enough to suit me. An instant later we were sprinting out the door together.

The half-block run gave me enough time to work out how I could do this without blowing Pyotr's cover. It was the total blackness of the night that gave me the idea. When we reached Callahan's I kept on running around to the back, yelling at him to follow As we burst in the door to the back room I located the main breaker and killed it, yanking a few fuses for insurance. The lights went out and the icebox stopped sighing. Fortunately I don't need light to find my way around Callahan's Place, and good night-sight must have been a favorable adaptation for anyone with Pyotr's basic mutation; we were out in the main room in seconds and in silence.

At least compared with the hubbub there; everybody was shouting at once. I cannoned into Callahan in the darkness—I saw the glowing cheroot-tip go past my cheek—and I hugged him close and said in his ear,

"Mike, trust me. Do *not* find the candles you've got behind the bar. And open the windows."

"Okay, Jake," he said calmly at once, and moved away in the blackness. With the windows open, matches blew out as fast as they could be lit. The shouting intensified. In the glow of one attempted match-lighting, I saw Tommy laid out on the bar in the same place Lady Macbeth had lain the night before, and I saw Pyotr reach him. I sprang across the room to the fireplace—thank God it was a warm night; no fire—and cupped my hands around my mouth.

"ALL RIGHT, PEOPLE," I roared as loud as I could, and silence fell.

Damned if I can remember what I said. I guess I told them that the Doc was on the way, and made up some story about the power failure, and told a few lies about guys I'd known who drank twice as much booze and survived, and stuff like that. All I know is that I *held* them, by sheer force of vocal personality, kept their attention focused on me there in the dark for perhaps four or five minutes of impassioned monologue. While behind them, Pyotr worked at the bar.

When I heard him clear his throat I began winding it down. I heard the distant sound of a door closing, the door that leads from the back room to the world outside. "So the important thing," I finished, locating one of those artificial logs in the dark and laying it on the hearth, "is not to panic and to wait for the ambulance," and I lit the giant crayon and stacked real maple and birch on top of it. The fire got going at once, and that sorted out most of the confusion. Callahan was bending over Tommy, rubbing at the base of his neck with a bar-rag, and he looked up and nodded. "I think he's okay, Jake. His breathing is a lot better."

A ragged cheer went up.

By the time we had the lights back on, the wagon arrived, Doc Webster bursting in the door like a crazed hippo with three attendants following him. I stuck around just long enough to hear him confirm that Tommy would pull through, promised Callahan I'd give him the yarn later, and slipped out the back.

Walking the half block was much more enjoyable than running it. I found Pyotr in his bedroom. Roaring drunk, of course, reeling around the room and swearing in Rumanian.

"Hi, Pyotr. Sorry I busted your window."

"Sodomize the window. Jake, is he—"

"Fine. You saved his life."

He frowned ferociously and sat down on the floor. "It is no good, Jake. I thank you for trying to keep my secret, but it will not work."

"No, it won't."

"I cannot continue. My conscience forbids. I have helped young Janssen. But it must end. I am ripping you all up."

"Off, Pyotr. Ripping us off. But don't kick yourself too hard. What choice did you have? And you saved a lot of the boys a lot of hangovers, laundering their blood the way you did. Just happens I've got a trick metabolism, so instead of skimming off my hangover, you gave me one. And doubled your own: the blood I gave you the last two nights must have been no prize."

"I stole it."

"Well, maybe. You didn't rob me of the booze—we *both* got drunk on it. You *did* rob me of a little nourishment—but I gather you also 'robbed' me of a considerable amount of poisonous byproducts of fatigue, poor diet, and prolonged despair. So maybe we come out even."

He winced and rolled his eyes. "These glands in my teeth—that was a very perceptive guess, Jake—are unfortunately not very selective. Alcoholism was not the only unpleasant thing I picked up working at the blood bank—another splendid guess—although it is the only one that has persisted. But it must end. Tomorrow night when I am capable I will go to Mr.

Callahan's Place and confess what I have been doing—and then I will move somewhere else to dry out, somewhere where they do not buy blood from winos. Perhaps back to the Old Country." He began to sob softly. "In many ways it will be a relief. It has been *hard,* has made me ashamed to see all of you thinking I was some kind of *altruist,* when all the time I was—" He wept.

"Pyotr, listen to me." I sat on the floor with him. "Do you know what the folks are going to do tomorrow night when you tell them?"

Headshake.

"Well, *I* do, sure as God made little green thingies to seal plastic bags with, and so do you if you think about it. I'm so certain, I'm prepared to bet you a hundred bucks in gold right now.,"

Puzzled stare; leaking tears.

"They'll take up a collection for you, asshole!"

Gape.

"You've been hanging out there for years, now, you *know* I'm right. Every eligible man and woman there is a blood donor already, the Doc sees to that—do you mean to tell me they'd begrudge another half liter or so for a man who'd leave a warm bed in the middle of the night to risk his cover and save a boy's life?"

He began to giggle drunkenly. "You know—hee, hee—I believe you are right." The giggle showed his fangs. Suddenly it vanished. "Oh," he cried, "I do not deserve such friends. Do you know what first attracted me about Callahan's Place? There is no mirror. No, no, not that silly superstition—mirrors reflect people like me as well as anyone. That's just it. *I was ashamed to look at my reflection in a mirror."*

I made him look at me. "Pyotr, listen to me. You worked *hard* for your cakes and ale, these last few years. You kept a lot of silly bastards from turning into highway statistics. Okay, you may have had *another* motive that we didn't know—but underneath it all, you're just like everybody else at Callahan's Place."

"Eh?"

"A sucker for your friends."

And it broke him up, thank God, and everything worked out just fine.

And a couple of weeks later, Pyotr played us all a couple of fabulous Rumanian folk songs—on Lady Macbeth.

Answers to the riddles left unsolved:

Category II

e) coffin; baby boy = pall; new man = *Paul Newman*

Category III (Male American Politicians)

a) irrigated; laser pistol = runneled; ray gun= *Ronald Reagan*

b) Nazi; cook lightly = Jerry; brown = *Jerry Brown*

c) British punk; knowledge; current = Teddy; ken; eddy = *Teddy Kennedy*

d) chicken coop; foreplay = hennery; kissing her = *Henry Kissinger*

e) wealthier; nuts to = richer; nix on = *Richard Nixon*

Ever feel like you don't fit in? Are you ever positive that there's no way you could be the same species as the madding crowd around you? SF readers often feel like that.... In this intriguing tale from the 1970s the real question is: are vampires catching up with the future— or is the future catching up with them?

Vanishing Breed

LESLIE ROY CARTER

Carl Rhyner was reading when his window vibrated with a soft thud. He ignored it, knowing what it meant, because at this moment he did not want to be disturbed. *With a plunge he seizes her neck in his fang-like teeth*— the window shuddered again, this time with such violence that Carl was afraid the glass would crack. He disgustedly put the book down and walked across his apartment to the window. The lights of the city, shining through the glass, distinctly outlined the dark object hovering outside. Carl stared at it, dislike pouring from his eyes onto the giant bat. "Go around!"

The bat skittered up and down the glass, its eyes burning red. Its mouth opened and closed, and a faint screech came through the window. "No, damn it, go around." The bat fluttered out into the lights of the city, disappearing among the neon stars. As Carl turned away, his eye caught a movement, and he hurled himself against the "raise" button. The window snapped open just as the bat flashed through into the room. It settled on the living

175

room floor and folded its wings across its body. The wavering mist flowed up from the ground, and Dr. Valpa stepped out.

Carl slammed his hand against the "lower" button and turned to his guest. "Hell, I told you to go around. I'm tired of this stupid rigmarole. If you keep coming in here like that, you'll give me away."

The good doctor scowled at Carl, displeasure written in the lines of his thin lips. "My dear boy—for you are one, you know, lad—all vampires come through windows."

"I don't," asserted Carl. "And furthermore, I don't come dressed in those ridiculous clothes."

Dr. Valpa looked down at his long, flowing black cape, opening his arms outward as if to present himself to an audience. "Enough—I knew you would start on that theme again." Valpa lowered himself into the easy chair, folding his cape behind him. He picked up the novel, turning to the cover. "*Varney the Vampyre!* and you question my methods—really, Carl, how hypocritical." Carl's face flamed. Valpa cut short a laugh and pointed. "There, there is the reason. What true vampire can blush like that? You young mutants are all alike—dress modern, scorn the old ways, run wild. Ah, in my youth—"

"Stop, Doctor. Your youth was a couple of thousand years ago. We, the new vampires, must live in this world, in this time. We can't go around wearing capes and acting strangely. We'd be picked up by the proctors in minutes if we did."

"Sad, but true, lad." Dr. Valpa nodded his head at this point. "Even I at the university must dress in the current fad in order to keep my job." He looked up sharply at Carl. "But I still hold to the old ways when I go on my rounds. At least you could do that."

Carl sat down opposite the old man and stared into his red eyes. "Dr. Valpa, you don't understand, do you? You still don't grasp what's happening. You wouldn't last a second in the city. If I followed the old ways of feeding, I'd be caught all too quickly. Here in the city, in this apartment complex, I have over five hundred people on which I feed. I take a sip here, a sip there—no one misses it, and if I overindulge a little, they chalk it up to iron-poor blood. No one guesses, or even can believe that I'm around."

Dr. Valpa sat back, his arms outstretched along the steep sides of the chair. "Another point, dear boy. But how can you say you are a vampire?" Valpa stood up and began pacing up and down. "A vampire involves himself with his prey; he lures it to him, seducing it with hypnotic trances that wrap them both in a world of their own. He—"

"Nonsense." Carl propped his leg across his other knee.

Dr. Valpa stopped before the easy chair, stricken to the heart. He turned slowly, his face paler than death. "Nonsense," he stuttered out. "Nonsense!" he roared.

"Nonsense," Carl repeated quietly. Valpa's mouth stood open, his eyes wide and staring. "We don't need it. After all, being human, we can enjoy the, ah—" Carl coughed into his hand, "say, better things of life."

Valpa stood rooted to the floor. His mouth slowly closed, and he seemed to melt down into the chair. "Is this what we have become, bastards upon the human race, losing our own identity and becoming more alien every day?" He lowered his head, his eyes riveted to the floral pattern on the tiles.

Carl stirred uneasily. "Doctor, what do you mean, alien? I know you and the other forefathers are dead come to life, but that makes you human still."

"No, Carl. You just don't really understand yourself. The true history of our race has never been written." Dr. Valpa's eyes became blank, and he seemed to sink into himself. His voice sounded as if he were speaking in an empty auditorium. Hollow, deep, and quiet. "Didn't they teach you anything when you were born?"

Carl shook his head. He stared uncomfortably at the old man. "You know, the usual—speed calculation, speed reading, computer technology—"

"No!" groaned Valpa. "Anything about being a vampire!"

"Well, no. Dr. Jamison, the psychologist attached to our coven, did try to stress the fact that although we were vampires, we had our place in society, that we were not truly deviants, misfits—"

"Curses upon him!" cried Dr. Valpa. "The old lure is lost. I told them to beware of Jamison, he would ruin us!" Valpa was raging now. Carl was afraid and tried to quiet him. Valpa struck down Carl's hands and grabbed his shoulders. "Didn't they teach you anything about history, boy? Anything?"

Carl pried the clawlike hands away. "Yes, they did. The general atomic wars feared in the '50s and '60s were averted, and the world turned instead to peace. All races were declared equal, and thereby all men. Now, in the twenty-second century, all people live their own lives as long as they bother no one. Each of us has his place—"

"Unholy Powers," Dr. Valpa sighed. "Carl, tomorrow night a warden will come to pick you up." His cape folded over his eyes as he sank down into the floor. The monstrous bat cried shrilly and fluttered up from the floor, striking the wall. The window opened, and the bat flitted out.

"Valpa, wait. Tell me—" Carl cried as the bat disappeared into the night. The cool night air breathed across Carl's face, chilling the sweat that streamed from his pores. He closed the window, and his reflection stared back at him—stark, hard features. Eyes bleak and cold. His flesh was firm upon his face. His teeth were even and white—no trace of fangs—no need, since the use of hyper-fine needles left no marks. "Damn, what did he mean?" Carl asked the still room.

The next night, around two, Carl was leaving on his evening rounds when he again heard the sounds at the windowpane. He hurried over and opened the window, through which a bat of large proportions flew. It settled in the living room and transformed into a middle-aged man, dressed in much the same attire as Dr. Valpa had worn. Only this man was a warden. Carl knew him from his days in the school where he had been instructed, along with the other young vampires, in the ways of men. The wardens were to the human vampires what the proctors were to society as a whole.

The tall vampire walked forward, his cape billowing out behind him. He touched Carl's arm. "You are to come."

Carl leaped as if he had been struck.

The warden eyed him for several moments, then quietly spoke to him. "You are summoned by the council. You must come."

Carl's ashen face convulsed into horror. "Valpa said so, but the council—the council has not been called for fifty years."

"I know." The warden turned and beckoned Carl to the window.

"I can't go that way, sir."

The warden grimaced. "I am not ignorant of your lacks. Come here and observe the dark aircar on the taxi strip. You are to walk down and board it immediately." As he spoke, he slowly vanished, and the bat flew out the window, crying shrilly into the night.

Stepping into the car, Carl saw Steven and Maria Collins. Their faces, like his own, were lined with worry. Maria cried out when she saw him, "Carl, a council—a full council has been called. We are summoned."

Carl sat down beside Maria and put his hand in hers. "He just came for me. I thought I had done something, maybe something I said to Dr. Valpa—"

"Dr. Valpa—the prime leader!"

Carl looked sharply. "Prime leader—since when? He was just an adviser when I heard last."

Steve shook his head. "He was levied into prime position last May. A power play among the old ones put him in. There has been a shake-up in the organization, and it looks like we are the cause of it."

"What do you mean, Steve—we? Do you mean us in particular—unlikely, since I have done little to cause trouble—or," here Carl hesitated, afraid to say it, "or is it the human vamps as a whole?"

Maria's eyes, looking into his, were red, but from crying. "All of us, Carl. We, the first group, and the last three groups they have created."

Carl sat gloomily in the car as it sped away from the city and into the hills. Steve and Maria were also quiet, each locked in his own thoughts, the idea that perhaps the experiment had failed.

The car turned into a deep valley and followed a steep, winding road up the hillside until it came to the house. One should say "castle," but none existed in North America. The house was dark and forboding, just as Carl, Steve, and Maria remembered it as young vampires playing in the surrounding hills. They always laughed at the antiquity of their elders and the place they chose to live.

Inside they were numbed by the sheer size of the gathering of vampires from all over the world. Great men and women they had only heard of in tales were present. Each one indefinably old, but still outwardly young. Bats whirled through the shadows under the vaulted ceiling. A dim flickering light was shed by a few antique candelabra, whose flames burned blue.

Carl and his friends stood in the rear of the great hall, for they were the last to arrive. No one really noticed them, because all eyes were fixed on Lord Ruthven, who stood before them on the raised dais.

He stretched out his arms, and the murmur of voices stopped. Silence filled the room as the earl's dead gray eyes searched over the gathering. His lips moved slowly, as if talking were an impossibility for him. In a dry voice, cracked and broken with ageless time, he whispered out over the gathering. As the words fell upon their ranks, a shock of silence hit the room. "The experiment has failed."

For a moment, an age, no one moved, talked, existed. For the true vampires, a dream of the centuries had been destroyed. The dream that had been fanned into being, nurtured, given hope and encouragement—gone. And for the human vamps, disbelief and anger. Shame filled their faces, and hatred filled the room. With the apathy and depression of their elders, their passion increased, and a tumult broke loose in the rear. The newer human vampires were pushing to the front. Shouts of, "Liar! Fabricator!" flooded the aisles. Carl stood up on a chair and shouted to be heard.

"Vamps, hear me. These old fools want the experiment to fail. They want us to believe that we cannot be human and still be vampires. They are filled with the ages of mankind and are beginning to believe their own legends."

Steve yelled affirmation, and the air vibrated with the noise of the human vamps crying in the night. Then the screech of a great bat split the air, and the vampires cowered to the floor. The earl stood tall on the platform, his great wings overshadowing the stage. His mouth, sharp-fanged and evil, gaped in anger.

"Fools—listen to me again. What is decided here will rule your lives from now to eternity." Ruthven gestured to a figure standing in the crowd near the stage. Meek it stood, beside Ruthven, a mere shadow of the image of him, but Carl recognized the prime leader.

"Thank you, my good Earl, but I think after I explain to these young hotheads why the experiment has failed, then they will cease this needless disorder." An atmosphere of a classroom seemed to pervade over all as the professor stood behind the podium and straightened his notes. He spoke.

"It seems a certain amount of history was deleted from our younger friends' education, and lacking this, a grave misunderstanding has arisen. I have found in many cases, such as Carl Rhyner's—" heads turned and looked at Carl's flushed face—"a seeking of understanding and self-explanation. The human vamps have been raised in *our* society, and they truly do not know who they are."

Dr. Valpa shuffled his notes and allowed the murmuring to die down. He glanced over his glasses at the rear

of the room and noticed the look of acknowledgment in
Carl's eyes.

"Yes, they read the old human classics and find only
the legends they accuse us of portraying—though in reality the legends are true, and what they read is really us.
But they cannot identify with these legends, because they
are human and do not believe in what are called 'fantasies' in the world. They are, however, truly vampires, in
that they exist by feeding on blood; but human, in that
they can't fly, have no problem with mirrors, eat garlic,
etc., etc." Dr. Valpa waved his hands as if dismissing the
traditional symptoms of vampirism. "Instead of ques-
tioning why vampires are affected this way, they took
their human 'souls' into hand and began to live their lives
in society as an integral part of it. They blended into the
background, became respected commoners, upheld the
UN and hated the perverts, all the time carrying on a
heritage which they accepted as being a norm for their
particular subculture. Human vampires. Now this we
wanted, expected, ahem, prayed for. But—" His hand
shot up, and the index finger quivered over the crowd.
Carl knew he would ball up his hand and slam it down
on the podium. Crash! "But, we did not expect them to
become so human as to not realize their true heritage—
that they are, and we are, all of us are aliens to this
world."

"Never!" shouted Carl. "I'm as human as anyone on
this planet. I'm, I'm—" Oh, my God, he's right. If the
legends are true, he must be.

"Carl, all of you, we are aliens. We came over ten
thousand years ago. We were forced from our last home
by the same thing which is facing us now. We are parasites, Carl, pure and simple. We draw our existence from
human life. If we are discovered, openly and under the
full light of human understanding, we will be wiped out
as cancer and heart disease were in the twenty-first century. No human being can abide the thought of a creature feeding on him. We would be hunted down and
destroyed."

Valpa paced the stage, his eyes now not seeing the crowd. His hands fluttered in the direction of Gilles de Rais and his group—the true vampires. "We would be the first to go. They have documented us pretty well. They know all about our peculiarities, and once mankind *really* believed in vampires, then we would quickly go. You," pointing to Carl, Valpa's red eyes glimmered, "would be safe—for a while. But not long enough. Medical checks would be made, impure blood diagnosed as vampire feeding, guards posted in sleeping areas, traps set. Oh, vampires of old, can we ever forget the persecutions of our forefathers on the twilight world of Antares Four!"

"That still doesn't explain, Doctor, why the experiment has failed." All eyes turned to Carl.

Dr. Valpa watched Carl for a moment, then turned to the crowd. The great hall waited for his reply. "They know we are here now. The experiment failed because one of the human vamps was analyzed by a psych-proctor. The vamp talked freely about his entire life. He complained of his feelings of non-belonging, his desire for acceptance. And he told the proctor every detail, not knowing what reaction he would get from the human. The vamp had been so humanized that he thought being a vampire was like being a homosexual, deviant but accepted and permitted. We didn't expect the proctor to believe him, but he did, and he forced the young man to reveal his adviser, Sir Romuald." Valpa's face turned paler than ever. "Sir Romuald was terminated, while sleeping, with a stake through his heart, and a real-time record of the execution stored in permanent cybernetic memory."

A cry of agony poured from the true vampires. "It is come, then."

The starship, though ultramodern and wondrous to the humans, was tired and old. It had been old long before its last trip, and it was even older now. But its gleaming hull stood beckoning to the vampires as they filed up from the valley and into the airlock. At the entry ramp Dr. Valpa stood, checking the boarding list against the men and women and whirling bats that thronged inside. Although busy, his eyes noted Carl's hesitant approach up the ramp. He felt a twinge of expectancy of what the young man was going to say. As the last of the humans were coming aboard, Valpa saw how Steven and Maria were gazing back at Carl, and he knew for certain now.

Carl stood beside him, and together they watched Steve and Maria walk into the vast cargo hold of the ship. Maria turned and waved, her small face bright with tears, then disappeared. Dr. Valpa pulled his cape around him, trying to ward off the chill wind blowing up from the valley. His blood-red eyes gazed back down the winding road, out across the valley, to the plasti-domed metropolis on the horizon.

"It was a good world, Carl. Good for our people. We watched it grow from distant Greece to powerful UN. Our people have aided the Terrans in many ways, most of which they will never know. Someday they may feel indebtedness to us. Perhaps, Carl, you may have a hand in that."

"Doctor, I—" Carl stopped. Valpa's arm was around his shoulder, and he felt, for the first time, a humanness, a warmth, coming from the old vampire.

"I know, Carl. You can't go. You can't leave this world for another—however near we can come to it in the universe. I know, because I too wanted to stay on our last journey. I could almost do so now." The old man shook his head sadly, the white curls floating in the chill night air. "Funny as it seems, Carl, I liked being a professor. Always have. However, I suppose I'll be a general or a medicine man or some other type on the next world." Carl couldn't help smiling at the picture of Valpa striding across the fields leading great hulking barbarians into battle.

"Then you will speak comfort to Maria for me, sir?"

Valpa nodded his head and turned to walk up the ramp. He still held Carl close around the shoulders, hugging him to his side. Carl could smell dank earth, a musty odor heavy in his nostrils, and he breathed deeply. Valpa let him go with a shake of the head, as if he were flinging tears from his eyes.

The door slid silently down before Carl, and he turned and raced down the ramp. The ship lifted on its anti-gravs, turning ever so slightly, searching with its starnavs for the correct hole in space. As it winked out of existence, Carl heard again the last words that Valpa had spoken to him:

"We will all think of you, Carl, for you will be something special. For us, for Earth, you will be all that remains of a legend."

Turnabout is fair play in this post-sixties, pre-AIDS walk on the wild side by bestselling SF & technothriller author Dean Ing.

Fleas

DEAN ING

The quarry swam more for show than for efficiency because he knew that Maels was quietly watching. Down the "Y" pool, then back, seeming to ignore the bearded older man as Maels, in turn, seemed to ignore the young swimmer.

Maels reviewed each datum: brachycephalic; under thirty years old; body mass well over the forty kilo minimum; skin tone excellent; plenty of hair. And unless Maels was deceived—he rarely was—the quarry offered subtle homosexual nuances which might simplify his isolation.

Maels smiled to himself and delivered an enormous body-stretching yawn that advertised his formidable biceps, triceps, laterals. The quarry approached swimming; symbolically, thought Maels, a breast stroke. Great.

Maels made a pedal gesture. A joke, really, since the gay world had developed the language of the foot for venues more crowded than this. The quarry bared small even teeth in his innocent approval. Better.

"I could watch you all evening," Maels rumbled, and added the necessary lie: "You swim exquisitely."

"But I can't go on forever," the youth replied in tones

186

that were, as Maels had expected, distinctly unbutchy. "I feel like relaxing." Treading water, he smiled a plea for precise communication. Perfect.

"You can with me," Maels said, and swept himself up with an ageless grace. He towered, masculine and commanding, above the suppliant swimmer. A strong grin split his beard as Maels turned toward the dressing room. He left the building quickly, then waited.

Invisible in a shop alcove, Maels enjoyed the quarry's anxious glances from the elevated platform of the "Y" steps. Maels strolled out then into the pale light of the streetlamp and the quarry, seeing him, danced down the steps toward his small destiny.

Later, kneeling beneath tree shadows as his fingers probed the dying throat-pulse, Maels thought: *All according to formula, to the old books.* Really no problem when you have the physical strength of a mature anaconda. Hell, it wasn't even much fun for an adult predator. At this introspection Maels chuckled. Adult for several normal lifespans, once he had discovered he was a feeder. With such long practice, self-assurance in the hunt took spice from the kill. Still probing the carotid artery, Maels thought: *Uncertainty is the oregano of pursuit.* He might work that into a scholarly paper one day.

Then Maels fed.

It was a simple matter for Maels to feed in a context that police could classify as psychosexual. Inaccurate, but—perhaps not wholly. Survival and sexuality: his gloved hands guiding scalpel and bone saw almost by rote, Maels composed the sort of trivia his sophomores would love.

> Research confirms the grimoires'
> Ancient sanity;
> Predation brings unending lust—
> An old causality

The hypothalamus, behind armoring bone, was crucial. Maels took it all. Adrenal medulla, a strip of mucous membrane, smear of marrow. Chewing reflectively,

Maels thought: *Eye of newt, toe of frog. A long way from the real guts of immortality.*

He had known a feeder, an academic like himself, who read so much Huxley he tried to substitute carp viscera for the only true prescription. Silly bastard had nearly died before Maels, soft-hearted Karl Maels, brought him the bloody requisites in a baggie. At some personal sacrifice, too: the girl had been Mael's best graduate student in a century.

Sacrifice, he reflected, was one criterion largely ignored by the Darwinists. They prattled so easily of a species as though the single individual mattered little. But if you are one of a rare subspecies, feeders whose members were few and camouflaged? A back-burner question, he decided. He could let it simmer. With admirable economy of motion Maels further vandalized the kill to disguise his motive. Minutes later he was in his rented sedan, en route back to his small college town. Maels felt virile, coruscating, efficient. The seasonal special feeding, in its way, had been a thing of beauty.

Ninety-three days later, Maels drove his own coupe to another city and left it, before dusk, in a parking lot. He was overdue to feed but thought it prudent to avoid patterns. The city, the time of day, even the moon phase should be different. If the feeding itself no longer gave joy, at least he might savor its planning.

He adjusted his turtleneck and inspected the result in a storefront reflection. Maybe he would shave the beard soon. It was a damned nuisance anyhow when he fed.

Maels recalled a student's sly criticism the day before: when was a beard a symbiote, and when parasitic? Maels had turned the question to good classroom use, sparking a lively debate on the definitions of parasite and predator. Maels cited the German Brown trout, predator on its own kind yet not a parasite. The flea was judged parasitic; for the hundredth time Maels was forced to smile through his irritation at misquotation of elegant Dean Swift:

So, naturalists observe, a flea
Hath smaller fleas that on him prey.
And these have smaller fleas to bite 'em,
And so proceed, *ad infinitum.*

Which only prompted the class to define parasites in terms of size. Maels accepted their judgment; trout and feeder preyed on smaller fry, predators by spurious definition.

Comfortably chewing on the trout analogy, Maels cruised the singles bars through their happy hour. He nurtured his image carefully, a massive gentle bear of a man with graceful hands and self-deprecating wit. At the third spa he maneuvered, on his right, a pliable file clerk with adenoids and lovely skin. She pronounced herself simply thrilled to meet a real, self-admitted traveling salesman. Maels found her rather too plump for ideal quarry, but no matter: she would do. He felt pale stirrings of excitement and honed them, titillated them. Perhaps he would grant her a sexual encounter before he fed. Perhaps.

Then Karl Maels glanced into the mirror behind the bar, and the pliant clerk was instantly and brutally forgotten. He sipped bourbon and his mouth was drier than before as he focused on the girl who had captured the seat to his left.

It was not merely that she was lovely. By all criteria she was also flawless quarry. Maels fought down his excitement and smiled his best smile. "I kept your place," he said with just enough pretended gruffness.

"Am I all that predictable?" Her voice seemed to vibrate in his belly. He estimated her age at twenty-two but, sharing her frank gaze, elevated that estimate a bit.

Maels wisely denied her predictability, asked where she found earrings of beaten gold aspen leaves, and learned that she was from Pueblo, Colorado. To obtain a small commitment he presently said, "The body is a duty, and duty calls. Will you keep my place?"

The long natural lashes barely flickered, the chin rose and dropped a minute fraction. Maels made his needless roundtrip to the men's room, but hesitated on his return. He saw the girl speak a bit crossly to a tall young man who would otherwise have taken Maels' seat. Maels assessed her fine strong calves, the fashionable wedge heels cupping voluptuous high insteps. His palms were sweating.

Maels waited until the younger man had turned away, then reclaimed his seat. After two more drinks he had her name, Barbara, and her weakness, seafood; and knew that he could claim his quarry as well.

He did not need to feign his easy laugh in saying, "Well, now you've made me ravenous. I believe there's a legendary crab cocktail at a restaurant near the wharf. Feeling like exploring?"

She did. It was only a short walk, he explained, silently adding that a taxi was risky. Barbara happily took his arm. The subtle elbow pressures, her matching of his stride, the increasing frequency of hip contact were clear messages of desire. When Maels drew her toward the fortuitous schoolyard, Barbara purred in pleasure. Moments later, their coats an improvised couch, they knelt in mutual exploration, then lay together in the silent mottled shadows.

He entered her cautiously, then profoundly, gazing down at his quarry with commingled lust and hunger. Smiling, she undid her blouse to reveal perfect breasts. She moved against him gently and, with great deliberation, thrust his sweater up from the broad striated rib-cage. Then she pressed erect nipples against his body. Maels cried out once.

When European gentlemen still wore rapiers, Maels had taken a blade in the shoulder. The memory flickered past him as her nipples, hypodermic-sharp, incredibly elongated, pierced him on lances of agony.

Skewered above her, Maels could not move. Indeed, he did not lose his functional virility, as the creature completed her own pleasure and then, grasping his arms, rolled him over without uncoupling. He felt tendons snap in his forearms but oddly the pain was distant. He could think clearly at first. Maels thought: *How easily she rends me.* She manipulated him as one might handle a brittle doll.

Maels felt a warm softening in his guts with a growing anaesthesia. Maels thought: *The creature is consuming me as I watch.*

Maels thought: *A new subspecies?* He wondered how often her kind must feed. *A very old subspecies?* He saw her smile.

Maels thought: *Is it possible that she feeds only on feeders? Does she read my thoughts?*

"Of course," she whispered, almost lovingly.

Some yards away, a tiny animal scrabbled in the leaves.

He thought at her: "*. . . and so on,* ad infinitum. *I wonder what feeds on you. . . .*"

As "And Not Quite Human" was one of the young Greg Cox's favorite stories, so I was moved by Susan Petrey's tales of benevolent vampires on the Russian steppes before I became an editor. I was extremely disappointed to learn that this unique voice had been silenced before her time, indeed before she had published enough stories to fill a book. However, several years after investigating her work for possible publication, I learned of a hardcover volume containing her complete works—including several previously unpublished stories and vignettes about the vampire tribe. The book, Gifts of Blood, was a labor of love produced by members of the SF fan community in Oregon as a tribute to one of their own. I was able to purchase the paperback rights for Baen and publish an author I had admired for years. If you find this story as intriguing as I did, I suggest you contact the publishers of the hardcover at Susan C. Petrey Clarion Scholarship Fund, P.O. Box 5703, Portland, OR 97228. All proceeds go to assist new writers to attend the Clarion Workshops. This story, "Leechcraft," is the culmination of her vampire series, and one of the best meldings I've seen of fantasy elements with a science fictional approach.

Leechcraft

SUSAN PETREY

Leechcraft: the art of healing (archaic); also the art of bloodletting.

—Words and Their Origins
by K.A. Haberthal

At 1:30 A.M. Myrna, the lab technologist, bent over the struggling patient, syringe in hand, and searched his arm for a vein. Dr. Meyer, one of the interns, held the man down as Myrna tried to tie the tourniquet.

"What's wrong with this guy?" she asked.

"DT's," said the intern.

"How come you don't tranquilize him?" asked Myrna.

"I don't like to coddle alcoholics."

Myrna found a vein in the emaciated arm and shoved the needle home, but the patient flinched away. When she pulled back the plunger, she drew no blood, only a vacuum.

"What's wrong, Vampira? Forgot to sharpen your teeth this evening?" quipped the intern.

Myrna groaned inwardly. Vampire jokes were an occupational hazard of medical technology. She withdrew the needle and tried again. This time she was successful.

"Now that's more like it," said Dr. Meyer. "I was afraid I was going to have to waste an hour, showing you how. Can we get STAT amylase, CBC and a crossmatch on that?"

Myrna injected the blood into tubes, some with antico-agulant, some without. "Why does he need a crossmatch,

193

STAT?" she asked. "Are you going to do surgery?" In hospital jargon STAT meant immediately.

"He needs it STAT because I ordered it STAT. Who's the doctor here, you or me?" said the intern.

"I want to know, because if I have to work my fanny off all night, I'd like to think it's for a good reason. Not just because some doctor decided to write STAT on the order."

"My, you're an assertive little lady," said Dr. Meyer. "If you must know, yes, we might have to do surgery. We think this guy has a 'hot' appendix, and the sooner you get those lab reports back, the sooner we'll know. So hustle back to the lab and get busy. You might win a date with a handsome, young doctor."

"Yuck!" said Myrna and walked away, leaving him standing there with a quizzical look on his face.

"Vampira, indeed!" she said under her breath as she stabbed at the elevator button. But when she thought about it, it made sense. A blood-drawer intent on collecting a specimen had to have a knowledge of veins and arteries, had to have a calming effect on agitated patients, and had to be able to coax blood out of the weakest, most scarred old veins; in effect, had to think somewhat like a Vampire.

When she got back to the lab, she plopped the tubes of blood into the centrifuge to spin down the clot. She threw a switch and a grumbling roar commenced as the centrifuge gained speed.

The lab was a small room crowded with machine consoles. Myrna took an anti-coagulated sample and fed it to "Clarabelle" the Coulter Counter, which slurped it up in pneumatic tubing. She watched as the little snake of red traveled up the tubing and into the reaction chambers. Winking indicated that the red and white blood cells were being counted. The printer chattered and spat out answers: Hematocrit 47.8, white cell count 16,700.

The hematocrit, the percentage of red blood cells, was normal but the white count was elevated. They would probably operate if the amylase was normal. A high amylase meant that the pancreas, not the appendix, was involved.

When the centrifuge clicked off at the end of ten minutes, Myrna reached in and slowed the spinning head with her hand to save precious minutes. She grabbed for squishy plastic bags of blood out of the refrigerator and lined them up on her desk to set up the crossmatch. Then she took serum to another console to run the amylase.

On the day shift, 30 people worked in the laboratory. On the graveyard shift, Myrna worked alone, handling the emergencies. She was a genius of time organization, as one had to be to keep up with the work of a whole hospital on a busy night. She often felt that the doctors and nurses got all the glory and that she was one of medicine's unsung heroes.

The amylase was normal. Myrna checked her crossmatch tubes and saw no clumping, a compatible reaction. She phoned Dr. Meyer with the report.

"Well, I guess you'll have to set up that crossmatch after all," he said.

"I already did," she said. "You've got four compatible units for surgery."

"My God, woman, you must be the fastest crossmatch in the West," he said. "How would you like to go out Saturday night?"

"I'm busy," said Myrna. "I've got to get my horse ready for a show."

"You mean you'd turn me down in favor of a horse?"

"Absolutely," and she hung up on him.

Shanty, a big Tennessee walking horse gelding, was the love interest in Myrna's life. His big free-swinging stride had carried her to the Plantation Walking Horse trophy last year. On the back of her tall graceful horse, Myrna felt a sense of accomplishment similar to that which she felt in her work. A lab tech working the night shift did not have much time to develop a social life, but Myrna sometimes went out of her way to avoid contact with men. And when she did go out, she was careful not to get involved. She had loved once and decided that was enough to play the fool.

She usually found herself the huntress, the predator, the seducer in her relationships. The men she ensnared on her forays into beery, cigarette-smelling nightspots were sometimes unkind. One had called her "hairy chested" after seeing the patch of silken mouse-like down that grew between her breasts. Before embracing them to that hirsute bosom, she sometimes warned, "Be careful, I bite." But after the orgasmic relief, she was always left feeling vaguely unsatisfied. Even the one man who had loved her had not fulfilled all her need, and she had backed out of the relationship feeling guilty and ungrateful. She sometimes wondered if she might be a changeling from some secret elder race.

Now that all her work was finished, she was free until the next emergency cropped up. Myrna loved the stressful nature of her work. When she had nothing to do, she would drift off into fantasies. She would imagine that she could travel back in time and bring modern medicine into a primitive setting.

Tonight she was working in an early 19th century laboratory with Robert Koch, founder of modern bacteriology. She was showing him how the growth of bread mold on a gelatin plate could inhibit the growth of bacterial colonies. Out of gratitude he pledged her his undying love and devotion (all in German) and crushed her against his bushy, bearded face, losing his *pince-nez* in the process.

Now that was silly!

She was feeling bored and hoped something would happen to get her through the rest of the night. "The said irony of it is," she thought, "that nothing fun happens around here unless someone's dying," and with this ghoulish thought in mind she put her Bell-boy beeper in her pocket and went downstairs to get hot brown water out of the coffee machine.

II

1845. Russia. The Caucasus.

Against dark hills burst occasional red flares as Imam Shamil's troops displayed their heavy artillery against the forces of Czar Alexander II. An orange blast of cannon fire exploded in the night, and in the distance could be heard the crack of musket fire and the shouts of men. Outside a large tent, a horse-drawn wagon pulled to a halt in the mud.

"There are two more wounded out here," a voice called. "One's taken a ball in the leg and the other has a saber wound in the gut."

"Thank you," another voice answered from the depths of the tent. "Please put them on my last two beds."

In the dark, stuffy tent Vaylance knelt by a pallet on the mud floor. One of his patients was dying. He peeled back the bloody piece of cloth and observed the neat flax string stitches that closed the wound. The man stirred in his uneasy sleep. The bleeding had stopped externally but not internally, and if it did not stop soon, he would have to resort to the dangerous process of transfusion.

"How's he doing?" asked Dr. Rimsky as he made his way among the pallets, holding a lantern high. Vaylance squinted away from the lantern. "He needs a transfusion."

The art of transfusion was seldom practiced in European medicine after the studies of Robert Boyle and others in the 17th century had shown it to be often fatal to the recipient. Vaylance, however, had learned his medical skill from a different tradition and had devised a method that worked fairly well in most cases.

"It's up to you to do it, then," said the doctor. "You have the best luck with it of anybody I've ever seen. I won't try my hand at it. Killed more than I ever saved with that method."

"Well, I guess I'd better find a donor then," Vaylance stood up. He was tall, lean and dark-haired with a sickly sallow complexion, and the most striking dark eyes—eyes that could read the soul. He staggered as he tried to stand, and Dr. Rimsky caught his arm to help him stabilize.

"I know you're not one of us, lad," said the doctor, "but even you must have your limits. You haven't been eating lately. Something is wrong."

"It bothers my conscience to feed, when you are all so sickly," said Vaylance. "When you were all fat and healthy, it was different. Now the cost is too high."

"Small good you'll be to us if you shrivel up and die of starvation," said the doctor. But he saw that his strange young friend was not to be persuaded. Vaylance, when he set his mind to follow his own inner law, was never waylaid by good advice. The fast would continue.

A year ago Vaylance had gone to Dr. Rimsky to tell him that he wished to serve in this war. Rimsky, an army surgeon, gray with age and much responsibility, had tried to discourage this young son of the Varkela from serving with the Russian soldiers.

"They would not accept you once they found you out, dear Vaylance," said the older man. "They would find out your hiding place and stake you while you slept. I cannot allow it. You must serve the Lord in some other way."

"You misunderstand my meaning," said Vaylance, fingering the wooden cross at his throat. "I would not serve as a soldier, but as a medical assistant with you. I must, for you, because you have saved me from the black-water sickness. You know my people are known for their herbal lore, leechcraft, and some for the healer's touch, and you have taught me much of the science of surgery. Let me come with you."

"The Varkela are known for other things besides their skill at healing," said Rimsky. "Even as a convert, you would be mistrusted by the men, and, besides, this is not your war, Vaylance. Your people are considered Tartar and not subject to the Czar." Rimsky hoped that Vaylance would survive the war and become a leader of his people, an ancient race that might become extinct. He had met Vaylance's father while stationed near the Caucasus. He had been surprised to find the old Varkela leechman living with a group of Kalmuck nomadic tribesman who still paid the ancient *blood-price* for his medical services.

Vaylance had not given up, however. "You forget," he said, "that I was born on Russian soil. And, remember, it has always been the custom of my people to heal the sick and wounded. When the Mongols came over the steppes and made war, did not we Varkela come in the night to ease pain and bind up wounds? All I require is that you provide me with a place to sleep, and I will keep the night watch while you work days."

"Very well," Dr. Rimsky had sighed. "You have my permission, and I will be very glad to have your assistance."

The volunteer came into the dimly lighted tent and sat on the campstool. Vaylance recognized the man.

"You can't give blood again so soon, Sarnov," he said. "It takes at least a month for your body to make more. Go and send someone else."

A few minutes later another man came and presented himself. Vaylance had him lie on the cot next to the wounded man and rolled up his sleeve. He applied the tourniquet and the veins bulged like rope cords. As he worked, Vaylance sang softly the "sleeping song" of his people, which had the effect of inducing a hypnotic state in the volunteer.

With his fingers he traced the swollen veins. He could actually hear the blood hum as it pulsed through the arteries like the rushing of water in subterranean caverns. His mouth began to water as he knelt next to the cot. Gentle as a kiss, his mouth touched the exposed arm, his hollow teeth entered the vein, and a swirl of blood flowed into his mouth. A taste was enough to tell him what he wanted to know. He withdrew his mouth and licked at the wound with his thin, dog-like tongue. Saliva from his lower gland bathed the prick and stopped the bleeding.

There were four blood types Vaylance could recognize by taste: salty, more salty, bitter and slightly sweet. This was the bitter, same as his patient, and without further delay he began to set up the transfusion. He had two hollow needles, and connecting the two was a crude form of rubber tubing. In the middle of the tubing was a glass reservoir with a pair of stopcock valves, a glassblower's nightmare. Vaylance selected the proper vein on the donor's arm and inserted the upper needle, and the lower he placed into the chosen vein of his patient. Slowly the reservoir filled with the dark fluid. Vaylance reversed the stopcock and forced air into a vent on the side of the reservoir, and it slowly emptied.

Knowing that there are four major blood types was a breakthrough in the art of transfusion, but it didn't rule out all danger. There was an antibody lurking in the serum of the patient. A more sophisticated test might have detected the telltale clumping in the bottom of a test tube, but Vaylance, limited to tasting the blood, missed it completely. For this reason he did not know anything was wrong until he saw the skin of his patient go all mottled with reddish splotches. He yanked the needle from the arm, but it was too late to save the man. Hemolyzed red blood cells had already dumped a toxic load of raw hemoglobin into the system. The patient burned with fever as the night wore on. His kidneys, confronted with the hemoglobin, failed, and he entered the coma from which there was no return. As the sun came up, the surgical assistant fought his weariness and stayed near his patient's side, but abruptly he ceased to breathe, and Vaylance admitted defeat. There was nothing to do but clean all the paraphernalia and remove the corpse for burial.

Vaylance went to Dr. Rimsky's tent and woke the doctor. After telling him of the failed transfusion, he prepared to sleep. He always slept in Dr. Rimsky's tent, which was strictly off-limits to everyone except himself and the doctor. Vaylance lay on his cot thinking. Presently his breathing slowed and his pulse dropped to 20 beats per minute. He slept as only the Varkela sleep.

Vaylance awoke with a start to find a crushing weight on his chest. The sun had gone down: it was time for him to work again, but something was wrong. Around him he heard the sounds of men groaning in pain. Hoofbeats approached and then receded in the distance. Then he heard a voice:

"The medical tent's been hit! Give us a hand."

Vaylance struggled with the weight on his chest and found it was a dead man.

"Over here!" he called to the voices.

Someone was moving the heavy tent cloth, and then strong hands reached in and pulled him from the wreckage. Vaylance then helped his rescuer, a large man in an ill-fitting black infantryman's uniform, to clear away the remains of the tent and find the wounded men.

"Shamil's broken through the front here," said the burly soldier as he hefted a stump-legged patient.

"Go and find me a wagon to move the wounded," Vaylance ordered.

Vaylance began to check his patients, who were lying scattered about on the muddy ground. Several of them had died, perhaps from shock or suffocation when the tent was hit. A cannon ball whistled overhead and burrowed into the clay of a nearby embankment. Suddenly he realized Dr. Rimsky was missing. He blundered back into the tent and floundered amid the fallen poles and tent cloth until he found the doctor lying face-down. He was wet all over and the smell of fresh blood hung heavy on the night air. Vaylance turned Rimsky over and saw where a tent pole had slashed an artery in his arm. He found the doctor's medical kit and began to work, quickly removing the pole and applying a pressure bandage to the wound. He prayed that the bleeding would stop.

Then he heard the approach of wagon wheels. The big soldier was back with two others, and they began to load the wounded into the cart. Vaylance lifted the doctor gingerly and placed him in the wagon. Then he climbed up and stayed at the doctor's side as the wagon creaked slowly over the soggy ground. By two hours past midnight they had reached an encampment of supply wagons.

A tall grimacing officer with epaulets on his shoulders approached the wagon on horseback.

"We are the Fourth Medical Unit," said Vaylance, "or rather what's left of it. The doctor is wounded. I am the surgical assistant."

The officer nodded and called to some men by the supply depot. In an hour they had the tent up and had made the patients as comfortable as possible. There were six patients left, including Dr. Rimsky. As Vaylance made his rounds, he was encouraged to see that one of his patients with the leg amputated at the knee was doing well. The man's fever had responded to an infusion of willow leaves, and the stump was healing without infection.

Vaylance was worried about Dr. Rimsky, however, and he decided to re-dress the wound. But when he set the new bandage in place, he saw where the blood still oozed to darken the fresh white cloth. And he realized his hunger. The nearness of blood was beginning to affect him again. He hastily finished the dressing and stepped out of the tent to gaze at the moon. The moon waned in the eastern sky, a thin scimitar of light. In a few nights would come the dark of the moon, the blood-moon, as his people called it.

The Varkela had originally been horse nomads of the Eurasian steppes, wandering from tribe to tribe, exchanging their skill at healing for the *blood-price*. For centuries they had survived, one here, a few there, in close association with humankind, yet always a race apart, a secret brotherhood. According to oral tradition, they had served in the legions of Attila the Hun around 400 A.D., and when Batu Khan, grandson of Genghis, invaded the Russian frontier, he found tribes that still employed the services of the old Varkela leechman. By Vaylance's time they had mostly died out or had interbred with humankind to the extent that the old genetic traits had been diluted out. One occasionally ran across Varkela characteristics among the Circassian people of the Caucasus or their Tartar neighbors on the steppes. Every now and then, a youth would have those dark, seductive eyes that seemed to exert so much power over the beholder. Or there would be a Tartar brave with such uncanny ability to train horses that people would say of him, "He speaks the horses' language." Blood-need was of course extremely uncommon. One Circassian folktale tells of the wolf-minded Tartar maid who lures a Cossack youth away into the night to drink his blood.

The Varkela had left their imprint on the Slavic racial memory in the form of Vampire stories.

By their strange nocturnal habits and their state of daylight dormancy, they had been regarded as "undead," the nosferatu. The old Greek word for Vampire, "Vrkola-kas," may be a corruption of Varkela, the *children of the night.*

As the gray dawn appeared, Vaylance left the medical tent and sought out the officer he had seen earlier. He found the man sitting on a wooden crate, cleaning a small flintlock handgun that rested on his knee. The officer forced a wet rag down the small bore with a straight alder stick, and with loving hands he polished the smudges of powder burn from the browned metal flashpan. His well-fed gray mare stood patiently tied to the supply wagon. It raised its head and swiveled its ears toward Vaylance, making a barely audible nicker. Vaylance scratched the animal's poll.

"A fine animal you've got here," he said. Then he proceeded with his lie:

"I must go to a nearby village and seek sheeting to make bandages. Could you please assign someone to stay with the wounded until I return?" He hoped this would be a good excuse to sneak away and take his daytime sleep. He no longer had Dr. Rimsky to explain away his odd habits. The taciturn officer nodded and continued his polishing. Vaylance turned to take his leave, then added:

"By the way, your horse has a stone wedged in her left fore hoof."

The road to the village branched, and Vaylance took the less traveled fork. Soon he was ascending a small hillock that was heavily wooded. The increasing light made it hard for him to see, and he welcomed the shadow of the trees. He found a dense thicket where he hoped he would not be discovered, and burrowing into the underbrush, he flattened the grasses and made a place to lie down. He drowsed, pondering his troubles. He might have to transfuse Dr. Rimsky, his dearest friend, yet he feared to take the risk without further knowledge. He would have to risk dreamwalk to find the answer. The trouble with dreamwalking was that he never knew where he might end up, and he needed someone else to help him do it, but it was the only course open to him. With resolution, Vaylance stopped breathing, slowed his heart and loosed his soul into the void.

He felt as if he were lifted up above the gently rolling hills of the Russian countryside, and he could see the grove where he slept far below. Then the landscape shimmered and disappeared, and in its place came the flat, dry grasslands of the open steppe. A yurt, a tentlike dwelling, stood like a bump in the flat plain, its felt cloth sides rippling in the wind. A few scruffy horses were grazing nearby, and a two-humped Bactrian camel lay sunning itself, its face toward the wind. The surroundings shimmered again, and Vaylance found himself inside the arched cane poles of the yurt. On a wicker couch lay an old man, whose leathern Tartar features, windburned and ancient, did not change, but acknowledged the presence in the yurt.

"My son, do you dreamwalk?" asked the old man.

"My father, I greet thee from the void," answered Vaylance. "I feel myself being pulled forward in the river of time, and I need your help." Vaylance explained his predicament to his father.

"The last time something like this happened," said Freneer, the father, "you almost brought back that unclean woman as your blood-love. You know I am against these outblood liaisons of yours. Favarka's been dead a long time, and I think you should take another mate. I am seeking a Varkela wife for you. You must consider, Vaylance, that we are dying out as a race; if the young men do not produce offspring, the 'old knowledge' will die with us."

"I don't intend to let you breed me like a horse, Father," said Vaylance. "Right now marriage is far away from my thoughts. I must find a way to save Dr. Rimsky."

"And yet you let that Russian doctor study you like some species of beetle—but I know he is your friend and I will help you—but you must promise to choose some wolf-minded girl, just as I chose your mother Odakai."

Vaylance remembered his mother, a Varkela woman who had left the steppes to live in Moscow, where she practiced as a medium and spiritual healer under the name of Anna Varkeerovna. He had lived with her until he was about thirteen, learning French and English in the drawing-room society of Moscow, and then she had taken him back to the steppe to study leechcraft with his father. One night on their journey to the steppes she had come across a wolf-cub which she had picked up and carried for a while across her saddle bow, saying to her young son: "This is the soul-beast of your blood-love, Vaylance." His parents insisted on a pedigree.

"Very well, a wolf-minded girl," Vaylance agreed, "but in my own time, Father, and in my own way."

"Well, then," said the old leechman, "let us begin." He took his staghorn rattles from the altar and sat cross-legged on the rug. Beating the horns together, he began to croon softly in the old language.

Vaylance sat on the rug opposite his father and concentrated on Dr. Rimsky. Gradually the singing got softer and Vaylance felt time, like a river, flowing around him. He let go and drifted with the current. Then he did not hear the singing anymore; in its stead came a sound like rushing water in his ears. He entrusted himself to the forward dream and waited.

III

Myrna sat up with a start. A face at the blood bank window was enough to jolt her from her reverie.

"Got a live one for you down in admitting!" said the intern, offering Myrna tubes of blood. "Not bleeding now but he seems to have lost a lot somewhere along the way. Hematocrit of sixteen. Dressed like he was going to a costume party. Also he didn't have any I.D. So we just gave him a number. And if you haven't already guessed, we want it STAT."

Myrna fed a sample to "Clarabelle" and got a reading: Hematocrit 15.9 percent, white cell count 4000.

"He won't live long at that rate," she said, as she plopped the tube into the centrifuge to spin. She was most concerned about the low hematocrit, the volume of red blood cells expressed as a percentage. Normal for an adult male was 45 percent. At 15.9 this patient wasn't doing at all well.

When the centrifuge stopped turning, Myrna retrieved the tube of blood, separated the serum from the clot and prepared to type the sample. She added typing serum, spun the tubes and frowned.

"Damn it! He doesn't type," she said, looking at the mixed-field agglutination in the A tube. "Must be a weak subtype of A; either that, or someone's been mixing A and O together." Uncertainty about a blood type was about the worst problem a tech could have when blood was needed for a transfusion.

Myrna had seen a reaction like this only twice before. Once had been when a patient of type O blood had been mistakenly given type A. The other had been when she had been new on the job, just out of training school. An intern had brought her a specimen to type for a "friend." She had at first been puzzled until she looked at the name on the tube. "I. M. Nosferatu." Then she had to laugh. Someone was pulling her leg. The intern had mixed A and O together as they might be expected to occur in the stomach of the fictitious Mr. Nosferatu. It was the ultimate vampire joke.

The man would have to be transfused with such a low hematocrit. So Myrna decided the best thing to do would be to collect a fresh specimen and repeat the tests. Hopefully someone had made a mistake the first time. She filled a tray with the tools of her trade: sterile needle encased in plastic, rubber tourniquet, vacutaner tubes, cotton swabs, alcohol and skin tape. Then she took the elevator to the intensive care unit.

The sweet, sickly odor of the patients hit her as she walked into the ICU. The most critical patients lay in full view of the nursing station, looking like a row of strange vegetables planted in a garden of wires and plastic tubing. The heart monitors peeped every few seconds, and electric recording devices hummed in the background.

"Hi, Rose," she said to the older woman at the nursing station. "I need a new specimen on your Mr. Number 3489."

"First door on your left, " said Rose, "and good luck. I don't think he's got any blood left."

She had expected him to be unconscious when she entered the room, but he was awake and looking at her. He looked to be about thirty, with a shaggy crop of black hair and the most striking dark eyes that glowed faintly as if there were light inside of him. There was something too intimate about looking into those eyes.

And then Myrna had one of those occasions that

people in her family called "second sight." She seemed
to see a woman, wearing a Cossack's baggy clothing and
a fur cap, sitting astride a horse facing into the wind. In
the crook of her arm was a wolf cub. The woman stroked
the cub and turned her head toward Myrna and smiled
at her with those same large dark eyes. She spoke a few
words and then the image faded. Myrna realized she was
standing there staring at the patient, who regarded her
with a whimsical smile.

"This must be an English hospital and you are the
leech," he said. He had an accent, although she couldn't
place it, and she instinctively knew that he used the word
"leech" in its oldest sense, the archaic term for "doctor."

"I suppose you could call me a leech of sorts," she
said, "but I'm not a doctor, I'm a medical technologist.
And this isn't England. You're in America, friend."

"America!" he exclaimed. "I thought there were only
wild Indians and revolutionaries living there. What year
is this?

"Nineteen seventy-nine," she said.

"My God!" he said. "When I went to sleep it was
1845."

"What did you do, fall asleep in a time machine? Or
are you Rip Van Winkle?"?

"Neither, I hope," he said. "If things are what I think
they are, then I'm dreamwalking, and I'm not really
here."

"We'll see about that," she said tying the tourniquet
around his arm and swabbing vigorously with alcohol.
She stuck the needle into his arm and pushed the vacutaner down snugly, breaking the vacuum. Blood was
sucked into the tube. Suddenly he clenched his arm,
causing the needle to pop out leaving a little trail of red.
His hand closed over her wrist tightly.

"Do not take from me, little blood-thief," he said. "I
don't have enough to give."

"You don't understand," she said. "I must test your
blood for the right type and do a crossmatch. Then they

will give you a transfusion because you have lost much blood."

"I have not lost any," he said. "But I have need of it. I have not taken blood in a month." After divulging this bit of information he stared at the few drops of blood in the tube. Perplexed, he said, "Perhaps I'm really here and Rimsky is over one hundred years dead." He lay back on the pillow and closed his eyes. He seemed to be concentrating on something very far away. For a moment she seemed to see his image fade before her eye so that she thought she could see through him, and then he was back, solid as before.

"It's all right," he said. "I can still hear my father's voice if I listen."

Something very odd was going on here. She wrinkled her brow and studied him for a moment. Then business-like and efficient, she retied the tourniquet.

"I don't know what's happening," she said, "but what-ever it is, my time-travelling friend, you had better give me some blood so I can get back to the lab, or you are going to be one sick turkey." She tried to maintain a calm appearance as she bent over him to obtain the specimen.

There was something about this woman that attracted Vaylance. For a brief moment, when he had looked into her eyes, he thought he had seen the "look of the wolf." And there was something else. Beneath the civilized odor of cologne and talc, he detected a fragrance, impercepti-ble to human-kind, of something definitely feral, as wild and sweet as the crushed leaves of his medicinal herbs, and this excited him. It called to mind a verse from one of the great Varkela love poems. He converted it into English in his mind and came up with: "Ah, woman, the scent of thy wolvish cunt hath turned my head." It was intended as a compliment, but was definitely not the sort of thing one said to an English-speaking lady in his time; so he kept it to himself.

As she bent over him, he observed that her hair was piled up on her head and held in place by a clip. The nape of her neck was lovely and vulnerable in the half-light, and he felt a strong urge to press his lips to her inviting throat and sink his cat-like teeth into the pulsing artery. Thinking this way caused him to have an erection, and he smiled inwardly at his attempt to stifle the impulse. This Christianity that he practiced was more difficult than the shamanistic religion of Freneer, his father. One of the saints had called the body "brother ass," an appropriate term for his, as it sometimes went stubbornly astray.

She finished drawing the blood sample and left the room, taking her fragrance with her. If she gave him blood, he would have to give her something in return. He knew some members of his race, especially those in the Balkan countries, stole blood like vile insects, giving neither love nor leechcraft in return.

It had been a long time since he had shared blood-love with a woman. Service in the Czar's army did not provide many opportunities. He had counted himself lucky when at the age of 17 he had won the love of Favarka, a full-blooded Varkela. Women were so rare that he'd shared her with another older man, according to their custom, but she'd called him "favorite." She was ten years dead, but he sometimes thought of her and the times he had laid his head on the soft fur between her breasts. He still carried the small scars where Favarka in her passion had marked him hers with love bites.

Back at the lab, Myrna fussed with her test tubes and got the same frustrating results. Holding the tubes up to the light, she saw little red flecks in the typing serum.

"This will have to do, I guess," she said.

Dr. Meyer was waiting at the window, impatiently drumming his fingers along the countertop.

"You'll have to sign for this one," said Myrna.

"That bad, huh?" he said.

"He doesn't type," she said. "I called my supervisor and she said give O-negative packed cells. At least he doesn't have any serum antibodies that I can detect."

"Maybe it's a hypoimmune response," said Dr. Meyer.

"You know, that guy is weird. 'Crit of 16, and he sits up in bed asking me questions all night. I'm surprised he can move his mouth, let alone sit up. You'd better loan him one of your books on blood-banking. He's asking things that are over my head."

At 5:00 A.M. when things had quieted down, Myrna was washing out the tubing on the auto-analyzer. She was finished and just about to get a cup of coffee, when she heard it. She did not exactly "hear" it, for there was no sound, but the definite words came to her: "Come to me," they said.

She got her coffee and sat down at the lab bench to think this over.

"Come to me."

It was a voice inside her head pleading subtly but insistently. *It was him.* It had to be him.

Her curiosity compelled her sufficiently that when Ernie the security guard came by, she asked him to watch the phone while she went upstairs.

The ICU was quiet except for the beep-beep of the heart monitors. When she entered the room, her patient was lying back on the bed with a smile on his face and a little white tooth projected over his lower lip. He had taken the IV needle from his arm and placed the tubing over one of his teeth. The blood bag, hung on a rack overhead, was emptying visibly. He seemed quite pleased with himself.

"You didn't come right away," he said. "That means you are somewhat wolf-minded—sit here." He pointed to the bed. His voice was quiet, but she could feel the command in it. And she felt an overwhelming desire to obey his commands, especially when she looked into those dark, seductive eyes. Somehow she resisted: he would not have fun at her expense. What is happening, she thought, is that he is trying to control my mind. With an effort, she raised her eyes from his.

"Suppose I refuse," she said.

His spell was broken, but he didn't look at all unhappy about it; in fact, quite the contrary.

"You know, you're one of the few people who can do that?" he said. "This is even better than I'd hoped." His eyes appraised her carefully, with a certain longing, laced with self-confidence.

She detested his smugness. "You'd better get that needle back in your arm before a nurse catches you."

He heaved a languorous sigh and winked at her.

She shivered and walked determinedly from the room. Halfway down the hall, she heard it again: "Come back."

The hell I will, thought Myrna.

"Please?"

No!

He was ecstatic to think that he could find a wolf-minded girl in this place.

At 8:00 A.M. Myrna went home from the hospital. She unlocked the door to her small apartment, crossed the room and turned on the television to keep her company. A blink of light, and the Morning Show came on. A psychiatrist was being interviewed about the effect of modern technology on the psyche. "We may find," he was saying, "that man needs mythology more than all the conveniences of our modern age." Myrna left the voices mumbling behind her, as she took the few steps to the kitchen. She stooped to open the small refrigerator that fitted under the counter and peered among the cottage cheese cartons and plastic-wrapped packages. She selected a package of two-day-old chicken, removed a drumstick, and shut the door.

Her small breakfast finished, she turned off the TV and opened the bedroom door. In one corner stood a clothes hamper stuffed to overflowing, and in the middle of the room lay a mattress under a heap of blankets. Beside it were piled the books she was currently reading. There was also the letter from Terry, in which he complained of her inability to say the word "love." The most she would say to someone she felt close to was, "I care for you." She had written back to him: "There is something wild in me that won't be caged by love."

Along one wall of her room was a bookcase that reached from floor to ceiling. She went to the wall and searched among the titles. Following one row with her finger, she stopped on *The Vampire, His Kith and Kin*, by Montagu Sommers. She tossed it on the bed and went to the bureau and opened the top drawer. She searched a while among the lipstick cases, pill bottles, and mismatched socks. It wasn't there. She pulled open the next drawer and sorted around the underwear until she found the little wooden jewelry box. Inside the box, tangled in a mass of neck chains and a string of pearls, she found the object of her search, a tiny silver cross, given to her when she was a little girl by her grandmother. She had never worn it, but she put it around her neck now. Then she began to undress. Removing her white nylon pants, she put on her flannel nightgown, rearranged the blankets, and settled into her nest to read. Eventually she fell mid-paragraph into a restless sleep.

The use of the cross as a religious symbol predates Christianity, going back as far as neolithic times. It was usually a glyph for the axe or hammer and, as such, signified power. To the Teutonic tribes of northern Europe, it represented the hammer of Thor. In the Shamanistic tradition of Eurasia it was Skaldi's hammer, the sun's hammer. To the Varkela, *children of the night*, the sun was viewed as an ancient enemy. For them the idea of a bright, sunny day had the same connotation as we might attribute to the phrase "dark of the moon." The sun hammer was regarded as a bad omen, as is echoed in the Varkela curses: "May the sun hammer smite thee," or "May the sun strike you blind." As a Christian symbol, the cross was supposed to ward off the devil, and so by converse logic the Varkela were regarded as "demonkind" because they avoided it.

That evening Myrna went early to the hospital. She went to the intensive care unit and inquired about the progress of her patient.

"He had a code 99 this morning, cardiac arrest," Rose reported. "They had to resuscitate him. Lucky they caught him when they did or he would have been gone."

Nervously Myrna entered the room and stood inside the doorway watching the figure on the bed. In her lab coat pocket she fingered her silver crucifix. He was sitting up in bed and he smiled when he recognized her.

"A person could get killed in a place like this," he said. "This morning when I was almost asleep, they came in and jolted me right out of it with that horrible shock machine."

"You're lucky," she said. "They could have decided you were dead and sent you to pathology for an autopsy. Then you would be all cut up and placed in little bottles by now."

"I see this age has its share of barbarous customs," he said.

Myrna took a step into the room, fumbling with the object in her pocket.

"You're a vampire, aren't you?" she said, stopping at what she hoped was a safe distance from the bed.

"I'm not a corpse come back to life, if that's what you mean," he said. "But I am Varkela, which is probably the source of all those silly legends."

Vaylance eyed her pocket mistrustfully, thinking it must contain a small hand pistol. When outbloods began using the word "vampire" it usually meant trouble, and only a fool would stick around trying to argue about technical differences. Therefore he was quite relieved when she took a small crucifix out of her pocket and extended her arm triumphantly in his direction.

Aha, he thought, someone comes to smite me down with the sun's hammer. He decided to have a little fun with her. Shrinking down in the bedclothes and feigning terror, he watched as she advanced in somnambulistic grandeur. When she was within range and the little cross dangled in front of his nose, he reached out and took it from her hand. An impudent grin spread across his face.

"Thank you," he said, "but as you can see, I already have one," and he pulled at the chain around his neck, bringing his own hand-carved cross into view.

Crestfallen, Myrna sat down on the bed, her mouth gaping.

"Little blood-thief," he said, "if you only knew how funny you looked just then."

"But I thought . . ." she began.

"I can be a Christian like anyone else," he said.

She didn't seem to hear him. She was still recovering from the shock.

"Hello," he waved a hand in front of her face. "You of all people don't have to be afraid of me. A wolf-minded girl can defend herself. I won't bite you or what-ever it is you are afraid of."

He was glad when he saw the wolvish look return to her eyes, but now she regarded him with such a stern expression that he stopped smiling. She was angry with him.

"I suppose you think this is a soup kitchen, where you can come for a free meal," she said. "I work hard to crossmatch blood for *sick* people. I'll have you know blood costs sixty dollars a pint, if you're interested. If you're hungry, go find someone who's healthy and bite them on the neck!"

He felt ashamed to have taken blood without payment.

"You don't need to haggle the price of blood with me," he said. "I know it comes dear, and I will find some way to repay, but right now I need your help."

He began to explain to her about the war in 1845, about his work in the medical tent, and about his dearest friend Dr. Rimsky who lay dying in another time. He watched her face for signs of comprehension. At first she raised a cynical eyebrow at his outpouring, but he rushed onward with his story, hoping to convince her by his urgency if not with logic. Soon her skepticism was replaced by doubt. She began to ask questions and to demand explanations on certain points. Eager to sway her his way, he supplied detail upon detail. Finally, as the torrent of his rhetoric abated, he thought he saw just the barest glimmer of belief in her eyes.

When he finished, Myrna was quiet for a moment. Then she said, "You know, you're not such a bad sort, and I'm half persuaded that you're telling the truth, but you make a horrible first impression. If you wanted my help, why didn't you ask me, instead of going through all that stupid 'come to me' business? You scared me half to death."

"I'm sorry about that," he said. "I was only thinking of myself. You see, I have not shared blood-love with anyone for a long time and your response was so typically Varkela, that I forgot for a moment that you are an out-blood and do not understand. Most of humankind cannot resist the 'call' and will come to us when summoned, but those who resist, the wolf-minded ones, are those we prefer to mate with, for they usually have some Varkela ancestry. But there are also wolf-minded outbloods here and there, and we also marry with them, because full-blood Varkela women are subject to an illness, and thus are very rare."

"It must be a sex-linked genetic defect," said Myrna.

"A what?"

"Never mind," she said. "Listen, if I'm going to help you, we're going to have to get you out of this place. Otherwise they'll keep trying to start your heart every morning, and you'll never get any rest."

"That's not the only thing," said Vaylance. "These doctors think I'm human. They are planning to transfuse me again tonight to raise my what-you-call-it."

"Hematocrit."

"Right. But I'm Varkela and don't need as much. It would be a waste of good blood and might even make me ill."

"I saw your chart and your 'crit is only eighteen. No doctor is going to sign your release," she said. "I can get your clothes from admitting and you can come and stay at my place for a while, but I don't know how to smuggle you past the nurses' station."

"That's no problem to me," he said, and so saying, he concentrated for a few minutes, and his image faded from view. Then he was back again. "I would have done it sooner, but I had no place to go."

"I have to go to work now," said Myrna, checking her watch. "But if you can slip past the nurses and meet me down at the lab, I'll have your things. I can teach you about transfusion, and maybe we can rig up a sort of crossmatch that would work back in 1845."

About 2:30 A.M. Ernie, the security guard, came by the lab to tell Myrna that one of the patients was missing from the ICU and that she should keep an eye out for him. After he left, Vaylance materialized behind the filing cabinet.

"I wish I knew that trick," said Myrna. "I'd vanish every time my supervisor came around with a stool specimen to analyze."

"It's merely an illusion of the dreamwalk," he said. "One shouldn't do it too often. It expends a frightful lot of energy."

Myrna seated Vaylance at the lab bench and prepared to teach him immuno-hematology.

"The four major blood groups, A, B, AB, and O, are probably what you are able to distinguish by taste," she said. "We differentiate them by adding typing sera to the blood specimen." She showed him how the blue serum precipitated group A; the yellow, group B. For type AB, both the blue and yellow serum precipitated and for type O, neither of them did.

"The next thing you have to worry about are antibodies," she said. "A person with type A has Anti-B antibodies in his or her serum; this is why you can't give type-B blood to a type-A person. A type-B person has Anti-A; therefore, you can't give type-A to a B person. A type-O person has both Anti-A and Anti-B; therefore, you can't give type A or B to an O person; but type O is sometimes called the "universal donor" because you can

give it to type A, B, and AB persons because they don't
have an Anti-O in their serum."

"Now you've got me really confused," said Vaylance.
"I'll never be able to remember all that."

"You won't have to," said Myrna, "because I am going
to teach you a simple crossmatch technique, which
should rule out some of the dangers." She then took two
different blood specimens and separated the serum from
the cells. Next, using a porcelain slide, she mixed the
donor cells with the patient serum on one side, and the
patient cells with the donor serum on the other.

"If either mixture reacts, then you know that the donor
is the wrong blood type, or that he has an antibody
against the patient, making an incompatible crossmatch."

She showed Vaylance how to let the blood clot and
take off the serum, and how to mix serum and cells
on the slide to make what she called a "major" and a
"minor" crossmatch.

"It's not perfect," said Myrna, "but it will pick out a
few antibodies and prevent errors in typing."

Most of the rest of the night they talked about blood
and transfusions and antibodies. She asked him how
drinking the blood could raise his hematocrit, and he
explained that the blood didn't go into his stomach, but
that most went through valves in his hollow teeth and
directly into his bloodstream. The serum antibodies were
apparently filtered out somewhere in the process. She
theorized that he probably had a deficiency of rubriblasts
in his bone marrow, which caused the blood-need he felt
from time to time. She was surprised to discover that a
"vampire" needed only two pints of blood in the course
of a month and could subsist on small amounts taken
from many, healthy, sleeping donors. Vaylance revealed
that he had two kinds of saliva: from the lower gland,
a rapid clotting agent, and from the upper gland, an
anticoagulant. Myrna was fascinated and asked if she
could take samples.

"You're as bad as Dr. Rimsky," said Vaylance. "He
experiments with my spit on men, rats, and horses. I've

spent hours drooling into bottles for the futherance of science."

Vaylance noticed that during their long conversation, she seemed to avoid any topics of a personal nature. There was a certain aloofness or distance that she tried to maintain. And he was reminded of how he had been after Favarka's death, the withdrawal from life and the inward nursing of pain. He was not sure how to broach the subject. So he decided on the bold, blunt approach.

"Have you ever loved anyone, Myrna?" he asked.

She pondered this for a long time and then answered: "Yes, once a long time ago."

"And he hurt you?" asked Vaylance gently.

"How did you know?"

"I don't know, I just sense it," he said.

There was a long silence, punctuated by the clicking of the peristaltic pump on the autoanalyser and the ringing of a distant telephone.

Finally he said, "And you've never allowed yourself to love anyone since." It was a statement of fact, not a question.

"Does that show too?" she asked defensively.

"It does," he said. "Don't you know that if you refuse to love, the wound may heal over on the surface, but inside an abscess grows, poisoning you from within?"

"Love is an illusion," said Myrna. "Two people come together to satisfy their own needs. The secret lies in not caring too much. That way you don't get hurt when they leave you."

He knew that this cynical answer was just her defense against deeper feelings, but it angered him, moving him to say:

"But in that way you defeat your own purpose. You hurt people and use them and drive them away. Don't you see that if you continue in that way, you will become more of a vampire than I am?"

He saw a flash of anger in her eyes, and then she

looked away, biting her lower lip. He saw that his words had had an effect: she wept silently.

Well and good, he thought, she will learn to care again. He reached out and put an arm around her shoulders.

"Heal thee, heal thee," he said after the custom of his people.

When she had dried her eyes and regained some of her composure, she said, "It's not fair of you to knock down a person's defenses like that."

"It's fair if my intentions are honorable, which they are," he said.

She had to laugh at "honorable intentions."

"Now I really believe you are from the nineteenth century," she said. "Welcome to the age of noncommitment, Vaylance."

At 8:00 A.M. Myrna took him home with her. At first he balked at the "horseless carriage," her Volkswagen Superbeetle, but she finally persuaded him to get into the metal contraption. At her apartment she prepared him a place to sleep on cushions on the living room floor. Then she went to take her own daytime rest.

She awoke to hear music. He had found her old guitar and returned it to resemble some instrument familiar to him. He strummed a minor chord and sang in his own language. It had the sound of cold wind howling across open plains.

"What is that you're singing?" she asked.

He translated for her:

> "The dun mare has died,
> Little sister of the wind
> She wanders the pasture of the spirit world.
> I hear her neigh sometimes
> When the north wind blows."

It moved her to confess to him. "I have a horse."

"Really?" he said. "You must take me out to meet him

tonight before I leave. But first I want to hear you sing for me."

She didn't like to think of his leaving. The more she got to know him, the more she felt he was the sort of man that she had always hoped to meet. She took the guitar from him and returned it, and played an old Scottish ballad, a favorite of hers called "The Waters of Tyne."

> *"Oh, I cannot see my love if I would dee.*
> *The waters of Tyne stand between him and me.*
> *And here I must sit with a tear in my ee,*
> *All sighin' and sobbin' my true love to see."*

Except that when she sang it her tongue stumbled so that it came out "the waters of time."

She took him out to the stable where she kept Shanty, her horse. Crickets were singing in the warm night, when they arrived, and Shanty trotted up to the fence to greet them, pushing his nose into Myrna's pocket to beg for sugar. Vaylance scratched Shanty's neck and then bent, sliding his hand down a foreleg to check the hoof.

"You'd better be careful. He's fussy about his feet," warned Myrna. She thought of the farrier, whom Shanty had chased out of the barn. The man refused to go near Shanty now unless the horse was hobbled.

Shanty, however, made no trouble, and at a softspoken word picked up his feet and allowed them to be examined.

"He isn't usually like this with strangers," said Myrna. "He's really taken to you."

Vaylance took hold of the horse's mane and vaulted up onto his back. Shanty made a half rear and pivoted, galloped to the far end of the field and came back at an easy lope. Vaylance bounced down next to her again.

"You can ride a strange horse without saddle or bridle!" exclaimed Myrna.

"Only to show off for you," he said. "Actually, I am not that good. Back home I could introduce you to some real riders. When you tell a Russian boy that he rides like a Cossack, he takes it as a compliment, but to Varkela it is an insult."

When they got back to the apartment they were hungry. Vaylance insisted on cooking for her.

"It is a custom of ours. I haven't prepared food for a woman in a long time. It would give me pleasure," he said.

They searched in the refrigerator and found lamb chops. Vaylance, as he set about to cook, consumed a quart of milk, explaining that on the steppes he had lived mostly on mare's milk. Myrna showed him how to work the electric stove and then found a snack for herself as she awaited the results of his experiment.

"What's that funny stuff you're eating?" he asked. "Surely that can't be good for you."

"Coca-Cola and potato chips. I eat them all the time."

"Ugh!" he said.

"What's wrong with it?" said Myrna, knowing full well but desiring to provoke him a little. They had been having contests of the will all day. It was some sort of Varkela custom having to do with courtship or flirting.

"If you were my blood-love, I'd make you eat lots of green, leafy foods, bran meal and meat," he said.

"Why?"

"So my love wouldn't weaken you, and your blood would grow back rich and strong. I'd not have it said that my woman faints. And of course you would have to eat lots of karacheer."

"What's that?"

"Jerked goat's liver."

"Bleccchhh!"

"If you wouldn't, I'd force it down your throat!"

"The hell you would!" she said.

He engaged her eyes and tried to stare her down. She felt the force of his will as he tried to "Call" her to him. She thought a fierce, sharp thought that sent him reeling backward.

"Ow, you *are* wolf-minded. Now you've gone and given me a headache just as Favarka used to do."

It was fun, but it made him look at her throat with such longing.

"You will eventually yield to me, won't you?" he asked hopefully. "It's not fair for you to be so good at the teasing game if you don't intend to yield."

"Wait and see," she said. She seemed to have the upper hand and she was enjoying it.

After dinner she had to admit he was a very good cook.

His presence had stimulated Myrna into a lovely fantasy. She had an idea:

"I wish I could dreamwalk and go back with you. I think I'd like helping you in the medical tent. I know first aid and I could teach you a lot about modern medicine."

Vaylance was surprised. He had been wishing he had more time with her. Then perhaps it might have worked.

"We don't know each other well enough," he said. "To dreamwalk requires love and trust in your guide. It can be dangerous."

"We could at least try," she said.

He tried half-heartedly to dissuade her. He really wished it could be so. Finally he agreed to try. He sat her in a chair and stared into her eyes, trying to put her into the proper trance. But she resisted. He could see that she didn't mean to, but she couldn't help it. The wolf in her that so strongly attracted him fought against him now.

"Keep trying," she insisted. "I feel something beginning to happen."

Carefully he tried to coax her soul into the void. Finally he seemed to be succeeding. She slumped forward in her chair.

Myrna found herself inside a long, dark tunnel. She moved toward gray light in the distance until she felt grass under her feet, and, looking up, she saw the night sky, a panoply of stars. In the distance a rider approached over the steppe. No sound came to her from the horse's hooves, only the small ringing of tiny bells. She could see the rider clearly now, outlined against the starry mist, a woman clad in baggy trousers wearing a fur cap. A loose Tartar jacket enclosed her arms, which held a small wolf cub. The sturdy horse of the steppes came to a halt before Myrna, shaking its mane with a sprinkle of wind chimes. The fierce, dark-eyed woman offered the cub to Myrna, who cradled it in her arms. No word was spoken. The rider spurred her mount and cantered away, making no sound except the jingle of tiny bells.

Myrna looked at the small wolf and thought she saw sentience begin to glow redly in the depth of its eyes. Abruptly its countenance changed so that it was no longer a cub, but the wizened face of a small demon.

"Are you then one of the chosen?" it asked of her.

Myrna screamed and flung down the cub. Where it fell the ground split open in a great rent. Something made a scratchy noise deep in the dark hole, and then Myrna saw it, a giant centipede-like creature with many-jointed legs. It began to come toward her. She turned and fled. As she ran, she could hear the gnashing of chitinous jaws just behind her. Then she was in the tunnel again, which seemed to wind on forever as the thing gained on her. Just as a whip-like antenna snaked out to touch her shoulder, she woke up sobbing in Vaylance's arms.

"I was afraid of something like this," he said. "Where did you go? I couldn't find you."

She told him about the dream as he held her close, comforting her.

"You have seen the ghost-soul of my mother, Odakai," said Vaylance, "but what it means, I do not know."

He lifted and carried her into the bedroom, and, setting her gently on the bed, he lay down beside her.

She had avoided any affectionate gestures from him all day, being both attracted and repelled by his vampire nature. But now, partly because she was upset, and partly because he would be leaving soon, she pressed closer in his arms.

"If you yield to me now," he said, "I will make your blood to sing."

She could feel his breath on her neck and she braced herself for what she knew must come next. But he didn't bite. He kissed her tenderly, and then he was kissing her mouth and her nose and her eyes and carefully undressing her. "Why you're tattooed!" she said, when he took off his shirt.

She traced with her finger where a stag raced across his chest.

"It's my soul-beast," he told her.

They played at love for a long time. He was gentle, teasing, the most sensitive lover she had ever known.

Vaylance, when he saw the soft fur of her bosom, made a little cry of joy. This and her scent proved to him that she was one of his own kind, and he banished his Christian conscience to a remote corner of his mind where it could not touch him.

When he finally pulled her over on top of him and entered her, she was so close that she could hardly contain it, but he sensed this and stopped, then brought her close to the knife's edge several times before allowing her to finish. And her blood sang, pulsing in her ears, a song of the open steppes. As she lay satiated on top of him, he sought the jugular vein in her throat and bit deeply. She didn't really mind. She felt so warm and sleepy that she was content to lie there and enjoy the intimacy of it. When he finished, he licked the wound clean with his pink dog-like tongue, and Myrna, having recovered, reached up and nipped him playfully in the throat.

"My poor little wolf with no teeth," he said. "I must help you." And he turned his head and bit his own shoulder so that the blood flowed.

"I share myself with you," he said.

She looked at the red trickle. She knew what he wanted her to do, but she didn't want to do it. So she just stared down at him.

"You reject me then?" he asked with such soft, wounded eyes that she couldn't refuse him. She pressed her lips to the small cut and drank a little of the warm liquid. The taste of his blood awoke in her some ancient need and she continued to drink until it was satisfied. For an instant it seemed as if she saw herself through his eyes. The moment passed and she was aware that he looked at her intently.

"Our souls have touched," he said.

They lay together a long time without talking.

Vaylance's conscience uncoiled from where it lay sleeping like a dormant asp and bit him.

"I have sinned and must repent," he said. "The Christians have such strange rules about love."

Then he looked at her and brushed back her hair to kiss her forehead. "And yet I don't think God would begrudge me to share blood-love with you," he said, "because it's such a comfort, and doesn't the Bible say, 'Comfort ye, comfort ye, my people, saith the Lord'?"

Myrna laughed.

"Have I made a joke?" he asked.

"Sort of," she said. "That's the first time I ever heard anyone quote the Bible to justify fornication."

Hurt, he rolled away from her, pulling the pillow down over his head.

"You make it sound like something people write on the wall of a latrine," he said.

Myrna pulled the pillow away and was going to clout him with it, when she saw that although his eyes were tightly closed, a tear wet the lashes.

"Hey, I'm sorry," she said. "I was only teasing you."

"It's nothing," he said. "Just my romantic nature showing. I'd hoped we could call it love, not fornication. But I know it's much too soon to know."

He was silent for a moment and then he said, "Do you know why it's so difficult for you to love, Myrna?"

"No," she said honestly, almost guiltily. "I thought it was because I'd been hurt once, but I know it goes much deeper than that."

"It's because the wolvish soul builds trust slowly," he said. "It rejects all but those who persistently continue to take the risk of courting it. It may be befriended, never tamed."

Myrna felt that, for the first time, someone had really understood her nature. It seemed impossible that he could be leaving.

"I wish we had more time," she said.

"So do I," he said, "but perhaps we may meet again someday. I think that dream you had gives us cause for hope. It may mean that Odakai accepts you, but you are just not ready yet."

They held each other for a long time in the dark, saying nothing.

From somewhere in the room, Myrna seemed to hear a faraway voice, singing in an unknown language, his language.

"I must leave you now," he said.

"I wish I could go with you," she said, "but if wishes were horses, then beggars would ride."

He didn't understand the English proverb, and she had to explain to him that back in the 17th century only those with enough money could afford a horse.

"It sounds funny to me," he said, "because where I come from even the beggars ride. I'll change the saying around and give you my blessing as a parting gift. May your wishes be horses, Myrna, and carry you wherever you desire to go."

"May your wishes be horses," she said. "I like the sound of that."

He gave her a parting kiss and an affectionate little nip on the neck, and then he was gone.

IV

In 1845 it was raining. Vaylance slogged back toward
camp in the evening drizzle. On the way to the medical
tent, he passed the cook's station. Old, fat Temboyov was
boiling a vat of some kind of lumpy gray porridge and
bragging to a new recruit about how he'd looted a set of
porcelain tea cups. Vaylance surreptitiously relieved him
of a few of the saucers.

The crossmatch worked just as she said it would. He
was able to rule out any incompatible donors by watching
for red clumps against the white porcelain background.
The transfusion was a success, and Dr. Rimsky was up
and around on the third day. Vaylance moved back into
the medical tent, after spending two days sleeping in a
hollow tree.

"I'm relieved to see that you are not slinking into camp
looking like a drowned rat anymore," said Rimsky. "But
why didn't you just take your bed and claim illness? I
would have thought up some way to cover for you."

"Because no one would believe me," said Vaylance. "I
look healthier than the lot of you."

It was true. His complexion was almost rosy. Thanks
to the transfusion in Myrna's hospital, Vaylance was in
better health than he'd been in a long time.

"What's that tune you keep humming?" asked Dr.
Rimsky one night as they worked together in the tent.

"I think it's called 'The Waters of Time,'" answered
Vaylance, a little sadly.

V

Externally, Myrna's life did not change much after
Vaylance left. Work was still a series of frantic rush
orders interspersed with periods of boredom. She
brought a book on Russian history to the hospital to read
when she wasn't needed.

Shanty still moved his big feet with the grace of a fairy dancer, and she won another blue ribbon at the shows. But he could not carry her to the place she really desired to go. One Saturday afternoon as she brushed the saddle marks out of his hair, she pressed her face into his neck and wet his mane with tears. It was then that she heard him make the little noise in the throat, as horses do when they wish to express sympathy, and she realized she had allowed herself to love again.

That night when she went to sleep, she dreamed that she walked through a long, dark tunnel. She came out into a large grassy place under a starry night sky. A horse and rider approached, making no sound except the jingling of faint harness bells. As the figure drew closer, Myrna recognized the Cossack woman who carried the wolf cub. The dark-eyed woman stopped her horse and offered the cub to Myrna, who took it and held it close to her heart. The woman pointed to a rutted wagon road, then turned her horse and rode away making no noise of hooves but only the ringing of tiny bells.

Myrna followed the road indicated until she came to a wagon parked by the roadside. A man was just climbing up to the driver's seat. Myrna put the cub on the wagon bed and boosted herself up. There were men, some lying, some sitting up, in the wagon. The man nearest her was crudely bandaged about the head and he muttered softly to himself. The driver clucked to the horses and the wagon creaked on its way. Myrna tucked the small wolf under the light flannel she was wearing. She felt its cold nose against her bare breasts. It was getting colder, so she moved closer to the man and placed her back against the side of the wagon. They lurched along until the road turned in at a large tent. Horse were tethered in a small grove of oak trees, and there was a fire a little ways from the tent. The driver pulled up and said something in Russian. A sturdy, gray-haired man with a bandaged arm came out of the tent and spoke to the driver, who climbed down from his seat.

Myrna reached for the wolf cub and found it was missing.

She looked down the front of her flannel gown and saw that in the hollow between her breasts, her little patch of gray fur was denser. Before she had time to think about this, she heard a voice she recognized from inside the tent. She jumped ⏤wn from the wagon, and, ignoring the gray-haired man who spoke to her, ducked under the flap and entered.

Inside, in the lantern light, she saw him, with his back toward her, bending over a patient. He turned to look her way and his mouth fell open in astonishment so that his blood teeth showed.

"Myrna!" he cried, and stepping around a cot, he hugged her to his white, blood-stained apron, then held her back to look at her.

"Like all dreamwalkers, you have come ill-prepared," he said, plucking at her flannel night gown. "And barefoot too."

She looked down past her ruffled hem to where her bare toes peeked out. He rummaged in a corner of the tent and tossed her a wool shirt, a pair of trousers and two heavy-knit woolen socks.

"This will have to do for now," he said. "We have incoming wounded and I have work to do." He was already busy with scissors, cutting back the sleeve of a soldier's uniform.

Myrna saw his surgical tools—forceps, scalpels, needles—all lying in neat order on a dirty piece of linen.

"You could stand to learn a few things about asepsis," she said, and made a mental note that she would have to teach him sterile technique. She hunted until she found a pot and water to boil, and took it out to put on the fire. Then she returned to where Vaylance bent over his patient, speaking soothing Russian phrases, as he pried at a musket ball in the ragged flesh. She found the bandaging cloth and made ready to assist him.

*Not only is this classic story probably the first ever writ-
ten about an alien vampire, it was also the first story
sold by the late C. L. Moore, who became one of the first
important female SF writers. That was over sixty years
ago. Science fiction—and vampires—have never been the
same since.*

Shambleau

C.L. MOORE

*Man has conquered space before. You may be sure of
that. Somewhere beyond the Egyptians, in that dimness
out of which come echoes of half-mythical names—Atlan-
tis, Mu—somewhere back of history's first beginnings
there must have been an age when mankind like us today,
built cities of steel to house its star-roving ships and knew
the names of the planets in their own native tongues—
heard Venus' people call their wet world "Sha-ardol" in
that soft, sweet, slurring speech and mimicked Mars' gut-
tural "Lakkdiz" from the harsh tongues of Mars' dryland
dwellers. You may be sure of it. Man has conquered
Space before, and out of that conquest faint, faint echoes
run still through a world that has forgotten the very fact
of a civilization which must have been as mighty as our
own. There have been too many myths and legends for
us to doubt it. The myth of the Medusa, for instance, can
never have had its roots in the soil of Earth. That tale
of the snake-haired Gorgon whose gaze turned the gazer
to stone never originated about any creature that Earth*

231

nourished. And those ancient Greeks who told the story must have remembered, dimly and half believing, a tale of antiquity about some strange being from one of the outlying planets their remotest ancestors once trod.

"Shambleau! Ha . . . Shambleau!" The wild hysteria of the mob rocketed from wall to wall of Lakkdarol's narrow streets and the storming of heavy boots over the slag-red pavement made an ominous undernote to that swelling bay, "Shambleau! Shambleau!"

Northwest Smith heard it coming and stepped into the nearest doorway, laying a wary hand on his heat-gun's grip, and his colorless eyes narrowed. Strange sounds were common enough in the streets of Earth's latest colony on Mars—a raw, red little town where anything might happen, and very often did. But Northwest Smith, whose name is known and respected in every dive and wild outpost on a dozen wild planets, was a cautious man, despite his reputation. He set his back against the wall and gripped his pistol, and heard the rising shout come nearer and nearer.

Then into his range of vision flashed a red running figure, dodging like a hunted hare from shelter to shelter in the narrow street. It was a girl—a berry-brown girl in a single tattered garment whose scarlet burnt the eyes with its brilliance. She ran wearily, and he could hear her gasping breath from where he stood. As she came into view he saw her hesitate and lean one hand against the wall for support, and glance wildly around for shelter. She must not have seen him in the depths of the doorway, for as the bay of the mob grew louder and the pounding of feet sounded almost at the corner she gave a despairing little moan and dodged into the recess at his very side.

When she saw him standing there, tall and leather-brown, hand on his heat-gun, she sobbed once, inarticulately, and collapsed at his feet, a huddle of burning scarlet and bare, brown limbs.

Smith had not seen her face, but she was a girl, and

sweetly made and in danger; and though he had not the
reputation of a chivalrous man, something in her hopeless huddle at his feet touched that chord of sympathy
for the underdog that stirs in every Earthman, and he
pushed her gently into the corner behind him and jerked
out his gun, just as the first of the running mob rounded
the corner.

It was a motley crowd, Earthmen and Martians and a
sprinkling of Venusian swampmen and strange, nameless
denizens of unnamed planets—a typical Lakkdarol mob.
When the first of them turned the corner and saw the
empty street before them there was a faltering in the
rush and the foremost spread out and began to search
the doorways on both sides of the street.

"Looking for something?" Smith's sardonic call
sounded clear above the clamor of the mob.

They turned. The shouting died for a moment as they
took in the scene before them—tall Earthman in the
space-explorer's leathern garb, all one color from the
burning of savage suns save for the sinister pallor of his
no-colored eyes in a scarred and resolute face, gun in
his steady hand and the scarlet girl crouched behind
him, panting.

The foremost of the crowd—a burly Earthman in tattered leather from which the Patrol insignia had been
ripped away—stared for a moment with a strange expression of incredulity on his face overspreading the savage
exultation of the chase. Then he let loose a deep-throated
bellow, "Shambleau!" and lunged forward. Behind him
the mob took up the cry again, "Shambleau! Shambleau!
Shambleau!" and surged after.

Smith, lounging negligently against the wall, arms
folded and gunhand draped over his left forearm, looked
incapable of swift motion, but at the leader's first forward
step the pistol swept in a practiced half-circle and the
dazzle of blue-white heat leaping from its muzzle seared
an arc in the slag pavement at his feet. It was an old
gesture, and not a man in the crowd but understood it.
The foremost recoiled swiftly against the surge of those

in the rear, and for a moment there was confusion as
the two tides met and struggled. Smith's mouth curled
into a grim curve as he watched. The man in the muti-
lated Patrol uniform lifted a threatening fist and stepped
to the very edge of the deadline, while the crowd rocked
to and fro behind him.

"Are you crossing that line?" queried Smith in an ominously gentle voice.

"We want that girl!"

"Come and get her!" Recklessly Smith grinned into
his face. He saw danger there, but his defiance was not
the foolhardy gesture . seemed. An expert psychologist
of mobs from long experience, he sensed no murder
here. Not a gun had appeared in any hand in the crowd.
They desired the girl with an inexplicable bloodthirstiness
he was at a loss to understand, but toward himself he
sensed no such fury. A mauling he might expect, but his
life was in no danger. Guns would have appeared before
now if they were coming out at all. So he grinned in the
man's angry face and leaned lazily against the wall.

Behind their self-appointed leader the crowd milled
impatiently, and threatening voices began to rise again.
Smith heard the girl moan at his feet.

"What do you want with her?" he demanded.

"She's Shambleau! Shambleau, you fool! Kick her out
of there—we'll take care of her!"

"I'm taking care of her," drawled Smith.

"She's Shambleau, I tell you! Damn your hide, man,
we never let those things live! Kick her out here!"

The repeated name had no meaning to him, but
Smith's innate stubbornness rose defiantly as the crowd
surged forward to the very edge of the arc, their clamor
growing louder, "Shambleau! Kick her out here! Give us
Shambleau! Shambleau!"

Smith dropped his indolent pose like a cloak and
planted both feet wide, swinging up his gun threaten-
ingly. "Keep back!" he yelled. "She's mine! Keep back!"

He had no intention of using that heat-beam. He knew
by now that they would not kill him unless he started

the gunplay himself, and he did not mean to give up his life for any girl alive. But a severe mauling he expected, and he braced himself instinctively as the mob heaved within itself.

To his astonishment a thing happened then that he had never known to happen before. At his shouted defiance the foremost of the mob—those who had heard him clearly—drew back a little, not in alarm but evidently surprised. The ex-Patrolman said, "Yours! She's *yours?*" in a voice from which puzzlement crowded out the anger.

Smith spread his booted legs wide before the crouching figure and flourished his gun.

"Yes," he said. "And I'm keeping her! Stand back there!"

The man stared at him wordlessly, and horror, disgust and incredulity mingled on his weather-beaten face. The incredulity triumphed for a moment and he said again, *"Yours!"*

Smith nodded defiance.

The man stepped back suddenly, unutterable contempt in his very pose. He waved an arm to the crowd and said loudly, "It's—his!" and the press melted away, gone silent, too, and the look of contempt spread from face to face.

The ex-Patrolman spat on the slag-paved street and turned his back indifferently. "Keep her, then," he advised briefly over one shoulder. "But don't let her out again in this town!"

Smith stared in perplexity almost open-mouthed as the suddenly scornful mob began to break up. His mind was in a whirl. That such bloodthirsty animosity should vanish in a breath he could not believe. And the curious mingling of contempt and disgust on the faces he saw baffled him even more. Lakkdarol was anything but a puritan town—it did not enter his head for a moment that his claiming the brown girl as his own had caused that strangely shocked revulsion to spread through the crowd. No, it was something more deeply-rooted than that.

Instinctive, instant disgust had been in the faces he saw—they would have looked less so if he had admitted cannibalism or *Pharol*-worship.

And they were leaving his vicinity as swiftly as if whatever unknowing sin he had committed were contagious. The street was emptying as rapidly as it had filled. He saw a sleek Venusian glance back over his shoulder as he turned the corner and sneer, "Shambleau!" and the word awoke a new line of speculation in Smith's mind. Shambleau! Vaguely of French origin, it must be. And strange enough to hear it from the lips of Venusians and Martian drylanders, but it was their use of it that puzzled him more. "We never let those things live," the ex-Patrolman had said. It reminded him dimly of something . . . an ancient line from some writing in his own tongue . . . "Thou shalt not suffer a witch to live." He smiled to himself at the similarity, and simultaneously was aware of the girl at his elbow.

She had risen soundlessly. He turned to face her, sheathing his gun, and stared at first with curiosity and then in the entirely frank openness with which men regard that which is not wholly human. For she was not. He knew it at a glance, though the brown, sweet body was shaped like a woman's and she wore the garment of scarlet—he saw it was leather—with an ease that few unhuman beings achieve toward clothing. He knew it from the moment he looked into her eyes, and a shiver of unrest went over him as he met them. They were frankly green as young grass, with slit-like, feline pupils that pulsed unceasingly, and there was a look of dark, animal wisdom in their depths—that look of the beast which sees more than man.

There was no hair upon her face—neither brows nor lashes, and he would have sworn that the tight scarlet turban bound around her head covered baldness. She had three fingers and a thumb, and her feet had four digits apiece too, and all sixteen of them were tipped with round claws that sheathed back into the flesh like a cat's. She ran her tongue over her lips—a thin, pink,

flat tongue as feline as her eyes—and spoke with difficulty. He felt that that throat and tongue had never been
shaped for human speech.

"Not—afraid now," she said softly, and her little teeth
were white and pointed as a kitten's.

"What did they want you for?" he asked her curiously.
"What had you done? Shambleau . . . is that your name?"

"I—not talk your—speech," she demurred hesitantly.

"Well, try to—I want to know. Why were they chasing
you? Will you be safe on the street now, or hadn't you
better get indoors somewhere? They looked dangerous."

"I—go with you." She brought it out with difficulty.

"Say you!" Smith grinned. "What are you, anyhow?
You look like a kitten to me."

"Shambleau." She said it somberly.

"Where d'you live? Are you a Martian?"

"I come from—from far—from long ago—far country—"

"Wait!" laughed Smith. "You're getting your wires
crossed. You're not a Martian?"

She drew herself up very straight beside him, lifting
the turbaned head, and there was something queenly in
the poise of her.

"Martian?" she said scornfully. "My people—are—
are—you have no word. Your speech—hard for me."

"What's yours? I might know it—try me."

She lifted her head and met his eyes squarely, and
there was in hers a subtle amusement—he could have
sworn it.

"Some day I—speak to you in—my own language,"
she promised, and the pink tongue flicked out over her
lips, swiftly, hungrily.

Approaching footsteps on the red pavement interrupted Smith's reply. A dryland Martian came past, reeling a little and exuding an aroma of *segir*-whisky, the
Venusian brand. When he caught the red flash of the
girl's tatters he turned his head sharply, and as his *segir*-
steeped brain took in the fact of her presence he lurched

toward the recess unsteadily, bawling, "Shambleau, by *Pharol!* Shambleau!" and reached out a clutching hand.

Smith struck it aside contemptuously.

"On your way, drylander," he advised.

The man drew back and stared, bleary-eyed.

"Yours, eh?" he croaked. "*Zut!* You're welcome to it!" And like the ex-Patrolman before him he spat on the pavement and turned away, muttering harshly in the blasphemous tongue of the drylands.

Smith watched him shuffle off, and there was a crease between his colorless eyes, a nameless unease rising within him.

"Come on," he said abruptly to the girl. "If this sort of thing is going to happen we'd better get indoors. Where shall I take you?"

"With—you," she murmured.

He stared down into the flat green eyes. Those ceaselessly pulsing pupils disturbed him, but it seemed to him, vaguely, that behind the animal shallows of her gaze was a shutter—a closed barrier that might at any moment open to reveal the very deeps of that dark knowledge he sensed there.

Roughly he said again, "Come on, then," and stepped down into the street.

She pattered along a pace or two behind him, making no effort to keep up with his long strides, and though Smith—as men know from Venus to Jupiter's moons—walks as softly as a cat, even in spacemen's boots, the girl at his heels slid like a shadow over the rough pavement, making so little sound that even the lightness of his footsteps was loud in the empty street.

Smith chose the less frequented ways of Lakkdarol, and somewhat shamefacedly thanked his nameless gods that his lodgings were not far away, for the few pedestrians he met turned and stared after the two with that by now familiar mingling of horror and contempt which he was as far as ever from understanding.

The room he had engaged was a single cubicle in a

lodging-house on the edge of the city. Lakkdarol, raw camp-town that it was in those days, could have furnished little better anywhere within its limits, and Smith's errand there was not one he wished to advertise. He had slept in worse places than this before, and knew that he would do so again.

There was no one in sight when he entered, and the girl slipped up the stairs at his heels and vanished through the door, shadowy, unseen by anyone in the house. Smith closed the door and leaned his broad shoulders against the panels, regarding her speculatively.

She took in what little the room had to offer in a glance—frowsy bed, rickety table, mirror hanging unevenly and cracked against the wall, unpainted chairs—a typical camp-town room in an Earth settlement abroad. She accepted its poverty in that single glance, dismissed it, then crossed to the window and leaned out for a moment, gazing across the low roof-tops toward the barren countryside beyond, red slag under the late afternoon sun.

"You can stay here," said Smith abruptly, "until I leave town. I'm waiting here for a friend to come in from Venus. Have you eaten?"

"Yes," said the girl quickly. "I shall—need no—food for—a while."

"Well—" Smith glanced around the room. "I'll be in sometime tonight. You can go or stay just as you please. Better lock the door behind me."

With no more formality than that he left her. The door closed and he heard the key turn, and smiled to himself. He did not expect, then, ever to see her again.

He went down the steps and out into the late-slanting sunlight with a mind so full of other matters that the brown girl receded very quickly into the background. Smith's errand in Lakkdarol, like most of his errands, is better not spoken of. Man lives as he must, and Smith's living was a perilous affair outside the law and ruled by the ray-gun only. It is enough to say that the shipping-port and its cargoes outbound interested him deeply just now, and that the friend he awaited was Yarol the Venusian, in that swift little Edsel ship the *Maid* that can flash from world to world with a derisive speed that laughs at Patrol boats and leaves pursuers floundering in the ether far behind. Smith and Yarol and the *Maid* were a trinity that had caused the Patrol leaders much worry and many gray hairs in the past, and the future looked very bright to Smith himself that evening as he left his lodging-house.

Lakkdarol roars by night, as Earthmen's camp-towns have a way of doing on every planet where Earth's outposts are, and it was beginning lustily as Smith went down among the awakening lights toward the center of town. His business there does not concern us. He mingled with the crowds where the lights were brightest, and there was the click of ivory counters and the mingle of silver, and red *segir* gurgled invitingly from black Venusian bottles, and much later Smith strolled homeward under the moving moons of Mars, and if the street wavered a little under his feet now and then—why, that is only understandable. Not even Smith could drink red *segir* at every bar from the *Martian Lamb* to the *New Chicago* and remain entirely steady on his feet. But he found his way back with very little difficulty—considering—and spent a good five minutes hunting for his key before he remembered he had left it in the inner lock for the girl.

He knocked then, and there was no sound of footsteps from within, but in a few moments the latch clicked and the door swung open. She retreated soundlessly before him as he entered, and took up her favorite place against the window, leaning back on the sill and outlined against the starry sky beyond. The room was in darkness.

Smith flipped the switch by the door and then leaned back against the panels, steadying himself. The cool night air had sobered him a little, and his head was clear enough—liquor went to Smith's feet, not his head, or he would never have come this far along the lawless way he had chosen. He lounged against the door now and regarded the girl in the sudden glare of the bulbs, blinding a little as much at the scarlet of her clothing as at the light.

"So you stayed," he said.

"I—waited," she answered softly, leaning farther back against the sill and clasping the rough wood with slim, three-fingered hands, pale brown against the darkness.

"Why?"

She did not answer that, but her mouth curved into a slow smile. On a woman it would have been reply enough—provocative, daring. On Shambleau there was something pitiful and horrible in it—so human on the face of one half-animal. And yet ... that sweet brown body curving so softly from the tatters of scarlet leather— the velvety texture of that brownness—the white-flashing smile ... Smith was aware of a stirring excitement within him. After all—time would be hanging heavy now until Yarol came.... Speculatively he allowed the steel-pale eyes to wander over her, with a slow regard that missed nothing. And when he spoke he was aware that his voice had deepened a little....

"Come here," he said.

She came forward slowly, on bare clawed feet that made no sound on the floor, and stood before him with downcast eyes and mouth trembling in that pitifully human smile. He took her by the shoulders—velvety soft shoulders, of a creamy smoothness that was not the texture of human flesh. A little tremor went over her, perceptibly, at the contact of his hands. Northwest Smith caught his breath suddenly and dragged her to him ... sweet yielding brownness in the circle of his arms ... heard her own breath catch and quicken as her velvety arms closed about his neck. And then he was looking down into her face, very near, and the green animal eyes met his with the pulsing pupils and the flicker of— something—deep behind their shallows—and through the rising clamor of his blood, even as he stooped his lips to hers, Smith felt something deep within him shudder away—inexplicable, instinctive, revolted. What it might be had no words to tell, but the very touch of her

was suddenly loathsome—so soft and velvet and unhuman—and it might have been an animal's face that lifted
itself to his mouth—the dark knowledge looked hungrily
from the darkness of those slit pupils—and for a mad
instant he knew that same wild, feverish revulsion he had
seen in the faces of the mob. . . .

"God!" he gasped, a far more ancient invocation
against evil than he realized, then or ever, and he ripped
her arms from his neck, swung her away with such a
force that she reeled half across the room. Smith fell
back against the door, breathing heavily, and stared at
her while the wild revolt died slowly within him.

She had fallen to the floor beneath the window, and
as she lay there against the wall with bent head he saw,
curiously, that her turban had slipped—the turban that
he had been so sure covered baldness—and a lock of
scarlet hair fell below the binding leather, hair as scarlet
as her garment, as unhumanly red as her eyes were
unhumanly green. He stared, and shook his head dizzily
and stared again, for it seemed to him that the thick
lock of crimson had moved, *squirmed* of itself against
her cheek.

At the contact of it her hands flew up and she tucked
it away with a very human gesture and then dropped her
head again into her hands. And from the deep shadow of
her fingers he thought she was staring up at him covertly.

Smith drew a deep breath and passed a hand across
his forehead. The inexplicable moment had gone as
quickly as it came—too swiftly for him to understand or
analyze it. "Got to lay off the *segir*," he told himself
unsteadily. Had he imagined that scarlet hair? After all,
she was no more than a pretty brown girl-creature from
one of the many half-human races peopling the planets.
No more than that, after all. A pretty little thing, but
animal. . . . He laughed a little shakily.

"No more of that," he said. "God knows I'm no angel,
but there's got to be a limit somewhere. Here." He
crossed to the bed and sorted out a pair of blankets from

the untidy heap, tossing them to the far corner of the room. "You can sleep there."

Wordlessly she rose from the floor and began to rearrange the blankets, the uncomprehending resignation of the animal eloquent in every line of her.

Smith had a strange dream that night. He thought he had awakened to a room full of darkness and moonlight and moving shadows, for the nearer moon of Mars was racing through the sky and everything on the planet below her was embued with a restless life in the dark. And something . . . some nameless, unthinkable *thing* . . . was coiled about his throat . . . something like a soft snake, wet and warm. It lay loose and light about his neck . . . and it was moving gently, very gently, with a soft, caressive pressure that sent little thrills of delight through every nerve and fiber of him, a perilous delight—beyond physical pleasure, deeper than joy of the mind. That warm softness was caressing the very roots of his soul with a terrible intimacy. The ecstasy of it left him weak, and yet he knew—in a flash of knowledge born of this impossible dream—that the soul should not be handled. . . . And with that knowledge a horror broke upon him, turning the pleasure into a rapture of revulsion, hateful, horrible—but still most foully sweet. He tried to lift his hands and tear the dream-monstrosity from his throat—tried but half-heartedly; for though his soul was revolted to its very deeps, yet the delight of his body was so great that his hands all but refused the attempt. But when at last he tried to lift his arms a cold shock went over him and he found that he could not stir . . . his body lay stony as marble beneath the blankets, a living marble that shuddered with a dreadful delight through every rigid vein.

The revulsion grew strong upon him as he struggled against the paralyzing dream—a struggle of soul against sluggish body—titanically, until the moving dark was streaked with blankness that clouded and closed about him at last and he sank back into the oblivion from which he had awakened.

Next morning, when the bright sunlight shining through Mars' clear thin air awakened him, Smith lay for a while trying to remember. The dream had been more vivid than reality, but he could not now quite recall . . . only that it had been more sweet and horrible than anything else in life. He lay puzzling for a while, until a soft sound from the corner aroused him from his thoughts and he sat up to see the girl lying in a catlike coil on her blankets, watching him with round, grave eyes. He regarded her somewhat ruefully.

"Morning," he said. "I've just had the devil of a dream. . . . Well, hungry?"

She shook her head silently, and he could have sworn there was a covert gleam of strange amusement in her eyes.

He stretched and yawned, dismissing the nightmare temporarily from his mind.

"What am I going to do with you?" he inquired, turning to more immediate matters. "I'm leaving here in a day or two and I can't take you along, you know. Where'd you come from in the first place?"

Again she shook her head.

"Not telling? Well, it's your own business. You can stay here until I give up the room. From then on you'll have to do your own worrying."

He swung his feet to the floor and reached for his clothes.

Ten minutes later, slipping the heat-gun into its holster at his thigh Smith turned to the girl. "There's food-concentrate in that box on the table. It ought to hold you until I get back. And you'd better lock the door again after I've gone."

Her wide, unwavering stare was his only answer, and he was not sure she had understood, but at any rate the lock clicked after him as before, and he went down the steps with a faint grin on his lips.

The memory of last night's extraordinary dream was

slipping from him, as such memories do, and by the time
he had reached the street the girl and the dream and all
of yesterday's happenings were blotted out by the sharp
necessities of the present.

Again the intricate business that had brought him here
claimed his attention. He went about it to the exclusion
of all else, and there was a good reason behind everything he did from the moment he stepped out into the
street until the time when he turned back again at evening; though had one chosen to follow him during the
day his apparently aimless rambling through Lakkdarol
would have seemed very pointless.

He must have spent two hours at the least idling by
the space-port, watching with sleepy, colorless eyes the
ships that came and went, the passengers, the vessels
lying at wait, the cargoes—particularly the cargoes. He
made the rounds of the town's saloons once more, consuming many glasses of varied liquors in the course of
the day and engaging in idle conversation with men of
all races and worlds, usually in their own languages, for
Smith was a linguist of repute among his contemporaries.
He heard the gossip of the spaceways, news from a dozen
planets of a thousand different events. He heard the latest joke about the Venusian Emperor and the latest
report on the Chino-Aryan war and the latest song hot
from the lips of Rose Robertson, whom every man on
the civilized planets adored as "the Georgia Rose." He
passed the day quite profitably, for his own purposes,
which do not concern us now, and it was not until late
evening, when he turned homeward again, that the
thought of the brown girl in his room took definite shape
in his mind, though it had been lurking there, formless
and submerged, all day.

He had no idea what comprised her usual diet, but he
bought a can of New York roast beef and one of Venusian
frog-broth and a dozen fresh canal-apples and two
pounds of that Earth lettuce that grows so vigorously in
the fertile canal-soil of Mars. He felt that she must surely
find something to her liking in this broad variety of edibles,

and—for his day had been very satisfactory—he hummed "The Green Hills of Earth" to himself in a surprisingly good baritone as he climbed the stairs.

The door was locked, as before, and he was reduced to kicking the lower panels gently with his boot, for his arms were full. She opened the door with that softness that was characteristic of her and stood regarding him in the semi-darkness as he stumbled to the table with his load. The room was unlit again.

"Why don't you turn on the lights?" he demanded irritably after he had barked his shin on the chair by the table in an effort to deposit his burden there.

"Light and—dark—they are alike—to me," she murmured.

"Cat eyes, eh? Well, you look the part. Here, I've brought you some dinner. Take your choice. Fond of roast beef? Or how about a little frog-broth?"

She shook her head and backed away a step.

"No," she said. "I can not—eat your food."

Smith's brows wrinkled. "Didn't you have any of the food tablets?"

Again the red turban shook negatively.

"Then you haven't had anything for—why, more than twenty-four hours! You must be starved."

"Not hungry," she denied.

"What can I find for you to eat, then? There's time yet if I hurry. You've got to eat, child."

"I shall—eat," she said softly. "Before long—I shall—feed. Have no—worry."

She turned away then and stood at the window, looking out over the moonlit landscape as if to end the conversation. Smith cast her a puzzled glance as he opened the can of roast beef. There had been an odd undernote in that assurance that, undefinably, he did not like. And the girl had teeth and tongue and presumably a fairly human digestive system, to judge from her human form. It was nonsense for her to pretend that he could find nothing that she could eat. She must have had some of the food concentrate after all, he decided, prying up the thermos lid of the inner container to release the long-sealed savor of the hot meat inside.

"Well, if you won't eat you won't," he observed philosophically as he poured hot broth and diced beef into the dishlike lid of the thermos can and extracted the spoon from its hiding-place between the inner and outer receptacles. She turned a little to watch him as he pulled up a rickety chair and sat down to the food, and after a while the realization that her green gaze was fixed so unwinkingly upon him made the man nervous, and he said between bites of creamy canal-apple, "Why don't you try a little of this? It's good."

"The food—I eat is—better," her soft voice told him in its hesitant murmur, and again he felt rather than heard a faint undernote of unpleasantness in the words. A sudden suspicion struck him as he pondered on that last remark—some vague memory of horror-tales told about campfires in the past—and he swung round in the chair to look at her, a tiny, creeping fear unaccountably arising. There had been that in her words—in her unspoken words, that menaced. . . .

She stood up beneath his gaze demurely, wide green eyes with their pulsing pupils meeting his without a falter. But her mouth was scarlet and her teeth were sharp. . . .

"What food do you eat?" he demanded. And then, after a pause, very softly, "Blood?"

She stared at him for a moment, uncomprehending; then something like amusement curled her lips and she said scornfully, "You think me—vampire, eh? No—I am Shambleau!"

Unmistakably there were scorn and amusement in her voice at the suggestion, but as unmistakably she knew what he meant—accepted it as a logical suspicion—vampires! Fairy-tales—but fairy tales this unhuman, outland creature was most familiar with. Smith was not a credulous man, nor a superstitious one, but he had seen too many strange things himself to doubt that the wildest legend might have a basis of fact. And there was something namelessly strange about her. . . .

He puzzled over it for a while between deep bites of the canal-apple. And though he wanted to question her about a great many things, he did not, for he knew how futile it would be.

He said nothing more until the meat was finished and another canal-apple had followed the first, and he had cleared away the meal by the simple expedient of tossing the empty can out of the window. Then he lay back in the chair and surveyed her from half-closed eyes, colorless in a face tanned like saddle-leather. And again he was conscious of the brown, soft curves of her, velvety-subtle arcs and planes of smooth flesh under the tatters of scarlet leather. Vampire she might be, unhuman she certainly was, but desirable beyond words as she sat submissive beneath his low regard, her red-turbaned head bent, her clawed fingers lying in her lap. They sat very still for a while, and the silence throbbed between them.

She was so like a woman—an Earth woman—sweet and submissive and demure, and softer than soft fur, if he could forget the three-fingered claws and the pulsing eyes—and that deeper strangeness beyond words. . . . (Had he dreamed that red lock of hair that moved? Had it been *segir* that woke the wild revulsion he knew when he held her in his arms? Why had the mob so thirsted for her?) He sat and stared, and despite the mystery of her and the half-suspicions that thronged his mind—for she was so beautifully soft and curved under those revealing tatters—he slowly realized that his pulses were mounting, became aware of a kindling within . . . brown girl-creature with downcast eyes . . . and then the lids lifted and the green flatness of a cat's gaze met his, and last night's revulsion woke swiftly again, like a warning

bell that clanged as their eyes met—animal, after all, too
sleek and soft for humanity, and that inner strangeness. . . .

Smith shrugged and sat up. His failings were legion,
but the weakness of the flesh was not among the major
ones. He motioned the girl to her pallet of blankets in
the corner and turned to his own bed.

From deeps of sound sleep he awoke much later. He
awoke suddenly and completely, and with that inner
excitement that presages something momentous. He
awoke to brilliant moonlight, turning the room so bright
that he could see the scarlet of the girl's rags as she sat
up on her pallet. She was awake, she was sitting with
her shoulder half turned to him and her head bent, and
some warning instinct crawled coldly up his spine as he
watched what she was doing. And yet it was a very ordinary thing for a girl to do—any girl, anywhere. She was
unbinding her turban. . . .

He watched, not breathing, a presentiment of something horrible stirring in his brain, inexplicably. . . . The
red folds loosened, and—he knew then that he had not
dreamed—again a scarlet lock swung down against her
cheek . . . a hair, was it? a lock of hair? . . . thick as a thick
worm it fell, plumply, against that smooth cheek . . . more
scarlet than blood and thick as a crawling worm . . . and
like a worm it crawled.

Smith rose on an elbow, not realizing the motion, and
fixed an unwinking stare, with a sort of sick, fascinated
incredulity, on that—that lock of hair. He had not
dreamed. Until now he had taken it for granted that it
was the *segir* which had made it seem to move on that
evening before. But now . . . it was lengthening, stretching, moving of itself. It must be hair, but it *crawled*; with
a sickening life of its own it squirmed down against her
cheek, caressingly, revoltingly, impossibly. . . . Wet, it
was, and round and thick and shining. . . .

She unfastened the fast fold and whipped the turban

off. From what he saw then Smith would have turned
his eyes away—and he had looked on dreadful things
before, without flinching—but he could not stir. He
could only lie there on his elbow staring at the mass
of scarlet, squirming—worms, hairs, what?—that writhed
over her head in a dreadful mockery of ringlets. And it
was lengthening, falling, somehow growing before his
eyes, down over her shoulders in a spilling cascade, a
mass that even at the beginning could never have been
hidden under the skull-tight turban she had worn. He
was beyond wondering, but he realized that. And still it
squirmed and lengthened and fell, and she shook it out
in a horrible travesty of a woman shaking out her
unbound hair—until the unspeakable tangle of it—twisting, writhing, obscenely scarlet—hung to her waist and
beyond, and still lengthened, an endless mass of crawling
horror that until now somehow, impossibly, had been
hidden under the tightbound turban. It was like a nest
of blind, restless red worms . . . it was—it was like naked
entrails endowed with an unnatural aliveness, terrible
beyond words.

Smith lay in the shadows, frozen without and within in
a sick numbness that came of utter shock and revulsion.

She shook out the obscene, unspeakable tangle over
her shoulders, and somehow he knew that she was going
to turn in a moment and that he must meet her eyes.
The thought of that meeting stopped his heart with
dread, more awfully than anything else in this nightmare
horror; for nightmare it must be, surely. But he knew
without trying that he could not wrench his eyes away—
the sickened fascination of that sight held him
motionless, and somehow there was a certain beauty. . . .

Her head was turning. The crawling awfulnesses rippled and squirmed at the motion, writhing thick and wet
and shining over the soft brown shoulders about which
they fell now in obscene cascades that all but hid her
body. Her head was turning. Smith lay numb. And very

slowly he saw the round of her cheek foreshorten and
her profile come into view, all the scarlet horrors twisting
ominously, and the profile shortened in turn and her
full face came slowly round toward the bed—moonlight
shining brilliantly as day on the pretty girl-face, demure
and sweet, framed in tangled obscenity that crawled. . . .

The green eyes met his. He felt a perceptible shock,
and a shudder rippled down his paralyzed spine, leaving
an icy numbness in its wake. He felt the goose-flesh
rising. But that numbness and cold horror he scarcely
realized, for the green eyes were locked with his in a
long, long look that somehow presaged nameless things—
not altogether unpleasant things—the voiceless voice of
her mind assailing him with little murmurous promises. . . .

For a moment he went down into a blind abyss of
submission; and then somehow the very sight of that
obscenity in eyes that did not then realize they saw it,
was dreadful enough to draw him out of the seductive
darkness . . . the sight of her crawling and alive with
unnamable horror.

She rose, and down about her in a cascade fell the
squirming scarlet of—of what grew upon her head. It
fell in a long, alive cloak to her bare feet on the floor,
hiding her in a wave of dreadful, wet, writhing life. She
put up her hands and like a swimmer she parted the
waterfall of it, tossing the masses back over her shoulders
to reveal her own brown body, sweetly curved. She
smiled exquisitely, and in starting waves back from her
forehead and down about her in a hideous background
writhed the snaky wetness of her living tresses. And
Smith knew that he looked upon Medusa.

The knowledge of that—the realization of vast back-
grounds reaching into misted history—shook him out of
his frozen horror for a moment, and in that moment he
met her eyes again, smiling, green as glass in the moonlight, half hooded under drooping lids. Through the
twisting scarlet she held out her arms. And there was

something soul-shakingly desirable about her, so that all
the blood surged to his head suddenly and he stumbled
to his feet like a sleeper in a dream as she swayed toward
him, infinitely graceful, infinitely sweet in her cloak of
living horror.

And somehow there was beauty in it, the wet scarlet
writhings with moonlight sliding and shining along the
thick, worm-round tresses and losing itself in the masses
only to glint again and move silvery along writhing tendrils—an awful, shuddering beauty more dreadful than
any ugliness could be.

But all this, again, he but half realized, for the insidious murmur was coiling again through his brain, promising, caressing, alluring, sweeter than honey; and the
green eyes that held his were clear and burning like the
depths of a jewel, and behind the pulsing slits of darkness
he was staring into a greater dark that held all things. . . .
He had known—dimly he had known when he first gazed
into those flat animal shallows that behind them lay
this—all beauty and terror, all horror and delight, in the
infinite darkness upon which her eyes opened like windows, paned with emerald glass.

Her lips moved, and in a murmur that blended indisti-
guishably with the silence and the sway of her body and
the dreadful sway of her—her hair—she whispered—
very softly, very passionately, "I shall—speak to you
now—in my own tongue,—oh, beloved!"

And in her living cloak she swayed to him, the murmur
swelling seductive and caressing in his innermost brain—
promising, compelling, sweeter than sweet. His flesh
crawled to the horror of her, but it was a perverted revulsion that clasped what it loathed. His arms slid round her
under the sliding cloak, wet, wet and warm and hideously
alive—and the sweet velvet body was clinging to his, her
arms locked about his neck—and with a whisper and a
rush the unspeakable horror closed about them both.

In nightmares until he died he remembered that

moment when the living tresses of Shambleau first folded him in their embrace. A nauseous, smothering odor as the wetness shut around him—thick, pulsing worms clasping every inch of his body, sliding, writhing, their wetness and warmth striking through his garments as if he stood naked to their embrace.

All this in a graven instant—and after that a tangled flash of conflicting sensation before oblivion closed over him. For he remembered the dream—and knew it for nightmare reality now, and the sliding, gently moving caresses of those wet, warm worms upon his flesh was an ecstasy above words—that deeper ecstasy that strikes beyond the body and beyond the mind and tickles the very roots of the soul with unnatural delight. So he stood, rigid as marble, as helplessly stony as any of Medusa's victims in ancient legends were, while the terrible pleasure of Shambleau thrilled and shuddered through every fiber of him; through every atom of his body and the intangible atoms of what men call the soul, through all that was Smith the dreadful pleasure ran. And it was truly dreadful. Dimly he knew it, even as his body answered to the root-deep ecstasy, a foul and dreadful wooing from which his very soul shuddered away—and yet in the innermost depths of that soul some grinning traitor shivered with delight. But deeply, behind all this, he knew horror and revulsion and despair beyond telling, while the intimate caresses crawled obscenely in the secret places of his soul—knew that the soul should not be handled—and shook with the perilous pleasure through it all.

And this conflict and knowledge, this mingling of rapture and revulsion all took place in the flashing of a moment while the scarlet worms coiled and crawled upon him, sending deep, obscene tremors of that infinite pleasure into every atom that made up Smith. And he could not stir in that slimy, ecstatic embrace—and a weakness was flooding that grew deeper after each succeeding wave of intense delight, and the traitor in his soul strengthened and drowned out the revulsion—and something within him ceased to struggle as he sank wholly into a blazing darkness that was oblivion to all else but that devouring rapture. . . .

The young Venusian climbing the stairs to his friend's lodging-room pulled out his key absent-mindedly, a pucker forming between his fine brows. He was slim, as all Venusians are, as fair and sleek as any of them, and as with most of his countrymen the look of cherubic innocence on his face was wholly deceptive. He had the face of a fallen angel, without Lucifer's majesty to redeem it; for a black devil grinned in his eyes and there were faint lines of ruthlessness and dissipation about his mouth to tell of the long years behind him that had run the gamut of experiences and made his name, next to Smith's, the most hated and the most respected in the records of the Patrol.

He mounted the stairs now with a puzzled frown between his eyes. He had come into Lakkdarol on the noon liner—the *Maid* in her hold very skillfully disguised with paint and otherwise—to find in lamentable disorder the affairs he had expected to be settled. And cautious inquiry elicited the information that Smith had not been seen for three days. That was not like his friend—he had never failed before, and the two stood to lose not only a large sum of money but also their personal safety by the inexplicable lapse on the part of Smith. Yarol could think of one solution only: fate had at last caught up with his friend. Nothing but physical disability could explain it.

Still puzzling, he fitted his key in the lock and swung the door open.

In that first moment, as the door opened, he sensed something very wrong. . . . The room was darkened, and for a while he could see nothing, but at the first breath he scented a strange, unnamable odor, half sickening, half sweet. And deep stirrings of ancestral memory awoke within him—ancient swamp-born memories from Venusian ancestors far away and long ago. . . .

Yarol laid his hand on his gun, lightly, and opened the door wider. In the dimness all he could see at first was a curious mound in the far corner. . . . Then his eyes grew accustomed to the dark, and he saw it more clearly, a mound that somehow heaved and stirred within itself. . . . A mound of—he caught his breath sharply—a mound like a mass of entrails, living, moving, writhing with an unspeakable aliveness. Then a hot Venusian oath broke from his lips and he cleared the door-sill in a swift stride, slammed the door and set his back against it, gun ready in his hand, although his flesh crawled—for he *knew*. . . .

"Smith!" he said softly, in a voice thick with horror. "Northwest!"

The moving mass stirred—shuddered—sank back into crawling quiescence again.

"Smith! Smith!" The Venusian's voice was gentle and insistent, and it quivered a little with terror.

An impatient ripple went over the whole mass of aliveness in the corner. It stirred again, reluctantly, and then tendril by writhing tendril it began to part itself and fall aside, and very slowly the brown of a spaceman's leather appeared beneath it, all slimed and shining.

"Smith! Northwest!" Yarol's persistent whisper came again, urgently, and with a dreamlike slowness the leather garments moved . . . a man sat up in the midst of the writhing worms, a man who once, long ago, might have been Northwest Smith. From head to foot he was slimy from the embrace of the crawling horror about him. His face was that of some creature beyond humanity—dead-alive, fixed in a gray stare, and the look of terrible ecstasy that overspread it seemed to come from somewhere far within, a faint reflection from immeasurable distances beyond the flesh. And as there is mystery and magic in the moonlight which is after all but a reflection of the

everyday sun, so in that gray face turned to the door was
a terror unnamable and sweet, a reflection of ecstasy
beyond the understanding of any who have known only
earthly ecstasy themselves. And as he sat there turning
a blank, eyeless face to Yarol the red worms writhed
ceaselessly about him, very gently, with a soft, caressive
motion that never slacked.

"Smith ... come here! Smith ... get up ... Smith,
Smith!" Yarol's whisper hissed in the silence, commanding, urgent—but he made no move to leave the door.

And with a dreadful slowness, like a dead man rising,
Smith stood up in the nest of slimy scarlet. He swayed
drunkenly on his feet, and two or three crimson tendrils
came writhing up his legs to the knees and wound themselves there, supportingly, moving with a ceaseless caress
that seemed to give him some hidden strength, for he
said then, without inflection,

"Go away. Go away. Leave me alone." And the dead
ecstatic face never changed.

"Smith!" Yarol's voice was desperate. "Smith, listen!
Smith, can't you hear me?"

"Go away," the monotonous voice said. "Go away. Go
away. Go—"

"Not unless you come too. Can't you hear? Smith!
Smith! I'll—"

He hushed in mid-phrase, and once more the ancestral
prickle of race-memory shivered down his back, for the
scarlet mass was moving again, violently, rising. ...

Yarol pressed back against the door and gripped his
gun, and the name of a god he had forgotten years ago
rose to his lips unbidden. For he knew what was coming
next, and the knowledge was more dreadful than any
ignorance could have been.

The red, writhing mass rose higher, and the tendrils
parted and a human face looked out—no, half human,

with green cat-eyes that shone in that dimness like lighted jewels, compellingly. . . .

Yarol breathed "Shar!" again, and flung up an arm across his face, and the tingle of meeting that green gaze for even an instant went thrilling through him perilously.

"Smith!" he called in despair. "Smith, can't you hear me?"

"Go away," said that voice that was not Smith's. "Go away."

And somehow, although he dared not look, Yarol knew that the—the other—had parted those worm-thick tresses and stood there in all the human sweetness of the brown, curved woman's body, cloaked in living horror. And he felt the eyes upon him, and something was crying insistently in his brain to lower that shielding arm. . . . He was lost—he knew it, and the knowledge gave him that courage which comes from despair. The voice in his brain was growing, swelling, deafening him with a roaring command that all but swept him before it—command to lower that arm—to meet the eyes that opened upon darkness—to submit—and a promise, murmurous and sweet and evil beyond words, of pleasure to come. . . .

But somehow he kept his head—somehow, dizzily, he was gripping his gun in his upflung hand—somehow, incredibly, crossing the narrow room with averted face, groping for Smith's shoulder. There was a moment of blind fumbling in emptiness, and then he found it, and gripped the leather that was slimy and dreadful and wet—and simultaneously he felt something loop gently about his ankle and a shock of repulsive pleasure went through him, and then another coil, and another, wound about his feet. . . .

Yarol set his teeth and gripped the shoulder hard, and his hand shuddered of itself, for the feel of that leather was slimy as the worms about his ankles, and a faint tingle of obscene delight went through him from the contact.

That caressive pressure on his legs was all he could feel, and the voice in his brain drowned out all other sounds, and his body obeyed him reluctantly—but somehow he gave one heave of tremendous effort and swung Smith, stumbling, out of that nest of horror. The twining tendrils ripped loose with a little sucking sound, and the whole mass quivered and reached after, and then Yarol forgot his friend utterly and turned his whole being to the hopeless task of freeing himself. For only a part of him was fighting, now—only a part of him struggled against the twining obscenities, and in his innermost brain the sweet, seductive murmur sounded, and his body clamored to surrender. . . .

"*Shar! Shar y'danis . . . Shar mor'la-rol—*" prayed Yarol, gasping and half unconscious that he spoke, boy's prayers that he had forgotten years ago, and with his back half turned to the central mass he kicked desperately with his heavy boots at the red, writhing worms about him. They gave back before him, quivering and curling themselves out of reach, and though he knew that more were reaching for his throat from behind, at least he could go on struggling until he was forced to meet those eyes. . . .

He stamped and kicked and stamped again, and for one instant he was free of the slimy grip as the bruised worms curled back from his heavy feet, and he lurched away dizzily, sick with revulsion and despair as he fought off the coils, and then he lifted his eyes and saw the cracked mirror on the wall. Dimly in its reflection he could see the writhing scarlet horror behind him, cat face peering out with its demure girl-smile, dreadfully human, and all the red tendrils reaching after him. And remembrance of something he had read long ago swept incongruously over him, and the gasp of relief and hope that he gave shook for a moment the grip of the command in his brain.

Without pausing for a breath he swung the gun over his shoulder, the reflected barrel in line with the reflected horror in the mirror, and flicked the catch.

In the mirror he saw its blue flame leap in a dazzling spate across the dimness, full into the midst of that squirming, reaching mass behind him. There was a hiss and a blaze and a high, thin scream of inhuman malice and despair—the flame cut a wide arc and went out as the gun fell from his hand, and Yarol pitched forward to the floor.

Northwest Smith opened his eyes to Martian sunlight streaming thinly through the dingy window. Something wet and cold was slapping his face, and the familiar fiery sting of *segir*-whisky burnt his throat.

"Smith!" Yarol's voice was saying from far away. "N. W.! Wake up, damn you! Wake up!"

"I'm—awake," Smith managed to articulate thickly. "Wha's the matter?"

Then a cup-rim was thrust against his teeth and Yarol said irritably, "Drink it, you fool!"

Smith swallowed obediently and more of the fire-hot *segir* flowed down his grateful throat. It spread a warmth through his body that awakened him from the numbness that had gripped him until now, and helped a little toward driving out the all-devouring weakness he was becoming aware of slowly. He lay still for a few minutes while the warmth of the whisky went through him, and memory sluggishly began to permeate his brain with the spread of the *segir*. Nightmare memories . . . sweet and terrible . . . memories of—

"God!" gasped Smith suddenly, and tried to sit up. Weakness smote him like a blow, and for an instant the room wheeled as he fell back against something firm and warm—Yarol's shoulder. The Venusian's arm supported

him while the room steadied, and after a while he twisted
a little and stared into the other's black gaze.

Yarol was holding him with one arm and finishing the
mug of *segir* himself, and the black eyes met his over
the rim and crinkled into sudden laughter, half hysterical
after that terror that was passed.

"By *Pharol!*" gasped Yarol, choking into his mug. "By
Pharol, N. W.! I'm never gonna let you forget this! Next
time you have to drag me out of a mess I'll say—"

"Let it go," said Smith. "What's been going on?
How—"

"Shambleau." Yarol's laughter died. "Shambleau! What
were you doing with a thing like that?"

"What was it?" Smith asked soberly.

"Mean to say you didn't know? But where'd you find
it? How—"

"Suppose you tell me first what you know," said Smith
firmly. "And another swig of that *segir*, too, please. I
need it."

"Can you hold the mug now? Feel better?"

"Yeah—some. I can hold it—thanks. Now go on."

"Well—I don't know just where to start. They call
them Shambleau—"

"Good God, is there more than one?"

"It's a—a sort of race, I think, one of the very oldest.
Where they come from nobody knows. The name sounds
a little French, doesn't it? But it goes back beyond the
start of history. There have always been Shambleau."

"I never heard of 'em."

"Not many people have. And those who know don't
care to talk about it much."

"Well, half this town knows. I hadn't any idea what
they were talking about, then. And I still don't understand, but—"

"Yes, it happens like this, sometimes. They'll appear,
and the news will spread and the town will get together

and hunt them down, and after that—well, the story doesn't get around very far. It's too—too unbelievable."

"But—my God, Yarol!—what was it? Where'd it come from? How—"

"Nobody knows just where they come from. Another planet—maybe some undiscovered one. Some say Venus—I know there are some rather awful legends of them handed down in our family—that's how I've heard about it. And the minute I opened that door, awhile back—I—I think I knew that smell. . . ."

"But—what *are* they?"

"God knows. Not human, though they have the human form. Or that may be only an illusion . . . or maybe I'm crazy. I don't know. They're a species of the vampire— or maybe the vampire is a species of—of them. Their normal form must be that—that mass, and in that form they draw nourishment from the—I suppose the life-forces of men. And they take some form—usually a woman form, I think, and key you up to the highest pitch of emotion before they—begin. That's to work the life-force up to intensity so it'll be easier. . . . And they give, always, that horrible, foul pleasure as they—feed. There are some men who, if they survive the first experience, take to it like a drug—can't give it up—keep the thing with them all their lives—which isn't long—feeding it for that ghastly satisfaction. Worse than smoking *ming* or— or 'praying to *Pharol*.' "

"Yes," said Smith. "I'm beginning to understand why that crowd was so surprised and—and disgusted when I said—well, never mind. Go on."

"Did you get to talk to—to it?" asked Yarol.

"I tried to. It couldn't speak very well. I asked it where it came from and it said—'from far away and long ago'— something like that."

"I wonder. Possibly some unknown planet—but I think not. You know there are so many wild stories with some basis of fact to start from, that I've sometimes wondered—

mightn't there be a lot more of even worse and wilder superstitions we've never even heard of? Things like this, blasphemous and foul, that those who know have to keep still about? Awful, fantastic things running around loose that we never hear rumors of at all!

"These things—they've been in existence for countless ages. No one knows when or where they first appeared. Those who've seen them, as we saw this one, don't talk about it. It's just one of those vague, misty rumors you find half hinted at in old books sometimes.... I believe they are an older race than man, spawned from ancient seed in times before ours, perhaps on planets that have gone to dust, and so horrible to man that when they are discovered the discoverers keep still about it—forget them again as quickly as they can.

"And they go back to time immemorial. I suppose you recognized the legend of Medusa? There isn't any question that the ancient Greeks knew of them. Does it mean that there have been civilizations before yours that set out from Earth and explored other planets? Or did one of the Shambleau somehow make its way into Greece three thousand years ago? If you think about it long enough you'll go off your head! I wonder how many other legends are based on things like this—things we don't suspect, things we'll never know.

"The Gorgon, Medusa, a beautiful woman with—with snakes for hair, and a gaze that turned men to stone, and Perseus finally killed her—I remembered this just by accident, N. W., and it saved your life and mine— Perseus killed her by using a mirror as he fought to reflect what he dared not look at directly. I wonder what the old Greek who first started that legend would have thought if he'd known that three thousand years later his story would save the lives of two men on another planet. I wonder what that Greek's own story was, and how he met the thing, and what happened....

"Well, there's a lot we'll never know. Wouldn't the

records of that race of—of *things*, whatever they are, be worth reading! Records of other planets and other ages and all the beginnings of mankind! But I don't suppose they've kept any records. I don't suppose they've even any place to keep them—from what little I know, or anyone knows about it, they're like the Wandering Jew, just bobbing up here and there at long intervals, and where they stay in the meantime I'd give my eyes to know! But I don't believe that terribly hypnotic power they have indicates any superhuman intelligence. It's their means of getting food—just like a frog's long tongue or a carnivorous flower's odor. Those are physical because the frog and the flower eat physical food. The Shambleau uses a—a mental reach to get mental food. I don't quite know how to put it. And just as a beast that eats the bodies of other animals acquires with each meal greater power over the bodies of the rest, so the Shambleau, stoking itself up with the life-forces of men, increases its power over the minds and the souls of other men. But I'm talking about things I can't define—things I'm not sure exist.

"I only know that when I felt—when those tentacles closed around my legs—I didn't want to pull loose, I felt sensations that—that—oh, I'm fouled and filthy to the very deepest part of me by that—pleasure—and yet—"

"I know," said Smith slowly. The effect of the *segir* was beginning to wear off, and weakness was washing back over him in waves, and when he spoke he was half meditating in a low voice, scarcely realizing that Yarol listened. "I know it—much better than you do—and there's something so indescribably awful that the thing emanates, something so utterly at odds with everything human—there aren't any words to say it. For a while I was a part of it, literally, sharing its thoughts and memories and emotions and hungers, and—well, it's over now and I don't remember very clearly, but the only part left free was that part of me that was but insane from the—

the obscenity of the thing. And yet it was a pleasure so sweet—I think there must be some nucleus of utter evil in me—in everyone—that needs only the proper stimulus to get complete control; because even while I was sick all through from the touch of those—things—there was something in me that was—was simply gibbering with delight.... Because of that I saw things—and knew things—horrible, wild things I can't quite remember— visited unbelievable places, looked backward through the memory of that—creature—I was one with, and saw— God, I wish I could remember!"

"You ought to thank your God you can't," said Yarol soberly.

His voice roused Smith from the half-trance he had fallen into, and he rose on his elbow, swaying a little from weakness. The room was wavering before him, and he closed his eyes, not to see it, but he asked, "You say they—they don't turn up again? No way of finding— another?"

Yarol did not answer for a moment. He laid his hands on the other man's shoulders and pressed him back, and then sat staring down into the dark, ravaged face with a new, strange, undefinable look upon it that he had never seen there before—whose meaning he knew, too well.

"Smith," he said finally, and his black eyes for once were steady and serious, and the little grinning devil had vanished from behind them, "Smith, I've never asked your word on anything before, but I've—I've earned the right to do it now, and I'm asking you to promise me one thing."

Smith's colorless eyes met the black gaze unsteadily. Irresolution was in them, and a little fear of what that promise might be. And for just a moment Yarol was looking, not into his friend's familiar eyes, but into a wide gray blankness that held all horror and delight—a pale sea with unspeakable pleasures sunk beneath it. Then the wide stare focused again and Smith's eyes met his squarely and Smith's voice said, "Go ahead. I'll promise."

"That if you ever should meet a Shambleau again—ever, anywhere—you'll draw your gun and burn it to hell the instant you realize what it is. Will you promise me that?"

There was a long silence. Yarol's somber black eyes bored relentlessly into the colorless ones of Smith, not wavering. And the veins stood out on Smith's tanned forehead. He never broke his word—he had given it perhaps half a dozen times in his life, but once he had given it, he was incapable of breaking it. And once more the gray seas flooded in a dim tide of memories, sweet and horrible beyond dreams. Once more Yarol was staring into blankness that hid nameless things. The room was very still.

The gray tide ebbed. Smith's eyes, pale and resolute as steel, met Yarol's levelly.

"I'll—try," he said. And his voice wavered.

Originally published under a pseudonym (as were many other stories in this volume—are serious SF writers embarrassed to be playing in the fields of supernatural fantasy?), Roger Zelazny, master of allusion, did indeed claim this delightful meditation for his own. Robots and androids are made in our image—why shouldn't they have inherited our nightmares?

The Stainless Steel Leech

ROGER ZELAZNY

They're really afraid of this place.

During the day they'll clank around the headstones, if they're ordered to, but even Central can't make them search at night, despite the ultras and the infras—and they'll never enter a mausoleum.

Which makes things nice for me.

They're superstitious; it's a part of the circuitry. They were designed to serve man, and during his brief time on earth, awe and devotion, as well as dread, were automatic things. Even the last man, dead Kennington, commanded every robot in existence while he lived. His person was a thing of veneration, and all his orders were obeyed.

And a man is a man, alive or dead—which is why the graveyards are a combination of hell, heaven, and strange feedback, and will remain apart from the cities so long as the earth endures.

But even as I mock them they are looking behind the

stones and peering into the gullies. They are searching
for—and afraid they might find—me.

I, the unjunked, am legend. Once out of a million
assemblies a defective such as I might appear and go
undetected, until too late.

At will, I could cut the circuit that connected me with
Central Control, and be a free 'bot, and master of my
own movements. I liked to visit the cemeteries, because
they were quiet and different from the maddening
stamp-stamp of the presses and the clanking of the
crowds; I liked to look at the green and red and yellow
and blue things that grew about the graves. And I did
not fear these places, for that circuit, too, was defective.
So when I was discovered they removed my vite-box and
threw me on the junk heap.

But the next day I was gone, and their fear was great.

I no longer possess a self-contained power unit, but
the freak coils within my chest act as storage batteries.
They require frequent recharging, however, and there is
only one way to do that.

The werebot is the most frightful legend whispered
among the gleaming steel towers, when the night wind
sighs with its burden of fears out of the past, from days
when non-metal beings walked the earth. The half-lifes;
the preyers upon order, still cry darkness within the vite-
box of every 'bot.

I, the discontent, the unjunked, live here in Rosewood
Park, among the dogwood and myrtle, the headstones
and broken angels, with Fritz—another legend—in our
deep and peaceful mausoleum.

Fritz is a vampire, which is a terrible and tragic thing.
He is so undernourished that he can no longer move
about, but he cannot die either, so he lies in his casket
and dreams of times gone by. One day, he will ask me
to carry him outside into the sunlight, and I will watch
him shrivel and dim into peace and nothingness and dust.
I hope he does not ask me soon.

We talk. At night, when the moon is full and he feels
strong enough, he tells me of his better days, in places

called Austria and Hungary, where he, too, was feared and hunted.

". . . But only a stainless steel leech can get blood out of a stone—or a robot," he said last night. "It is a proud and lonely thing to be a stainless steel leech—you are possibly the only one of your kind in existence. Live up to your reputation! Hound them! Drain them! Leave your mark on a thousand steel throats!"

And he was right. He is always right. And he knows more about these things than I.

"Kennington!" his thin, bloodless lips smiled. "Oh, what a duel we fought! He was the last man on earth, and I the last vampire. For ten years I tried to drain him. I got at him twice, but he was from the Old Country and knew what precautions to take. Once he learned of my existence, he issued a wooden stake to every robot—but I had forty-two graves in those days and they never found me. They did come close, though. . . .

"But at night, ah, at night!" he chuckled. "Then things were reversed! I was the hunter and he the prey!

"I remember his frantic questing after the last few sprays of garlic and wolfsbane on earth, the crucifix assembly lines he kept in operation around the clock— irreligious soul that he was! I was genuinely sorry when he died, in peace. Not so much because I hadn't gotten to drain him properly, but because he was a worthy opponent and a suitable antagonist. What a game we played!"

His husky voice weakened.

"He sleeps a scant three hundred paces from here, bleaching and dry. His is the great marble tomb by the gate. . . . Please gather roses tomorrow and place them upon it."

I agreed that I would, for there is a closer kinship between the two of us than between myself and any 'bot, despite the dictates of resemblance. And I must keep my word, before this day passes into evening and although there are searchers above, for such is the law of my nature.

* * *

"Damn them! (He taught me that word.) Damn them!" I say. "I'm coming up! Beware, gentle 'bots! I shall walk among you and you shall not know me. I shall join in the search, and you will think I am one of you. I shall gather the red flowers for dead Kennington, rubbing shoulders with you, and Fritz will smile at the joke."

I climb the cracked and hollow steps, the east already spilling twilight, and the sun half-lidded in the west.

I emerge.

The roses live on the wall across the road. From great twisting tubes of vine, with heads brighter than any rust, they burn like danger lights on a control panel, but moistly.

One, two, three roses for Kennington. Four, five . . .

"What are you doing, 'bot?"

"Gathering roses."

"You are supposed to be searching for the werebot. Has something damaged you?"

"No, I'm all right," I say, and I fix him where he stands, by bumping against his shoulder. The circuit completed, I drain his vite-box until I am filled.

"You are the werebot!" he intones weakly.

He falls with a crash.

. . . Six, seven, eight roses for Kennington, dead Kennington, dead as the 'bot at my feet—more dead—for he once lived a full, organic life, nearer to Fritz's or my own than to theirs.

"What happened here, 'bot?"

"He is stopped, and I am picking roses," I tell them.

There are four 'bots and an Over.

"It is time you left this place," I say. "Shortly it will be night and the werebot will walk. Leave, or he will end you."

"You stopped him!" says the Over. "You are the werebot!"

I bunch all the flowers against my chest with one arm and turn to face them. The Over, a large special-order 'bot, moves toward me. Others are approaching from all directions. He had sent out a call.

"You are a strange and terrible thing," he is saying, "and you must be junked, for the sake of the community."

He seizes me and I drop Kennington's flowers.

I cannot drain him. My coils are already loaded near their capacity, and he is specially insulated.

There are dozens around me now, fearing and hating. They will junk me and I will lie beside Kennington.

"Rust in peace," they will say. . . . I am sorry that I cannot keep my promise to Fritz.

"Release him!"

No!

It is shrouded and moldering Fritz in the doorway of the mausoleum, swaying, clutching at the stone. He always knows. . . .

"Release him! I, a human, order it."

He is ashen and gasping, and the sunlight is doing awful things to him.

—The ancient circuits click and suddenly I am free.

"Yes, master," says the Over. "We did not know. . . ."

"Seize that robot!"

He points a shaking emaciated finger at him.

"'He is the werebot," he gasps. "Destroy him! The one gathering flowers was obeying my orders. Leave him here with me."

He falls to his knees and the final darts of day pierce his flesh.

"And go! All the rest of you! Quickly! It is my order that no robot ever enter another graveyard again!"

He collapses within and I know that now there are only bones and bits of rotted shroud on the doorstep of our home.

Fritz has had his final joke—a human masquerade.

I take the roses to Kennington, as the silent 'bots file out through the gate forever, bearing the unprotesting Overbot with them. I place the roses at the foot of the monument—Kennington's and Fritz's—the monument of the last, strange, truly living ones.

Now only I remain unjunked.

In the final light of the sun I see them drive a stake through the Over's vite-box and bury him at the crossroads.

Then they hurry back toward their towers of steel, of plastic.

I gather up what remains of Fritz and carry him down to his box. The bones are brittle and silent.

... It is a very proud and very lonely thing to be a stainless steel leech.

An Anthropological Approach to Vampirism

T.K.F. Weisskopf

Among the Lalakai of New Britain in the midst of the Pacific they are called *vis*, spirits who fly at night and scratch the living's eyes out with their long nails. Crossing the oceans to Ireland in the Atlantic, you will find stories told of the *leanhaun sidhe,* a female fairy who lives off the life spirit of the men she seduces. And in the rest of Europe we find the vampire. From the dim mists of the pre-Biblical Middle East and cults of blood sacrifice, through the rise of Christianity and reports of spirits of the excommunicated rising from the dead, through the age of great plagues and Vlad the Impaler, and on into the Age of Rationalism and Romantic literature, the myth and metaphor of the vampire has been refined—and grown in its power to move people.

This volume has tried to illustrate how the symbol of the vampire, present in almost every culture in the world, still is pertinent to us living in a modern, global community, in an age of technical miracles. This collection is not simply a compilation of supernatural stories. Although all these stories concern a supposedly mythic construct, they are also true science fiction, SF performing the function of SF: interpreting the world in a rational manner.

It has been said that SF is the modern equivalent of ancient myth-making. As a literary genre it helps us interpret our universe, and to make it comprehensible. Frederik Pohl, Isaac Asimov and many other students of the field have also called SF a literature of change, irresistible change being the central fact of modern life. Science fiction in general accustoms the reader not to any specific future or technology that may be coming out way, but to the mere fact that chance is inevitable.

But even in the midst of constant change there is some continuity in our culture. Besides creating new icons and symbols to help us interpret the universe and accustom us to this unstoppable change (not necessarily *progress*, mind you), science fiction has also commandeered icons and symbols from all preceding ages of which we have record and reinterpreted them.

For the most part, the vampires of early legend and primitive myth are female bloodsuckers or leechers of life, while the modern European vampire is male: Dracula, not Carmilla, reigns in the popular imagination as the ideal vampire. But in this volume "Shambleau" & "Fleas" follow the model. In Ireland the female *leanhaun sidhe* act the part of muses (according to Yeats), and the victim, if ambivalent, is at least in part willing to exchange his life's blood for inspiration. So, too, in "Shambleau," the man goes semi-willingly to his doom. The fascination of the vampire is not just that it is horrific, but also that it is seductive. To quote C. L. Moore: "Dimly he knew it, even as his body answered to the root-deep ecstasy, a foul and dreadful wooing from which his very soul shuddered away—and yet in the innermost depths of that soul some grinning traitor shivered with delight." Part of the human is evil and welcomes the darkness—the apotheosis of the forward-looking, problem-solving, rugged individual that is the quintessential science fictional hero. We see the dark side of the spaceship.

In Moore's story, and even in Zelazny's humorous contribution, "The Stainless Steel Leech," the mythic nightmare has been reinterpreted to reflect the specific fears of our modern culture—the end of civilization, the extinction of humanity, the horrors to be found on the new frontier. Of course, by the mere naming of fears you have started on the road to taming them. Which is one of the functions of science fiction. In several other stories included here, the author goes farther, and seeks to explain the nightmare—it's a perfectly straightforward alien, a disease, a mutation, and so forth—and thereby demystify it. And to my mind, the stories that seek to explain the nightmare, solve the mystery of the myth, do more than just qualify as SF, they perform its *primary* function: to help us understand and thereby shape our environment and our destiny.

(That, after all, is what the human animal does: the thing that separates us from the rest of Earth's biota is not morphology, but what we've done with our upright stance and larger brains and opposable thumbs. We are the animals who drastically change the environment to suit ourselves—we are the animals with culture.)

SF as a whole has of course not only altered older symbols but introduced new ones into the culture. The robot, the artificial intelligence, the cute little alien, and so on, are part of a modern human's psyche as much as—*more* than—fairies, witches and gods. The best science fiction shows that a combination of symbol plus metaphor is one of the most effective linguistic tools humans have for interpreting reality. And this volume has tried to illustrate how this treatment of the vampire can be persuasive.

But I wonder, what will the *next* symbol be for humankind's struggle for control over fate and itself?

THE BEST OF THE BEST

For *anyone* who reads science fiction, this is an absolutely indispensable book. Since 1953, the annual Hugo Awards presented at the World Science Fiction Convention have been as coveted by SF writers as is the Oscar in the motion picture field—and SF fans recognize it as a certain indicator of quality in science fiction. Now the members of the World Science Fiction Convention— the people who *award* the Hugos—select the best of the best: *The Super Hugos*! Included in this volume are stories by such SF legends as Arthur C. Clarke, Isaac Asimov, Larry Niven, Clifford D. Simak, Harlan Ellison, Daniel Keyes, Anne McCaffrey and more. Presented and with an introduction by Charles Sheffield. This essential volume also includes a complete listing of all the Hugo winners to date in all categories and breakdowns and analyses of the voting in all categories, including the novel category.

And don't miss *The New Hugo Winners Volume I* (all the Hugo winning stories for the years 1983–1985) and *The New Hugo Winners Volume II* (all the Hugo winning stories for the years 1986–1988), both presented by Isaac Asimov.

The Super Hugos • 72135-6 • 432 pp. • $4.99 ☐
The New Hugo Winners Volume I • 72081-3 • 320 pp. • $4.50 ☐
The New Hugo Winners Volume II • 72103-8 • 384 pp. • $4.99 ☐

Available at your local bookstore. If not, fill out this coupon and send a check or money order for the cover price to Baen Books, Dept. BA, P.O. Box 1403, Riverdale, NY 10471.

NAME: _____

ADDRESS: _____

_____

I have enclosed a check or money order in the amount of $_____